The House Of Cards Murder

A Jonas Lauer Mystery

Jesse A. Hester

Available on amazon.com
Createspace.com
Ingram Distribution

Copyright © 2016 Jesse A. Hester

All rights reserved.

ISBN: 1539710769
ISBN 13: 9781539710769

*This book is dedicated to the memory of my friend,
Saunook Pedigo Guy, who is sadly, no longer with us.
I would also like to thank David and Debbie, whose unwavering
faith in me, is never forgotten or taken for granted.
And to you, the reader, none of these books
would be possible, without you.*

Other books by the author.
The Bottoms Up Murder
The Whiskey Barrel Murder
The Open Window Murder

Prologue

The confidence man, is another name for the grifter, the charlatan and of course the southern favorite, the carpetbagger. Though the last one is slightly unfair, as history has shown, most of the people who came down from the north during the Reconstruction Period, were decent people. These people wanted to help the south recover from the devastating civil war. Of course there were those who took advantage of southerners, buying up the land, at quite literally, dirt cheap prices. Many were morally deficient politicians, who wrote the laws to seize as many assets as they could. I suppose one could say nothing has changed in today's time. In truth, there have always been those, who use illicit means, to obtain property that isn't theirs. From a snake in a garden with two naked lovers, to slick traveling salesmen, who peddle a magical elixir, as a cure-all for every medical condition known to man; to infomercials touting the small donation for a promise to the pathway to a perfect life. The eternal relationship between the "con" and the "mark" have been with us since the dawn of man and will no doubt be with us until the end of time.

Monroe County, Tennessee had its very own confidence man back in 1999 and the scandal is still whispered about today. In a seven-month period, a man worked his articulate magic over the town of Vonore, in a way that the county had never seen before or since. People lost their homes, farmers lost their cattle, several people lost their savings and that is just the tip of the proverbial iceberg, that capsized the town. The man ingrained, at the very root of this convoluted weed, was Alston Mesmer. He was a man of average looks, with a square jaw, flat cheeks and penetrating eyes. Barely five feet ten inches in height, Alston was the type of man most wouldn't remember meeting, but he is also a reminder of the slogan about judgment and book covers. Alston had the ability to make people believe every word, which exited his lips.

Alston arrived in Vonore in the fall of 1998. He rented a cottage on Niles Ferry Road, which had a boat dock bordering Tellico Lake. He was often seen standing on the dock, surveying all that was around him. He made his first public appearance at the Fall Fest held at Vonore Park. He made quite the impression, draped in designer labeled slacks, blue button down shirt and wearing leather shoes polished to the point they were almost glowing. Vonore was and still is a small city, where everyone knows everyone, so Alston stood out like the proverbial sore thumb. The locals initially had their guard up, when they first met this newcomer, but it didn't take Alston long to get them to open up. By the time the festival was over, he knew most of the names of the town officials and had them laughing along, with what would eventually be discovered as "tall tales".

The dapper conman introduced himself as a land developer and was looking to invest serious money into creating a subdivision, near the heart of the city. This wasn't to be just any subdivision, but one set right on the lake, with a marina allowing the residents to cruise Tellico Lake, at their leisure. Alston spoke of a steamboat to host parties, live shows under the moonlight, and perhaps a small casino, if the county would permit. There would also be an eighteen-hole golf course, with an open country club and adjoining restaurant. He had preliminary sketches drawn of his designs and had commissioned models to scale for a visual aid. These grand designs ignited the imagination, hopes, and dreams, of those who resided on the land needed for this expansion. Over time they began to warm to the idea, of turning their city into a boomtown, as well as swelling their personal bank accounts. Not only did he convince them to offer up their land, he even persuaded some to invest their own money into this project, thereby increasing their profits. In other words, the hook was set.

The land was the key ingredient in this magnificent recipe and Alston knew it was also the easiest one to acquire. Donovan Birch owned four hundred acres of prime farmland near the lake, which made him Alston's first call. Donovan was sixty-three years old at the time, with two children, who had moved to different towns and had no interest in continuing the family farm. Donovan was still a robust man, with a marginally protruding belly, that was as solid as a steel barrel, much like the rest of his physique. His hands thick and calloused from hard farm work, possessed fingers that were strong enough to crush an average man's hand. When he first laid eyes on Alston Mesmer, Donovan was not immediately impressed by the well-dressed business man, but after several visits and the promise of a more golden year, Donovan agreed. He remortgaged his land and used the money to invest in the subdivision. He envisioned a multi-million dollar return on his investment.

As word spread about Donovan Birch's potential windfall, others soon jumped on the bandwagon, including a young Martin Udall and his wife Odette, who was five months pregnant. Six other families also jumped at the opportunity, for the brass ring to the good life. The grand total for the investment for those six was an additional six million. As with Donovan, Alston provided them the legal documents to sign, and reiterated, they wouldn't regret their decision. It seemed, too good to be true and as is most often the case, it was. As fate and time would reveal, it wasn't very long before everyone's dreams came tumbling down like a house of cards.

Ten weeks after the final agreement had been signed, representatives from Jenkins LLC showed up, saying the investors had thirty days to leave the premises before forceful eviction would be initiated. Guy Jenkins, the owner of Jenkins Reality LLC, was a land developer from Chattanooga, with the documentation proving ownership for all the properties involved in the scam. However, according to the agreement, the sole owner, of all said property, was none other than Alston Mesmer. It was around then that the investors noticed, they hadn't seen Alston in a few days. He didn't have a cellphone, which as peculiar as it sounds now, in 1998 cellular phones were still in their infancy, and not everybody and their brother had one. So they went to the house he had been renting, only to discover it vacated. The furniture was coated with dust, a mound of envelopes protruding from the mailbox, and the closet vacant of garments.

As for the property sale, Alston had insisted that in order to be sure the property to be used in the investment, was on the up and up, he be allowed access to the deeds. It was later learned he had an identic memory, and was able to transpose the information to a bill of sale, thus giving the property solely to Mesmer LLC, where Alston Mesmer was the principle owner. And since the investors had signed agreements with him, he had samples of their signatures which he forged on the transferal documents.

He next contacted Guy Jenkins of Jenkins Reality LLC, and before the ink was dry, he had sold all of the parcels of land for a reported seven million dollars. Needless to say, Mr. Jenkins was as surprised as the residents of the properties, when he leaned of the deception. Alston had already cashed the check, but Jenkins did try to trace the money. However, the conman was ahead of him and had already transferred the cash through a bank in the Cayman Islands, making it impossible to track down. Alston had left them all holding empty moneybags.

After going to the police, it was discovered his real name was Alston O'Brian, with a long record in theft, extortion, forgery, and of course swindling. The officers of the Vonore City Police Department wanted to take the lead in the investigation, but found they couldn't, after it was revealed the chief of police Valance Udall, was Martin Udall's father. Because his son, daughter-in-law, and future grandchild were just robbed of half their savings, the chief's objectivity was now in question, which is how it became the Monroe County Sheriff Department's case. Bill Hayes was at the helm and he wasted no time. After five weeks of interagency cooperation and hundreds of hours of manpower, Alston O'Brian was discovered hiding out in Tucson, Arizona, using the name Adam Dobb. He was already working on a similar scheme with a logging company when the Arizona state police arrested him. Brought back to Monroe County, he went to trial and was sentenced to nineteen years in prison, for theft, forgery, and larceny.

Of course that only ended the criminal side of the case. Guy Jenkins believed, since he had documentation proving the land was his, he should be able to keep it. The citizens of Vonore took civil action against him, in a case that lasted two years, during which time no one could live on the property until the case was settled. Eventually Jenkins LLC had to file bankruptcy and shut down, resulting in the case being dismissed. A year later, Guy Jenkins would go on to open up another limited liability corporation and make his money back, before eventually dying of a heart attack. He had no living relatives, so his business went into default.

Having been forced off their own property, many of the victims had either moved away or flat out given up any hope of getting their land or money returned. Those that remained in town, were in such bad financial straits, they had to either file for bankruptcy or have their property foreclosed on. But after all this time, Vonore along with Monroe County had put the tainted memory of the grifter behind them.

Yet the tentacles, of the past, have a very long reach on the road we travel and it is almost always guaranteed, to rear its head, just around the bend. Time may move on, but the echoes of our memories remain. This memory chose to reveal itself on a cold January morning, as I looked through the steam of my hot coffee, to see Alston O'Brian pumping gas at the Shell station in Madisonville.

I was returning to my truck to fill up the tank, after prepaying the attendant and buying a cup of coffee for some warmth, when a tungsten color Toyota Camry parked at the pump next to mine. Inserting the nozzle into the tank, I selected my fuel and set the grip, feeling the movement of the fuel vibrate the bed of my truck. I glanced over at the sedan to see a man with a healthy gray beard and bald head, which he quickly covered with a black toboggan, as he pulled the collar of his pea coat up around his neck. I was only half paying attention to him, as he inserted his credit card into the pump and selected his fuel. It wasn't until after he turned around to get his gas, that I got a good look at his face. Staring through the vapors of my coffee, I found myself studying the man's physical features longer than was appropriate, but I couldn't help myself. In my line of work, names can become confusing. Women change their last names upon marriage, criminals use aliases and despite what you may see in the cinema, most of us can't remember every name that comes across our desk. Faces, however are an entirely different matter. For me, if I see someone's face, I can often remember it much easier, than the name. The old man across from me seemed familiar, but the memory was covered with several layers of cobwebs, thus obscuring the identity. I took a sip from my coffee, turning back to the pump to watch the gauge for a few seconds, before casting my eyes once again on the man across from me. He was watching the line of vehicles stopped at the traffic light, giving me an excellent view of his profile, but I still couldn't remember the name. When he looked over at me, I gave him a mock salute with my coffee hand and smiled. "Cold enough for you?"

He gave shiver, for effect, as he tapped his fingers on the roof of his car. "If it isn't, it'll sure do until the real cold gets here. What's the temperature?"

I tipped my head toward the gas station. "The thermometer outside the door says twenty-eight."

He took a deep breath of the cold air. "It doesn't feel twenty-eight to these old bones. The arthritis in my knees says it's eight."

The House Of Cards Murder

I smiled at his joke, setting my cup on the roof of my truck. "Well, it is January, so I suppose we should expect a little chill in the air."

He glanced down at the fuel gage and then tapped his right shoulder, as he turned back to me. "Yeah, we should, but that doesn't mean my shoulder likes it."

The sunlight was shimmering through the opaque fog that had settled over the area, giving the low riding cloud an amber tint. I took a moment to admire the sight, before I looked back to the stranger. "I thought it was your knees that had arthritis."

He gave me a smile, all old men give to the younger generation, finding humor in our callowness, about the life that is ahead of us. "When you get my age, there aren't many of your bones that don't ache anymore."

I had to concede his point and looked down as the nozzle lever clicked closed. "I suppose, I'll learn that myself in a few years. You passing through?"

Looking up at me, he hunched his shoulders, as he returned his nozzle to the pump. "I'm not sure. I was in Monroe County a few years back and it left an impression on me."

I walked around to the driver's door of my truck, keeping my coat over my badge and sidearm. "So it's nostalgic reasons that bring you here?"

The man gave me a guarded look. "I suppose. You ask a lot of questions."

I feigned embarrassment, putting my gloved hand inside the pocket of my overcoat. "Sorry. Didn't mean to be nosey. Enjoy your stay here Mr. ?"

The humor, of the universe, always decides to reveal itself at the most inopportune moments and today was no different. Just as the man across from me was about to give, what I assume was a name, Brent Talent, the owner of the gas station, stepped out to get into his Durango and waved at me. "Hey sheriff. Congratulations again on the election."

xiii

I waved at him, smiling at the ironical fact, that Brent had been opposed to my re-election, but had now given me away. "Thanks Brent. Good morning to you."

The old man stared at Brent, as he fired up his Durango, before refocusing his eyes on me. "You're the sheriff?"

Clearly there was no point in hiding the obvious, I opened my coat revealing the gold star on my belt. "According to this I am."

He looked at me from head to toe, rolling his tongue over his lips. "You look a little young to be the sheriff."

I smiled at him placing my hand in my pocket. "I don't know if thirty-five is exactly young. I'm almost thirty-six."

Oscillating his eyes, he released the lever on the nozzle and returned it to the pump. "Sheriff, I'm sixty-six. That's young."

I took a sip of coffee, enjoying the warmth that flooded down my chest. "Well I'm growing out of it Mr…what did you say your name was again?"

He kept his eyes away from mine, while he closed the cover to the gas tank. "I didn't."

I moved behind the Camry, as he removed his credit card receipt. "Sir, I'm sorry for the deception. It's just your face seems familiar to me. One thing I've learned since becoming sheriff, is sometimes people clam up, if they know I'm a cop. Even if they've done nothing wrong."

Stopping with his hand resting on the door handle, he pursed his lips before exhaling a deep breath. "Son, I know what you were doing. You're old enough to remember seeing my face in the newspapers and on the news, but you can't place my name. I'll save you the trouble. It's Alston O'Brian."

The memories began to rise from the ashes of my mind, as I recalled some of the headlines from the local papers. "Also known as Alston Mesmer."

Alston's face grew taut, at the mention of his alias. "I don't use that epithet anymore."

I swirled my coffee, in the cup, not moving from my positon. "I suppose it does bring up some bad memories. If you don't mind me asking Mr. O'Brian, what's the reason you're back in Monroe County? It seems you'd want to stay away from here."

He turned to me, the tinge of yellow that enveloped the iris of his hazel eyes, seemed to glow, as he tilted his head back. "It's like I said before sheriff, it's a personal matter."

Realizing we had come to the natural end of our conversation, I reached into my inner coat pocket and removed a business card to give him. "Well, if you ever need some assistance, feel free to give me a call."

He glanced down at the cream colored card. "Sheriff Lauer, I'm not trying to start another scam. Those days are long behind me."

"I never meant to imply you were Mr. O'Brian. But there may be some people, in the county, that won't be too pleased to see you again. I worked a cold case a few months back and it taught me that sometimes, the past doesn't like to be disturbed. You get into any trouble give me a call."

Offering him my hand, he stared at it for a moment before shaking it and taking the card. He opened the door to his sedan and gave me one last look as he got in. I returned to my truck and wrote down the number of the temporary license tag in the back window. From there I watched him drive up to the traffic light, then turn left, heading north, in the direction of the city of Vonore.

Chapter One

I had intended to go back to the office to do some background on Alston, but I got a call from Glen, saying he needed my assistance at the courthouse, with Gary Dawson. Upon hearing the name, my shoulders felt like an anchor had just been attached to them. I moved my head slowly forward to rest on the steering wheel, as shivers of trepidation ran though my veins. Gary Dawson was a chronic problem, that the department had addressed, for the last ten years, long before my tenure as sheriff.

For years the Ten Commandments hung in the Monroe County Courthouse, even though federal law says church and state must be separate. ACLU lawyers had walked through the halls, seemingly benign to their existence, until Councilman Brent Nelson made a big to do about it in 2005. To give this tale some context, at the time, there was a lot of news coverage on what a lot of people were calling the war on Christianity. The proponents stated that this country was founded on the Judeo Christian law, meaning the ten commandments should stay in our courthouses. The Supreme Court disagreed, stating any form of medium that displayed the commandments, was to be removed from every federal and state facility.

Councilman Nelson, a lean man, with graying temples, could not understand what the big deal was. He wrote an op/ed piece in the Knoxville News Sentinel, stating how the commandments had been hanging in the courthouse for years and no one had a problem with them being there. As I have mentioned, the ACLU knew our courthouse displayed God's law, but had turned a blind eye to it, for reasons unknown to this day. Yet, when the councilman flaunted it to the public, it left the nonprofit organization little choice, but to sue the county to remove the banner, which it reluctantly did in the latter part of 2005.

Several citizens were upset by this, but the ruling really stuck in Gary Dawson's craw. He has held dozens of marching protests around the courthouse, holding a small scale Ten Commandment sign in his hand, demanding the county officials to return what was taken away. Patience wears thin with time and after a decade and countless miles, he had walked around the block, Gary was starting to become more aggressive in his protests. For the last four months he has been going into the courthouse and staging sit-ins, on the bench, underneath where the commandments used to hang. I've personally escorted Gary Dawson from the courthouse more times than I can remember. I've even arrested him twice, which seems to only solidify his fortitude. It didn't help that his father owned one of the largest trucking companies in East Tennessee. When he died nine years ago, he left the company to Gary, who sold it for a nice sum of money. Meaning, he had plenty of time on his hands to stage his protests.

I took the concrete steps two at a time and entered through the front door. The court officers let me bypass the metal detector and move into the vestibule, where Glen was standing in front of the bench where Gary Dawson sat. The heat was on full blast, so I unbuttoned my coat and rested my palm over the grip of my sidearm, as I joined my deputy. "All right fellas, what's the problem?"

Deputy Glen Coop had his department bomber's jacket unzipped with his hands crossed over his protruding stomach. He adjusted the bill of his khaki cap over his sandy blond hair, as he scratched the edges of his goatee. "It's the usual Jonas. Gary wants the Lord's top ten put back on the wall behind him."

Gary Dawson, with his silver hair combed back, his blade thin face translucent of any emotion, focused his brown eyes on the wall behind us. "I've said it before sheriff. I want the word of God brought back into this courthouse, where it belongs."

I inhaled a deep breath and looked down at him. "I'm afraid the justices of the Supreme Court haven't changed their opinion. Which means they have to stay down."

He shook his head, eyes focused on the wall. "I still don't understand how a man of the law can stand by and let this travesty happen."

I shifted my weight to my back foot. "Gary you do know, at the time the Commandments were taken down, I was just a forensic technician. It was former Sheriff Bill Hayes, who was ordered to remove them."

"But you are the sheriff now and can put them back. They are upstairs in the attic covered with a sheet. Just walk up there, get them, and hang them up."

"I should also add Gary, that if I had been the sheriff back then, I would've done the same thing as Bill."

Gary looked first at me then to my deputy. "And you agree with him?"

Glen gave him a small smile, and used his thumb to point at me. "I follow him wherever he leads."

I felt a small snigger catch in the back of my throat, at hearing Glen's support of me, which I carefully pushed down to take care of the business at hand. "Gary let's just skip to the end. The Commandments are going to stay upstairs, that is final. What happens to you, however, is entirely in your power. You can get up and leave on your own volition. No charges will be filed and everyone can go about their day. If you chose to stay, I'll have to arrest you...again for I believe the third time."

Gary returned to staring at the wall, firmly planting his feet into the floor and gripped the bench tighter. "I will not be deterred from my mission."

After releasing a heavy sigh, I gave Glen a nod and he proceeded to remove his cuffs from the pouch on his gun belt. "OK Gary, you know what to do. Stand and put your hands behind your back."

Following the directive, Gary rose and turned around for Glen to clasp the cuffs around his wrists. He advised him of his rights, as he escorted him out the front door, to his cruiser. I was following when a voice shouted from the second floor. "Hey Jonas."

I turned to see Anthony Deland, the assistant Attorney General for the county standing at top of the steps, where criminal court is held. He waved me up to join him, with a thick file folder in his hand. When I met him, he used his finger to beckon me to follow. "Let's talk in here."

Since criminal court wasn't in session this week, the courtroom was empty. Inside the wooden benches were vacant, as was the judge's bench with the seat turned to face the back wall, where the Tennessee state seal hung. Anthony rested his bifocals atop his gray head, as he sat down on the edge of the defense table, while patting the folder on his knee. "I see Mr. Dawson has decided to have yet another sit-in."

I placed my left hand in the pocket of my jeans. "As annoying as it can be sometimes, I can't help but admire his conviction. There aren't many people that would keep up a fight, for nearly a decade."

Anthony smiled, scratching his round chin. "I guess it can be called conviction. I'll admit there is a part of me that agrees with him, but our hands are tied on the matter."

"Obviously Gary doesn't see it that way." I moved to the bench in front of him and took a seat. "I think I'm correct in assuming, you didn't ask me in here to talk about Gary's crusade."

He shook his head, holding up the file for me to see. "I just got a call from the warden of the Whiteville Correctional Facility, giving me a courtesy call, about an inmate that was just released. A man by the name of Alston O'Brian. Apparently, he ran a confidence scam a few years back and just got his release three days ago."

I pursed my lips as I nodded. "Well that was serendipitous timing. I just ran into him at the gas station before coming here."

Anthony stared at me for a long moment, his mouth open. "Come again."

I pointed in the direction of the Shell station in town. "I ran into him, not fifteen minutes ago at the gas pump. He said he was in town for personal reasons."

Anthony's bushy eyebrows elevated up to his hairline. "You spoke to him?"

"I thought I recognized his face, so I struck up a conversation with him. When he learned I was the sheriff, he told me his name and that he was back in Monroe County, for unfinished business. What that is I don't know."

"He actually said unfinished business?"

"Those may not have been his exact words, but that was what I intuited from it." I narrowed my eyes on the folder, as I thought about what Anthony had said, about the call from the warden. "Why the courtesy heads up for a grifter? From what I remember about the case, there was no foul play. So why did the warden give you a call?"

"For a confidence scam, normally you'd be right, the warden wouldn't even give it a second thought, but Elizabeth felt this one needed mentioning."

It was my eyebrows that were now meeting my hairline, as I angled my head over my shoulder. "Elizabeth?"

He gripped the folder, a bit tighter with both hands, before placing it beside him on the table. "Warden King and I went to college together. We've kept in touch over the years."

I decided to stop prying into the prosecution's personal life and returned to the business at hand. "So why did Warden King feel compelled to call you about Alston O'Brian? Was he a problem inmate?"

"Quite the opposite. He was a model inmate who never got into trouble. They shaved off the last year of his sentence for good behavior and released him on the sixth of January."

I looked over at the state seal, the synaptic roads of my mind going into overdrive. "He was released three days ago? Did someone pick him up?"

Anthony pinched his eyebrows together, shrugging his shoulders. "She didn't say. Why?"

I shook my head. "It's nothing."

The prosecuting attorney slouched back, his face revealing an almost scolding look. "Please sheriff, if you asked the question, it must mean something."

I leaned into the armrest of the bench, rubbing the bottom of my chin with my hand. "He gets out early, on good behavior three days ago, gets himself a nice wardrobe, and a car to drive out to the very place, that led to his incarceration. It's certainly atypical of your average prisoner release."

Anthony hunched his shoulders, picking at some lint on his knee. "It's possible he had a benefactor on the outside. We can look into it, but does it really matter?"

I'll never understand why people ask your opinion, then ask: what does it matter? If you don't care, why ask? "I suppose not. So why the interest in Mr. O'Brian?"

"The reason for the heads up call, is Mr. O'Brian's own words. When asked about his plans, he indicated he wanted to make amends to the people of Vonore."

I leaned back, stretching my arms across the top of the bench. "Forgiveness would be up there with unfinished business. Are you afraid that some of the victims might be looking for revenge?"

Anthony tapped the folder on the table with his finger. "This all happened before I was stationed here. There were a lot of victims back in 99. It has been eighteen years, but some wounds don't heal. There was something else that also caught my attention."

He opened the file, to the marked section and handed it to me. "Take a look at the highlighted section."

The section, in question, was the summation of the money that Alston O'Brian was convicted of stealing. The police at the time, were able to retrieve most of it. However, it turned out there was some money, that was never recovered. The best the investigators could determine, was six hundred thousand dollars, that was never discovered. "Well, six hundred grand would qualify for unfinished business too."

Anthony rolled his tongue inside his cheek, while elevating his eyebrows once again. "A very hefty amount of unfinished business, if I might say. It could also be a further motive for revenge."

Now we were getting to the crux of this meeting. "The victims obviously know about the missing money. If word gets out about Alston's return, someone might decide to get their pound of flesh and some of the money, they feel is theirs."

"It would tempt even the noblest of men. Or women." He stood and put his hands in his pockets. "Which leaves us with a tough decision."

I looked at him once again, unsure of his intentions. "Decision? What do we have to decide?"

"What our next move should be, with regards to Alston O'Brian. Do you think we should do something about him being here?"

"Anthony, I don't have to tell you, that there isn't a thing we can do. He's served his sentence, meaning he's legally a free man, allowed to go anywhere he pleases. We can't arrest him because he may have left some money around. Even if he did find the money, the statute of limitations has expired, so it won't be considered ill-gotten gains. The same goes for the victims or the families of the victims. We can't arrest them because we're afraid they are going to seek retribution."

From the long exhale, it appeared the attorney general did indeed know this. "You're right of course. It's just this has the makings of a powder keg sheriff. Perhaps you could have your deputies keep tabs on him, while he's here."

"It's the same as before. He's done nothing illegal."

Anthony moved toward the judicial bench, his hands cocooned inside his pockets. "I have to tell you, I don't like this Sheriff Lauer. I don't like this at all."

There was a slow moving sensation beginning to take root in my gut, that had proven reliable more often than not. "Is there something else Anthony?"

Turning around, he stared at me, while hunching his shoulders. "Why would there be something else?"

I leaned forward and clasped my hands between my knees. "You've been doing this too long, to not know our hands are legally tied. Is there something else going on?"

He pursed his lips, as he slowly expanded the distance between us, moving toward the county clerk's seat. "Of course not sheriff, I just thought you'd like to know Mr. O'Brian was in town."

That feeling in my stomach was still there and I didn't need it to know, there was more to this than just a courtesy, heads up. I also knew that Anthony wasn't going to give me anything more, so for now I had to drop it. I stood up and let my hands hang loose by my side, as I moved to the center aisle. "Well, I do appreciate the notification, Anthony. If anything turns up, I'll let you know. At least Alston knows we're aware he's in Monroe County, so if he's up to no good, that may make him think twice. I even gave him my business card."

He looked at me and nodded. "I guess that is all that can be done for now."

I turned to leave, but Anthony called me back. "How is Ms. Corbett handling the unexpected layover?"

I faced him and let out a deep breath. "Ah, about as well as can be expected. That ice storm came out of nowhere and layered everything. I spoke with her last night and the weather is warming up a bit. The road crews hope to have a path cleared by the end of tomorrow, at the latest. She should be back by Wednesday."

Anthony looked down at the tops of his black leather shoes, a slight grin on his face. "I'll bet she wishes, I had never sent her to that conference in Nashville. The weather reports never even mentioned any rain, much less an ice storm."

I shrugged, as I started for the door again. "It's Tennessee weather Anthony. There's no way you could've predicted it. At least they still have power in her hotel. I'll let her know you were asking about her."

Lydia Corbett is an investigator for the attorney general's office and the liaison to the sheriff's department. Last Wednesday, Anthony sent her to Nashville to attend a legal conference, which was supposed to have lasted a day and a half, with her returning Friday afternoon. But late Thursday night and during the early morning hours of Friday, there was an unexpected shift in the weather, bringing a cold front into the area, dropping the temperatures to below freezing. The rain that came, turned to ice almost immediately on contact with the surface. The interstate and the streets were coated with an inch of ice, as were the trees. Thirty thousand people lost power and as of Monday morning, ten thousand were still off grid. Lydia was lucky that Nashville hadn't been hit too hard, but with the roads closed, she was stuck and from the conversation I had with her last night, it was starting to chip away at her nerves. The fact, that we had planned a romantic getaway for ourselves this past weekend, I'm sure only compounded the impact, but in the bout of humanity versus Mother Nature, humanity often comes in last.

I paused a moment at the top of the steps and looked over at the county clerk's office and decided to take a small detour. Heather Koch was the legal secretary in the County Clerk's office, and she was sitting at her desk, with her strawberry blond hair tied back in a ponytail, typing on her computer when I stepped up to the counter. "Morning Heather."

She looked up from her screen, her gray eyes focusing on me through black rimmed glasses, a grin developing on her oval face, as she waved. "Hey Jonas. What brings you here?"

"Gary Dawson decided to stage another sit-in for the return of God's law."

She rolled her eyes, sitting back in her swivel chair. "That man is committed to his beliefs, I have to give him that. I even sympathize with his plight, but our hands are tied."

I nodded, leaning into the counter top. "I've tried to explain that to him, but I might as well be talking to a wall. Anyway, that's not what I'm here about. I would like you to look up an old case for me, Heather."

She stood up, adjusting her sweater over the slightly round stomach as she approached the counter. "What case is it?"

"The People Vs. Alston O'Brian. It's an older case that happened in '99. I'd like all that you still have on file."

She wrote the name down on a post-it note, paused to stare, her forehead wrinkled in deep thought. "Alston O'Brian. The name is familiar."

"He pulled that con job in Vonore."

Her eyes widened, as her she tapped the note with her pen. "That's right. Talk about a blast from the past. Has something new turned up?"

I shook my head, as I drummed my gloved fingers on the wooden top, deciding discretion was the better part of valor, for now. "Nothing like that. I just need to refresh my memory on the case."

"Well, if you give me ten minutes, I can have the file ready for you."

Smiling I displayed my hands palms up. "Sounds good to me."

Chapter Two

I had the boxed trial transcripts in my hands as I stepped into the stationhouse. Glen had just about completed processing Gary Dawson, for unlawful protest and was entering his mugshot into the system. Jack Barnes, the desk sergeant, was sitting behind the glass partition working on the morning reports. "Got any messages Jack?"

He scratched his shaved obsidian head, as he looked up at me. "All is quiet on the home front Jonas."

"Well that's different for a change."

Jack grinned, as he signed the report he was working on. "Well, don't get too use to it. Something is going to get stirred up soon. It always does."

I laughed, as I headed to my office. "Amen to that."

An hour later I was a quarter of the way through the transcripts and had seen nothing about undiscovered money. I did however, read the testimony of some of the victims of Alston's game. One victim was a single mom, Agnes Macon, whose son Adam had Down syndrome. She invested nine thousand, three hundred and twenty-three dollars into Alston's scheme, almost half her life savings. In the wake of the con, Agnes had to sell her home, so she and her son could move into a small one-bedroom apartment.

There were several more victims with identic stories of loss, that would pull the heartstrings of even the most stoic soul. Yet, there was one name among those who testified that stood out like a golden effigy, and explained the peculiar feeling I had gotten from the assistant attorney general. Gretchen Deland, a sixty-year-old court reporter and mother of a then young, up and coming prosecuting attorney, named Anthony. She was a more fortunate victim, having only been swindled out of five thousand dollars and was able to keep her property. Yet, I can speak from experience as a son, no matter what our age, occupation, educational background, or personal philosophy, there is one fundamental rule: you don't mess with a southern boy's mother.

The nebulosity, that had blanketed Anthony's interest in the affairs of Alston O'Brian was revealed, as was the courtesy notice from the warden about the prisoner's release. Unfortunately, this revelation only increased the tense sensation inside my gut. I hoped Anthony would be able to keep his objectivity, however, from our last conversation, it might not be possible.

I spent the next hour reading the rest of the transcripts, which revealed nothing new. Alston didn't testify in his own behalf and had exhibited no emotion, as the jury foreman read the guilty verdict. Returning the transcripts to the cardboard box, I couldn't really say what I had hoped for when I started reading, other than familiarizing myself with the case. It wasn't like I didn't have a desk full of open cases. I placed the box over beside my filing cabinet, to return to the clerk's office later.

The knock on my door preceded Deputy Tom Kirk's entrance. "Is it all right if I come in for a minute, Jonas?"

I waved him in. "What can I do for you?"

He took a seat across from me, scratching his left temple with the pad of his thumb. He was staring at an incident report, as he pursed his lips in confusion. "There was a break-in last night at O'Reilly's Automotive. It happened afterhours, so no one was hurt. The cash was locked up in the safe, so no money was taken. In fact, all that was taken were a set of aluminum wheels and a couple of air wrenches."

"All right, we need to get word out to the local scrapyards, to be on the lookout, for someone trying to pilfer new wheels. The air wrenches are going to be harder, to unload that way, unless it's a private sale."

Tom shook his head, as he placed the report in his lap. "No, I've already done that. It's just that we were able to get some surveillance of the robbers."

I elevated my eyebrows at our good fortune. "Even better. Get some photos of our robbers and we can put them in the local paper. Maybe someone will turn them in."

Tom rubbed his chin, as he pulled a four by six print from his shirt pocket and handed it to me. "That's where the problem is, Jonas. They've covered their faces."

I looked, at the black and white still, for quite some time, not sure of what I was seeing. In my four years as sheriff, I have seen all types of masks used to obscure the face of those committing crimes. From United States presidents to Sponge Bob, the spectrum of guises out there is infinite. However, the dual robbers, I was now looking at, had decided to take a more original route in their cover. I looked up at my deputy wanting to be sure of what I was seeing. "Are these two idiots really using boxer shorts for masks?"

Tom rolled his eyes, as he exhaled a deep breath. "I'm afraid so. It took me a minute to figure out what they were wearing too."

I looked at the photo again, easily able to deduce from their build, that the two perpetrators were male. Using the shelves, in the photo as a scale, I would say one was just at six feet and the other one was probably five feet nine or so. The shorts they were wearing appeared to be a plaid striped, with the crotch directly over where their eyes would be. "So if we're looking at this correctly, they must be using the front opening as their peep hole. Like a perverted cyclops."

Tom shrugged. "I guess. It doesn't work too good though. They stumbled around and nearly fell several times. The taller one dropped one of the wheels on his partner's foot. He hopped around for a while, hitting the other guy over the back of the head, before they exited out the back."

I put the picture down on my desk and rubbed my chin with my fingers. "If a wheel landed on his foot, then there's a good chance it's broke. Those aluminum wheels can weigh over twenty-five pounds. Put out a word to the emergency rooms. Maybe they'll recall a moron with a broken foot."

Tom grinned, reaching over my desk to retrieve the photograph. "I just can't figure out what they were thinking. I mean I've seen people use a panty-hose for masks, but not this."

I stared at my deputy for a long spell, before hunching my shoulders. "All I can say is, it takes all kinds to keep the world turning Tom. Even the imbecilic have their purposes. What that purpose is I haven't a clue, but I'm pretty sure it exists."

* * *

Other than the return of Alston O'Brian, the boxer robbery, and Gary Dawson it had been an unusually quiet day at the stationhouse. I was able to get home at a reasonable time, with just enough daylight for me to take Mick, the American Bull Mastiff, who resides with me, for a quick walk. The nights were coming much quicker, so I took a flashlight and we hoofed it over the small hills behind my house. The twilight sky was, a mosaic of violet, peppered with white diamond stars outlined in pink, from the fading sun. The cool air was taking on a sharper chill, as we marched along the trail of damp leaves. Mick was trying to find the squirrels, that had been searching the foliage for food, but they had turned in for the evening. On our way back to the house, a band of coyotes started singing their high octave pitches several miles away, yet the quiet chilly air brought the sound closer, as if they were just on the other side of the trees. Soon the other dogs, in the area joined the chorus, including Mick, who had to stop his leisurely trot and throw his massive head back, to release a deep howl, that made his voice crack. "That a boy. Let's go, in case they decide to come this way."

After setting down the dog's bowl full of kibble, I made myself some chicken soup and a grilled cheese sandwich for my dinner. Two helpings later, I washed up the dishes and poured myself a glass of water, as I checked the time on the wall clock. It was almost eight, so I quickly grabbed two cubes of ice from the fridge, as I made my way to my office and opened my laptop. I brought up my home screen and clicked the video chat icon.

Soon the image of a woman, with golden hair sitting at a hotel desk, was looking at me through the screen. "Hey, right on time."

I took a sip of water and smiled at her. "Of course. This is our only way of seeing each other nowadays. How is the weather now?"

The woman speaking to me from a hundred and seventy-five miles away is Lydia Corbett, who is without a doubt the best thing to ever happen to me. She joined the AG's office not long after I became the sheriff, our paths crossed and she later asked me out. I'm not ashamed to admit the woman made the first move, just for the record. Lydia rested her chin on her hand and let out a deep sigh. "It's finally thawing out, but it's going slow. I might get out of here late tomorrow morning, but more than likely it'll be the day after."

"Cabin fever has finally set in, I take it."

She lowered her head, so she was looking directly into the camera. "There are only so many country music bars and shows a girl can take."

"You were always a little bit rock and roll, but sounds like you only have to put up with it one more day. You've been lucky that you had power."

She nodded releasing a light sigh. "Yeah, that is true. But I think the hotel has been trying to conserve power. The thermostat barely gets above sixty-eight. I have to wear my thermal socks and two pairs of pants just to stay warm. Although, since some people got stranded in their cars overnight, I guess I can't complain."

I rotated my glass, on the coaster, leaning back in my chair. "Well did you meet some interesting people, at least, while on your unexpected delay?"

"Yeah. There is a couple from Heidelberg, that I chatted with. It was a good chance to practice my German. Of course, they're like everyone else now and just want to get home."

There are times I forget that Lydia spent the earliest part of her life in the United States Army, as both the daughter of a three star general and later as a Warrant Officer in the Criminal Investigation Division. Having traveled abroad, she speaks fluent German, Spanish, and Italian. It was a marvel, as to how she ended up in Monroe County, in the first place. Staring at her face, admiring the angle of her jaw and bright eyes, I glanced at my image in the upper corner of my screen and saw square blocked features and wondered what she saw in me. "What's wrong?"

I smiled, hunching my shoulders. "Nothing. I was just thinking, that if you get too cold you could sandwich yourself between the German couple for warmth."

Her bronze eyes narrowed, as she got a little sneer on her face. "That's not funny. The only one I wanted to curl up against this weekend, was you."

"I was looking forward to that too, but obviously the universe had other plans. Keep in mind, we can try and do that this weekend."

She cocked an eyebrow, as a mischievous grin enveloped her lips. "Oh, feeling hopeful I see."

I took a swallow of water, enjoying the cold liquid running down my dry throat. "In all fairness, I'm always hopeful when it comes to seeing you without attire."

She laughed and pointed her finger at me in a mock scolding fashion. "You're awful."

"She says as she laughs," I replied.

Lydia ran her finger in invisible circles on the table top, staring down at the keyboard. "It wasn't just intimacy I was looking for… there was…."

She left it hanging in the air, like an albatross. I glanced over at my right desk drawer, gently running my fingers over the handle. "There was what?"

Looking back into the screen she shrugged and cleared her throat. "It doesn't matter. Anything happen in town today?"

The deflection was about as subtle, as a bull in a China shop, but I knew nothing could come of it, with her in Middle Tennessee and me here. So I opted to tell her about my encounter with Alston O'Brian and my brief conversation with her boss, Mr. Deland. "So not only is the conman, who swindled the town of Vonore back, but my boss's mother was one of his victims?"

"That's what it looks like."

Lydia was silent for a moment, as she stared at the screen in deep thought. "You don't think Mr. Deland will do something rash do you? He's never struck me as the kind of guy, who would go rogue, but when it comes to family, the rules go out the window."

I exhaled a deep breath, as I scratched my lower back. "I didn't get that sense from him. I think he was hoping there was a way I could run him out of town, but as far as I'm aware, the man hasn't done anything illegal. Of course, he could be here looking for the alleged six hundred grand, that went missing from the original trial. The problem with that is, the statute of limitations has expired on that case, so if the money is real, it's fair game."

Lydia sat back and crossed her arms over her abdomen. "So we have a conman, an upset attorney general, and there is a possibility of a hidden treasure. Is that about it?"

"You've summed it up." I held up my glass to her, "Happy days."

* * *

The arms of Morpheus had a good hold on me that night, as I slept better than I had in a while, with light dreams that I couldn't really recall, but left a good impression on my psyche. The serenity that had engulfed my inner self, quickly evaporated when my phone started ringing. My eyelids at half-mast, I saw the time was 4:37 in the morning and let out a groan, as I reached for the phone. The late night calls or early morning calls, depending on your point of view, were one part of the job I could do without. I hit the talk button keeping my head on the pillow. "Jonas."

"It's Glen, Jonas, sorry for waking you, but there's a situation on Niles Ferry Road. that needs your attention."

"What's happened?"

"We received a phone call from Janice Yolanda, saying her neighbor was walking around his backyard yelling about the Second Coming."

I rubbed the sleep from my eyes. "You said this was on Niles Ferry Road? I take it Phil's having an episode?"

"Afraid so Jonas. I've been here for about fifteen minutes, hoping it would work itself out of his system, but it looks like he's got a long sermon in him this time."

I laid my head back and stared up at the ceiling, fighting off the sleep, that I wanted to desperately reclaim. "All right. I'll get some pants on and meet you out there."

A car passing on the road could be heard through my receiver, as I threw back the covers and sat on the edge of the bed. "There's something else Jonas. The backdoor to Phil's place looks like it has been jimmied. I think he might've been robbed."

* * *

I parked beside Glen's cruiser in Phil's gravel driveway. I stepped out of my truck and met my deputy, who was standing near the front entrance. I could hear Phil's voice coming from the back of the house. "Has he calmed down any?"

Glen glanced up at me, his eyes unsure if I was serious or joking. "I've never been able to tell if he's up or down, when he's having one of his religious spells. But the rants seem to be getting more subsided. I tried talking to him, but it did no good. For some reason, you're the only one that seems to get through to him, when he's like this. Well, besides Bill that is."

I glanced at the log cabin, fighting the chill running up my legs to my lower back. "Does it look like anything's missing?"

A cloud of vapor snaked through his fingers, as he blew into his hands. "The flat screen's gone, but they left the VCR player. That's about all I can say for certain. Who still has a VCR player?"

I started toward the back of the house, Glen following. "Was any of Phil's herbal medicine lying around?"

"There was a pipe and what looked like some roaches in the ashtray. And there was the smell as well."

I looked up at the sky, the stars effervescing through the curtain of night. "We'll deal with that later."

Phil Woody is Monroe County's town character. Most of the time he's a mild tempered retiree, who preaches part-time and does volunteer work for Meals On Wheels and various other charities. In case you haven't deduced, the herbal medicine I referenced, is marijuana, Phil's narcotic of choice, which he started indulging in during the sixties. I've never been able to prove it, but I believe Phil dabbled in some of the more hallucinogenic drugs, LSD more than likely, with its residual side effects still felt today. My reasoning for this belief is because Phil has periodic episodes of delusions, where he prophesizes about the Second Coming, saying he is the thirteenth apostle of Christ, which has earned him the nickname, Apostle Phil. He is not a danger to anyone, whenever he goes into one of these episodes, save for himself, because he is completely unaware of his surroundings and for one reason or another, is often in his skivvies or his birthday suit.

As I rounded the corner of his wraparound porch, I saw Phil had decided to keep the briefs on, but seeing a sixty plus year old man running around in his tighty whities was an image I didn't want to see before dawn. Phil had his arms outstretched, speaking to an invisible congregation. "We have to ready ourselves for the time of our Savior's return. Not just our physical bodies, but the very nexus that is our being: the soul. When the Lord descends from the clouds on the wings of love, He'll only take those who are righteous and repentant. It is in His image we are made and His image we must do our best to emulate for our very salvation. As it says in Isaiah, *I will ascend above the heights of the clouds; I will make myself like the Most High.*

I stepped wide, keeping Phil just out of arm's length, as I stood in front of him. His hazel eyes were devoid of emotion, as they stared through me. I clapped my hands together, in applause which caused him to drop his arms and stop his sermon. "That was excellent Phil. Some of your finest work, but it's time to come back."

His body was shaking from the exposure and the tips of his toes had a blueish hue. Phil was about to begin again, but I interjected. "Don't you see the congregation has retired for the evening Phil? See the empty pews? It's time to call it at day."

There was slack in his bottom jaw, as he looked at the brown grass under his feet, a slight flicker of lucidity, beginning to resonate in his eyes. "That's it Phil. Come on back to us. The end of times will get here just fine, without your help."

He shook his head and closed his mouth to swallow, as he turned to me, rubbing his arms to fight the chill. "Sheriff?"

I nodded, as I took off my coat and draped it around his shoulders. "That's right Phil. Why don't we get you out of this cold before you freeze to death."

I turned him around and guided him onto his porch, toward the backdoor. "How long did this one last?"

"Maybe an hour," I replied, removing my coat, as he stepped over the threshold. "Phil it looks like there may be some stuff missing. Was there anyone in your house earlier tonight?"

He glanced back, scratching his sagging behind and pasty belly. "Yeah...yeah there was. I caught two of them in here. I think they woke me up and—"

I held up my hand for him to pause. "First, I think you need to get some clothes on. While you're at it, do a light sweep of the house and see what else is missing, or needs to be put away. Glen and I will wait out here."

Phil's eyes fell on the coffee table with the ashtray and pipe, before his reddening face turned to me and nodded. "That's probably a good idea. I'll only be a minute."

He shut the door, but it wouldn't close, because the latch had been compromised. The markings were your classic signs of a crowbar; it's not elegant, but still effective. I stood on the porch putting my coat back on, waving Glen to join me. "He'll let us in when he's decent."

Glen had a sheepish grin on his face, as he broached the steps. "And hides his stash?"

I shrugged, as I rested my palm over the hammer of my sidearm. "If that happens, I won't complain."

Glen leaned against the handrail placing his hands in the pockets of his department issued bomber's jacket. "You know, we could get into a world of trouble, if the wrong people heard about us turning a blind eye to Phil's ganja use."

I glanced at my deputy, before casting my gaze down on the top step near the front porch. "Yeah we could. And I'd be lying if I said I didn't wonder about it once in a while. The way I look at it, however, is like this: we have Phil Woody, who smokes some grass, but as far as I know, never once hurt another living soul. Then you have your murderers, rapists, child molesters, politicians, and stockbrokers. The way I see it, an old man who likes to smoke some grass, is a waste of the department's time. Besides the way things are going, marijuana is going to be legal across the country in the next few years anyway."

"You really think so?"

I turned so I was facing him, a chill running down my spine again, from the cold. "The state has already legalized cannabis oil for medicinal purposes. Now there is talk of medicinal marijuana being legalized. After people get use to that, it'll be just plain legal. We're in the bible belt, so Tennessee will probably be one of the last hold-outs, but it's going to happen."

Glen stared at the tops of his boots for a moment, scratching his chin through his goatee. "And how do you feel about that?"

I blew out a ribbon of smoke from the chill and shrugged. "Honestly I don't know Glen. All I can say with certainty is, we've been waging a war on drugs since the Reagan administration and I for one, can't tell it's any different *now* than *then*, except for the fact the bad guys are getting smarter at hiding it. If we are going to win it, we need to come up with a better game plan, but I'm the first one to tell you, I'm not smart enough to come up with that plan. So for now, if an old man wants to use reefer…well that's the least of my problems."

After a few minutes Phil opened the door, wearing faded green sweatpants and a white t-shirt, with thermal socks over his feet. "Come on in guys. Sorry about all of this."

Wiping my feet on the doormat, I stepped into his house, with Glen right behind me. Despite the absence of the paraphernalia and the use of a deodorizer, there was still ambient waves of a sweet burning scent in the air, that I had to ignore. I stood before the now vacant space where a flat screen had once resided. "If you feel up to it Phil, we need to go over what happened here. Besides the TV, is there anything else missing?"

Taking a seat on his well-worn plaid couch, Phil let out a deep breath, as he stared back at me. "Looks like they took an old silver pocket watch, that belonged to my grandfather and a Rolex watch I've had for years. The cash in my wallet's gone too, but they left my debit card and credit card, so that's a mixed blessing I suppose."

I took my Moleskine notebook and pen from the inside pocket of my coat. "From the looks of the backdoor, that was their point of entry. Can you tell me what time the break in happened?"

He looked over at the door, his face seeming to grow longer. "I honestly can't say for sure. I was...sleeping at the time. It's a bit foggy."

Glen elevated his eyebrows, as he looked down at the apostle. "Foggy? Like you were sleepy foggy or maybe a pharmaceutical foggy?"

Phil's face grew slightly red, as he stared at his hands. I moved to the similarly upholstered chair and rested my notebook on my knee. "Phil, we're not looking to stitch you up here. We just need you to remember, as best as you can, what happened here tonight."

He glanced back at Glen, before refocusing on me. "I know it was after one. I was having trouble sleeping and I needed some aid, so I came in here to...mellow out. The last time I checked, the clock said 1:14 a.m. And then I remember hearing something out back."

"Did you go and check it out?" I asked, as I took notes.

He laid his head back on the sofa to look up at the ceiling. "No. I never answer the door, when it's that late. I figured it was someone who got lost and wanted directions or something and would move on, when no one answered. Then, I heard the wood on the door frame being splintered. Before I knew it, the backdoor was opened and two guys were in my house shouting at me."

Glen moved to the door and looked at the frame and knelt down to look at the tool marks. "I guess I can fingerprint the door handle and see if they left some prints. I can also dust around the wall where the TV was too."

I nodded to him before returning to Phil. "When they came in, did they attack or threaten you in any way?"

He squinted his face, raised his hands up in frustration. "Not that I can recall. I'm pretty sure I just stayed here on the couch. I was tripping and scared all at the same time, which is probably what triggered my spell outside."

I made reference in my notes, more for his benefit than mine and stared at the page for a moment. "Can you remember what they looked like?"

I observed his face, which once again become red, as he closed his eyes while releasing a long sigh. "This is where I must've really started feeling the effects of the...medicine. Because it doesn't make any sense at all. Jonas, I could swear they had boxer shorts over their heads."

I stopped writing to look at him. "Boxer shorts? Was one of them limping?"

Phil looked down at his knees, undoubtedly trying to assemble the kaleidoscope that was his memory of the past few hours. "I think so, though I wouldn't swear to it. From what I can recollect they were both stumbling around, but I think one might have been complaining about his foot hurting."

"The prints on the door are too smudged Jonas. I'll try the TV panel," Glen said as he moved to the wall in front of Phil.

"Would you recognize their voices if you heard them again, Phil?"

He shook his head, resting his socked feet on the coffee table. "Probably not."

I closed my notebook and returned it to my inside pocket. "Phil, not to come off as rude, but it's pretty much common knowledge about the natural herbs you consume. Did those guys take your stash?"

Phil got a grin on his face, as he crossed his left ankle over his right. "Sheriff I can't say."

I rolled my tongue inside my cheek, as disbelief flooded my face. "Phil."

He tapped his chest before pointing to the mileage lines on his rectangular face. "Sheriff, look at me. I'm getting closer to seventy than I am sixty and the memory fades. It's like in the book of Matthew, *After a certain number of years, our faces become our biographies.*

I looked down at the top of my denim clad knee and gave my head a light shake. The greatest paradox for me, when it came to Phil's condition, is his misquotes. When he's in his psychotic state, he can quote the bible word for word. Yet the moment he's coherent, he's all over the map. "Phil, I'm not certain, but I'm fairly sure it was Cynthia Ozick who said that. Now can you please answer my question?"

He stared at me for a moment, his eyes pinched together. "I'd have sworn that was from Matthew."

"I need you to focus Phil. Did they take your drugs?"

"Jonas, I'm not lying, when I say I don't remember. The bible also says *No man has a good enough memory to be a successful liar.*

I scratched the skin between my eyes, as I stared at the ceiling. "Putting aside that it was Abraham Lincoln who said that, there's something you need to understand. This is the second breaking and entering for these guys. It was O'Reilly's last night, now you. So far no one has gotten hurt, but that might not be the case next time. So, if these guys are drug heads, then I need to know Phil."

He enveloped his chest with his arms, as he frowned in deep thought. "They really rob O'Reilly's?"

I nodded. "They're getting more brazen Phil. An empty store is one thing, but to bust into someone's house, while they are still in it, is another matter entirely. How would you feel, if a someone got hurt, because you held out on me?"

He looked at me, all pretense of confusion vanished from his face. "My supply has been depleted more than I recall from earlier this evening. Does that help you?"

"It does Phil. It suggests they singled you out for your weed. We'll get some extra patrols out your way for the next few days, in case they decide to come back. If I was you, I'd get a better lock for that door. Maybe even a deadbolt, if you can."

He looked at his disfigured door, his shoulders slouching a bit. "It's not a good sign of the times, when an old man can't be safe in his own house."

"Phil, we're going to get these guys, of that I have no doubt. From their choice of disguise, it's obvious, they're not criminal masterminds. You just have to be cautious, for the next few days, until we apprehend them."

I could tell my words had little effect in alleviating his feeling of violation, which in all honesty I could understand. Security is what we all want, yet it is the most difficult to acquire. As much as I hate to admit it, in many ways my job is the equivalent of a glorified janitor. More often than not, I arrive on the scene, long after some tragedy happens and it is left up to me and my department, to put the pieces together, to figure out what happened. Also more often than not, there is no rational explanation for the pain and fear of the victims, whether it be over money, drugs or just a moment of rage. In the end, it doesn't change the past or where you're standing in that moment of your life.

Phil smiled at me, as he patted me on my arm, the way old men do. He sat forward, resting his elbows on his thighs. "Jonas, I know you mean well, but I don't expect a miracle. You've only got so many deputies and a lot of territory to cover and they can't be everywhere at once. Absolute protection only comes from the Lord and that is for our immortal souls. Those who expect you to do it all are fools, even if they don't know it. It was in Ezekiel that it was said, *A fellow who is always declaring he's no fool, usually has his suspicions.*"

It wasn't from Ezekiel and I couldn't place the original author, but his point was nonetheless true.

Chapter Three

When I got home, there was no sense, in even trying to squeeze in any more winks of sleep. Instead, I opted to go to my basement and stretch, before doing some jumping jacks and sparing with the punching bag. Next, I did my repetitions with the weights. Then I took Mick on another walk, as the sun crested the hills, using the shadows of the naked trees, to stencil the valley with jagged black lines. After returning home, I ate breakfast and showered.

I dressed and put on my watch, before I slipped my badge on the left side of my belt, along with the double pouch, which held my two extra magazines for my sidearm. I opened the drawer to reveal my 1911 forty-five, a recent gift from Lydia's father, Alexander. The jet black ceramic coat over the slide complimented, the stainless match grade barrel, giving the gun a professional quality look. Lydia had been after me to get a handgun, with a light rail and ambidextrous safety, but I had been putting it off. The general, decided I needed a better firearm, to help ensure I made it home to his daughter. I could not offer up an argument or complaint. I performed a brass check and found a round in the chamber, plus a magazine filled with eight rounds of hollow point .45 ammunition, for a total of nine, then holstered the weapon. Making myself a cup of coffee, for my travel mug, I then made sure Mick had food and plenty of water to drink. I double checked his doggy door before I got in the truck.

I drove straight to the stationhouse, but instead of heading into the office, I crossed the street to where our forensic laboratory was located. Entering the mud red brick building, the warmth from the heat felt like a warm towel caressing my cold cheeks. I moved passed the front desk, down the corridor, to the supervisor's office and knocked on the door. The head of the facility, Molly Newman, behind her desk and typing on the computer, looked up and waved me in. "Morning Jonas."

I entered her office, noticing she had on fuchsia colored scrubs, I hadn't seen before. "Get yourself a new outfit, Molly?"

She glanced down at her attire, scratching her neck beneath her curtain of rich brown hair. "Yeah. I got tired of the same old green ones. I thought I'd just go a little wild and try something new." She paused to look at my face, narrowing her brown eyes. "You get much rest last night?"

I smiled and took a seat across from the desk. "I was, until around four this morning, when I had to handle a breaking and entering call at Phil's house."

She stopped her typing, and rested the flats of her hands on the desk. "Was that the same break in, Glen retrieved the fingerprints from?"

I nodded.

"Is Phil all right?"

I nodded, yawing into my fist. "Yeah. He was giving a sermon in his briefs, but I was able to settle him down and get him back inside his house."

Molly looked down at her keyboard, scratching her forehead with her fingertips. "You know he's getting some age on him now Jonas. One of these days, he's liable to go into one of his dissociative states and get hurt, before you're able to get there."

"I've thought the same thing more than once, Molly. Unfortunately, there isn't a whole lot I can do about it right now. He's lucid most of the time and is able to keep a roof over his head, pay his bills and so forth. If I wanted to push it, I could probably have his mental competency brought up before a judge. With his history, it wouldn't be too hard to have him declared incompetent, but then that brings up the question of what would happen to him? Where would we put him? He has family in Ohio, but we can't legally make them take him in and if they don't, that means a state home."

Molly cocked her head over her left shoulder, pushing her chair back from her desk to cross her leg. "I see your point. It's a rock and multiple hard places."

I took a long sip from my coffee and rested the cup on my knee. "As much as I hate to say it, for now, all we can do is wait and see."

"I hate that expression."

We all hate it. It's because, it reminds us of how powerless, we really are in the grand scheme of the world. "The breaking and entering, at Phil's place, seems to have been done by the same guys, who broke into O'Reily's the day before. Phil remembers the robbers wore boxer shorts for masks. I know it's early, but have you had a chance to compare the fingerprints at both scenes?"

"Give me ten minutes." Molly stood up and walked into the lab. Exactly ten minutes later, she came back into her office. "The prints at both scenes came from the same two people. Of course, that probably didn't come as much of a surprise, since both assailants were wearing boxer shorts for masks. What's with that?"

I shook my head staring up at the heavens. "I have no idea. I've got Glen doing some background, to see if there's been any more reported sightings or robberies in the surrounding counties or if we're lucky enough to be the birthplace, of this particular crime wave."

She smiled, revealing a slightly off center front tooth, as she handed me the folder. "Well, I'm afraid there isn't any luck when it comes to their identities. A.F.I.S. gave us no hits. The nimrods don't have a record."

I opened the file to the photographic copies of the zebra pattern oval prints. "Not yet, at least. We need to get these guys off the streets fast."

Molly took a pen and flipped it, like a pendulum, between two fingers. "Don't worry about it Jonas. There's no way you won't be able to catch these guys."

"I have no doubt about that Molly, it's what will happen between now and then, that's got me concerned. These guys have gone from robbing stores afterhours, to personal homes, in a short span of time. That's a heck of an escalation. I'm afraid they might actually hurt someone, if we don't nip this in the bud fast."

A lopsided grin illuminated her face, as she leaned her chair back on two legs. "It looks like, if Glen doesn't find anything in his search, then all you can do is wait and see what happens."

I narrowed my blue eyes at her, before standing to leave. "Touché"

Jack had no messages for me, so I decided to stop by Glen's desk. "Good morning Glen."

Glen looked over his shoulder at me, nodding. "Morning. If you're wondering if the two bozos, with underwear breath, have been running around the other counties, I'm afraid the answer is no."

"That's what I figured. There's no way their disguise wouldn't have registered, on someone's radar before now. So, we're the lucky county where these guys decided to launch their careers."

Glen twirled his finger in the air, as he returned to his work. "Yeah, we're the lucky ones all right."

I took another long sip from my coffee and started to head to my office, when Jack stood up at his desk. "Hey Jonas, I just got a call for you, saying you're needed at the Hardees in Vonore."

I wrinkled my forehead, perplexity filling my brain. "Let the Vonore City Police Department handle it, that's their jurisdiction."

Jack held up the phone, a puzzled look all over his face. "That's what I said, but this is the manager and she said she's called the VCPD three times and no one has showed up."

"Three times? What seems to be the problem?"

Jack arched his eyebrows, as he handed me the phone. "Apparently, there's seems be a disturbance with one of the customers. The manager fears there's going to be a riot."

I took the receiver, setting my coffee cup on Jack's desk. "Sheriff Lauer. What seems to be the problem?"

"Sheriff, this is Greta Bibi, the shift manager here at Hardees. I need someone to get down here and help us out. I'm afraid they're going to hurt this guy."

I heard elevated voices, in the background, that seemed to be growing in fervor by the second. "Who is the customer that seems to be causing the trouble?"

"I really don't know. I can hear some of the people calling him Alston in between the screams."

* * *

Erring on the side of caution, I hitched a ride with Deputy Tom Kirk in his cruiser. We made the normally fifteen-minute drive to Vonore, in six minutes, aided by both siren and lights. Upon parking, next to the front door, I exited the vehicle, before Tom had the ignition switched off, unbuttoned my overcoat, to allow easier access to my sidearm, if it was necessary. The muffled shouting of the patrons inside, could be heard coming through the double glass doors of the vestibule.

Hardees is famously known for its scrumptious, artery clogging breakfasts and is almost always full in the mornings. Today was no different, yet instead of forming a line, there was a corral of people surrounding two men, next to the public restrooms. I instantly recognized the bearded man, as Alston O'Brian. The other man, who was about half his age with a two-day stubble of gray shadowing his jaw and a blue toboggan over his smooth head, was unrecognizable to me. He had his hands on the lapel of Alston's pea coat shaking him back and forth like a ragdoll. "Why the hell did you come back here, you son-of-a-bitch? Taking my family's money and land wasn't enough? You have to rub our faces in it by prancing around town."

Alston wasn't saying anything or seeming to offer up much of a physical defense either. I started shoving patrons aside, my badge in my left hand. "Move aside. Sheriff's department step out of the way."

Tom was there helping me wade into the eye of the storm. Once there, I secured my badge to my belt, so my hands were free and moved to the two men before me. "Sir, release him right now."

The toboggan man turned to me, flashing his yellow tinted teeth beneath feral green eyes. "Piss off. I've wanted to get my hands on this piece of shit for eighteen years."

He shoved Alston against the wall, knocking a reproduction of a Norman Rockwell painting down onto the cobblestone tile floor. The man, then charged the conman like a bull, but I was close enough to intervene. Setting my feet, I pivoted hard with my left arm outstretched and circled it around the throat of the raging man. I felt a jarring wave ascend up my arm and into my shoulder. The charging man was knocked back on his heels, waving his arms in a reverse circular motion, attempting to propel himself forward. I grabbed his forearm, with my right hand and put my left on his shoulder, as my left foot hooked behind his right ankle. The momentum forced him onto his back, where I rolled him over and put the cuffs on him. "Hey, he didn't do anything wrong."

I looked up to see a man, with long gray hair and a matching beard, moving toward me, as a few hagglers inched behind him. Tom had his hand over the grip of his gun, while sending out an officer needs assistance call on the radio. "You need to stop right there boys."

The small group, kept closing the divide between us and I slowly removed the curtain of my overcoat, to reveal the afzelia wood grip of my forty-five, as I placed my palm, just over the underside of the hammer. "I think everyone needs to settle down, before things get real messy around here."

The group halted their advance, but I could see in their eyes, that the mob mentality had yet to recede the fog of rage, which had engulfed their reasoning. "Folks, I realize a lot of you have a grievance with this man. A part of me even sympathizes with you. The fact is Alston O'Brian has served his time, for the crimes he was convicted of. As angry as you are with him, you can't take matters into your own hands."

I had my knee on the back of the man I had cuffed, as he lifted his head to speak. "Are you going to arrest us all? Looks like you're out numbered sheriff."

The others cheered him on. I inhaled a deep breath, as I felt a buoyance of anxiety swell in my stomach, then ever so slowly dissipate, as I exhaled, leaving behind a familiar serenity. "Before any of you make another move, you need to ponder the situation you're in. Whatever steps you take now are going to affect the course of your lives. You need to understand, if you step any closer to me or my deputy, no matter the outcome, it will have irrevocable consequences, that will follow you for the rest of your days."

The man with a ponytail shouted, as he sucked in air between his teeth. "You really expect us to believe you'll shoot us?"

There was surge, of adrenalin beginning to course through my veins, turning the skin along the back of my neck and forehead hot. I relaxed the fingers of my right hand, allowing the tips to touch the cool steel of my handgun. "I suppose there's only way for us to find out, isn't there?"

I've been in a few precarious situations, as sheriff, with my back to the wall. In every situation, I find my mind flickers to the most peculiar places. Often, I see flashes of my parents and Lydia through the blinking of my eyelids. However, during the nanoseconds I waited for their decision, I found myself trying to decipher how I wound up in the cliché, of being the lawman facing down this angry mob.

"I'm not pressing charges."

All eyes turned to Alston, who had remained silent, on the floor, up to that moment. His words seem to have the effect of water on flames. The group suddenly developed laryngitis, as they stared at the man they believed was the nucleus of their righteous anger. I looked down at my prisoner, to see he was trying to twist around for a look at the man he wanted to pummel. "Mr. O'Brian, are you sure you don't want me to arrest this man for assaulting you?"

Alston leaned against the wall, in an effort to stand. "Yes. I don't want to press any charges against anyone here."

Everyone looked at one another, not sure of what they should do, so I took the reins of this runaway stagecoach. I grabbed the man below me and helped him to his feet. "All right, you're free to go. Mr. ?"

His toboggan was off center over his left ear, as a result of his face being planted into the floor. "I don't have to give you a name. I'm not under arrest."

I nodded holding the key to the cuffs in my hand. "Not yet, you're not."

His eyes became elliptical, as he turned to look at me. "He just said he wasn't going to press charges."

I nodded, allowing the handcuff key to dangle loosely in my hand, as I stared at him. "That is correct sir; *he's* not going to press charges. *I* can still charge you for inciting a riot and noncompliance with an order from a police officer. Or you can give me your name."

Looking down at the floor, he spat out a small burst of air, before looking at me with his jaw set. "Harrison Birch."

I eyed him for a minute, recalling the name from the casefile I had read yesterday. "You any relation to Donovan Birch?"

Harrison's oval face grew stern, as he spoke through gritted teeth. "He's my father. Or he was. After losing all of his property, to that piece of trash over there, he was never the same. It was like the life was sapped out of him and he just wasted away."

From the corner of my eye, I noticed Alston was standing silently, his hands in the pockets of his coat, displaying no emotion on his face. Tom was standing beside him, his hand still resting on the grip of his Smith & Wesson. I turned my attention to the man with the ponytail, who seemed to be a co-conspirator. "And your name sir?"

He looked to Harrison, for a moment, before turning toward me. "Patrick Winchell."

The name wasn't ringing any bells from the case. "And do you have a connection to Mr. O'Brian."

"That's not really any of your business is it?" Patrick said.

Fair enough. I turned Harrison around and removed his restraints. He stepped toward Patrick, rubbing his wrists. I turned toward the staff of the restaurant, as a black woman, with swaths of gray in her shortcut dark curly hair stepped forward. "Are you Greta Bibi?"

She nodded, leaning on the countertop beside the cash register. "Yes sir. I don't know what this is all about, but I can say, that it was those two who started it. The older gentleman was at the register trying to order his breakfast. The man in the toboggan, Mr. Birch, was sitting with his friend over at the table by the backdoor, when he jumped out of the booth and started yelling. I called the city police, but no one came."

I nodded toward the broken picture frame. "How do you want to handle this Ms. Bibi? Other than the painting, is there any other damage done to the establishment?"

Alston took a silver money clip from the inside pocket of his coat, filled with crisp greenbacks. He removed three one hundred dollar bills and placed them on the counter. "That should cover any damages. If it is all right with you, I think we all just want to put this behind us."

All eyes, including mine, were on those green Benjamin Franklins. Greta tapped her fingers on the countertop for a few moments, before she looked up at Alston. "I guess that is all right. But the two who started this are no longer welcome here. Sir, I know you're the victim here—"

"Victim?" Harrison placed his hands on his hips.

Greta got a look on her face, which left me no doubt she was a mother, because it made both men take a step back. "I personally saw you two attack this man. I don't know what he did to you in the past, but you totally attacked him for no reason. Isn't that the definition of a victim?"

Tom looked over at Harrison and Patrick, his body language more relaxed, now that a lot of the tension had been alleviated. "Yes, it is."

Greta kept her gaze targeted on the two men, as she pointed to Tom. "That settles it. You two are no longer welcome here. As for you sir, I know this isn't fair and I can't ban you, but I would ask that you not come back here. I'm sorry."

Alston replaced his money clip in his pocket nodding, with no ill inflection in his voice. "I completely understand ma'am. It's me who should apologize to you."

I looked at the two men and the crowd, as the AC unit streamed more heat into the building. "All right, for those of you who've already eaten, there's nothing left to see, so go about your business. The rest of you enjoy your sausage biscuits. Mr. O'Brian, follow me and Deputy Kirk outside, please."

The cold air slapped me in the face, as I stepped out on the front sidewalk, causing me to pull the lapel of my coat over my neck. Tom zipped up his bomber's jacket, as we made our way to the cruiser. We all glanced back at the restaurant as Harrison and Patrick exited. Alston followed, keeping his hands in his pockets. "Mr. O'Brian can we offer you a lift?"

Alston stood beside our cruiser, looking out at the highway seeming to stare at the traffic light. "No, my car is over there by the payphone. If it's all right, I'll just wait here until they're gone."

Harrison got into his faded blue pickup truck, with rust speckled along the tire well. He ignited the engine, giving Alston a double barrel stare, as he revved the motor several times for effect, before putting the gear in reverse. He pulled up to the traffic light and turned right to cross the bridge. Patrick was resting his hands on the roof of his green Mazda pick-up. After about a minute or so, he got behind the wheel and took a left into Madisonville.

When I looked at Alston, I noticed a thin ribbon of red drippling down his cheek, touching the collar of his orange shirt. I put my hand on his shoulder, to keep him from moving. "Mr. O'Brian, you're injured."

He shrugged out of my grip and headed to his sedan. "I'll be all right sheriff. Thank you for your time."

I stepped ahead of him to cut him off. "Mr. O'Brian—"

He paused to look at me, a small smile on his face. "Sheriff, I think after what just happened, you can call me Alston."

I exhaled a deep breath, stepping back on my left foot. "Alston, you should really see a doctor about that."

He gently racked his head with his knuckles. "It'll take more than a knock on this head to take me out. I'll be just fine."

He stepped around me, but I walked with him. "You make me curious Alston."

"How so?"

I scratched the back of my neck, adjusting the collar of my shirt underneath my coat. "It just seems a bit odd to me, that a man who got out of prison just a few days ago, would return to the place that led to his incarceration. And even more peculiar is that you're driving a very nice car, wearing good quality clothing and have a money clip filled with hundred dollar bills. Can you see why that might peak my curiosity sir?"

Alston shrugged, as he pulled the car keys out of his pocket. "I suppose it would make me a bit perplexed too, sheriff."

He clicked the unlock button on the key, and the car emitted a beep, before the doors released the locks. I blocked his attempt to reach the handle. "It's peculiar enough to make a man wonder, if all those stories about the missing money were true. I mean, why else would someone come back to the place, where the people have so much animosity against him, unless it was to retrieve six hundred thousand dollars."

A subtle smile developed on Alston's face, as he squared against me, putting his hands in his pockets. "I see you've looked at the casefiles."

I returned his smile. "It's not often that we have an individual, of your celebrity coming through our county, Alston. It's only natural to want to do some background on you."

"Plus when you have a person in town, that may cause trouble, it helps if you know what you're getting yourself into."

I shrugged, as I realized there were no flies on him. "True. So, if I may be so bold Alston, is it the money that brings you back to Vonore?"

"Sheriff, with all due respect, my business here is mine, not yours. As I'm sure you're aware, if I had hidden away some money, as it was believed, the statute of limitations has expired, so there is no penalty for me retrieving it."

"If it exists you mean?"

He smiled again, before looking over at the BP gas station beside us. "Right. Why are you interested in it sheriff? You thinking of what it would be like if you could get your hands on it? Maybe retire early, on an island, where a pretty waitress in a bikini, would be at your beck and call?"

I pursed my lips, as I shook my head. "The idea never entered my mind Alston. I haven't spent much time around those with money, but the few times I have, it always seems to me that they were always consumed with dread, that they either didn't have enough, or someone was going to try to take it from them. I'm quite comfortable, as I am, for the time being."

The mileage lines on his forehead grew deeper, as he seemed to study me through squinted eyes. "You know, I believe you just may be telling the truth."

"I've no reason to lie."

This seemed to have hit his funny button, because he chuckled softly. "I'm sorry, but you have to know that in my experience, the cops lie, just as much as I did with my cons. The only difference is the state says it's legal. Although, I do take it back about one cop. It was the sheriff back then, that took over the case. Bill Hayes"

I felt the cold slowly working its way up my legs, causing them to grow slightly numb, so I stomped them on the hard asphalt, to get the blood circulating again. "He was my predecessor."

He pointed at me and nodded. "Now *he* treated me cordially, save for the time I tried to escape, that is."

I felt my eyes expand to the size of silver dollars. "Escape? I don't remember seeing a charge for that in your file?"

He hunched his shoulders, as he once again retrieved his key from his pocket. "That's what I mean, when I said he treated me well. It was just two days after my extradition went through. I tried to make a run for it, while they were taking be back to holding, after being questioned by the prosecuting attorney all day. It was late and the department was pretty much empty, save for the sheriff and a couple of deputies. They didn't have me in leg irons, so as I was escorted back to my cell, I made a run for the door. It was a stupid and futile play, but I was desperate. I made it to the front door and thought I was home free, but then I felt two strong hands grip my shoulders and shove me to the floor."

I felt myself smile, as I listened to him. "Bill is a strong one. He worked on a dairy farm, for years, before being elected sheriff. I believe he could crush walnuts with his bare hands, if he chose to. What happened next?"

Alston waved his hand out, the key reflecting in the sunlight. "Took me back to my cell and asked me why I ran. I told him the honest truth, that I didn't know. He just stood on the other side of the bars and looked at me for a long time, before he shook his head and went back to his office. I figured I would be charged with fleeing arrest or something, but it was never bought up at trial. I never found out why he decided to not press charges."

"I'm sure he had his reasons."

"Is he still alive?"

"Yes. I took office after he him, but he's still with us."

Alston gave me a thumbs up. "Good. Like I said I've never had the best experience with cops, but he was all right. You kind of remind me of him in a way."

I felt my cheeks grow red, glad for the cold wind to camouflage my discomfort. There was a silence, that was beginning to settle between us, signaling our conversation was at the crossroads of us going our separate ways. Like our first meeting, I had nothing to hold him on, or compel him to divulge the reason for his return. "I can't make you tell me why you're here Alston, but I can offer you some unsolicited advice. Whatever the reason you're here, you better wrap it up quick. The next time you get in trouble, I might not get there in time to help you."

I offered him another business card, but he waved his hand, patting his back pocket where I assumed his wallet was. "I still got the one you gave me yesterday. Thanks for the help sheriff and have a good day."

I moved aside and let him get into his car and watched him leave. I returned to the department cruiser, where Tom was waiting, with his usually benign face taunt with frustration. "What is it?"

"I cancelled the officer needs assistance call. The only reply I got was from Jack and two Madisonville P.D. patrolmen."

I stared at him, thinking about what he had just said. "No one from the Vonore City Police Department was responding to our call?"

Tom shook his head, tucking his fists into his coat pocket. "No sir. I called the VCPD headquarters and asked why they didn't reply and you want to know what they said?"

I watched the capillaries of my deputy's face develop a dark rouge tint, as his voice became more elevated. "What did they say?"

He spat out a disgusted breath before replying, "They never heard the call. There must've been a technical malfunction."

Now I felt my own skin grow warm, as the muscles of my chest and shoulders tighten with tension. "Let's take a trip to the VCPD station."

* * *

The Vonore City Police Department's building is located on Church Street, through the overpass for the railroad tracks, just past Davis Recycling and Farnsworth Firearms. If it weren't for the sign out front, the station would look like a two-story white house. It is positioned right across from the public library, with a view of Tellico Lake. Tom parked in the visitor parking lot. We both entered the station through the glass door, where a man of solid build, in a blue uniform, was typing. His red hair was cut close to his scalp and freckles were sprinkled all over his face, which judging from the absence of any wrinkles, told me he was barely in his late twenties. His nameplate said Hensley. "Officer Hensley, I'd like to speak with Chief West please."

His eyes remained glued to his screen as he replied, "Chief West is busy right now sir. May I take a message?"

I looked toward the office with the word Chief painted on it and saw the man himself sitting behind his desk, casually reading a report. Looking back at Hensley I smiled at him, resting my hand on his desk. "Officer, I believe you might have a wire crossed, because I see the chief right over there, at his desk and he doesn't appear to be too busy. Maybe you should check again."

Still remaining transfixed by his work, Hensley bobbed his head and typed away. "So you're saying, I don't know how to do my job?"

"I didn't say that officer. I just want to speak with Chief West for a few minutes."

He finally looked at me, his green eyes as hard and emotionless as emerald stones. "Really? You want to speak with him now, after you stepped in on our jurisdiction?"

Tom stepped to the side of me, so he could look at the officer. "We called it in on the radio. The manager at Hardees called you guys first, but apparently you fellows had something *else* to do beside your job."

Hensley's face began to match the tint of his hair. He stood up, leaning onto his desk, bracing himself with the knuckles of his fists. "So now, you think you can come in here and tell us how to do our jobs? Who the hell do you think you are? You're just a deputy."

Tom, whose own face was red with rage, moved to step up to the desk, but I intercepted him and leveled my eyes on Hensley. "You're correct, he is a deputy." I removed my badge from my belt and held it up so he could see it. "What does it say on there, officer?"

He looked at the gold seven pointed star medallion for a brief moment, before he returned my glare. Exhaling a long breath, he swallowed hard and parted his lips. "It says sheriff."

I placed the badge back on my belt. "Yes, it does and I'd appreciate, if you showed me the respect that title deserves. I don't have to get permission to come into your jurisdiction, because the entire county is my jurisdiction. I'll see Chief West now."

I stepped through the swinging door, but Hensley seemed to think he still had a say in the matter. "Hey you can't go back there."

I saw Tom in my peripheral vision, set his jaw and plant his hands on his hips. "Are you serious?"

Having enough, I turned and moved toward him, where the officer took a step back. "Son, I don't know who or what put that bee in your bonnet and frankly, I don't care. I'm going to see your chief."

The interior of the office had four empty desks covered in police folders and various other paperwork. The Vonore City Police

Department consisted of eight officers, including the chief, so you rarely saw more than one or two officers in the building, at any given time, as the rest were patrolling the streets. I knocked on the doorframe, then entered the chief's office. "Chief West."

He glanced up at me, before resuming his reading. "Sheriff Lauer."

Saul West was a robust man in his mid-forties, with sandy blond hair cut military style and a solid figure, that still resembled the former running back he had been in high school. I took a seat in the chair after unbuttoning my coat. "Having a good morning today, Saul?"

He seesawed his head, as he turned the page of his report. "About the usual. I heard you had an interesting breakfast."

"It wasn't so much interesting, as it was confounding." I crossed my leg and rested my hand on my knee. "I can't figure out why a sworn officer of the law didn't respond to a disturbance call. Care to fill me in?"

Closing the folder, Saul looked at me, his square face stoic, as he inhaled a deep breath. "I can only answer that question with another one. What concern is it of yours?"

I had my own poker face in full throttle, as I plucked a loose thread from my pants. "When a man is being attacked in a restaurant and the city police don't respond, it makes me very concerned."

"As Officer Hensley explained to your deputy, we never received that call."

"Deputy Kirk called for assistance on the radio."

"Our radios weren't working."

Suddenly, an officer called in a vehicle breaking the speed limit, loud and clear on the scuffed black radio, resulting in my right eyebrow elevating up to my hairline. "You wish to revise that last statement?"

Saul got a grin on his face, that was very close to a sneer and shrugged. "We just got it fixed."

He didn't miss a beat; I have to give him that. "Okay Saul, can we skip all of this and just get to the chase? Why did you ignore the call from Greta at Hardee's?"

Saul leaned back in his chair, swiveling it back and forth for a few moments, before he nodded. "All right. Maybe, just maybe we decided to drag our feet on the disturbance call. I mean come on Jonas, that guy ruined a lot of lives in this town and he has the gall to come back and doesn't expect to get roughed up a bit?"

"When I got there Saul, it was about to escalate, into something more than just a roughing up."

"Tempers flare, but that doesn't mean it would've led to anything serious."

I was tapping my finger on my knee, as I kept my eyes focused on him. "And the other patrons and staff watching scared and confused, as to why the police didn't show up?"

He rolled his eyes and held up his hands. "All right, all right. In hindsight it may have been a mistake. But you guys got there in time, so no harm no foul right?"

I looked around his office, the walls only decorated with a muscle car calendar. The vibrations from the steady cadence of a train, could be heard traversing the iron track across from the station, causing me to wait a moment, so I wouldn't have to yell over the noise. "I suppose we'll have to agree to disagree on that one Saul. Forgive me for being so direct, but it's been one of those mornings. Is there another reason why you didn't reply to the disturbance?"

He stopped his swiveling and tapped his fingers on his desk, as he sucked in his cheek. "I'm not sure I understand what you're asking?"

"I'm just curious if you know anyone or if any of your relatives were swindled by Alston O'Brian. I only read the court transcripts yesterday and I don't recollect anyone named West being listed, but wouldn't swear to it."

Saul gazed at the corner of his desk in silence. I had him and he knew it. If he lied all I would have to do is recheck the transcripts or even pull the original casefile, to see if anyone related to him was a victim in Alston's con. He lifted his brown eyes, as he sucked on his cheek once again. "The Udalls."

I narrowed my eyes, as I filtered through the long list of victims I had read. "You mean Martin Udall and his wife? The old police chief's son and daughter-n-law?"

He nodded. "I was close with the family. They were good people."

I lowered my head to look at the tops of my shoes, resisting the urge to sigh, for fear it would make the situation worse. "I'm sorry to hear this. They lost their home right?"

Saul's jaw became rigid, as he grit his teeth. "Yeah. The strain almost drove the two of them to divorce. They had to move back in with Martin's dad for nearly three years, before they got their feet underneath them again."

I pointed to the front door. "Does Officer Hensley have a connection to the O'Brian case? He seemed to have a lot of anger in him about the situation."

Saul looked over my shoulder, to where the officer in question, was still stationed. "Officer Daniel Hensley went to school with kids, whose parents were victims of Mr. O'Brian. You see sheriff, I don't think you fully grasp how deep these waters are. It wasn't just a few people that O'Brian cheated. It was their families and friends, who had to help keep them afloat. I know of several people, who nearly had to file for bankruptcy, because they had to assist family members, who lost their shirts to that man. So, can you understand, why him being here again stirs up a lot of hard feelings?"

I scratched the corner of my eye, with my knuckle. "That brings up another interesting question Saul. How did the people find out so quickly that Alston O'Brian was back in Vonore? I only found out from Mr. Deland yesterday, that he had returned. Did he tell you as well?"

The chief rested his forearms on the desktop, interlacing his fingers to roll his thumbs over one another. "Yeah. It was just a heads-up."

I planted my feet flat on the faux hardwood floor and scooted to the edge of my seat. "Did the A.G. ask you to give the victims a heads-up too? News travels fast in a small town, but the man has barely been back for twenty-four hours and already the people are after him? Did you call them or was it Mr. Deland?"

The muscles around his jaw line appeared to knot up, as he gripped his fingers tighter on his desk. "What are you implying, Jonas?"

I held up my right hand, palm out. "I'm not implying anything Saul. I'm just trying to get a better understanding of what's happening here."

The chief stood, pulling up his gun belt before resting his hands on his hips. "I appreciate your concern Jonas, but we can take care of our neck of the woods. Now if you'll excuse me, it's my turn to patrol this morning."

I stood up and offered him my hand, which he shook and released as quickly as he could. "Don't let me keep you Saul."

Tom and I were in the cruiser, watching Saul exiting the station, zipping his jacket before he entered his own cruiser and ignited the engine. Tom stared through the slightly fogged windshield, shaking his head. "Can you believe he actually thought we were going to believe the radios were down?"

I reached over and hit the defrost button and watched the white vapors slowly recede from the windows. "I don't think he really cared, if we believed him or not. Let's head back."

Tom put the car in gear and headed back on Highway 411. We were at the traffic light, near Weigels, when he asked, "Did I hear you right when you said to O'Brian there was supposedly six hundred thousand dollars missing from the loot he stole?"

I tilted my head over my left shoulder, watching a Food Lion delivery truck pull off 321 onto the four lane highway. "According to the transcripts, the prosecution stated there was money missing from the accounts they were able to trace after Alston was captured."

Tom released a slow whistle, gripping the steering wheel tighter. "That's even more of an incentive for the victims and anyone else for that matter, to go after the man. You think it's possible that the money is still here, after all these years?"

"You mean if it exists? I don't know Tom. Your guess is as good as mine. Real or not, you said it yourself, all it's done is put a target on the man's back."

Tom's face grew quiet and still, as he lowered his voice. "You think the chief may be after the money?"

I looked at him pointing my finger in his direction. "I don't know, but you keep that between us for now. We've nothing to support the theory that Saul is after the money. Besides, we've stirred up enough dust, for the time being."

"So what now?"

I smiled, looking out the window. "I think it's time I visited an old friend, who was there when all of this went down."

Chapter Four

I sat waiting, in the brick lined room, watching the sun engulf the bars on the window, etching charcoal shadows across the wall. I slowly oscillated the styrophoam cup of coffee on the table. Another cup of coffee was sitting on the other side, awaiting the arrival of one of the best detectives to ever bless Monroe County. I've lost count of the times the two of us have met, to discuss investigations, while I was still just a forensic investigator, for the sheriff's department. Of course we were both a bit younger and the circumstances have changed, but I always gain insight from our conversations. I can only hope I've been as helpful to him over the years.

The buzzer chimed a half second before the steel door opened. He was sandwiched between two guards, who then released his wrists from the chain around his waist, before attaching the cuffs, to the ring in the center of the table. I nodded to the guards, as they exited the room. Spying the coffee, he took it in hand and drank a long sip, before exhaling a deep breath afterward. "Thanks Jonas. I really needed that."

I raised my own cup in salute. "Any time Bill."

Bill Hayes sat garbed in an orange jumpsuit, his hair in a small ponytail, and his face covered with a silver beard. He was the sheriff before me, for almost two decades, with hardly a blemish on his record, until one day he came home early and found Ana, his wife of nearly thirty-three years, in their marital bed, with another man. Upon seeing her betrayal, he drew his service weapon and killed the two of them. I was running against him and just mere weeks before the election, we discovered their skeletal remains in a banana box, after a fire broke out in the master bedroom. Bill engaged in a standoff, with the police and the Tennessee Bureau of Investigation for several hours, before requesting to turn himself in to me. He removed his name from the ballet and with my name being the only one left, I won the election. Bill got twenty to life and as far as I know, has never held any bitterness toward me for arresting him.

Taking another sip from his coffee, he inhaled a deep breath and glanced out at the sun. "How is the world out there?"

I shrugged, following his gaze to the window. "About the same as before, only much colder. Lydia's stuck in Nashville because of the ice storm."

Bill grinned, tapping his finger on the side of the cup. "From what you've told me about her, that has to be driving her crazy."

I shook my head, unable to keep a smile from my face. "Oh yes it is. I love her, but she is a bit of a control freak and when she's reminded that we have very little control over the events of our lives, she can't stand it. We'll keep that between us."

Bill smiled, looking around at our surroundings. "I think I can guarantee that."

We spent the next few minutes going over the idle catching up, before I brought up a case from his past. "Monroe County has a new visitor. Or to be more specific Vonore has."

"Who's that?"

"Alston O'Brian."

I watched the flesh around his eyes grow tense, as he sat up straight, the serious cop face in full onset. "Alston O'Brian? Are you certain?"

I placed my hand on the tabletop, slowly bobbing my head. "I saw the man with my own eyes just yesterday morning. Then this morning, I had to stop an attack on him, at the Hardees in Vonore."

Bill's mouth dropped open, his shoulders slouching. "The man went back to Vonore? Has prison made him suicidal?"

I sat up straight on the bench and rotated my neck. "I didn't get the sense he's suicidal. In all honesty, I couldn't get a real bead on him."

Bill exhaled a light chuckle, as he massaged the skin between his eyes with his thumb. "Yeah, that's about the way I remember him. I believe I interviewed him three times and to this day, I'm still not quite sure who was really in charge of the interrogation."

"He said that you were the only lawman to ever treat him with respect. He also mentioned that I reminded him of you. Of course, I believe he was trying to pull one over on me, so I'd let him go."

Bill grinned again, hunching his shoulders. "That is the thing with those con artists. You can never be certain if they are telling the truth or spinning a web."

I shrugged. "The best lies are the ones with strings of truth woven in them."

Bill looked down at his fingers, splayed on the table top for a few seconds, his forehead wrinkled in deep thought. "He got twenty years for his sentence. So I take it he did the full bit?"

"According to the assistant attorney general, he was released four days ago, on early release for being a model prisoner."

Bill stared up at the ceiling and shook his head. "A model prisoner? That's always seemed like an oxymoron."

I slowly rubbed my finger in small circles on the table. There was a tone to his voice, that said there was more behind that last remark. We were friends in our own unique way, but the unspoken truth is, that though Bill may understand how I live my life outside the walls of cinderblocks and steel bars, I'll never understand his world behind them. I gave him another moment before I proceeded. "During my conversation with Mr. Deland I couldn't help but notice, he seemed a bit over zealous in his wish to have Alston run out of town or arrested.

Either scenario seemed appealing to him, so I took a look at the trial transcripts and gleamed some valuable intelligence."

Bill looked at me for a few seconds then hunched his shoulders. "Do I have to guess?"

"One of the victims from Alston's con, was Gretchen Deland."

The former sheriff closed his eyes, as he rested his chin on his chest. "That's right. I had completely forgotten about that. Anthony had only been with the AG's office for a short while. I had only met him a couple of times, but I do remember Gretchen. She was a nice lady, with a good heart. It was a damn shame what happened to her. It was a shame what happened to all of the victims."

"At least she didn't lose as much as the other victims. Still, it does bring Anthony's objectivity into question. I mean, you swindle a man's mom, and it's going to leave a bad taste in your mouth, no matter how long it's been."

Bill exhaled a sardonic sigh and gave me a smile. "You just want to arrest another attorney general, don't you?"

I narrowed my eyes, not seeing any humor in his last statement. "Once was more than enough, thank you very much."

Bill held up his hands in faux surrender. "I'm just kidding son. You did what you had to do with Sam Phillips. A lot of cops would've been tempted to let the prosecuting attorney skate on the charges. You didn't. That's nothing to be ashamed of."

I waved my hand, palm down, saying it was OK. "Well, I have more than Anthony Deland to worry about this time. During the fight at Hardees none of the Vonore P.D. showed up after repeated calls from the manager. When Tom and I arrived we called for officer needs assistance and still no response. After things settled down, I made a trip to the station to speak directly with the chief."

"What did the chief say?"

I tilted my head to my right, displayed my hands on the table. "He said the radios were down at that time."

Bill rolled his eyes. "Well that's original. Who is the chief now?"

"Saul West."

Bill looked at me, his face growing taut, as he leaned into the table. "Saul West is the chief of police in Vonore?"

The hushed tone in his voice sent a chill down my spine. I leaned forward, leveling my eyes with his. "Why is that a bad thing?"

He moved closer to me, lowering his voice to one octave above a whisper. "Saul West's mother, Tammy, went into labor while on the way to the hospital. A police officer noticed the car driving erratically, pulled it over believing the driver was drunk. Turns out he ended up having to deliver the baby. There were complications, the uterine wall ruptured and Tammy bled out. No one was at fault, it was just a tragic accident. Saul's father was out of the picture long before the first trimester, so he was officially a ward of the state. The officer involved felt bad for Saul and he adopted the baby."

I felt the chill along my spine drop another five degrees, as I had an inclination where this was going. "Was the officer who delivered the baby, former chief of police, Valance Udall?"

Bill nodded his head. "The one and the same. He raised Saul like he was his own."

I rested my forehead on the thumbs of my interlaced hands, feeling the beginnings of a headache. "Saul didn't mention that, when I asked him if he had any connections to the original case."

Bill sat back, the chains of his leg irons clanking on the floor. "That doesn't sound good."

"Then why don't they have the same last name?"

Bill shrugged, as he leaned back. "I don't know. Maybe he felt like Saul should keep his mother's name. Either way, Alston O'Brian isn't a welcome guest in the town of Vonore."

I pointed at him, as a realization came to light. "And since Saul wasn't a direct victim, his name was never mentioned in any of the casefiles."

"Bingo."

I set my cup to the side, rubbing my head with the tips of my fingers. "So...what you're saying, is not only do I have an assistant attorney general, whose objectivity is in question, but I also have a police chief, who may have a personal vendetta against Alston O'Brian."

Bill shook his head drumming his fingers on the table. "We don't know anything for sure Jonas. I just thought you needed to know the full scope of what's going on."

I looked out the window, feeling a balloon of apprehension inflating in my stomach, as I was about to broach a subject I knew was sensitive. "Bill, what can you tell me about this money that couldn't be found?"

The former sheriff closed his eyes, releasing a long sigh. "Ah, yes, Alston's infamous hidden money. That was the subject of many a watercooler conversation for years. Nearly six hundred grand supposedly stashed away somewhere. I recall Valance telling me stories about people scouring the lands, that Alton had conned people out of, searching for the money. He said they dug up the yard, tore out the walls of the foreclosed houses, you name it, trying to find just a dollar bill of that cash."

"Was any of it ever found?"

A car alarm going off, made us both look toward the window, until five seconds later it was deactivated. "Not as far as I know. We had forensic accountants go over every transaction Alston conducted, looking for that missing funds, but they always came up dry."

I adjusted myself on the bench, interlacing my fingers on the table. "You talk to Alston about the money?"

"Several times. He never told me anything. The TBI took a crack at him too, but they came up empty handed also. Alston refused to tell us anything."

I rolled my tongue along the side of my cheek, taking a moment to process this information. "Did he ever deny the money existed?"

"He never said anything about it Jonas."

I inhaled a deep breath, gently rubbing my palms together, looking down at the table. "Do you think the money even exists at all? Could it just be a rumor?"

He scratched his chin through his beard, slightly bobbing his head. "It is a possibility. Or he could've spent it. Keep in mind, it was over a month before we caught him. He was staying at a local hotel under an assumed name. When we searched his belongings, we found five more high quality fake identification cards and licenses. Those weren't cheap, even before this holographic paper."

I couldn't resist a half smile. "Wouldn't that be something? The elusive treasure was already spent on illicit materials, that Alston didn't disclose out of fear of additional charges."

Bill pursed his lips, shaking his head. "Yeah, but I'd think most had forgotten about the money by now. At least they had, before Alston returned, but now he has dredged up a lot of bad memories. Even if the money doesn't exist, there may be people out there, who still want to believe it does. And belief is a powerful drug, Jonas."

"And you add in the desire for revenge, it's the equivalent of adding gasoline to a fire."

Bill flattened his palms on the table keeping his voice low. "If and when you see Alston again, you might need to strongly suggest he leave Monroe County. He was lucky you were there to stop today's assault, but you and your deputies can't be everywhere."

I told Bill I made that suggestion to Alston. "But I don't think it'll do any good. Even after the altercation at Hardees, he showed no signs of backing down. Whatever his motives for coming back, he's not leaving until he accomplishes his goal."

Bill exhaled a long breath and sat back. "If that's the case, then I hope he gets it done, before someone else takes a shot at him."

I exhaled a sigh of my own, acknowledging the tranquility, that had blanketed the county for the last few weeks, had just been lifted.

Chapter Five

The next morning found me standing outside the reception office of the Horton Recycling Center, located two miles from the McMinn County line. Barely 8:00 a.m., the temperature was right at thirty-two degrees, and the wind coming out of the north at ten miles an hour made it feel like it was twenty-two, despite the fact the sun was in full bloom. We received a call from Oscar Horton at 7:30 a.m., reporting a break-in on his property. When Tom and I arrived, we discovered that Oscar had left out a few details.

The Horton Recycling Center was a metal recycling facility and car parts yard. Oscar bought junk metal, scrap cars, copper, batteries, brass, aluminum cans, and various other metallic materials. Needless to say a lot of cash moves around in a place like that, meaning there is a lot of temptation for theft. On the phone Oscar said there were signs of forced entry into the office. We expected to see the front door being forced in or perhaps a broken window. Instead, what my deputy and I saw, upon arrival, was a twelve by twelve concrete building with a five-foot hole in the side. Approximately twenty yards from the crater was a black safe lying face up.

Oscar stood before the fissure in his wall, hands in the pockets of his plaid coat, and stared into the darkness. I stepped out of my truck, unable to move, as I assessed the carnage that had been wreaked upon the facility. Busted chunks of concrete block were strewn over the graveled lot, as was a beat-up filing cabinet, with several documents scattered about. I approached Oscar, who was staring mutedly at the destruction, his gray whiskered chin moving as he chewed his gum. "Oscar."

He adjusted the brim of his outback hat further down on his head. "Hey sheriff. Heck of a way to start the day huh?"

"It's not how I saw *my* morning panning out. Anyone hurt?"

Oscar wrapped his coat tighter around his torso, the wind flapping the tips of gray hair peeking out from under his hat. "Nah. The place was empty. So there's that, at least."

I lifted the collar of my overcoat to shield my neck from the cold, while I surveyed the scene. "Did they manage to get into your safe?"

Oscar glanced back at the steel box and shook his head. "Nope. They tried, but that sucker is strong enough to withstand a stick of dynamite."

I found myself focusing on Oscar more than the building. "I have to say Oscar, you're taking this remarkably well. If it was me, I'd be bouncing all over the place."

"Shoot Jonas, no one got hurt. I've got insurance that'll cover the damages and I still have the money. It'll take a while, but I'll be back on my feet."

"I wish everyone took that point of view about these situations. If you wouldn't mind waiting here while we check out the scene?"

He pointed to the destruction with his chin. "That's why I called you."

I signaled Tom, who was standing by the cruiser, to come over. Joining me at the jagged opening in the wall, Tom stood with his hands resting on his gun belt, shaking his head at the destruction. "What do you think did this?"

The gray gravel didn't reveal any vehicle tracks in the soil, but there was evidence of subtle dips in the ground leading up to the opening. There were two sets, each about ten inches in width, with about sixty inches between the two tracks. The center of the tracks clearly displayed gravel covered with a dark stain. Kneeling down, I picked up one of the rocks and brought it up for the smell test. "This is oil."

Tom's face wrinkled in confusion, as he looked at the rock. "Oil. You think they used a truck or something and pulled the wall down."

I slowly shook my head, as I continued to examine the gravel. "I don't think so Tom. If that was the case, we'd see signs of the tires spinning in the gravel. These tracks look to be smooth and even. It had to have been a pretty heavy vehicle to make these tracks."

Tom tapped my shoulder and pointed to the shed by the chain-link fence. "Or equipment."

I turned to see a yellow Komatsu front loader parked under the shed with the scoop attached. I started to stand, but my eyes caught a glimpse of something in the shadows of the office. I took out my flashlight and shined it inside the structure and found a small camera encased in a black plastic dome case. "Looks like Oscar had some security cameras for the office Tom. Why don't you go and ask him, if we can look at the footage, while I take a look at the front loader."

"Yes sir."

A closer examination of the front loader, revealed fresh concrete dust on the blade of the scoop. I took out my leather gloved hand, drew a line in the dust, to see it wasn't damp from the morning frost. The yellow, heavy duty equipment is the size of a small tank, with four thick solid rubber tires used to carry the machine. Concrete had been poured for the floor of the outdoor work shed, so when I moved to the side and shined my light under the Komatsu, I saw small droplets of oil pooling underneath.

"Hey Jonas."

I turned to see Tom at the office door waving me over. "You get the footage?"

"Oh yeah. You definitely need to take a look at it."

A mild sense of direness ran up my spine, but was quickly replaced by an icy shiver, from the gust of wind that traveled up my coat, as I crossed the yard to the office. "What have you got?" I asked when I joined my deputy.

"Oscar's cameras got the intruders on video," he said."

I nodded, sticking my hands in my pockets. "You recognize them?"

"Sort of. Come on I'll show you."

I followed Tom into the building, through the pay room, stepping over papers and debris from the demolished wall, into another office. Oscar was behind the desk, moving his mouse around while studying the screen of his computer. "Heard you managed to record the break-in."

Oscar nodded, his eyes pinched together, studying the screen, like it was an enigma. "Yeah. Don't know how much help it's going to be though."

As I stood behind Oscar, he hit play and I saw the room I had just walked through, only it was still intact. When the time stamp displayed 2:24 a.m., that is when we saw the blade of the bucket puncture the concrete, tilt down and roll back, taking the wall with it. Once the dust settled, two figures in insulated coveralls and leather gloves ran into the room, their heads swathed in plaid boxer shorts. Seeing the two effigies on screen once again, I dropped my chin to my chest and exhaled a slow breath. "Good lord, not those two idiots again."

Tom, observing the screen with his arms across his chest, slowly shook his head. "They do seem to get around."

The two boxer bandits, stumbled on their feet, probably due to their narrow vision through the opening in the crotch. They then took a heavy chain and wrapped it around the safe, which was located to the immediate left of the opening. One of the robbers snaked the chain around the bottom and then the top, before bolting the ends together. When both were outside, the chain grew taut for a half a second, before the safe was ripped out of the floor and out onto the gravel.

Oscar stopped the display and swiveled around to face us. "That's the end of the show. I don't have any cameras on the front gate."

I looked back through the open door to the pay window. "Oscar did you walk through the point of entry after you got here this morning?"

He shook his head, as he stood up. "No Jonas. When I saw the damage to the wall and the safe in the driveway, I called you."

I looked at Tom. "We saw from the video, they were wearing gloves, meaning there are no fingerprints, but they did walk through the dust covering the floor where the safe was located."

Tom winked at me. "Meaning we can get some shoeprints. I'll get on it."

I removed my gloves and took my Moleskine notebook from my inside coat pocket along with my pen. "Okay Oscar, I'm going to need to ask you a few questions."

Oscar tilted his chair back to look up at me. "Fire away."

"Can you think of anyone who would want to rob you? Have there been any customers that have given you trouble lately?"

Oscar looked down at the tops of his steel toed work boots, for several seconds, before shaking his head. "None that stand out. You have the pain in the rear end customer, who doesn't like the price of scrap from time to time, but that's part of the business. I can't think of any who would go this far."

I made a reference in my notebook. "How about employees? You have any trouble with them or perhaps a former employee?"

Oscar shook his head. "Nah, I've had the same employees for twelve years and I've never had a problem like this."

I pointed back to the carnage, as I observed him. "You sure about that Oscar? Those two seem to know from the outside, exactly where the safe was located. It makes me think there is a chance they have seen the layout of that part of the building."

Oscar drew his eyebrows closer together, frowning down at the floor. "I hadn't thought about that, but you're right. They did seem to know where everything was. Then again, it could be a regular customer, Jonas. The safe is out of sight, but if they are paying attention, it wouldn't be hard for them to figure out where we keep it."

I could see the validity in his logic, as I closed my notebook and tapped it on my thigh. "Well, Oscar once we've collected the shoe impressions and taken some photographs, we'll get out of your way. If you can think of anything that might help, don't hesitate to give us a call."

Oscar nodded, as he pulled a bag of chewing tobacco from his back pocket and removed a plug. "From the way you talked, it sounded like this isn't the first time you've seen those two in the video."

"Unfortunately no. They started out a few days ago, robbing O'Reilly's in Madisonville. Then stole some things from a private residence and now here."

"Busy boys. Any idea why the dumbasses are wearing boxer shorts for masks?"

I let out a light laugh, as I shrugged. "I have no clue. I wasn't sure…." I turned back to look at the front pay window again.

Oscar moved to the side, so he could look out the door too. "What is it?"

"Do you buy aluminum rims here?"

"Sure. They're one of my big money items at sixty-five cents a pound right now. Why?"

"One of the items stolen at O'Reilly's, were some aluminum wheels. Has anyone brought those in to you in the last few days?"

His face grew serious, as a light of ingenuity flashed in his green eyes. "Yes, I did turn down a set of aluminum wheels the day before yesterday."

I flipped open my notebook. "Who brought them in?"

Oscar shook his head as he grabbed a paper coffee cup and spat in it. "Never saw them before then. They drove on the lot in red Chevy S10. There were two of them, both guys."

I scribbled this down, underlining the make of the truck. "Can you give me a description?"

He shook his head, spitting once again into the cup. "After a while the faces start to jumble. Sorry."

I wrote down unidentified and underlined it. "Why didn't you buy the wheels?"

He spat again in the cup, before wiping his mouth with his coat sleeve. "Because they looked brand new. No one brings new aluminum wheels here for scrap, unless something isn't on the up and up. You can get three times as much selling them out of the trunk of your car, then what I could give."

I wrote this down as well and tapped the notebook with the back of my pen. "How did they react to you turning them down?"

Oscar scoffed, shifting his weight to his back leg. "They got pissed. I didn't think anything of it. There's not a week that goes by, when someone isn't upset about the prices or try to argue about the final weight. Most of them just shout out a few curse words and move on, only to come back in couple of weeks with another load of scrap."

I scratched my chin with the tip of my pen, as I looked over my notes. "It looks like these guys may have taken it a step further."

He shook his head, before spitting out more tobacco juice into the cup. "I forgot about the robbery at the O'Reilly's store. If I had remembered, you could've arrested those two thieves and none of this would've happened."

I flipped my notebook closed, returning it to my pocket, and took out one of my business cards. "If you do remember anything else about them Oscar, give me a call. If it's all right, I'd like to get a copy of the footage of them breaking in. Once we get the footwear impressions, we can let you get around to cleaning up."

He took my card and put it in his lapel pocket. "I will make a copy, now."

Out near the crime scene, Tom was lifting a shoeprint with a gel tab and securing it in an evidence box. "You done here Tom?"

"Last one Jonas."

"All right. We'll fill out the report and get those to Molly. You never know, they might come in handy later on."

As we were heading back to our vehicles, a silver F150 pulled into the lot and braked hard, upon seeing the carnage. After a moment, the driver proceeded into the lot and parked beside my truck. A woman in her late thirties with red hair peeking out from under her blue toboggan, stepped out on the gravel, staring with her mouth opened at the scene. "My god what happened?"

I pulled out my badge for her to see. "Sheriff Lauer ma'am. Looks like there was an attempted robbery here last night. And you are?"

Casting her blue eyes in my direction, she swallowed hard, before looking back at the punctured wall. "I'm Katy Spear. I'm the office manager. Is that the safe?"

I looked toward the large black steel box, lying five feet away from us. "Yes it is. But nothing was taken."

She interlaced her fingers and slowly tightened, then relaxed her grip, as she scanned the yard. "Is Mr. Horton all right?"

Tom joined us, after securing the gel lifts. "Yes, he is Ms. Spear. If you feel up to it, I'd like to ask you a few questions."

Katy once again gripped her gloved hands so tightly, I could hear the leather becoming taut, even over the wind. "Me?"

"It'll only take a moment. We can step back inside your truck, if you want to get out of the weather," I replied.

Her eyes darted between the two of us, before facing me, and placing her hands back in the pockets of her green parka. "No, I'm fine here."

I removed my Moleskine once again, to take some notes. "Do you recall two men coming in here two days ago, with some aluminum wheels that Oscar turned down?"

I watched as she stared at the gravel driveway for a few moments, before slowly nodding her head. "Yeah I seem to. They came in a red truck, if I'm remembering correctly."

"Did you know them or perhaps get a good look at them?"

She shook her head, looking back at the building. "No. The scales are around the back of the building. I just work the office and pay window. I noticed them coming in and maybe ten minutes later they were tearing out of here. The reason I remember them, is because I could hear the wheels hitting one another in the truck bed."

I quietly scribbled this down in my all but illegible handwriting. "You happen to catch the license plate?"

Hunching her shoulders, she gave me a grim look, before blowing out a cloud of breath. "I wasn't really paying attention to that. Sorry. You think it was those guys who did this?"

"We have to look into everything ma'am," Tom replied.

I returned my notebook to my pocket and looked at my watch, noting it was almost 9:17 a.m. "Ms. Spear, according to the signs the scrapyard opens at eight and it's now well past nine. May I ask why you're late?"

She turned to her truck and kicked the whitewall tire. "The battery died on this heap. My neighbor Jim, tried to help me boost it off, but it was like beating a dead horse. So Jim gave me a lift to the Walmart, where I bought another one. I called Mr. Horton at 7:30 a.m. to let him know."

My BlackBerry emitted Lydia's ringtone, while I fished out a business card. "If you can remember anything else, please give us a call. If you would, give Deputy Kirk your information while I take this call."

I stepped away from them, as I hit send on my phone. "Morning."

"Good morning to you too," she replied with a heavy layer of jubilation in her voice.

I grinned into the receiver. "I'm going to take a shot in the dark and say the roads are finally clear enough for you to travel."

She gave a curt laugh. "Screw that, I'm already past Cookeville."

I felt tension begin to rise in my chest. "Cookeville? The only way you could be there is if you left before sunrise."

Lydia blew out a deep breath into my ear. "Jonas, don't start. The roads were clear enough."

I was griping my phone tighter, the tension growing. "Lydia, even with the dissolving solution, the roads are slippery, especially when the sun is down."

"Jonas, you know I'm a better driver than most of those guys who drive the salt trucks. My dad took me up into the hills and taught me how to drive when I was fifteen."

"I'm not worried about you; it's the other idiots on the road. All it takes is one nimrod looking down at his cellphone."

She blew out a deep breath. "Jonas, don't make me start wishing for the ice storm to come back."

I took a breath of my own, trying to push down the tide of anxiety. Lydia was one of the most careful drivers I had ever seen and I probably was overreacting. Yet, in the years I've been in law enforcement, I've lost count of the fatal collisions I've had to oversee. Many of whom were responsible drivers, who still wound up having to be scraped off the bloodstained asphalt. I didn't want her homecoming, to be overshadowed with an argument, so I opted to let it go. I knew no matter what was said, Lydia would go her own way, which is what I had always admired about her. "OK, point taken."

"I know you're concerned and it isn't unappreciated, but I can take care of myself."

"I never said you couldn't. Just....Is there much traffic?" I asked, deciding a neutral subject was the best route to take.

"No, it's fairly light. I think I got ahead of it."

I uttered a silent sigh of relieve, for that bit of good news. "Good. I guess you'll be home in about two hours."

I heard her scoff. "Less than that."

I kicked at the gravel smiling into the receiver. "Well it'll be good to have you home."

"It'll be good to be home and to see you again. You got any plans for tonight?"

I hunched my shoulders, despite the fact she was on the phone, over a hundred miles away. "None."

Even through the phone, I could see her smiling in my mind's eye. "You do now. Keep your powder dry until then."

I frowned into the phone. "I've never really understood that expression."

She let out a playful laugh, before saying, "You will tonight. See you then."

I looked down at my phone after she ended the call. We've been seeing one another for nearly five years and the woman still confounds me. Realizing that is how it will always be, I returned my phone to my pocket. The steady roaring of a diesel engine made me turn around to find Oscar, driving a small green fork-truck towards us. He set the brake, two feet from the safe, hopped out and adjusted the forks to the proper width, then returned to the driver's seat. He put the truck in gear but stopped, when he saw Katy Spear talking to my deputy. "Shoot, Katy I should've called you and told you to take the day off. We're closed for the day."

She moved to the safe, raising her voice over the engine. "That's all right Mr. Horton. Since I'm here, I might as well help."

"You sure? I won't fault you for wanting to go home, especially in this cold."

Katy shook her head. "It's the least I can do. Where do you want me?"

Oscar shrugged before pointing to the office. "You can do an inventory on the office. See what equipment is still working and what needs to be replaced. Then we can start getting a cover over that big hole."

"Yes sir." Katy got into her truck and headed to the office.

Oscar slowly scooped the safe up with the forks and elevated it four feet above the ground. "Sheriff," he said before putting the fork truck in reverse.

"Oscar, if you wouldn't mind, let me know when you have that inventory complete. It could help us assess the damage done to the office."

He nodded in my direction. "I'll fax it over when Katy finishes."

"Tom, lets head back to the stationhouse."

Tom was visibly shaking from the chilly morning air. "You don't have to tell me twice."

When I got back to my truck, I had my hand on the handle, but stopped to take another look at the wall. Katy Spear had turned the lights on inside the office, as she walked through the rubble, picking up the papers spread across the floor. Tom must've noticed me looking. "What's wrong?"

"It's something Katy Spear said a minute ago. About how staying was the least she could do."

Tom looked in her direction, tapping his gloved fingers on the hood of my truck. "What about it?"

I rolled my tongue inside my cheek, as I massaged my thumb along the door handle. "Seemed an unusual expression to me is all. When we get back, check her out for any priors."

Tom adjusted the bill of his cap over his forehead. "Think she's in on the break in?'

I gave him a slight grin, as I opened my door. "Anything's possible, Tom. That's something this job has taught me."

* * *

Back at the stationhouse, I immediately recognized the jet black Lincoln Town Car parked in the court officer's parking space, as the one belonging to Anthony Deland. This was a bit of a surprise. Usually we met at his office in the courthouse. Once inside the vestibule, I looked at Jack, who pointed to my office. I nodded, but grabbed myself a cup of coffee, before going in to meet the attorney general.

Anthony was sitting in one of the chairs in front of my desk, adorned in a charcoal black suit, with a blue tie. He had his legs crossed, drumming his fingers on his knee cap, while shaking his foot up and down. "Good morning Anthony."

He stood up, as I closed the door. "Morning sheriff. Sorry to come unannounced."

I set my cup on the desk, so I could remove my coat and put it on the coat rack in the corner. "Not a problem. Sorry for the wait, but we had an early call this morning."

"Was it serious?"

I took a sip of coffee, as I sat down. "Two men broke into Oscar Horton's scrapyard and tried to make off with the safe."

He elevated a single eyebrow. "Tried?"

I set my coffee cup, on the rubber coaster, before stretching my upper back. "I believe they underestimated how difficult it is to break open a two thousand pound safe."

Anthony placed his arms on the armrests of his seat. "You have any suspects?"

I nodded my head. "Got some video footage. It looks to be the same people that broke into O'Reilly's and Phil Woody's house."

Anthony's forehead furrowed, for a moment. "You mean those guys wearing underwear on their heads?"

I sighed, slowly nodding my head. Only in Monroe County would we get thieves like this. "Afraid so. It doesn't look like they stole anything today. Oscar said he'd let us know the total damage estimates, when he has the figures."

"Do you have any leads, as to who they may be?"

"There is a strong probability that the two tried to sell the aluminum wheels, they stole from the auto shop, to Horton two days ago, but he turned them away. The attempted robbery on the scrapyard could be retaliation."

Anthony lightly rubbed his fingers on the armrests, as he looked down at the top of his shoe. "Did they leave fingerprints?"

I shook my head, slowly rocking in my chair. "The video showed they were wearing gloves. We were able to lift prints at Phil's house and O'Reilly's, but there were no hits in A.F.I.S. Whoever these guys are, they've not been arrested, but I am more than hopeful that we'll remedy that problem real soon."

Anthony frowned again and shrugged. "Why are you so confident? Sounds like they've left you little to work with."

I glanced around at the faded white walls, with the paint chipping along the edges, as I hunched my shoulders. "They're getting more brazen with every crime. They'll eventually get overconfident and make a mistake. The only problem with that is, it could lead to someone getting hurt. I've got Tom looking into alternative avenues, in hope it might lead to an ID, but I wouldn't hold my breath, just yet."

Anthony closed his eyes, as he exhaled a deep breath. "I've never gotten use to the waiting part of this job."

I held up my cup in agreement to him. "Me either. So what can I do for you this morning?"

Clearing his throat, he set his feet flat on the floor and took on his prosecutorial tone of voice. "I understand there was an altercation with Alston O'Brian yesterday in Vonore."

I set my cup down, turning my chair to face him. "Some people tried to assault him yesterday morning. Alston chose not to press charges, despite the fact he was the victim."

Anthony arched his eyebrows. "Press charges? You mean Mr. O'Brian didn't instigate the altercation?"

I narrowed my eyes, as I focused on the assistant attorney general. "No. Witnesses said Alston was trying to purchase his breakfast, when he was accosted by a Harrison Birch. You might remember his father was one of the victims, from the original case in '99. What did you hear? While you're at it, who did you hear it from?"

He cleared his throat, a bit more emphatically, adjusting his tie. "Chief West told me about it."

This wasn't a revelation given what I had learned. "Saul told you about it? He said Alston was the instigator?"

Anthony shook his head, his face beginning to acquire a crimson flush. "Not in those words. He just indicated that Mr. O'Brian was in the center of the altercation."

"But Saul didn't do anything to dissuade you from believing Alston started the altercation, did he?"

He chose to remain silent, which I interpreted as a yes. "Well Anthony, when Saul told you about the incident, did he mention how he neglected to respond to the 911 call the manger made? That Greta Bibi got so desperate, she had to call my office to get assistance?"

Anthony slowly shook his head, casting his eyes down on the floor. "No he didn't. I'm sure that was just a mix up or something."

I leaned forward and propped my arms on the desk. "So what was it about the incident at Hardees, that you wished to discuss?"

"I was hoping you had persuaded Mr. O'Brian to leave town. I said the other day, his return to Monroe County, might resuscitate some bitter feelings in the Vonore community."

It seemed the common thread in this case was that everyone wanted Alston O'Brian out of town. "I'm afraid you're out of luck counselor. If anything, he seemed even more determined to stay."

He lowered his head, blowing out a deep breath. "What is he after? The money?"

I pursed my lips, listening to the train whistle announce the arrival of the morning CSX locomotive moving through town. "I mentioned the cash, but he just brushed it off. It did seem odd that he didn't press charges though."

The prosecuting attorney picked at some lint on his pant leg. "He probably assumed it would stoke the fire even more. Or, it could've been a ruse to throw everyone off."

"It's a possibility. He's a conman, so it's hard to read if his intentions were sincere or manipulative." I looked at him for a few seconds, before deciding to let the cat out of the bag. "I read the court transcripts from the trial, Anthony."

He looked up at me, eyes dilating, before he leaned back in his seat. "I see. So you know my mother was a victim then."

I nodded, picking up a paper clip from the desk and slowly rotating it between my fingers. "I also know Saul West was later adopted by Chief Valance Udall and raised as one of his own. Since Valance's son Martin was a victim too, it only stands to reason that there would be some bad blood between Saul and Alston."

Anthony rubbed his chin with the back of his fingers, before clearing his throat again. "So naturally you believe our judgment is in question."

"No offense Anthony, but if the roles were reversed, wouldn't you be wondering the same thing?"

The prosecuting attorney stared at the floor for a moment, before he looked up at me, with translucency in his eyes. "I suppose I would. What is your next move?"

I furrowed my brow, keeping my eyes focused on him. "Next move?"

"I'm assuming you're going to ask, that I recuse myself from the Alston O'Brian situation."

I leaned forward, clasping my hands on the desk. As I've said before, there isn't an Alston O'Brian situation Anthony. At least not yet. He's served his time and has done nothing illegal, that I know of since his release. If you have any sway with Saul, you need to tell him he needs to tread carefully. If Tom and I hadn't arrived when we did yesterday, things could've gotten out of hand and his negligence, in responding to the call, could've opened up the city and county to a lawsuit."

He cocked his head over his left shoulder, giving me a double barrel stare. "You really think Alston O'Brian would sue?"

I held up my hands in befuddlement. "I don't think so, but there is no sense in presenting him with the perfect opportunity to do so."

"Fair enough. That would be ironic, if the man who swindled millions from the city of Vonore, returned to sue them."

"Alston would have a solid case too."

Anthony stood and put his hands in his pockets. "I know. Sorry for the deception sheriff. I thought I had put this behind me, but when I learned of Alston's release, all those memories and the anger just flooded back."

I stood up resting my hands on my hips. "You've nothing to apologize about Anthony. It's called being human."

He made his way to the door, but snapped his fingers and returned to his spot. "I almost forgot, there was another reason I came by."

"Oh?"

He scratched his forehead with his thumb. "Garry Dawson posted his bail and paid the fines, for his protests over the removal of the Ten Commandments, a little over an hour ago. He said he's getting tired of the police persecuting him and said he intends to sue the county for harassment and false arrest."

I felt my eyes oscillate in their sockets, but stopped them at mid revolution. "Well, that's about par for the course isn't it? He's threatened to do that since the first time we had to arrest him. "

Anthony seesawed his head, his lips pursed. "That's true, but there was something different in his demeanor. I think he might be serious this time. I'm not telling you how to do your job. If you have to arrest him, then do so. I'm just giving you a heads-up."

"Thanks Anthony."

Chapter Six

Lydia Corbett is a woman, who never meanders in her endeavors. When her enlistment was up in the United States Army and the tension between her father, retired General Alexander Corbett, was at its zenith, she decided she needed a change. So she moved from Memphis to Monroe County, taking a job as investigator/liaison with the attorney general's office, where we eventually met. It was she who initially asked me out, much to my surprise. I wasn't blessed with the good looks stick, I'm not horrendous, but I'm no Bradley Cooper either. So when this beautiful woman, with golden brown eyes asked me out, I was initially thrown for a loop. Being an army kid, she was well traveled and exposed to many cultures. Other than a brief trip to Italy, after graduating high school, I had never been out of the states, so I couldn't for the life of me figure out what she saw in me. All this time later, I still don't know. Yet, when Lydia sets her sights on something, nothing will stop her, save for some sort of Higher Intervention and I have my doubts, that even that would stop her. I was about to get another pleasant reminder of her determination.

The rest of the day had been the usual, so I was able to get home at a decent hour. Lydia had said she was coming over, so I texted her to be there around seven and I would have some dinner ready. I was in an Italian mood that evening, so I placed a pot of water on the stove turning the dial to eight. While waiting for the water to boil, I got out the makings for a salad and began to chop the romaine and iceberg lettuce, then proceeded to dice the tomatoes. I was working on shredding the carrots, when I heard a car rolling over the gravel of my driveway. Mick pricked his ears forward and followed me to the door, where we saw Lydia's green sedan, frosted with road salt, parking beside my truck. I held the door open for her and Mick moved to the threshold and started whimpering in glee, his tail wagging, at the sight of her.

She scratched his massive head, before rubbing his jaw. "Hey boy. Good to see you too."

When she stepped inside, she gave me a big hug, allowing me to inhale the clean scent of her hair and the fragrance of her perfume. "I'm not complaining, but you're a bit early. I've not gotten the spaghetti on yet and the bread isn't in the oven."

Leaning back, while keeping her arms around my waist, Lydia smiled. "Then I got here just in time."

I shut the door while she removed her coat, to reveal an off white sweater and blue jeans. She removed her insulated boots and joined me in the kitchen, where I was about to place the spaghetti into the water. She turned the oven and stovetop off, before removing the pasta from my hand and putting them back in the plastic bag. She then placed the bowls in the refrigerator. "I take it you weren't in the mood for Italian?"

She shut the refrigerator, the smile on her face was more definitive and her eyes had a tint of mischief in them. She reached around and pulled the string of my apron. "Oh, we can have some Italian. We can call out for a pizza later."

I raised my eyebrow, at her as I felt my skin grow warm, from the arousal of my blood pressure. "Later? What's about to happen now?"

She let out a small giggle, as she stood on top of my shoes in her sock feet and draped her arms around my shoulders. Tilting her head, she gave me strong kiss, that would've sucked the air out of a tire, her tongue lightly touching my parted lips. When she leaned back, Lydia kept her nose at the edge of mine, looking directly into my eyes. "Care to guess what's about to happen?"

I smiled back at her, allowing my hands to glide along her back. "I'm not quite sure. Can you tell me again?"

She kissed me again before stepping back and taking my hand. "Follow me and I'll show you."

* * *

The pizza arrived just after eight o'clock. I paid the delivery man and waited until he was gone, to let Mick out. "Ten minutes boy. Do your stuff."

I shut the door and Lydia came into the dining room adorned in my blue button down shirt and her socks, while I had switched to a T-shirt and lounge pants. I opened the box to reveal a sausage and pepperoni pizza, before I retrieved our salad bowels from the refrigerator. I listened to what she had learned from her seminar, then I gave her the rundown of my day, about how the boxer boys had struck again.

She wrinkled her forehead, swallowing a piece of pizza. "For lame disguises, those guys are getting more ambitious."

I swallowed the bite of pizza, along with a sip of soda. "I know. They've been smart enough to keep the shorts on until after they're off camera. I don't know which one of them came up with the idea for using underwear as masks, but I have to say it is original. Moronic, but original."

After letting Mick in, I decided I needed to discuss what I had learned about her boss, even though it was going to dampen the mood. Still, I believe she should hear it from me first. After I divulged what I had learned from my conversation, she sat back in her seat, her mouth agape. "You told Mr. Deland you know about his mother and that you think the Vonore P.D. chief was negligent?"

I nodded, as I took another sip of soda. "Pretty much. Though I didn't say Saul was negligent, I said he could be sued for negligence."

She gave mean sardonic look. "That isn't much better."

"I know. I didn't want to confront Anthony, but he was getting so adamant, about me running Alston out of town, I had to."

Lydia rested her elbows on the table, shaking her head. "I know you did what you thought was right. I just hope this Alston man leaves before history repeats itself."

I leaned into the table. "That is the last thing I want to happen."

She reached across the table to take my hand. "I know. You didn't set out to arrest Mr. Phillips, but you had no choice. If Mr. Deland follows a similar path, then you'll have no choice but to arrest him too."

A line of tension was lacing its way up my spine, as I listened to her. It had been with Lydia's assistance, that I was able to arrest her former boss, Sam Phillips for the manufacturing and distribution of narcotics, only a few weeks after she first started working for him. I know it made the situation in her office tenuous at best, some seeing it as a betrayal, but I never once heard her complain about it. I know she's no shrieking violet, but I still had no desire to put her in that situation again. "We're a long way from me having to cuff the assistant attorney general. I just wish I knew what Alston's game was."

Lydia picked up a piece of pizza crust and casually brushed it over her plate. "You told me the other day there was money that was never discovered from the original trial. You think that could be it?"

I scratched the end of my ear, leaning back in my seat. "Maybe. But I'm wondering if he hasn't already found the money."

"What makes you think that?"

"The man's barely out of prison, yet he's driving a very nice car and wearing nice clothes. Yesterday at Hardees, he pulled out a money clip full of hundred dollar bills. There had to be two thousand dollars in that clip."

Her eyes expanded in diameter. "Two grand?"

"If it was a dollar. I don't know how else an ex-con, just released from prison could have access to such funds, unless he had some stashed away. Or...."

She twirled the crust for me to go on. "Or what?"

I ran my finger over the rim of my glass, allowing a thought to play out in my head. "I was thinking about that scam he ran on everyone back in the nineties. It'd be pretty hard to do by yourself."

"You're thinking maybe he had an accomplice and that's where the money has been all this time? You think if he had a partner, they would wait for him to get out? Wouldn't you think they'd just run off with the money, while all the attention was focused on him?"

I hunched my shoulders. "I don't know. There was never a mention of an accomplice in the trial and Alston never fingered anyone as an accessory. As for the theory, of the anonymous accomplice waiting to spend the money, what if Alston was the only one who knew the location? That could explain why they would have to wait until his release."

She was tapping her plate with the crust as she made her counterpoint. "If there was an accomplice. No matter how you look at it, there's not much you can do until someone makes a move."

I smiled and raised my glass in salute. "The burden of being sheriff: waiting for the other shoe to drop."

She smiled. "A lot of the time that's what your job entails."

I slowly rotated my glass on the table as I stared at her, admiring the sight of her ruffled hair draped over the shoulders of my shirt. "After hearing all of this, I bet you wish you could've stayed in Nashville, until the dust settled."

She furrowed her brow, moving her plate forward. "And miss out on all the fun. Besides, we're a team. What kind of person would I be, if I let you face this all alone?"

She stood up and walked toward me, allowing her fingers to slowly trace the edge of the table. "Besides, if I had stayed, we would've missed out on the fun we had a couple of hours ago."

I scooted my seat back as she sat in my lap, to rest her head, on my shoulder. I leaned over to inhale her fragrance, before kissing her temple. "I got lucky the day you came into my office, you know that?"

Lydia muzzled my neck and cheek before she looked into my eyes. "You weren't the only one Jonas." She leaned her head back and closed her eyes as I kissed her.

* * *

A week later, another storm front moved through the area, powdering the mountains with sleet and snow, making narrow roads slippery, while leaving the valley virtually untouched. A little sidenote about the school system of Monroe County. With four towns forging the county, if winter weather closes one school down, then all the schools in the county will be closed. It was a Friday, so not only did the kids get a day from school, they also got a three-day weekend. Probably to the chagrin of more than a few parents. I used to love snow days until, I got into the workforce and had to traipse to work, regardless of the road conditions. Yet despite the weather, everything else appeared to be tranquil in my county. The boxer twins hadn't hit any other places and there had been no other signs of Alston O'Brian, since the incident at the restaurant. The optimist in me was hoping this meant, the robbers had given up on their criminal endeavors and that Alston had left the county limits, as I had suggested. Yet deep down, I knew we weren't going to be that lucky.

Oscar Horton had sent an invoice for the destruction to his facility. The total damages and reconstruction was going to amount to nine thousand dollars. The background Tom conducted on Katy Spear, revealed no criminal history or associations with known criminals, so that appeared to be a dead end.

I was reading over the previous month's department expenditures, when Jack buzzed the phone on my desk. "What can I do for you Jack?"

"I'm afraid Gary Dawson has decided to once again protest the removal of the commandments."

I set the reports down and exhaled a long breath. So much for things staying quiet, I thought to myself. "Well, that didn't take long. Have Glen go out there and see what's going on."

Jack cleared his throat, as he emitted a low moan. "I'm afraid it's going to be more complicated than that, Jonas. I suppose Gary has decided his protesting on the spot where the Ten Commandments were hanging wasn't working, so he has decided to move it to another location."

There was a ball of ice slowly rolling around the pit of my stomach, as I tightened my grip on the phone. "Please tell me he hasn't interrupted a court session."

"Oh, no. He's set up shop in the county clerk's office. It's Amber who called it in."

I stood up to leave. "Tell her I'm on my way. Have Glen meet me there."

* * *

The county clerk's office is located on the second floor of the courthouse, where Amber Gillian has been the clerk for nearly sixteen years. A quite woman with short auburn hair, with thin ribbons of silver swirled around her temples, Amber has always been courteous and spoke with a calm voice. So it was, a great surprise to hear her speaking in an agitated voice, as Glen and I ascended the steps.

At the threshold of the office door, we saw Amber standing with her hands planted on her hips, with her chin jutted out, and Heather holding her shoulders to keep her back. Gary Dawson was standing before her, with his smartphone out, recording the spectacle, which made my blood turn cold, at the thought of this winding up on YouTube or Facebook. The two were speaking simultaneously over one another, so I wasn't able to decipher what they were saying, but it was plainly obvious neither party was happy. There were five people inside the office standing near the walls observing the commotion, as if it was a play.

I moved to Gary, signaling my deputy to stay by Amber. "What's going on here?"

Gary turned the black camera-phone on me, speaking in a clear, authoritative voice, like he was making a documentary. "I'm exercising my constitutional right, to protest over the removal of our nation's commandments from the courthouse. I've tried everything in my power to get you to perform your legal and obligatory duty, to place the Ten Commandments back on the wall downstairs."

Amber started to step closer to Gary, but Glen interceded with his arm. "This man came in here, jumped the line, and started shouting out accusations, that were completely false and meritless."

"Every word I said was completely true," Gary said.

I held up my hand to him. "Gary, I'll get to you in second. Amber what exactly did he say?"

She pointed a long finger at Gary, her face becoming redder by the second. "He said we were guilty of violating the law of the land, by continuing to work in a building that refuses to acknowledge the law of the Lord. He went on, saying we were sacrilegious and would burn in hell for our actions. I'll have you know I've been a lifelong member of the First Baptist Church sir, and I personally hated it when the commandments were taken down, but this is a state building and the law is clear. Church and state must be kept separate. If you don't like it, try writing your congressman and senator."

Gary seemed unfettered by her words, as he slowly panned his phone around the room, to ensure everyone's image was recorded. "It was their incompetence that started this. If they had any backbone at all, they would've fought the Supreme Court at every turn."

Amber was about to speak, but I held up my hand for her to wait. "Gary, none of this explains what you're doing up here in the first place."

He refocused the camera on me. "I came here for a copy of the judicial order that sanctioned the removal of the commandments."

I looked into the lens of the camera, slowly rotating my shoulders. "That's all this is about? A copy of the court order?"

Gary eyed me over the camera, tiny lines of sweat rolling down his face, from either the heat or his rising temper. "Yes. We're going to put a case together to petition the court to put the commandments back up."

I felt my stomach churn, as I narrowed my eyes at him. "You said we?"

"I've been talking with other people, online, who believe like I do, that it isn't right for the Ten Commandments to be taken down, seeing as how our laws were based on the Christian Law. We have decided to take matters into our own hands and take our case to court to get the commandments back."

I thought about pointing out the oxymoronic concept, of taking a case to the very court that agreed to the removal of the item in question, but I realized I would probably only embolden Gary even more. I had recalled Anthony's warning that Gary may try to sue me and the county and this could very well be his way to incite a reason, for me to arrest him, so he could serve me with legal documents. Yet his decree for the judicial ruling, gave me a plausible peaceful resolution, if I could get him to follow my path.

"I just want to be clear Gary, all you want is the judge's ruling and you'll be satisfied?"

"Yes," he replied.

I glanced back at the people waiting, before turning to Amber. "How many were in front of Mr. Dawson before he arrived Amber?"

She looked at the small crowd, exhaling a long sigh. "All of them. But there were at least two more, who left before you got here."

I nodded. "All right, Gary for the sake of civility, these people were here first. I think it's only fair they be allowed to conduct their business. Amber while you're helping them, you could have Heather go back and get the court order, so it would be ready for Mr. Dawson when his turn is up. Is that agreeable?"

Amber had her left elbow cocked on her hip, sucking in her cheek, a mammalian gleam emanating from her brown eyes. "I can agree to that."

I swiveled my head to Gary, who was still pretending to be Spielberg. "Mr. Dawson?"

He waited several seconds, either for annoyance or dramatic flair, before replying, "I can agree to those terms."

I felt an internal sigh run down my core. I stood to the side guiding Gary with me, so the other patrons could resume their line. "Great. Let's just stand over here, while Heather gets that court ruling."

To say the wait was a bit tense, was putting it mildly. The people waiting in line kept their eyes on Gary, who still had his camera, on the desk, as Amber worked. Some of their faces were red as they gave the cameraphone, quick side glances. The twenty minutes it took for it to be Gary's turn felt like an hour, with Glen and I exchanging glances at one another, both hoping that it didn't implode, into another arrest.

When Gary reached the counter, he turned to pan the room, focusing on me and then my deputy, before refocusing on Amber. He looked down at his watch as he began his dictation. "At 12:13 p.m. on January fifteenth, I am receiving a copy of the court order that violated the very soul of our nation. With it we are going to take the steps of bringing the nation's law back."

Amber was working hard to keep her temper in check, as she set her jaw. "This concludes our agreement Mr. Dawson."

I stepped forward. "Amber is right Gary. She did fulfill her part of the deal. Now it's your turn."

Gary panned the camera around the room once again, before zeroing in on me. "I will leave on my own volition, but I reserve the right to free demonstration outside"

I kept my expression translucent, resting my palm in front of my sidearm. "You're free to demonstrate all you want, Gary, but it has to be outside and you can't block access to the courthouse."

Ceasing his documentation, Gary placed his smartphone in the front pocket of his coat. He simply nodded his head to us and walked past me and Glen, heading down the steps. I could hear the double wooden doors at the front open and slam shut.

It took a few more minutes for me to calm Amber, as her temper was beginning to reach volcanic levels. I could tell she wasn't appeased by my assurances, that I would do the best I could to make sure Gary didn't disturb her place of business, but it was a catch 22 situation. The courthouse is a public building, meaning there were limits to what could be done to control problematic citizens. The most I could legally do, was make sure Gary didn't obstruct the business, that was conducted in the courthouse or that he didn't make a menace of himself. Small comfort, I'm sure, but I'm only the sheriff. Though it is the second most powerful position in the county, my authority is finite, no matter what some may believe.

When Glen and I stood out on the front step, we saw Gary silently marching on the sidewalk, holding a sign that displayed the Ten Commandments. It was barely forty degrees, with a crisp wind coming out of the north, which was making his face grow red. Glen shook his head, as he tucked his hands in the pockets of his bomber's jacket. "I do appreciate his moxie, but sometimes you have to just give it up."

I gave him a sympathetic smile. "It's been over eleven years since the commandments were taken down Glen, and he's shown no signs of backing down. Like it or not, I say this won't be the last time we get a call about Gary."

"I'd say you're right."

As I got into my truck, my BlackBerry rang. I had to dig down to my shirt pocket. I didn't recognize the number, as I pressed the send button. "Sheriff Lauer."

"Sheriff this is Alston O'Brian."

"Mr. O'Brian? Is everything all right?"

"Yes everything is fine sheriff. How are you doing?"

It was hard to decipher over the phone, but it seemed like there was a slight quiver in his voice. "Oh, I'm just dealing with the usual, nothing exciting. Is there something I can do for you Mr. O'Brian?"

I could hear the light undertone of a song mixed in with the clicking of blinker, telling me he was driving somewhere. "Well…I tell you what, just forget I called you Sheriff Lauer."

A chill ran down my spine from the cold inside the cab. I turned on the ignition, so I could get some heat. "Are you sure? I'll be glad to help any way I can."

The line was mute, for a brief period, before he replied, "It's all right. I said it myself, I have unfinished business. I need to see to it personally."

I adjusted the vents in my truck, so the heat wasn't billowing up my nose. "You obviously had something on your mind Mr. O'Brian or you wouldn't have called. We're already talking, so why not go ahead and tell me about it?"

Silence was once again the initial reply. I figured I was about to lose him, so I decided to try one last play. "Sir, are you in town?"

"I will be in about twenty minutes. Why?"

"It's almost lunchtime. Why don't we meet and have a bite? You pick the place and I'll buy."

I heard a sigh over the line, that quickly mingled with the horn of a train engine. I had a good view of the train track that ran through town and saw the railway lights were not illuminated. "I suppose that's all right. You know where Pizzeria Venti's is?"

"Yeah. It's that Italian restaurant in Vonore. Vonore, Mr. O'Brian, where they really don't like you."

"That place is all right sheriff. The owners didn't move into town until well after my incursion into the city. It's the middle of the week, so there won't be many people there."

The idea of heading back into the lion's den brought up flashes of the altercation at Hardees a few days earlier. The fact that the restaurant, in question, was quite literally across the street just on the other side of the second of two traffic lights in Vonore, only made me more uneasy. However, since I had Alston agree to a meeting, I decided a compromise was in order. "All right. I can be there in fifteen minutes."

"I'll meet you there."

I called Jack, saying I would be out for an hour, as I headed out of Madisonville. The traffic light caught me and as I waited I heard the train approaching town, heading south. Meaning if Alston was heading back into the county limits, he was most likely on Highway 411. Several arterial roads branched out from the main highway leading to Loudon, Greenback, and Blount County, just to name a few. Curiosity was buzzing in my head, as I accelerated the truck, when the light switched green. When I glanced back in the rearview mirror, I saw Gary Dawson, marching in his solitary protest, his sign of the commandments held high in his left hand, his right clutching his coat tighter around his chest.

* * *

I arrived at Pizzeria Venti a few minutes quicker than I had thought, so I went ahead and stepped inside. The restaurant had been in business for ten years and was infamous for their pasta and pizza pies. I had passed the place more times than I could count, but this was the first time I had been inside. The place was decorated with a modern appeal, with the earth tone tablecloths, and stone tile flooring.

Guests were free to sit where they wanted, so I selected a seat at the bar, with a view of the front door. I placed my coat on the empty space beside me. A woman in her late forties or early fifties, dressed in black with her blond hair tied in a bun, approached me with a menu.

"Good afternoon. I'm Carol, and I'll be serving you this afternoon. Can I get you something to drink while you look at the menu?"

"I'll have a water, please."

I noticed her stealing a glance at my sidearm and badge. "Of course sir. I'll be right back with that."

There were about twelve people besides me eating in the restaurant. I didn't recognize any of the faces, so I looked down at the menu, whereupon I decided, I would try the pasta salad. I looked to the front door, when I heard a car park outside, expecting to see Alston. Instead it was a woman picking up the lunch for her coworkers. I glanced at my watch, and saw I had been there for roughly ten minutes. When the waitress returned, I told her I was waiting for someone and would need a few more minutes. Fifteen minutes after that, I began to get a cold feeling in my stomach, so I took out my BlackBerry and called Alston's number. When it went straight to voicemail, I felt that cold feeling, turn glacial. I waved the waitress over to me, as I put my phone away. "How much do I owe?"

"The water's on the house officer."

I stood up and put on my coat. "Thank you."

Noticing my haste, Carol said, "Have you got stood up?"

I adjusted my paddle holster, so the grip of my gun wasn't digging into my side, as I made for the door. "Looks like it. The problem is, I don't know if it was voluntary or forced."

I left her standing at the booth, with quizzical look on her face.

Chapter Seven

I stood on the front porch of the restaurant and glanced at the cars in the parking area, still no sign of Alston's Camry. I went to my truck, dialing his number, only to once again get his voicemail. I opted to leave a message this time. "Alston, Jonas here. You said you were only twenty minutes out. That was over forty minutes ago. Give me a call when you get this message."

I sat in my truck, tapping my fingers on the steering wheel, not sure of my next move. It could be that Alston just decided to not come to lunch and was ignoring my calls. Which wouldn't bother me, had he not initiated the whole thing, by calling for my assistance. Of course, he could've just changes his mind, but why not call and let me know? Alston was too smart of a man, to not know that his absence would raise suspicion. If what he said was true, and he was heading into town, the train told me he was heading south on 411. I started my engine and pulled onto the highway, heading north.

I honestly didn't know what to expect. There were over a dozen feed roads that connected to Highway 411, anyone of which Alston could've used, but this rationale didn't seem to resonate with my actions. I kept my speed at around forty-five, looking for any signs of the golden sedan. I was on the other side of the bridge and I had still turned up nothing. I continued down the road, until I reached the Loudon County limits and turned around. I looked down the other side roads, yet as before, there were no signs of the enigmatic conman.

Realizing the futility of trekking every road in the northern end of the county, I decided to head back to the office. Spotting the Vonore chief of police's black and white Tahoe, at the McDonalds\ Exon gas station, I pulled in and parked beside it. Inside I could see Saul sitting by himself at a booth, working on a Big Mac. When he saw me walking up to his booth, he almost choked on the bite of food in his mouth. "Afternoon Saul."

He took a long sip from his cup and grimaced, as he swallowed hard. "Jonas. What brings you here?"

I glanced around at the other patrons, who weren't paying too much attention to us. "I was in town to have lunch with Alston O'Brian, but he never showed up."

He dipped a French fry into some ketchup, before twirling it around and eating it. "You and Alston were at lunch?"

I shook my head. "No. We were *supposed* to have lunch, but he was a no show."

Saul wiped his mouth with a paper napkin. "And I need to know about this because?"

I pointed to the empty bench across from him. "May I have a seat?"

I didn't wait for him to reply before sitting down. "Normally, I wouldn't think much of it myself. The thing of it is: Alston called me a little over an hour ago, asking me for help."

Saul set his half eaten burger down, letting out along sigh. "And I guess you want me to ask what he needed help for."

I rested my arms on the tabletop, shrugging. "He never got around to telling me, Saul. He seemed reluctant at first, which is why I suggested that we meet for lunch. I'm pretty sure he was heading south on 411 and said he was twenty minutes from the restaurant, so he should've beaten me there, but alas he was nowhere to be seen."

Saul frowned at me and pursed his lips. "How do you know he was driving south on 411? Were you tracing the call?"

"No. I heard the train horn as it rode the tracks that are parallel to the highway. A few minutes later that same train came through Madisonville."

Saul smiled, as he took another sip from his beverage. "I heard you were a details man."

I returned his smile. "I try to do my best. The reason I'm here Saul is, given what happened a few days ago at Hardees, I can't help but wonder if there were any more incidents involving Alston. Have there been any other people harassing Alston O'Brian?"

Saul cocked an eyebrow, his face turning to stone. "Harassing?"

"When people are belligerent to an individual, who is minding his own business and threatening to do him bodily harm, I would say that is harassment Saul."

He leaned into the table, staring directly into my eyes. "A couple of guys lost their temper. That doesn't mean they were harassing the guy."

I wasn't interested in engaging in a conversation over semantics, so I bypassed it. "That's beside the point Saul. People in Vonore had a grievance with Alston and didn't care who knew it. No one is saying their anger isn't justified. Now, he calls me up, asking for help and he doesn't show up. It makes my cop radar start to beep Saul. How about yours?"

The chief stared at me a few seconds, then he picked up his burger and took a big bite. He took his time chewing slowly, before swallowing. "Not really sheriff. I mean the guy's an ex-con, so that doesn't lend him a lot of credibility. Plus, there are a lot of reasons why the guy didn't show. Maybe he had car trouble. Maybe he got another call and had to make detour. Or maybe he just changed his mind. In my experience, criminals usually don't like to deal with the police."

I nodded, ignoring his condescending tone, as I interlaced my fingers on the table. "That is true. Maybe he changed his mind. Like I said, I was just wondering if there had been any more incidents in town involving Alston."

"None that I know of."

I stared out the window at the gas pumps and the traffic moving along the highway. "Would you mind keeping an eye out for him? I just want to make sure he's all right."

Saul gave me a crisp laugh, as he finished the last bite of his sandwich. "Sure. That is, if you think I'm up to doing the job."

I looked at him, my forehead furrowing in confusion. "What?"

"Anthony Deland gave me a call the other day and told me that you were aware, of what Alston O'Brian did to our families. Why did you have the AG tell me, instead of calling me yourself? Didn't have the balls?"

With difficulty, I ignored the venom in his words. "Nothing like that. Anthony said he would call you and I thought it might come easier from him instead of me. As for your competency, to be honest, I'm on the fence about that Saul."

I watched the skin along his temples begin to grow tense and his jaw become firm. He set his large hands flat on the table, as he glared at me. "I can't believe you said that to me. I've been a cop for nearly eighteen years. I've had six commendations administrated to me and not one write up on my record. You have the gall to sit there and say I'm not a fit officer."

I held his gaze, keeping my voice neutral. "What about that morning Alston was attacked? Are you going to sit there and let on, that it was really mechanical failure that you didn't respond to our request for assistance? Or that the 911 call the manager made, just somehow got lost in the atmosphere?"

Saul stood up, leaving his tray and wrappers on the table. "Valance Udall was a good man, who raised me like his own. My brother Martin was a good man, who worked hard to provide for his family. That damn grifter came into town and took their savings and ran like the coward he is. They lost their starter house and had to move back in with Dad. It was four years before they were able to get back on their feet again. *Four years.* And here you are worried about the man who caused them and many more, so much pain."

The other patrons all turned to look at us, while we stared at each other, like rams about to butt heads. I never intended this to spiral so rapidly. In hindsight, I probably should've known it was a possibility. We're all guilty of naivety from time to time in our lives and mine was believing that Saul could keep his emotions in check. I stood up keeping my hand loose by my side, but ready in case this came to something more physical. "Saul, I didn't mean to stir up old feelings. I'm sorry for what happened to your family, but like it or not, sometimes we have to do things that we would rather not do."

Saul pointed his finger at me, the flesh of his face growing redder. "Don't stand there and lecture me about being a cop."

"You misunderstand me Saul. I'm not lecturing you. I'm reminding you." I held back my coat so he could see my badge. "Every time we put this star on, we're holding ourselves up to a higher standard. There is an abundance of power and responsibility that comes with this golden star. I've been sliding it on my belt for nearly five years and there are days it still sends a chill down my spine, when I realize all the baggage that comes with it. I can sympathize with you wanting to look the other way at times. There's not a cop who hasn't wanted to look away, at one time or another. If we do that, then we might as well chuck this in the trash."

He gazed at me in silence, his breathing was rapid, but the indignation in his eyes seemed to be softening. I figured this was a good place to make my exit, so I closed my coat and clasped my hands in front of me. "I didn't mean to disturb your lunch Saul. I'll see you around."

The other diners were watching me leave, but it was Officer Daniel Hensley standing by the front door, who drew my attention. I hadn't noticed him come in. His eyes had the dead stare of a shark, as I walked past him. He stepped forward to block my path. "Who are you to talk to him like that?"

I stopped and returned his gaze, causing him to take a step back. "The sheriff and a fellow officer. Do yourself a favor son, and think about what I said."

* * *

In my quest to find Alston O'Brian, I had neglected to get anything to eat. So when I returned to the stationhouse, I scoured through the freezer for a steak and potato microwave dinner. I was able to ingest it, though I believe the digestion was going to prove to be difficult. I tried dialing Alston's number, but got the same result as before. I spent the rest of the day performing administrative duties, unable to wipe the predicament, of Alston completely from my mind.

It was still lingering in the recesses of my mind, while I was Skyping with my parents. Mom was talking about the trip she and Dad were going on this spring, but the words were all muffled to my ears. "Jonas? Jonas are you even listening to a word I'm saying?"

I looked to the screen and saw their crystalline pixel images. Mom had her hair tied back, with her green glasses resting on the bridge of her nose. Dad's hair was a bit ruffled, most likely from the wind outside, while gathering firewood. "Sorry folks. It's been a bizarre day. What were you saying again?"

Mom put on that stern face, I got as a child, whenever I wasn't paying attention. "I was saying we just got the confirmation for our reservations at Harrah's Hotel today. We'll need you to check on the house for us, while we're gone."

Abigail Lauer was a teacher for thirty years before retiring. She now spends her time renovating our family home. I suppose for accuracy, I should say she's making my father, Patrick renovate the house. After working for over thirty years at Sea Ray, Dad retired believing his hard working days were over. He quickly put that thought behind him. My parents only live ten miles from my house, yet the reason we're Skyping, is because they want to use it while they're away on their vacation. I've been walking them through the process, which has been arduous at times. When I feel my temper beginning to grow short, I try to remember all the times they helped me with my homework or afterschool projects, when they were both tired. I looked at the screen and smiled. "That won't be any trouble Mom. But the week of the trip is over eight weeks away, so I think you're getting ahead of yourself, just a bit."

Dad looked over at his wife of forty-three years, cocking an eyebrow. "That's what I told her, but she's always had trouble listening."

"I do listen, honey. The things that make sense I pay attention to. If I don't agree with it I set it free," Mom said not missing a beat. "So, what's distracting you?"

I scratched the end of my nose, before I shook my head. "It's a work thing Mom."

She let out a curt laugh. "What else is new? Want to talk about it?"

"Come on Mom, you know I can't talk about on going cases."

Dad crossed his arms, as he shook his head. "How many times do we have to do this?"

"What?" I said.

"Yeah, what?" Mom replied.

Dad pointed to Mom, then to me. "This. Every time he has a case that's nagging him, you ask him to talk about it. Then you Jonas, say you can't because it's an active investigation. Then the two of you go a back and forth for about two minutes, and you finally tell her about the case. So, just once, do your old man a favor and just talk about it all ready."

Mom turned in her seat to look at him. "We don't banter for two minutes."

"All right, I admit it might be less than two minutes."

Mom's jaw was starting to set and her tone of voice was getting higher. "You're making it sound like I nag the boy. I never make him talk."

I was beginning to have flashbacks of the arguments I had witnessed as a child, while observing them through this seventeen-inch screen. I'm halfway through my thirties, but whenever I hear my parents argue, I feel that instinctive need deep inside, to go to my room and close the door. I know it's a testament to them that they've stayed together, but it was still hard to witness. "Guys, let's take it down a couple of notches. I'll tell you what I can. It involves Alston O'Brian. You might remember him as Alston Mesmer."

Both of their faces grew serious, as they filtered through the recesses of their minds, for the corresponding memory. Dad was the first one to make the connection. "The name is familiar. It was in Vonore right? He stole something?"

"Close. He performed a long con on several people. Some lost their homes and life savings."

Mom nodded her head. "Yeah, I sort of recall that. Lord that was, what? Nineteen, twenty years ago? Why are you looking into that?"

I gave them the cliff notes on what had happened, ending it with Alston's call and his no show at the restaurant. "So you can see why I'm a bit perplexed?"

"It is a bit unusual," Dad said.

"That would be my assessment," I retorted, scratching my chin.

Mom studied me through the screen. "You think something's happened to him don't you? That's why it's bothering you."

No matter what your age, it's always difficult to hide your feelings from your mother. "I believe there is a strong possibility. For now, all I can do is wait."

Mom cocked her eyebrow and Dad, arched his brow in genuine surprise. Their expressions perplexing me, I felt a vacant look draw across my face. "What is it?"

The looked at each other before Mom said, "Well, and don't take this the wrong way, but usually when you get in situations like this where you can't do anything, you start beating yourself up. You literally, whip yourself over it."

I tilted my head over my left shoulder. "I can't argue with you on that one. I guess after doing this job for a while, I've learned there are limits to what I can control. Don't get me wrong, I'm never going to like the waiting game, but unless Alston calls me again, then there's not a thing I can do about it."

Mom smiled, nodding her head. "Well, look at that Pat. Our boy just accepted that he's human."

"We all have to eventually," he said.

Amen to that.

Chapter Eight

The weekend went by with no sightings of Alston O'Brian, nor did he return my calls. I distracted myself with my work, which is always bountiful in lovely Monroe County. Yet, as hard as I tried, Alston was always nudging the back of my brain. I've been accused of being an over thinker, on more than one occasion, and I've never been able to defend myself against that title. Often, it is a good trait to have in my profession, but it can also be nuisance. So, it was a relief when the boxer boys struck again. It was another home invasion, fortunately this time, no one was home.

Hannah Cathcart worked the graveyard shift at the Phyzer factory near Tellico Village. It was after eight in the morning, when she reached her home on Carol Street, and she immediately sensed something was wrong. Her first thought was that her central heating had gone out, but when she saw her backdoor had been jimmied, she dialed 911. Hannah has an eighteen-year-old daughter Amy, who just moved into a dormitory at the University of Tennessee. When her child was a toddler, she had purchased one of those kiddie cameras. Instead of throwing it away when her daughter was older, Hannah decided to use it as a security camera for her home.

Tom was the first to respond to the call and after making sure the house was clear, Hannah told him about the camera, she had hid in the living room, angled so it could pan most of the bottom floor. When she played the recording, Tom immediately called me. I arrived on the scene fifteen minutes later.

Jesse A. Hester

I found Tom and Hannah sitting on the blue sofa, staring at a laptop computer. The entertainment center of the home was missing a TV and DVD player, the cords unplugged, lying limp on the floor. The desk to the right had the drawers open, with pens and papers strewn across the floor.. "What's the situation Tom?"

My deputy looked up at me and slowly shook his head. "Hey Jonas. Looks like they've struck again."

I looked to Hannah, who had the red lines of fatigue coloring her eyes. She had her strawberry blond hair tied back and her oval face had the stern look of someone in a bad mood. "Sheriff. I get off from work and find out my house has been broken into by the dumbass brothers."

I kept my hands in my pockets, giving her a sympathetic nod. "I'm sorry this happened to you Ms. Cathcart. I understand you have some video of the robbers."

"We just finished watching it. It's definitely them," Tom said.

The video indeed, showed two men with boxers covering their faces, walking into the living room, removing the TV and DVD player. It seems the robbers had decided to alter their disguises. One was wearing a pair of boxers littered with hearts, while his companion donned a pair with the banner of the USA. It was easy to see they were wearing black leather gloves, as they scavenged the desk, pulling out the drawers, throwing papers and pens on the floor. The one wearing the hearts approached the fireplace and sat down directly across from where we were now seated. The angle of the camera prevented us from viewing exactly what it was he was rummaging through, but soon he was back in focus, holding a clear plastic bag containing a powder like substance. The two seemed to be particularly fascinated by this discovery. A few moments later, they left the living room, not to be seen again.

Hannah inhaled a deep breath, tears welling in her eyes. "Those sons-of-bitches stole my Momma."

I looked at her and found her staring at the fireplace, where a solitary rosewood box sat in the center. "Pardon me?"

She pointed to the box, fighting hard to control her tears. "My momma. I kept her ashes in that box after she was cremated, two years ago. Those bastards took her. Why on earth would they steal ashes?"

I stared at the box for a long time, unable to ascertain the motivation for stealing cremated remains. A quick side glance at Tom told me, he was as confounded as I was. "Ms. Cathcart, I can't even begin to imagine what it is you're going through. We're going to do everything we can to get your mother's remains back to you. Was there anything else taken from your home?"

She wiped the corner of her eye with her knuckle and cleared her throat. "They took some jewelry out of my bedroom. I think they might've taken some more stuff, but I can't be sure. They threw so much of my stuff around, it's hard to know what's missing."

"Deputy Kirk, will make out a report of the break in and the items you know for certain have been stolen. When you notice other things that are gone, you can call us and we'll amend the report," I said. "If it's all right, I'd like to take a look around ma'am."

Hannah nodded, letting out an angry laugh. "Please. If it'll help you catch them, do whatever you need to."

I left them on the sofa, as I went to the kitchen, where the point of entry had been. The French door was made of oak, painted evergreen. The pane of glass beside the doorknob had been broken out, so the boxer twins could release the deadbolt, to enter the house. I took out my flashlight and examined the glass on the floor and the remaining shards in the door, looking for any signs of blood, in hopes our intruders had cut themselves. The slivers of glass appeared to be clean, save for dirt stains. So despite the absurdity of their masks, the two did appear to be conscientious about their physical wellbeing.

Yet there were some nice shoeprints on the tile floor, from the dirt in the backyard. I stepped over them and opened the door, not worrying about fingerprints, since the boxer twins wore gloves. Outside, I could see two sets of boot treads, in the wet ground leading from the backdoor into the small cluster of trees, at the edge of the property. I followed the tracks, through the trees and dead underbrush, to the other side. There, I found a tire impression in the mud along the shoulder of the road. I took out my BlackBerry and a quarter, before I stood over the tire treads. Setting the quarter beside the tire impression for scale, I set the focus on my camera to thirty-five millimeters and snapped a picture. After making sure the resolution was clear, I sent it to Molly Newman's email.

Molly has been the supervisor of the forensic laboratory since it was built five years ago. Located just across the street from the sheriff's stationhouse, I had lobbied for its construction, to aid in our investigations. In the past, we would have to send all evidence collected, to the state lab in Nashville, where the waiting period, at best was four to six months. At worst it could be over a year before getting the results back. Now, depending on Molly's caseload, which is always hectic, we can get results within days. In any investigation, time is always a determining factor in solving a case.

I called her office phone, but it went to voicemail, meaning she was busy in the lab, so I left a message. "Molly, Jonas here. I sent you an email that contains a photo of a tire track."

I returned to the house, to see Tom taking photos of the boot prints using an evidence marker. "There's a tire impression just on the other side of those trees. I took a picture and sent it to Molly. You have any dental stone in your car?"

He nodded, as he checked the photos in his LCD screen. "I think I have some in the kit."

"Is the kit in your trunk?"

He pointed to the kitchen counter behind him, where the stainless steel case sat. "Right there."

I held out my hand for the case. "Hand it over. I'll take care of it."

With the case in hand, I went to my truck and removed a gallon bucket that I keep in a large plastic bag. I filled it halfway with water from the kitchen, before I returned to the tire track. I removed the plastic frame from the kit and used it to corral a one foot section of the tread. I took out a bag of plaster, very similar to dental stone and poured it into the bucket of water. Using a paddle stick, I stirred the liquid until it became a pasty substance. The mixture for the plaster has to be precise. If it's too lumpy, then the clumps could ruin the prints. If it's too thick, it'll not settle and lift the print. The best mix is when the solution looks very similar to pancake batter. When I had the right combination, I removed a small funnel from the kit and set it on the inside edge of the frame. I poured the white paste through the funnel, so it could pool into the ridges of the tread, where it would eventually set and give us an excellent cast. Once the print was covered, I took out a mechanic's rag and wiped the residual content from the bucket. Now the waiting commenced, which because of the cold, was going to take longer than usual. It could take the majority of the day, but I had an idea that could speed it up. I took out my cell and called Tom. "You almost done Tom?"

"Yeah, I've about to wrap it up."

A silver crossover came down the road and honked at me and I waved in return. "I need you to make a quick stop at the stationhouse and get the portable heater. The one that has the port plug. Bring it out where the cast is. We're going to speed up the drying process."

"I'll be there in ten."

I put my hands in my pockets and stood watch over the white plaster. I'm sure to some it would seem odd for me to be standing guard over a tire tread, but evidence has to be secured, if you want it to be admissible in court. In the leisure, I focused on the most recent robbery of the boxer twins. The fact they pilfered the TV, DVD player, and jewelry wasn't unusual, but why take the cremated ashes? It was unusual to say the least, even for this duo. First, they hit the auto parts store, for the aluminum wheels. Their next move was Phil Woody's house, where they removed his TV and marijuana. Horton Recycling was the next place to get hit, most likely in retaliation, for Oscar refusing to buy the aluminum wheels they had stolen. It appeared the two were eclectic, when it came to selecting the places they robbed, but sometimes the lack of a pattern could be a significant clue.

I spotted Tom's cruiser turning onto the road and in a minute, he stopped beside me. "You need a heater?"

I felt a shiver work down my spine, smiling at him. "I could use it, but we'll put it to better use."

Opening the passenger side door, I saw the heater on the passenger seat and took it out. I placed it near the frame, aiming the vents down onto the white liquid. "Plug it into the port, Tom."

Once he had, I turned the heater on high and held my hand in front of it. The invisible waves of heat cascading over my fingers, told me the machine was working as it should. Tom took out two small orange cones and set them out at both the front and the rear of the sheriff's department vehicle. I then flipped the switch for the light bar, so the blue orbs would illuminate his presence to those passing on the road.

Tom joined me at the tire track. "I was able to get some gelatin lifts from the boot tracks in the house. How long do you think this will take to set?"

I hunched my shoulders. "In a few hours the cast should be dry enough to move. You'll still need to be careful it doesn't break, but it can finish drying at the lab."

Tom stared at the track and looked in the direction of Hannah's house. "What is the deal with these guys, Jonas?"

I let out a curt breath, as I shook my head. "I'm still stumped on that one Tom. From all appearances they seem to be all over the map, but they're smart enough to hide their faces and evade us. I just can't get an angle on them."

The deputy glanced down the road, which was barren for the moment. "I tell you what, I'd like to get a hold of them. Ms. Cathcart is still crying over them taking her mother's ashes. I mean what kind of people steal ashes of the dead? What could they possibly use them for?"

"Again, I have no idea. When they broke into Phil's house and stole his stash of pot, I could get my head around that. This doesn't make any sense at all."

Tom zipped his bomber's jacket up to his neck, before rubbing his gloved hands together. "Maybe we need to put this in the papers. Let everyone be aware of what's going on with these two idiots."

I mulled it over for a moment. "That's about as good a plan as I have. We're certainly not doing any good trailing behind them. The fact that they stole the remains of someone's mother might help get us the break we need."

Tom sniffed, stamping his feet on the asphalt. "Yeah it could. You don't mess around with the dead in the South. Especially if the deceased is a person's Mama. That's sacred around these parts."

I smiled looking up at the blue sky. "If only we would show that much appreciation to the living, think what a wonderful place the world would be."

My phone started ringing. After retrieving it from the inside pocket of my coat, I saw the number on the caller ID belonged to Saul West. "Chief West, what can I do for you this morning?"

There was no reply. "Saul can you hear me?"

Saul took a deep breath before he replied. "Jonas...I'm afraid I've got some unsettling news."

It only took an instant for me to deduce what the call was about. It's about Alston, isn't it?"

There was another long pause. "I'm afraid it is."

My stomach began to churn, as I realized my worst fears were coming true. "Have you found him?"

Tom was looking at me, as I listened to Saul let out a long sigh. "Yeah. We did. He's dead, Jonas. Someone literally dropped a house on him."

I clenched my jaw hard and inhaled a deep breath then slowly exhaled. "Where?"

"Sheriff, it's in our jurisdiction and we have it covered."

I could feel the blood flooding my face, as I headed back to my truck, leaving Tom with the tire track, his face full of confusion. "Don't make me ask again Saul."

Chapter Nine

Saul was still reluctant to give me the address, but when he realized I was coming to Vonore, despite his objections, he gave in. I had my light bar and siren on, as I phoned Tom on his cell and informed him why I had left him in such a hurry. Since I was hardly popular with the VCPD, I radioed Glen, asking him to assist me. The scene of the crime was located on Church Street four miles south of the Vonore City Police headquarters.

Three city police cruisers were parked in front of the driveway, so I had to park along the shoulder. Despite being near the main road, the property in question was in a geographically isolated location. The five acre lot was nestled at the bottom of a hill, surrounded by trees and wild brush, with the train track just ten yards behind it. You could drive by it on the main road and not even see it. The yard was covered with knee high pale yellow grass, with tree limbs scattered from the two oak trees rooted in the front yard. The brick house had been sitting on stilts, but was now lopsided. Several pieces of shingles were missing and the shutters were lying on the ground. The windows of the house had a white film over them. From all appearances, the property and home had been abandoned for years.

There was one officer standing in the driveway, with a yellow legal pad tucked under his arm. His hands were busy with a glazed donut and cup of steaming coffee, living up to the classic cliché. I held up my badge, as I approached him. "Is that the sign in sheet?"

He had just taken a large bite from his donut, so all he could do was nod, as he chewed. He turned to the side, so I could grab the legal pad, from under his arm. After signing my name and the time of arrival, I placed the pad back under his arm. "Where is Saul?"

Still chewing on his donut, the officer turned and pointed down to the house, but there was no one there. I exhaled a long breath, as I stared at him. "Is he inside the house or outside officer?"

Finally, he swallowed his bite, leaving flakes of glaze stuck to the corners of his mouth. "They're on the other side of the house, sheriff."

I looked down at the soft ground. "Do you have any shoe covers?"

He stared at me, like I was speaking a foreign tongue. "Yeah, but not here. Why would we need them?"

I went to my truck and removed a pair of shoe covers and gloves from the field kit I keep behind the seat. At the driveway, I put them on, as the officer watched me, with amusement. "Thanks officer."

Since the house was on braces, that meant at one time, someone must've been preparing to move it, but signs of weathering on the wooden braces, indicates the project was abandoned some time ago. As a result of the impact, several of the windows were cracked, along with part of the foundation. As I made my way around the back, I found Saul and Officer Daniel Hensley, standing near the backdoor, staring at the ground. Neither of them had on shoe covers.

One of the braces, on the east end of the house, had been forcibly removed. The sudden removal and lack of support in that section, resulted in a domino effect, as the weight shift allowed the house to slide down to the ground. When I was only a few feet from the chief and his officer, I noticed the fine leather shoes on the legs sticking out from under the house. The entire upper half of the body was under the foundation of the house, all but severing it into two pieces. The scene reminded me of that scene in Oz, when the house fell on the eastern witch.

Saul looked from the cadaver to me, his face slightly pale. "Sheriff. Looks like we found out what happened to Alston O'Brian."

I walked a path to the other side of the body, carefully studying the scene. "How can you be sure it's him?"

He held up an evidence bag, with a black wallet inside. "Found his driver's license in here. His prints are on file, so the M.E. can compare them at the autopsy, but I believe it's him."

I knelt down, allowing my flashlight to cast a bright glow across the edge of the house. Officer Hensley leaned over my shoulder. "You see something?"

I shook my head, as I scrutinized every blade of grass and the surrounding soil. "It's what I don't see that has me confused. There doesn't appear to be a lot of blood around the remains or on the house or the ground."

Saul was quick to catch up with me. "You're thinking he was dead, before the house landed on him."

"Karen will tell us for certain, but my money is on that scenario." I next examined the braces, that had once supported the house, but which now lay scattered on the ground. "How were the braces removed from under the house?"

Saul pointed to the yellow evidence markers, that dotted the land, twenty feet straight out, from where the braces had once set. "There are some heavy tire impressions, in the grass and mud that appear to belong to a pickup truck. Looks like someone wrapped a chain around the brace and yanked it out from under the house."

I stood up, to survey the surrounding real estate, noting the closest house was roughly a mile up the road, in the direction I had come from. A CSX train blew its horn, causing my eardrums to contract in pain, as every beat of the wheels reverberated through my body. "Whoever did this put some thought into it. Whose house is this?"

Daniel stared down at the top of his tactical boots, as Saul kept his face translucent. "Technically it belongs to the bank. It was foreclosed on a long time ago."

I stared at house, trying to note any other structural damage. "Any idea who the original owner was, before the bank foreclosed on it?"

Neither party replied to my question, causing me to turn toward them. Daniel had his hands pocketed in his coat and Saul was rubbing his chin with the back of his hand. "Who was the original owner guys?"

"What difference does it make? The place has been abandoned for years," Daniel replied.

"Hensley," Saul retorted.

The young officer turned to his chief, shaking his head emphatically, as he pointed to me. "Come on Saul, you know where he's going to go with this."

The chief turned to face his deputy. "He's going to find out one way or the other, so it might as well come from us."

I stared at the two of them, my patience starting to wear thin. "Will someone please tell me who used to live in this house?"

Saul looked at me, his eyes and face neutral. "Gary Winchell used to live here back in 1998."

I raised my eyebrows, as I glanced back at the house. "Winchell? Is he any relation to Patrick Winchell?"

"He's his father, Jonas," Saul replied.

I looked down at the body, then up to the brick house, unable to recall reading the Winchell name in the original casefile. "Was either Gary or Patrick a victim of Alston's?"

Daniel's face was turning as red as his hair, as he looked up to the sky waving his hands. "You see? He's already trying to finger someone in town for this. We can't let him do this, Saul."

Saul placed his finger in front of Daniel's face, as he admonished him. "That is enough. I want you to go and wait by the squad car, until I say otherwise, while the sheriff and I talk."

Daniel's mouth dropped open, as he stared at Saul, disbelief dripping from his eyes. "Chief—"

"That's an order, Officer Hensley."

Daniel looked from his commanding officer to me, his face red from both anger and embarrassment, before he stomped toward the front of the house. Saul stared after him, then turned to me, his lips taunt as he swallowed hard. "I can't put all the blame on him. I've not been setting the best example here lately, particularly when Alston O'Brian was involved. Still, I do apologize for his behavior. Like I said before, when it comes to the victim, there are still plenty of hard feelings."

I took out my Moleskine notebook and opened it to a blank page. "So I've noticed, Saul. As I asked earlier, did either Gary or Patrick Winchell have contact with Alston O'Brian?"

Saul shook his head. "Not directly. Gary worked for Kaleb Tate. Do you remember the Tate Sock factory?"

I had to dust off the cobwebs in my head to recall the name. "Vaguely. It was located over where the Lowes warehouse is now, right?"

"That's the one. Kaleb was one of Alston's investor's. Like everyone else, he lost his investment and he started hitting the bottle pretty hard. It wasn't long before he was showing up at work drunk. Shipments didn't get out on time, employees quit. The whole plant had to be shut down in six months."

I wrote this down in my illegible handwriting, pausing to tap the pad with the end of the pen. "I'm starting to remember it now. Three hundred people lost their jobs. It made the local newspaper and I think WBIR did a report on it as well. What ever happened to Kaleb?"

Saul stared at the ground, clearing his throat. "He was driving late one night on Old Highway 68 and missed the curb, hitting a rock embankment head-on. He had an empty six pack and a bottle of Wild Turkey on the floor board."

A silence engulfed us for a moment, as Saul sniffled and cleared his throat once again. I asked, "Did you know Kaleb?"

He angled his head to the left. "Just when I saw him. I never heard anybody say anything bad about him, even after he started drinking."

I looked back at the asymmetrical house, allowing another moment of silence before I asked my follow up questions. "Was Gary Winchell one of the employees, who quit after Kaleb started drinking?"

"I can't say Jonas. All I know is after the factory was shutdown, his house was foreclosed on and he and his family moved into a small apartment in Madisonville. His wife divorced him a year later and moved to Dayton is what I heard. Gary had a stroke and died six months after that."

I glanced down at the corpse, amazed at the destruction one man could release onto one little town. "Other than Patrick, do the Winchells have any other relatives in the area?"

Saul took a moment, before slowly shaking his head. "No. I believe Patrick is the last one in the area, as best as I recall. I'm pretty sure he doesn't have any kids."

I wrote this down. "How about Kaleb Tate? He have any kin left?"

He stared at the dead grass, his forehead wrinkled in concentration. "None that I'm aware of. I know Kaleb was pretty tight with Donovan Birch though."

My mind immediately brought up the name of the man I had to restrain in Hardees. "Harrison Birch's father?"

Saul nodded. "Yeah. He was Donovan's boy, that's right. How did you know?"

I thought perhaps, it was better to not bring up our past disputes over the late Alston O'Brian. "We've ran into each other before. How long has the house been on stilts?"

He blew out a gust of air. "As long as I can remember. Like I said the bank owns it now. They tried to auction it off a while back, but I don't think there were any takers."

"You remember which bank foreclosed on it?"

He slowly shook his head. "No Jonas. It was so long ago; I don't even know if that branch is still in town."

I made a note to call the county registrar. I was about to ask if he knew the whereabouts of Patrick Winchell and Harrison Birch, when Glen came around the corner, followed by Anthony Deland. I was relieved to see both of them wearing shoe covers. "Glen. Anthony, this is a surprise."

"I called him," Saul said.

Glen nodded at us, before looking down at the remains, a scowl spreading across his face. "Jonas, Saul. Man this is a new one for me."

Anthony stared down at the body for several seconds, his face morphing from pale to a faint green. I thought he was about to upchuck, but he swallowed hard and turned toward me and the chief. "Sheriff Lauer, Chief West. Is that really Alston O'Brian?"

Saul held up the plastic encased wallet. "This is his wallet Tony. I'm certain the fingerprints will make it official."

Anthony looked at the scene one more time, then turned toward us, stepping away from the body. "I've come to a decision Saul and you're not going to like it."

Saul parted his lips, as if to speak, but decided to keep it to himself. He covered his left hand with his right, as he awaited the decision. The attorney general placed his hands in his pockets and looked at the both of us. "I want Sheriff Lauer and his office, to take the lead in this investigation, Saul."

The chief's face turned two shades of red and the muscles around his jaw tightened. "Tony, we can handle this."

Anthony kept his voice low, but firm. "Your competency isn't in question Saul. This case is going to be scrutinized by both the public and the courts. With our previous history, with the victim, our objectivity may be called into question. Sheriff Lauer was neither a victim nor an investigating officer for the case in 1999, so he is impartial."

Saul looked toward me for a moment, a kaleidoscope of emotions emanating from his eyes, before he spoke to Anthony. "I see your point Tony. We'll assist the sheriff's department in any way we can."

The prosecuting attorney stepped forward, extending his hand, which Saul accepted. "I'm glad you see it that way Saul. We need to make sure everything is done by the book on this one. Starting with both of us giving the sheriff our alibis."

Both Saul and I were taken aback by Anthony's words, though I was more than a bit relieved by his suggestion. I was going to need to ask their whereabouts, so this saved me some time and inconvenience. "We don't have to do this here Anthony. We can meet up in Saul's office, where we have a bit more privacy."

Saul handed me the evidence bag containing the wallet. "It's all right, Jonas. I was on patrol last night till about midnight. I was home by 12:30 a.m., until I left for work this morning at 7:00 a.m."

I tapped the end of my pen on the notebook, as I read his statement. "Do you usually patrol that late in the evening?"

Saul nodded, clasping his hands behind his back. "I always work a few late shifts. We're a small department, so everyone has to pull their weight."

I wrote this down in my notebook and looked to Anthony, who took my cue. "I was working late on a deposition. Ms. Corbett was with me until 6:30 p.m. After that I went home and spent the night reading the newspaper and watching some TV. Alone I'm afraid."

I addressed the question to the both of them. "Before this morning, had either of you had any contact with Alston, in person or otherwise?"

They simultaneously shook their heads, which I noted and made a check mark beside it. When you're a detective, after a while, you can't help but get what I call, a cautionary mistrust of people. We all have a tendency to fib a little, especially if it casts a beneficial light upon us. This is never truer, then when it comes to a murder investigation. It pained me to think that a fellow officer and the attorney general might be lying, but it isn't unheard of. I know for a fact, the two have been in contact with one another, about Alston O'Brian and given the animosity I had witnessed, it wasn't a giant leap to think the two may have collaborated to get their stories straight.

"Alston went missing last Friday. Can you tell me where you were then?"

Saul tucked his hand into his pockets, shrugging. "That's easy. I was at the station, filling out reports. Daniel was there too. Up until you found us at McDonalds that day."

"And I was before Judge Belcher, giving closing arguments on a burglary case," Anthony replied in turn.

I made a note, before turning to Glen. "You need to call the forensic unit and Karen. Also call Greg Hinshaw, at the rescue squad and have him come out here. We're going to need his expertise, to lift this house, so we can remove the body."

"Yes sir." Glen got out his cell, as he stepped away.

I faced Saul, while flipping to a fresh page in my notebook. "All right Saul, I need to know the events that led to the discovery of the body."

Saul placed his hands in his pockets, and turned around, so he was not facing the body. "After you told me about Mr. O'Brian contacting you and then vanishing, I had an APB put out on his vehicle. Nothing ever came from it, but I still had my officers keep an eye out for him. That too, unfortunately yielded no information, as to his whereabouts."

I made abbreviated references in my notepad. "So what led you to the crime scene?"

The chief pointed to the sky. "Buzzards. Officer Hensley was about to go on patrol at 8:30 a.m., when he noticed about half a dozen of them circling the sky. He thought it a bit odd for there to be so many during winter, so he radioed it in and came out here to check for himself. He called me, as soon as he discovered the body."

I glanced up at the few trees surrounding the scene and saw no signs of the feathered scavengers. "Did you see the birds, Saul?"

He shook his head. "No, they were gone by the time I got here."

"Did you notice them when you came into work?"

The flesh along his forehead rippled in confusion. "No. Why?"

"I'm just trying to be thorough Saul." I pointed to the remains with my pen. "Besides, you and Officer Hensley, did any more of your men come around the body?"

"No. We kept the scene secured."

I put the pen and notepad in one hand and tapped my leg. "When forensics gets here, we're going to need to take impressions of your and Officer Hensley's boots, so we can separate them from the rest of the scene."

"You want our boot prints to separate them? Not because we're suspects?"

Anthony decided to intervene. "Saul, you know he has no choice in this matter. This has to be by the book and since you and your officer were on the scene, without proper foot protection, he has to take exemplars from you both. If he doesn't and this goes to trial, a good defense attorney can easily say the crime scene was contaminated and get any evidence recovered thrown out of court."

Though his face was still red, Saul voice was more subdued, even as he spoke through clenched teeth. "All right Tony. I see your point. We'll let you take a cast of our boots."

I gave the attorney general a quick nod of thanks. "I appreciate this Saul. I'm going to need to speak with Officer Hensley too, but I think I'll give him a few more minutes to cool off, while I take a look at the scene."

The chief looked toward his officer and nodded. "That's probably not a bad idea."

I returned to the house, for a closer inspection of the braces, which now lay on the ground. I took gloves from my pocket and put them on. The wooden braces used to support the house, showed heavy signs of weathering. The two by four boards which crisscrossed over one another, revealed heavy signs of mold from moisture, that had seeped in over time. I wasn't able to move the braces before they were photographed, but it didn't take long to locate the pieces, that had distinctive rifts running along their sides. It did look like a chain had been used, to remove the wooden supports, from underneath the house.

I walked a straight line back away from the house, until I came to a part of the lawn, where the grass had been cut by tires, which left clumps of red clay and mud, indicating the trajectory of the vehicle. First glance, told me Saul was correct, in surmising that it was a pickup truck used to remove the support. I followed the tracks, until they disappeared into the tall grass, but I was still able to follow them by using the bent and twisted blades the truck had left in its wake. I stepped alongside the tracks, as they made a half moon across the ground, until they stopped approximately ten feet from the braces. I knelt down and looked at the width between the tires.

"Glen," I said.

My deputy came from around the side of the house his hands resting on his gun belt. "Yes sir."

"You got a tape measurer in your field kit?"

He nodded. "Yes sir."

"Go get it for me please."

Anthony watched Glen head to his cruiser, before he looked back to me. "What is it, sheriff?"

I kept my focus on the tire impressions, as I scratched the back of my ear with my gloved finger. "I want to check the measurements of these tire tracks."

A minute later Glen returned with a silver tape measure in his hand. "You stand on that end and extend it to me, Glen."

We measured the distance of the tire treads and I wrote it down. I got out my BlackBerry and after a web search, I came to a quick conclusion. "I'm not sure it was a truck that did this."

Saul and Anthony glanced at one another, a look of surprise on their faces. Anthony, put his hands in his pockets, and looked at the tire track. "Why do you say that?"

I pointed to the tread marks I was standing beside. "The dimension between the tires don't match those found on most trucks. We'll send the measurements and casts to Molly, so she can do a more thorough analysis. For now, I'm thinking we're looking for an SUV."

Saul glanced at the rifts in the ground, chewing on the corner of his lip. "Well, you narrowed that down pretty quick."

I still was uncertain, as to where Saul stood, on the circumstances surrounding Alston's death and clarification did not appear to be coming anytime soon. "It's just an educated guess for now."

Glen looked around at the area. "The nearest house is about a mile away. How come no one reported hearing the noise? I mean yanking out the braces, would've made a heck of a racket."

I remembered seeing the white house, just up the road across the street, when I first arrived on the scene. "Just because they didn't report the noise, doesn't mean they didn't hear something. We need to start canvasing the neighbors and document what they saw or heard."

Glen put the tape measure in his coat pocket and started toward the road. "Ten four."

When I looked back, Saul was removing a stick of gum from a yellow package. "Tony?"

The AG, declined his offer, as did I. "Saul, who did you have on duty last night?"

Folding the wrapper, he put it in his coat pocket, as he started to soften the gum. "Like I said, I was on patrol up until midnight. Officer Gentry was manning the phones and radio until six this morning, then Daniel relieved him. I came in at a little after seven."

I scribbled all of this down in my notebook, unable to not mentally acknowledge, just how close the VPD stationhouse was to the crime scene. "I'd like to speak with Officer Gentry and I'd also like a copy of all your calls, from midnight, until the body was discovered."

Saul nodded. "I'll get you a copy. As for Gentry, he's the man standing guard in the driveway."

I recalled the donut eating cop, who could barely answer any of my questions and was already dreading the interview, that was to come. "I'll get to him, after I speak with Officer Hensley."

I found myself studying the house, which now encompassed the body of Alston O'Brian. "Anthony, I'm going to need a warrant to search the house, after we've removed the body."

He took his cellphone from the inside lapel pocket of his overcoat. "I'll find a judge."

Saul moved closer to me, focusing on the lopsided home. "You think the killer took a stroll inside the place, before landing it on O'Brian's head?"

"I really don't know what to think Saul, except that I don't believe this house was chosen at random. The way I see it, the killer either used it because of the connection Alston had to it, or the killer knew about it being on braces and decided to use it to his advantage. Either way, we need to take a look inside, just to be sure."

I spotted Officer Hensley leaning against the hood of his cruiser, with his arms crossed. I believed I had given him enough time to cool off and if it wasn't then, too bad. We had a homicide to investigate. "If you'll excuse me, I think it's time your officer and I talked."

Saul moved, as if he was about to join me. "You want me to come with you?"

I waved my hand for him to stay. "Thanks, but we'll be all right."

When I reached the cruiser, Officer Hensley did not acknowledge my presence. With his eyes shielded by dark sunglasses, he appeared to be staring at the train tracks. "Officer, we need to go over what happened this morning."

He barely turned his head in my direction, a long breath exhaling from his nostrils, like an angry bull. "All right."

Flipping to another clean page in my notepad, I wrote his name in the top corner. "What time did your shift end yesterday?"

"I checked out at 6:00 p.m. last night."

The sun was eclipsed by a white cloud, shadowing the valley for a few seconds, as I stared at my notebook. "And what time did you come into work today?"

Hensley crossed his ankles, digging his heel into the gravel driveway. "Six o'clock."

The bitterness lining his responses was starting to irritate me, but I chose to ignore it, for the time being. "Walk me through your day, this morning."

The young officer finally looked me square in the face, his eyebrows pinched together, as if he hadn't comprehended my words. "Walk you through my morning? Why?"

I kept my pen just above the pad, as I gave him a small smile. "I like to be thorough."

He exhaled another curt breath, as he gazed up at the sky. The curtain of the cloud had been removed and it allowed me to see his eyes, oscillating behind his sunglasses. "I came in this morning and got myself a cup of coffee from the breakroom, as usual. I checked last night's incident reports. Then I went to my desk and checked my emails, before starting on my own paperwork, until the chief came in."

I chose then to interrupt him. "You and Saul talk about anything?"

He hunched his shoulders, crossing his feet the other way, kicking gravel over my shoes. "Yeah, it was just your usual good mornings. We griped that we're ready for warm weather."

I gave my head a light nod, writing all he said down in short hand. "When did you leave for patrol?"

He looked down at his feet, folding his arms across his stomach. "Around half past eight. I got into my cruiser and headed south, on Church Street toward 411 and noticed the house was setting different. At first, I thought maybe the supports gave way. I can't remember how long the house has been setting like that. When I walked around to the back, I saw the legs protruding out from under the foundation. I called it in and you know the rest."

I studied his statement for a moment, then glanced up at the sky. All I could see on the blue canvas was white marshmallow clouds, two jets streaming through the sky, and the egg yolk yellow sun. Not a vulture or a bird of any kind was visible, but according to Saul, it was the flying scavengers, that first drew Hensley's attention, to the house. He had failed to mention any birds just now. "So it was the house being of kilter, that first caught your attention?"

"Yes sir."

I tapped the notebook with my pen and allowed a moment of silence between us. "So it wasn't the kettle in the sky, that caught your eye, Officer Hensley?"

He frowned at me, as if I had lapsed into a foreign tongue, removing his sunglasses to stare into my face. "Now what?"

I pointed upward, as I explained, hoping his frustration could be used to my advantage. "Kettle. It's what you call a flock of vultures flying circles in the sky. You didn't see any of them, hovering around the body from the stationhouse?"

I watched as his eyes quickly looked down and to the left, as the flesh around his neck grew red. "Vultures? Yeah…yeah that's right. There were a few of them circling in this vicinity. I thought it was kind of odd, with it being so cold. I mean I know they don't all fly south, but there had to be nearly half a dozen or so. I guess they were hungry. Of course, they only would've gotten half a meal, as only the legs were exposed."

The tasteless joke is often a cop's defense mechanism, against the brutality of what we see every day. Seeing humanity at its worst is a burden and sometimes you have to make light of it, in order to get through the ordeal. But it didn't take a genius, to see, that Hensley was using humor to deflect my questions. You become accustomed to being lied to when you're a cop, but when the lies come from fellow officers, it really gets under your skin. "So, you did see the buzzards, before noticing the house was tilting? Or you saw the house had fallen off the supports and then saw the buzzards?"

Hensley's opened his mouth, only to close it, before taking a deep swallow. "It was…now what did you say again?"

I stared at him, tracing invisible circles on the sheet of paper, with the back of my pen. "What did you see first officer, the buzzards or the fallen house?"

Tiny beads of sweat appeared along his hairline, as he released the top button of his coat. "I saw the buzzards. I thought I said that all ready."

"Actually you originally said it was the house having shifted that caught your eye. You never mentioned anything about the vultures, until I did." I kept my eye on him, noting he was having difficulty meeting my gaze. "The only reason it even occurred to me to ask about the vultures, is because of what Saul said."

Hensley's eyes shot to Saul, who was still at the house with Anthony. The chief gave his officer a quick glance and judging from the stern look on his face, he didn't appear to like the look of distress, on the young officer's face. Saul began making his way toward us, meaning I had to kick it in fifth gear. "Your chief said, that you stated, it was the vultures circling the house that drew your attention, Officer Hensley. So that leaves us in a bit of a pickle here. Did you lie to your chief before? If so, why?"

Removing his sunglasses, Officer Hensley's eyes narrowed into daggers, as he looked at me. "I didn't tell a damn lie. I just got confused is all. It happens to everybody now and then."

Saul had joined us by then, and positioned himself between us. "What is going on here?"

I put my pen inside my notebook, as I rested my hands at my side and gave the chief a quick glance. "I'm trying to conduct an interview, Saul."

Saul positioned his body in front of Daniel, acting as a shield. "It looks more to me, like you're upsetting my officer. What have you been talking about?"

I rolled my thumb over the ink pen. "I'm trying to determine the circumstances, that drew Officer Hensley to this house and discover the body."

Saul squared his shoulders and hooked his thumbs under his gun belt. "I already told you how he found the body. So what's the problem?"

I contemplated Saul, then Hensley, who had now returned his sunglasses to his face and was looking down. "The problem is, Officer Hensley just told me that it was the house appearing uneven that alerted him, to the crime scene, not the vultures. He didn't even mention them in fact."

Saul looked back at Hensley, who tried to cower behind the collar of his coat. His cheeks so red hot, you could fry bacon on them. "I'm sure it just slipped his mind."

"He said as much, just before you stepped in," I replied. "If you wouldn't mind Officer Hensley, you said you were heading toward Highway 411 to begin patrol. Why did you head south from the stationhouse? Isn't it faster to get to the highway, if you turn north?"

"I…I was conducting a sweep of the neighborhood," he said.

Saul stepped directly in front of me, so he had all but obscured Officer Hensley, from my line of sight. "What's the big deal here, Jonas? What difference does it make which way he turned? So the kid forgot to mention the birds. So what?"

I found myself staring at the chief of police for a moment, unable to believe what he had just said. "We're talking about the circumstances that led a police officer to discover a dead body. You say it was buzzards. He is saying something else entirely. If we don't get this straightened out now, a good defense attorney will get all of this thrown out, before it even gets to trial. I'd say that is a very big deal, Saul."

He exhaled a deep breath, laced with a strong coffee smell, which was slightly nauseating. "No one is lying. He just misspoke. You just need to get onboard."

I felt the muscles along my neck and my stomach grow taunt, like the inside of a helium balloon. "Onboard? You mean, get our stories straight?"

Saul shook his head, his mouth dropping down in disgust. "No one is saying anything like that. I'm just saying you need to cut a fellow officer some slack. He's had a heck of a morning."

I was at a true loss for words. Was the chief of police actually saying, it was not a big deal, that the first officer on the scene, to a homicide, couldn't make up his mind how he discovered the body? Saul was too experienced a lawman, to not realize the consequences, of Officer Hensley's different renditions, of what brought him to the premises. This in turn led me to a train of thought, that made my skin grow cold, and it had nothing to do with the weather. Was Saul covering his officer's slip of the tongue? Or was he concealing something more sinister?

I flipped to the next page of my notebook and stepped to the side, so I had a view of Officer Hensley. "I have a few more questions. Officer, before this morning, did you ever have any contact with a man known as Alston O'Brian?"

He wrapped his arms around his body, as if he was cold, while shaking his head. "No."

Both Daniel and Saul's faces were strained, indicating they would rather have been anywhere else. Daniel's demeanor had an air of nervousness about him, whereas every breath Saul took was laced with annoyance. "And to be clear, it was the tilted house that first caught your attention?"

Saul scoffed, looking away, before he focused his eyes on me. "You don't give up, do you?"

I didn't reply to his question, keeping my gaze on Hensley. "Is that the order of events, officer?"

Hensley looked at the back of Saul's neck, as if expecting the chief to intervene, only to find he was on his own. He licked his lips and scratched the tip of his nose. "No sir. I saw the buzzards flying over the house first, sir. Then I noticed the house was tilted."

"And your whereabouts last night officer?" I asked, scribbling away.

"I got off at six, like I said. Spent the evening home, alone," he spat out.

Things were not starting out good in this investigation. Barely thirty minutes into the case and not only was the city police department stonewalling my inquiries, but I was fairly certain that at least one officer was lying to me. So that meant, the bridge of interagency cooperation was all but incinerated and it didn't appear like it was going to be restored anytime soon. Spotting the evidence recovery van's arrival, it seemed this would be a good time to end the interview. "I'll need you both to come down to the stationhouse and give a formal statement. If there any further questions, I'll be in touch."

The van stopped at the edge of the driveway, where Officer Gentry handed the driver the notepad for the techs to sign. Spying Dr. Karen Long in the passenger seat, I stepped up to the passenger door, as she lowered the window. "Morning, Jonas."

I braced myself against the dark blue van. "Karen. I was expecting you to come in your vehicle."

Karen is half Caucasian and half Cherokee, which gave her skin a beautiful tan complexion, no matter what time of year it was. She gave me a small grin as she playfully rolled her eyes. "Nick's car broke down the other day, so I lent her mine. I've been after her for a year, to get rid of that piece of junk she drives. It spends more time in the shop, than it does on the road. I'd thought I'd hitch a ride back with the ambulance, after the body was secured. Where is it?"

Nick is short for Nicole, Karen's life partner, for the last twenty years. It's a sign of the times, that an openly lesbian couple, can live in the once ultraconservative Monroe County. When I was a kid, no way that would've been allowed. I wrinkled my nose, as I nodded toward the house. "On the back side of the property, under the house."

Karen's ebony eyes took on the diameter of silver dollars. "*Under the house?*"

"Afraid so. The rescue squad is in route. They should be able to elevate the house enough, so we can pull him out. Or at least what's left of him."

She stared at the house for bit, before shrugging it off. "Well, this sets itself apart from the other body recovery calls, you've sent me on."

I allowed myself a sardonic smile, as I lowered my voice. "Well, it is always good to spice things up. You can go on around and take your photographs."

After informing the forensic unit, to take casts and measurements of the tire tracks, along with retrieving the wood used for the braces, I headed toward Officer Gentry. He had finished his donut, so I hoped that meant, I would be able to get more than one syllable responses from him. "Officer, I understand you were monitoring the calls last night, for the VCPD."

He faced me, with his hand resting on his belly. "Yes sir I was."

I again took out my Moleskine notebook and glanced back at Saul and Hensley, who were still standing by the cruiser, glaring at yours truly. "If you would, give me your full name."

"Officer Elvis Gentry."

I paused after writing his first name, narrowing my eyes at him, one second away from disciplining him. "Seriously?"

He let out a slight laugh, his round face seeming to light up, as he shrugged. "Both of my parents are Elvis Presley fans. It wasn't easy going to school with that name, but I kind of like it, now."

I gave him a slight nod, seeking no more elaboration. "How did the shift go last night, sir?"

He gave his head a slight shake, as he adjusted his belt over his stomach. "It was a pretty quiet night. There was one call to Danny's Bar, just down 411, around 1:00 a.m. And I recall a few domestic calls, but nothing else springs to mind, right now. We have a complete log at the station."

I pointed to the property behind him, now littered with law enforcement and shades of blue from the light bars on the cruisers. "Were there any calls about this property? Or even on this road last night?"

"No sir. If there had been, it'd been the first thing I told you."

I turned, so I could keep Saul and Hensley in the corner of my vision, as I asked my next question. "Were you there when Officer Hensley called in the discovery of the body?"

Gentry nodded, as he glanced over at Hensley and the chief. "Yes sir. I was just about to go off duty, when it came in. I can't complain though. I need the overtime, just like everybody else."

I gave him a quick grin and tilted my head. "We all do man."

This got a laugh out of him, as I hoped it would. "Yeah man. It's crazy how the prices of everything keep going up, but we don't hardly ever get a raise."

I nodded, hoping to coax him along. "That's the way it's always been. Or it sure seems like it. Hey, I asked Hensley this already, but forgot to write it down. He seems upset, so I don't want to bother him again, but I thought maybe you could help me. What did he say it was, that drew his attention to this place?"

Gentry scratched the back of his head, as he stared up at the sky. "Ahh, he saw some buzzards in the sky. If you can believe that."

I paused for a moment to look at him, wondering if that last remark was more than just an afterthought. I wrote this down and underlined it twice. "If you wouldn't mind Officer Gentry, come down to the stationhouse and give us a statement. Just so we have our ducks in a row."

He nodded, tapping the back of the legal pad with his fingers. "No problem."

"Thanks." I went to my truck, so I could review what I had learned, undisturbed but still able to keep the chief and Hensley in view. That cold feeling, which had been consuming me, did not dissipate, as I reread my notes. Glen came up to me, his hand resting above his gun, finger lightly tapping the sights as he glanced in Saul's direction. "I couldn't help but notice, that the chief and Hensley are shooting bullets at you, with their eyes. I take it the interviews didn't go well?"

I got a sardonic smile on my face. "Apparently, I'm not supposed to point out discrepancies, in a fellow officer's statement. That was the impression they gave me anyway."

"You think they're lying?"

I closed my notebook and used the end to scratch my forehead. "Hensley is for sure. I just don't know if Saul is backing him up or lying with him."

Glen turned, so he was facing me, and kept his voice low. "Did either of them say they had any contact with the victim?"

"Both said they didn't see the victim, prior to his death."

His face seemed to go elliptical, as he releases a long breath. The change in his demeanor, made the balloon of unease nestled, in my chest swell from the size of a golf ball to a basketball. "Why? Has someone said otherwise?"

He pointed down the road to the closest house, where a gentleman was standing by his driveway, smoking a pipe. "I just spoke to that old man standing in his driveway. He said last night he saw two people standing by the house, just after the eleven o'clock news."

"Did he get a good look at them?"

Glen pivoted his hand back and forth. "Sort of. It was dark and all. But, Jonas he was sure one of them was driving a police cruiser."

Chapter Ten

The rescue squad arrived, along with a Moyer's Housing truck, which had the uniformed hydraulic jacks, needed to lift the house up off the remains. While they were setting up, I decided to pay a visit to the old man, who had observed two people talking, at the crime scene last night. The old man settled down on his front porch to talk. He was puffing away on his black pipe, as he scratched his chin through his thick gray beard. He was over six feet tall, so he almost towered over Glen and myself, but he had gentle gray eyes and the soft voice of a kind man. "I've been alive for nearly seven decades and I've never heard of a man getting crushed by a house."

His name was Abel Brenton. He was a retired custodian, from the Vonore Elementary School. He had the strong hands of a man, who had done a lot of manual work. I nodded in agreement, as I stood to the side, to avoid the smoke drifting from his pipe. "It's a first for me too, Mr. Brenton. Now, I understand you told my deputy, you saw two men talking, at the crime scene, last night."

He nodded, taking a long draw, the smoke slithering from the corners of his mouth. "Yes sir. My wife doesn't like the smoke smelling up her furniture, so I come out on the front porch at night, to light up."

I couldn't help but elevate an eyebrow at this. "Sir, it was nearly twenty degrees last night and you still came out for a smoke?"

Abel revealed yellow tinted teeth, as he smiled at me. "We all have our quirks, son. It's what makes us unique. Besides, I always sleep better, after a late night puff, on this old pipe here. Plus, I really enjoy smoking. At my age, it's one of the few pleasures I have left."

I gave him a slight nod. "And at what time last night did you see the two men talking, sir?"

"Just past 11:00 p.m."

I wrote this down in my notebook. I was sure Glen had already written it down too, but it helps my mind process things better, if I put pen to paper. "Now, Mr. Brenton, I don't mean to keep pressing the point, but I need to know how you are so certain of the time."

He turned and pointed to his house with his pipe. "Because Beverly, that's my wife, had just turned the news on channel 10. We usually go to bed, just after they give the weather, so I put on my boots and grabbed my pipe and lighter, for one last puff."

I lightly stomped my feet on the gravel driveway, to help alleviate the cold numbness. "I know you've already gone over this with my deputy, but if you could, tell me exactly what you saw last night."

He took one long draw, before exhaling a small gray cloud of smoke, then pointed over to the crime scene, with his pipe as he spoke. "Like I said, I came out here to have a quick smoke. I was on the front step, staring up at the stars, when I heard two men talking over there. They were too far away for me, to make out what they were saying, but from the way one of them was waving his arms about, it looked like he was mad about something."

Another train roared its way down the tracks, making my ear drums feel, like there was a symphony playing in my head. I waited for the front engine, to move on down the tracks, then raised my voice over the train cars being towed. "About how long were they standing there talking?"

Abel squinted his right eye, as he looked up, at the naked treetops in his yard. "Oh, about five minutes, before they left."

"You think it was possible they saw you, Mr. Brenton?"

He shrugged. "I can't say for sure. It didn't appear like they knew I was out here. I didn't bother turning on the porch light, but I can't swear to anything."

"Could you tell what kind of vehicles they were driving?" I asked, after writing his statement.

"One was definitely a truck or one of those SUVs. I couldn't tell which. The other one was definitely a car. It was easy enough to tell, because it was parked in front of that truck, with its headlights on."

I tapped my notebook, with the tip of my pen for a moment, rubbing my dry lips with my tongue. Glen had said Able mentioned the car might've been a cruiser. I didn't want to lead the witness, so I thought about my words, before my next question. "I don't suppose you were able to tell what kind of vehicles they were, I mean the make and models?"

He took one last drag, before tapping his pipe on the heel of his worn leather work boot. "Of the SUV, no. Anymore they all look alike to me, besides it was too far away and dark. Now the car, I think it might've been a cop car."

I started writing again. "What makes you say that, sir?"

"Because I saw those long light boxes, you guys have on your cars, setting on top of that one."

I turned back to look at the driveway leading to the crime scene. "Where were the vehicles parked last night, Mr. Brenton?"

He lifted a long bony finger, with a swollen arthritic knuckle and pointed to the house. "Just on yon side of the driveway."

That was the better part of a mile away, give or take a foot or two. I looked to the older gentleman before me, who from all appearances seemed to be of sound mind. However, it was his vision that I now had to question, because a defense attorney certainly will, if and when this goes to trial. "Mr. Brenton, please don't be offended by this, but it was dark last night and you said you were about to go to bed. So, I have to ask, how can you be sure it was a police cruiser you saw?"

He got a smile on his face, emanating no offense was taken. "Son, you don't have to beat around the bush. You want to know, if my old eyes can see that far at night, right?"

I smiled in return and hunched my shoulders. "Well, yeah."

He kicked some gravel across the road, as he laughed. "I would too, if I was in your shoes. The answer is, I have to wear glasses when I have to read or drive at night. But that night both the truck and the car had their headlights on. So even though the images were a bit blurry, I was still able to make out the lights on top of the car. Like I said, would I stake my life on it: no. But I would wager a good bet the car was a police car."

I wrote this down and underlined it. I couldn't help but like the old man. He was right, in not placing his life on the line. A good defense attorney would make his eyesight a liability to the prosecution, but the conviction in his voice was enough for me to believe him. "Have you yourself ever had any run-ins with the law?"

He furrowed his brow, adding to the wrinkles time had produced. "No. Why?"

I waved my hand, showing I meant no offense. "I have to ask. And you heard nothing last night? No strange or loud noises?"

Able shook his head. "I take Tylenol PM before bedtime and it knocks me right out. The wife likes to listen to one of those sound machines, that sound like a waterfall. She takes out her hearing aids at night, so she could barely hear a cannon go off, right beside her, much less anything outside."

I scribbled this down and tapped my pen on the notebook. "We're going to need to speak with your wife too, Mr. Brenton, just so we can mark her off the list. If you wouldn't mind coming down to the sheriff's department stationhouse, we can type up your statement for you to sign and we'll be in touch, if we have any other questions."

"Sarah's inside right now, so you can go on in. I've got to pick up some medicine at the pharmacy this afternoon. Is it all right, if we swing by around two o'clock?"

I extended my hand, which he accepted. "That'll do just fine. Thanks again for your time, Mr. Brenton. If it's all right Deputy Coop will speak with your wife in a moment."

"Not a problem."

Glen and I stepped off the porch, as Abel opened the door and entered his house. We kept our voices low, but did our best to act like nothing was amiss. Glen hooked his thumbs under his belt. "So what now?"

I put my notebook away, before placing my hands in the pockets of my coat. "For now, we work this investigation, like any other case."

Glen allowed his eyes to stray over to the Vonore City Police cruiser parked, in front of the crime scene. "And if it turns out someone, on the VCPD, had a hand in killing Alston O'Brian?"

I didn't need to ponder for my reply. "We arrest them. No matter if it's a cop or civilian, we find proof of who the murderer is, we take them into custody."

He tilted his head over his left shoulder and blew out a light sigh. "That's not going to win you any popularity points, among the police department, or the people of Vonore for that matter."

I looked toward the VCPD stationhouse and then back to the crime scene. "You can't have this job and not make some enemies. Of course, I never expected to make them inside the police force."

My deputy stared at the faded, gray asphalt, shaking his head, as if he didn't want to believe what he was about to say. "Do you really think it was a cop he saw last night?"

I rolled my tongue along the inside of my cheek, recalling Abel Brenton's demeanor, as I had interviewed him. I didn't notice a hint of deception, as he reiterated what he had seen the previous night. Of course, he could just be an exceptional liar, but a quick background check will reveal if he's had any dealing with the law. Until I discover a reason not to, my initial reaction to his statement, is he is telling the truth. "I believe he meant what he said Glen. Of course we're still a long way from proving anything and like you, I'm hoping this case doesn't involve an officer. Yet, let's face the facts, neither the chief nor his officer have hidden their disdain for Alston O'Brian."

Glen worked hard to not roll his eyes, as he tapped the toe of his shoe, on the asphalt. "They weren't exactly the model for efficiency, that morning at the Hardees, that's for sure. From the way the chief was glaring at you earlier, it looked like he didn't like the questions you were asking Hensley."

"No, he certainly did not. But we can't get ahead of ourselves here. Karen still has to examine the body. We've got to search the house too and see if the killer or victim were inside. Has there been any luck in finding Alston's vehicle?"

Glen shook his head, as he looked up the street. "No. And it would be hard to miss it on this road. Not a lot of places to hide a car."

I examined my notes, where I had written down the information about Alston's Camry, from our initial meeting, at the gas station. I made Glen write this information on his own notepad. "I want all units, to be on the lookout for his car. Saul said he put out a BOLO for it, but I want it issued again. We find it, maybe we find out where he was killed. After that, go and see what Mrs. Brenton has to say."

Glen took out the speaker to his radio and stepped away, speaking clearly into the microphone. I returned to the house, passing Saul and Hensley, neither of them looked in my direction. I guess they were still upset over my refusal, to get on the same page. At the back of the house, the men from the moving company were working to balance the house. Or I should say, some of the men were working. There were six men standing outside, all in company uniforms and hardhats, but only two were placing the hydraulic jacks under the foundation of the house. The others stood watching, with their hands in their pockets, staring down at their coworkers. Karen was standing to the side, waiting for the house to be stabilized, so she could examine the remains. I moseyed over beside her, as I watched the men at work. "Why are there so many men here and only two working?"

Karen scoffed, as she cocked her eyebrow. "I've asked myself, that same question, I don't know, how many times, especially when I pass a construction site."

I nodded, a slight grin spreading across my face. "Yeah, my mother was very vocal about that, on every vacation we took, when I was a kid. I guess it wouldn't be funny, if it weren't true. Of course, I'm also standing around with my hands in my pockets, so I suppose I can't say much."

Karen gave me a quick side glance, before nudging me in the ribs with her elbow. "You're waiting for them, to move the house, so you can look at the body. There is a difference. Though I'm sure, that trait is in your DNA, as it is with all those, of the male persuasion."

I looked down at her. "Nice backhanded compliment."

She smiled. "Thank you."

When the last jack was set, one of the men left the herd, and went to the control box, that had several black hoses veining out across the lawn. After hitting two buttons and flipping a switch, the hoses jerked, as the air pressure began to engage the lifts under the house. I spotted Anthony working his way toward me, as he put his phone away. He placed a finger over his ear canal, as he passed the motor for the jacks. "We get the warrant, Anthony?"

He leaned in to avoid shouting. "You're good to go, once the house is stabilized. I've got one of the junior assistants bringing it down, as we speak."

I gave him a thumbs up. "Good to know."

He looked toward the house, as it slowly began to ascend, then turned back to me. "You got anything yet?"

Having no desire, to broadcast my suspicions over the valley, I just nodded. "It's still early. I'm hoping we might learn more, inside the house. We've also got a BOLO out on his car."

"How did the interview go with Saul and Officer Hensley?"

Jesse A. Hester

I thought about my answer for a moment, then replied, with the only response I could think of. "About as well as can be expected."

* * *

An hour later, the house was elevated and secured, allowing Karen, to now examine the body. The waist and lower abdomen of the corpse was almost crushed flat. The face, wasn't as disfigured, as one would've thought and was recognizable as Alston O'Brian. The house had been elevated, for some time, allowing the rains to erode most of the soil from beneath it, thus forming a small pocket. Alston's body was lying in the center of that pocket, which allowed his face and the upper part of his torso to be intact. The same couldn't be said for his life. He was wearing a blue button down shirt, untucked, with dried blood down the front and up on the shoulders. His dark pants were torn around the knees, revealing scratched knee caps. There was also the distinct scent of urine coming from the body.

After the preliminary photographs and measurements were taken, Karen put on a set of gloves and took on the stoic doctor's face, as she knelt down, to get a closer examination of the remains. With a flashlight, Karen looked into his hazel eyes, now covered with a foggy white sheen. She carefully placed her gloved hands on his forearm and lifted it two inches off the ground. "The limbs are stiff and his eyes have that milky white tint to them. I'd put time of death to be approximately twelve to twenty-four hours ago. With the cold temps, that's the best I can do, for now. I should be able to be more precise, after I open him up."

I noticed deep circular gashes on the back of his hands, where congealed blood was scabbing over. "Are those hammer marks Karen?"

She looked at them very closely. "They appear to be. The injuries have already started to heal. Suggesting it happened a few hours, before his death. Someone broke his hand, while he was alive, Jonas."

"They wanted him to feel the pain." I had my flashlight out, studying the foundation, where it had come in contact with the body. There wasn't as much blood spatter, as you'd expect to see, from a house dropping on a body. I inspected the soil at the edges of the remains and found the same vacancy of blood, thus confirming my earlier suspicions. "Karen, I don't think he died from the house falling on him."

She shook her head, as she unbuttoned his shirt. "I don't think so either. I can't say for certain yet, what killed him, but it wasn't from being crushed."

After she had the deceased's shirt open, she sat back and stared at his chest. "But he definitely suffered more than a broken hand, prior to his death."

I crawled to the other side of her, to get a better view of Alston and saw what Karen was referring to. Along his chest and the section of abdomen that weren't crushed, were several bruises consistent with being hit with a fist. There were other bruises marbling his torso, that had an almost dome shape to them. I blew out a long breath, as I rubbed my chin with the palm of my hand. "Looks like the final hours of Alston's life were not peaceful."

The good doctor stared, at the black patterns of the wounds and took photographs of them. "No. He's been struck at least twelve times, with a fist and what looks to be a weapon. I'll do thermal photography on him, back at the morgue, to see if any more bruises might show up on the prints. This guy had some serious enemies."

I adjusted my position, to relieve the tension in my back. "More like serious bad blood. He was a conman, who swindled a lot of people in Vonore out of their money and property. More important, he took their pride and dignity. This very house was in foreclosure, as a result of the con, he ran back in 1999. It's fair to say, there will likely be a lot of people glad, that Alston O'Brian is no longer alive."

Karen looked at the cadaver for another moment, before she looked to me, with her same translucent expression. "In other words, you have your work cut out for you, on this one."

I closed my eyes, almost dreading the work ahead. "That sounds right."

Karen looked up at the house only inches above her head, a slight wrinkle forming across her brow. "Why did they drop the house on him? Some sort of twisted way of saying, screw you?"

I looked around at the red clay stained foundation, not entirely convinced, that was the only motivation for the house being used in the crime. "Perhaps. Or it could've been used in hopes that it would help conceal the evidence, that he was beaten shortly before his death. Another possibility is, this could all be a smoke screen."

Karen removed two sterile paper bags from her kit and wrapped one of Alston's hands in each, for preservation of any trace evidence. "I don't follow you."

I pointed upward toward the house, as I stared at the body. "It was widely known, in Vonore, that Alston was back in town. What if this has nothing to do with the con from '99? The killer could've known the history of the house and used it, to make us think, it was about Alston's past, when it was something else."

"That's…pretty smart, if you think about it. A bit extreme too, though. The simplest thing to do, would be been to weight the body down and put it in the lake."

I stared at her, a bit alarmed, at how quick she came up with that scenario. "Is that what you would've done?"

She got a sly smile on her face, while sealing the bags around his hands. "I'm a doctor, Jonas. If I was going to kill someone, I'd cut the body up and scatter it all over the valley."

I felt a slight chill run down my spine, as I took a long look at her. "It sounds like you've put some thought into that, Karen."

She smiled and gave me a quick wink. "You always need to be prepared."

I made a mental note, to not ever piss Karen Long off, just as a mild spasm worked its way down my back. "I've got to get outside and stretch, Karen."

"I've done all I can here. I'll let you know, what I find during the post mortem," she said, as I crawled out from under the house.

When I was clear, I straightened up, feeling the vertebrae, in the center of my spine pop. I walked away from the body, toward the truck treads, feeling the tension move down my lower back. Turning around to look at the now, level house, I had to concede, to the validity of Karen's reasoning. The use of the house, as a way to conceal the injuries, seemed a bit farfetched, even for my active imagination. Then again, we have two morons, who have eluded arrest while robbing people's homes, using boxer shorts as masks, so I suppose it would be better, to keep an open mind.

As I watched the rescue squad lift Alston's body and place it in the black cadaver bag, my mind drifted back to our last conversation. He wanted to tell me something, but wouldn't do it over the phone. The mere fact he called me, after adamantly saying, he didn't want help from the police, meant, whatever was bothering him was serious. Was it serious enough, that it cost you your life Alston? Were you abducted that morning or did you just decline to show up, at the last minute? If you had told me what was bothering you, would you still be alive? I quickly pushed that last question out of my head, as there was nothing that could be done about it now. The goal, now, was to figure out, who killed the former convict.

Anthony came around from the front of the house and stopped Karen, as she headed to the ambulance with the body. After a brief word, she took out her digital camera and let the prosecuting attorney take a look at the display screen. She gave me a quick glance, as Anthony scrolled through the photos. I gave her a light shrug, realizing she didn't have much choice in the matter.

Anthony handed the camera back to her and walked toward me. I couldn't help but notice his face had a pallid look. He reached into the inside pocket of his overcoat and pulled out a folded document. "My assistant dropped off the warrant Jonas. I thought you would want it in your possession, before you begin the search."

I took the piece of paper, that allowed me to legally trespass, and read it, to make sure all the pertinent information was correct. "Thanks. You all right?"

He nodded, clearing his throat, as he coughed into his gloved fist. "Yes. It was just the way his waist was all flat." Anthony looked back at the house, before he turned back to me. "You have to close this one, Jonas."

The skin around the corner of his eyes was tight and I noticed his jugular artery was beating harder, than it was before. Being a seasoned prosecuting attorney, he had seen his share of gruesome crime scene photographs over the years. Yet his reaction to Alston's photos seemed out of sync. "You sure you're okay, Anthony?"

He looked down at the dried grass for a moment, before he shook his head. "He was tortured before he was killed Jonas. I wasn't glad that Alston O'Brian came back to Monroe County, but I didn't wish this on him either. I can't help but think, I may have contributed to this, by letting it be known he was back. You have to close this case, Jonas. And you have to do it by the book."

I looked at him for a long time, as I clasped my hands in front of me. "That's the only way I know how to do it, counselor."

Chapter Eleven

When Glen returned, from his interview with Sarah Brenton, he said she confirmed her husband's statement. We had to wait an hour, before the house was safe enough, for us to enforce the search warrant. I borrowed a ladder from the moving company and climbed up to the front door. The brass door knob was unlocked, so it moved with ease. I had my forensic kit in my left hand, which I set inside the foyer. As quietly as I could, I eased my Simian frame, into the elevated abode and waited on Glen to follow suite. It was times like these, I realized how big I really was. I watch what I eat and exercise regularly, but my broad shoulders and solid frame, make it hard to conceal my size. I helped Glen up and once he caught his breath, I gave him shoe covers, for his tactical boots and I took out a clean set, for my shoes. The new covers were necessary, to avoid cross contamination from the ground outside. If we did find dirt from outside, inside the house, we know it didn't come from our shoes. I signaled, I wanted to make sure the house was empty. It was highly unlikely there was anyone inside, after all the noise and calamity, that had been going on this morning, but the front door was unlocked. We had to accept the outside possibility, that someone could be on the premises.

We separated, Glen taking the west section of the house, me the east. I eased my forty-five out of its leather holster and let it hang loose by my side. The house was barren of furniture, and no pictures on the walls. The stale musty scent, that fills a home that had been unlived in, infiltrated my nostrils. Cobwebs draped the upper corners and dust bunnies adorned the faded gray carpet. I searched what had once been the living room and moved on into the kitchen and dining room. I checked the pantry and storage closet, to confirm the place was empty. Glen came back a minute later and shook his head. "It's all clear Jonas. But one of the bedrooms contains a heavy bleach smell."

Sheathing my sidearm, I opened my kit and got out a pair of nitrite gloves for Glen and myself. We started walking the room, looking for any signs of intrusion. The living room and dining room both appeared to be clean, so I followed Glen to the room, where he had detected the odor. Upon entering the room, I found my deputy was correct in his assessment, bleach had been used. The sour, chlorinated liquid was so heavy in the room, my eyes began to burn. Also there were four distinct indentions, in the carpet, all evenly spaced. The closer you moved to the indentions, the stronger the smell became. I got down on my hands and knees, near the imprints and inhaled. I immediately coughed from the chlorinated liquid. "Yep, we've definitely got bleach here."

Glen eyed the floor and the indentions, walking a circle around them. "Someone or something was setting there for a while, in order to leave marks that deep."

I moved to the walls, taking another whiff, and found the same aroma as before. The problem was the smell of bleach was so strong, it was difficult to tell, if the scent from the carpet was also on the walls. However, when I looked up at an angle I was able to see more signs of disturbance. I took out my flashlight and shined it along the wall, revealing that one section of the faded white wall appeared to be whiter. "Someone has cleaned this wall too. You can see where the dust was disturbed."

I shined my light upwards, on the faded lime green ceiling and immediately noticed, dark rusty brown flecks, sporadically spaced. I moved to the wall, on the opposite side of the indentions in the carpet and found more signs of disturbance in the dust. "Someone tried to clean up after themselves. They did a good job on the walls, but forgot the ceiling."

Glen craned his head upward to look. "You always said people tend to forget to look up. Looks like this proves the rule."

I returned to the foyer for my kit. Once back in the room, I removed the high intensity flashlight from its compartment, along with amber tinted glasses. After putting the amber glasses on, I handed Glen my overcoat. "Put that over the window, please."

Glen was able to cover the window enough, to create darkness in the room. I turned the light on and beamed it along the carpet, around the indentations, which revealed a bright pour pattern, near the edge of the space, where the chair would've set. I knelt down and placed a marker beside it. I placed an amber lens filter on the digital camera and used it to take photographs of the pattern, before making a note of it. I took out some sterile swabs along with a bottle of distilled water. Soaking one of the swabs with the water, I next took a sample from the carpet, then placed a safety capsule over that sample. I labeled the carpet section it came from and placed it in my kit, before turning to Glen. "Your arms hold up a bit longer?"

He nodded, as he let out a small grunt. "I'm fine."

"I'll move as fast as I can." I again beamed the light over the carpet and found more flecks around the chair indentations. I checked the entire floor, which revealed more specimens, but they were too faint to use. The walls were my next area to check, but nothing more was discovered. I removed my glasses and turned off the light. "Rest your arms Glen."

He grunted, as he slowly lowered his arms. He folded the coat over his right arm, as he rotated his left shoulder. "Good timing. My shoulders about had it."

I gave him a sympathetic nod. "I've been there a few times myself, over the years of processing crime scenes. I tried to move as fast as I could."

Glen shook his head, as he continued to rotate his arms. "Comes with the job, Jonas. What was that you found by the chair impression?"

"I'm fairly certain it's urine," I replied, as I returned the light source to my kit. "I smelled it on the body outside. My guess is they tied Alston to a chair and beat him. But eventually nature had to take its course, so he urinated on himself."

Glen stared at the indentations, his face a scowl of disgust. "They didn't even let the old man go to the bathroom? I know the guy hurt a lot of people, but no one deserves to be treated like that."

I nodded toward the invisible stain. "Apparently, there are some who disagree with you. I doubt there will be any way to get a DNA match, since bleach was used, but maybe Molly can confirm it was urine. Also after we finish here, I want you to take the light and check the bathrooms and sinks. If other people were here, maybe they had to answer the call of nature too. See if they used the house. If not, then they probably used the woods."

Glen's face grew even more disgusted. "Lucky me."

I looked up at the ceiling. "Those stains are our best bet at finding any DNA and blood type. Our killers bleached out the walls and carpet, so that's degraded the evidence quite a bit, but those are still pristine."

Glen pointed in the direction of the front door. "You want me to get the ladder, so you can get a sample?"

I shook my head, as I took a utility knife from my kit. "Not yet. I want to finish up on the floor and walls first. Once I have a sample of the carpet, I'm going to need you to cover the window with my coat again."

Glen folded my coat over his right arm and rested his left hand on his hip. "Just say when."

I knelt down next, to the plastic yellow ID number and cut a three inch by three-inch swath of the carpet, with the utility knife. I took out a scraper and pulled the end of the carpet up, so I could get my fingers underneath it. Once the carpet was pulled loose, I flipped it over, which revealed where the blood had settled. On TV and the cinema, blood at crime scenes is often depicted, as a deep red. In reality, blood turns a reddish brown, as it oxidizes. People also often believe that cleaning the carpet gets rid of the stain. What really happens, is the stain is pushed down to the underside of the carpet. I photographed the evidence, and placed the swath in a brown paper bag, sealing it with red evidence tape. I then measured the distance between the four marks in the carpet and wrote it down in my notebook.

I took the bag along with the swabs and placed them outside the door in the hallway, before removing two filtered face masks and a bottle of luminol, from my kit. I gave one mask to Glen, who put it on his face. I did the same and proceeded to squeeze the handle of the spray bottle, allowing a mist to cascade over the carpet, around the chair imprints and over to the door. I did the same for the walls, then put the bottle down and pointed to the window. "All right Glen, cover it up, one more time, please."

Glen cloaked the room in enough darkness, to allow the luminol to react with the iron in the hemoglobin. Another misconception, is that bleach erases bloodstains. While it will remove the stains from the visible eye and often degrade any hope of a DNA test, luminol, allows the removed blood pattern to become visible once again. The only downside, to using the chemical compound, is that, it too, can further degrade the chances of getting DNA or blood typing. Which is why I took the samples before spraying, the area. The room fluoresced neon blue across the carpet and up the walls. The blue areas around the indentations, looked smeared from someone attempting to get the stains out. The walls revealed similar signs of blue swipes over an eight-foot diameter. I took the digital camera and began taking preliminary shots. Next I marked the smear patterns, with plastic yellow numbers and took more photos.

The section of carpet leading to the door, had a faint pattern, which was now much more prominent. I stood over the glowing pattern, which revealed a fairly decent shoe impression. I photographed both with and without a scale, because this is the only way to enter it into evidence. There were other faint traces, of what appeared to be shoe impressions, but even with the aid of the luminol, they were too faint to document. "That'll do Glen."

Glen shook his arms again, in an attempt to relieve the strain from his muscles. "I was looking over my shoulder, but was that a footprint you were taking a picture of?"

I nodded my head, as I took an evidence report form, from my kit and began filling it out. "Yep. Looks like someone got some faint traces of blood on their shoes."

Glen pointed, to where the shoe impression had been. "If we're lucky, we might locate them in time, to find traces of blood still on the shoes."

"We can only hope. After your arms have rested, go to the front door and get that ladder. I'm going to need to get some samples from the ceiling."

I was still filling out the report, when Glen returned with the stepladder and placed it under the blood spatter. "Thanks."

I took my pictures and scaled the droplets, before taking another swab, using distilled water, to collect the sample and labeled its location. After collecting another sample, I climbed down and took out a bottle of phenolphthalein and squeezed a few drops on the swab. I watched the solution react to the alkaline, in the blood, turning the swab from a dingy red stain, to a bright pink. "That's definitely blood. We'll have Molly do a test, in the lab, to confirm it."

Glen was looking down at the four indentations, rubbing his chin through his goatee. "These marks are strange, Jonas."

I stared at them, as I made the notations in my report. "How so?"

"When you asked me to get the ladder, I did another quick sweep of the premises. There's not a chair in this house. There isn't furniture of any kind."

I nodded, as I continued writing. "So you're thinking, it was all premeditated."

Glen thrust his hands out, before resting them on his hips. "It's the only thing that makes sense. We've got evidence that suggest one truck was used to remove the braces. All one had to do was pitch the chair in the truck bed and take it with them, after they dropped the house on the victim."

I turned the page over, as I continued to write. "If that is true, which I believe it is, then whoever did this had a strong sense of irony."

Glen scratched the skin between his eyes, with his finger. "How so?"

I pointed to the floor, with my pen, before I resumed writing. "Before the bank reclaimed this house, it once belonged to Gary Winchell, the father of Patrick Winchell, one of the men who attacked Alston at Hardees, the morning Tom and I were called."

Glen's shoulders slouched, as he closed his eyes and looked up to the ceiling. "Gary was a victim of Alston O'Brian's?"

"Not directly. But as a result of Alston's actions, Gary lost his job, his house and his marriage. He eventually died, of a stroke. At least, that's what Saul told me."

My deputy slouched back, on his left leg and looked around the room again. "It looks like we've stumbled into a hornet's nest on this one, Jonas. From what you have said happened at Hardees, there were a lot of hard feelings out there against the victim, including the chief of police, who is definitely, not a fan of ours, right now."

I placed the report in a compartment of my kit. "It seems to me, we were actually thrown face first into the hornet's nest, rather than stumbled into it."

Glen looked down at the evidence bag and swabs. "You going to have Molly do a DNA test on the blood?"

I shook my head, as I set the evidence to the side. "Not yet. We'll do a blood typing first and see if it matches the victim. If it does, then we'll hold off on a sending the samples out to a serologist. If it doesn't, we'll cross that bridge, when we get there."

He looked at the swabs and got a small smile on his face. "We do have to watch the money, don't we?"

The popularity of forensic TV shows and movies has led to the misconception, that DNA testing is a customary request for law enforcement. While the advances of science have made it easier for scientists, to retrieve DNA from the smallest samples, it is still an expensive test to run. Being a rural county, on a limited budget, I have to allocate my resources carefully. "Yes we do. As of right now, there is nothing, that suggests Alston wasn't in this room being tortured and killed. If the blood type doesn't match, then we'll spend the resources, for a DNA test. Right now, we need to get this to Molly, along with Alston's clothing and see, if she can find any traces of the carpet, from the house. We work this case hard and pray for a quick resolution."

Glen scoffed and raised his hand in the air. "Amen to that."

* * *

Glen took the UV light and checked the bathrooms and sinks, but found no signs of defecation, suggesting the perpetrators went outside, to relieve themselves, while leaving Alston bound to a chair. We dusted all the door handles and locks for fingerprints, but unfortunately we came up with nothing. The intruders either wore gloves or cleaned their prints afterwards. Knowing Saul was more than likely, still sore about our last discussion, I let Glen take the exemplars from his boots, as well as Officers Hensley and Gentry. Then, I had Glen call Tom and ask him to track down Patrick Winchell and Harrison Birch, for questioning. I felt given my last encounter with them, it was appropriate two deputies were there, in case there was a trouble.

After that I called Jack and had him try, to find out, who owned the house now and what were the circumstances surrounding the foreclosure. Saul said it belonged to Gary Winchell, but given our history, I thought it would be more prudent, to do our own research into the matter.

I stayed behind in the room, and began the arduous process of measuring the blood evidence. Bloodstains do have the ability to tell you what happened in a room. It's the elliptical stains that reveal the most evidence. How they are formed, gives you their directionality. There weren't many left behind, but there were a few on the left wall as you enter the room, that hadn't been wiped away, plus there were the stains on the ceiling. Circling the stains that would work best, I placed evidence stickers by them and made the necessary references, in my report.

With a magnifying lens and ruler, I measured the stains I had selected, the width first, then the length. Dividing the two, I entered the results into the equation and after each one, I was able to get an approximation, as to where the assailant was standing, within a two-foot diameter. This placed him or her standing directly in front of the indentation marks. Whoever, did the beating, Alston had a clear view of them, as they tortured him.

Chapter Twelve

It was pushing 4:30, when I placed a seal on the front door of the house and made an X over the door with yellow police tape. After climbing down, I took the evidence, that had been collected from inside the house and secured it my truck. The rescue squad had left, as had Saul and his men, meaning Officer Gentry wasn't there for me to sign the entry log. I guess Saul didn't feel protocol was a necessity. I noted the time on my watch and wrote it down, as the time I left the crime scene.

Both ends of the road fed into Highway 411, so I put the gear in drive and continued around the curve, heading to the stop sign, but brought my vehicle to an abrupt halt twenty feet from the highway. On the asphalt were a set of heavy skid marks. I set the emergency blinkers on my truck and got out to study the dual marks inked onto the pavement. I knelt down by one of the marks and gently ran my finger over it. The tar residue easily wiped off the road. I brought it up to my nose and the strong, burnt, tar aroma, told me the skid marks were fresh. I grabbed the tape measure and spread it across the length of the tracks and found the measurements matched, the measurements for the tracks in the grass. I took out the digital camera to document the skid marks and made notations, in my report. Normally, I wouldn't have given skid marks tattooed on the road much attention, but when I factored in the fact, they were fairly fresh and matched, the width of the tire span, for the marks at the crime scene, I decided thoroughness was necessary.

I walked to the shoulder of the road, examined the ditch and found shards of glass, from a headlight. There were also traces, of what appeared to be blood, on the dried grass. I documented this and collected the glass, for evidence, along with samples of the grass. Whatever vehicle caused the marks, it looked like they had hit something, but I could find no signs of a body. Of course, if it was an animal, it could've crawled into the woods and died or may have been only slightly injured and limped away. Either way, the skids marks and blood, didn't bode well, especially, when so close to a crime scene.

I gave the skid marks one last look and noticed a portion, of the asphalt, appeared to have a white film over it. Kneeling down, I applied distilled water to a swab and swiped it over the stain. Inhaling from the cotton tip, I smelled the chlorinated scent of bleach. I looked back to the crime scene, that wasn't even a tenth of a mile away, where bleach had been used and I knew this wasn't a coincidence. I secured the swab in an evidence container.

Afterward, I drove to the forensic laboratory, located directly across from the stationhouse. Whenever I entered the lab, I was always greeted with the sterile smell of alcohol and disinfectant. I turned all the evidence in to the lab supervisor, Molly Newman, to be cataloged. With her cinnamon brown hair under her black hairnet, Molly looked over the inventory, before signing the forms. "You've had a busy day."

I had the digital camera out and connected the USB cord, to her computer, to upload the photographs from the crime scene. "I like to keep a hectic schedule, whenever possible, Molly."

She handed me a pink copy, of the evidence transfer form, to file at the stationhouse. "Anything specific you want me to run?"

I watched the empty bar, on the computer screen fill green, as the pictures were copied. "On the swabs I have taken, I want a blood type comparison to the victim, after you get the report from the autopsy. Also compare the blood type, to the blood found, on the sample of carpet as well. Determine if it's all the same type. Maybe we'll luck up and the killer left some of his own blood behind. Also, if you can, try to get a blood type from the grass and the road. I doubt you can, but you never know until you try. I also have a swab of what I believe to be urine. Test to see if it is and see if there is any blood in it, to compare to the other samples, I took."

"You want DNA?"

I shook my head. "Not yet. If we need to send it out we will, but lets see what the other evidence tells us first."

The computer beeped saying the upload was complete. I disconnected the camera and rolled up the USB cable. "There are shoeprints for Saul West, Daniel Hensley, and Elvis Gentry."

Her forehead wrinkled, as she looked over the top of the computer screen. "Saul's the chief. Aren't the other two with the Vonore Police Department?"

I placed the camera back in the carry bag, along with the cable. "Yeah. They were walking through the crime scene with no shoe covers, so I had no choice, but to take their shoeprints."

She shook her head, while hunching her shoulders. "I guess they didn't think it was important."

"I suppose not. I also have a shoe impression in luminol, from the carpet in the house. Check it against all impressions collected."

Molly looked at me, silently tapping her fingers on her blue scrubs. "The only impression you have, are from the VCPD?"

I nodded, slinking the camera bag strap over my shoulder. "You know me, Molly. I like to be thorough. The press is probably going to be all over this and they'll add enough conjecture of their own. We need to dot every i and cross every t. We don't need mistakes broadcasted on television."

Molly crossed her arms, narrowing her eyes at me. "There's nothing else going on?"

Lying has never been my forte, which has been pointed out by both my mother and Lydia. Molly has hinted the very same thing herself, on numerous occasions. For some reason, the women in my life can see through me. This has always left me feeling disconcerted, whenever I think about it, which is why I try my best to not think about it. I wasn't ready to divulge my suspicions of the VCPD to anyone, outside the department right not, but there was also no reason to attempt to deceive Molly Newman. "Molly, you've known me long enough to know, there is always something else going on. For the moment though, I need to keep it on the down low. I want to see what you and Karen find out first, before I say anything."

She continued, to scrutinize me, with those cobalt blue eyes for a second or two, but then gave me a nod. "I'm fine with that. You've never given me a reason to doubt you."

I felt an internal sigh surge through my body, as a compromise had been reached. "When you get the clothing, from the victim, do a full trace evidence search on it. Compare it to the carpet samples. I want to confirm, if he was inside the house."

"That's not a problem. I'll also examine the tire casts you took, when the plaster dries enough for me to clean them. Then I will for sure be able to get you a make on them."

"Any help is appreciated, Molly." I started for the door. "Call me when you've got something."

"Oh, Jonas, I just remembered, Tom brought in a cast from a tire taken a few hours ago."

I snapped my fingers, shaking my head at my memory lapse. "Yeah. It's a separate case. Those two guys, using boxer shorts for masks, have struck again. Stole a woman's jewelry and her mother's ashes this morning. We found those tire treads in the mud, a few yards away from the house."

Molly set her hands on her hips, tilting her head to the left, with a quizzical look scrolled across her face. "They took her mother's cremated ashes? What in the world for?"

I hunched my shoulders, waving my hands out. "I haven't a clue. I was trying to figure that out, when I got the call about the murder."

She looked down at the floor for a moment, as I recognized the look of concentration, which told me, she was trying to recall a fact from her impressive knowledge bank. "There are urban legends and myths, about people ingesting the ashes of the dead, to be close to them or open a spiritual doorway, but as far as I know, it's never been substantiated."

"Somehow, these guys don't strike me as the spiritual type." I was about to say something else, but it was immediately lost, as an idea began to take root and grow. "You said they ingested the ashes. Could that by any chance also mean snorting?"

She nodded. "It's a popular myth too, if I'm remembering it correctly."

The more I thought about my flash of intuition, the crazier it seemed. However, given the people we were after, I didn't figure it was any weirder than the getup they've been wearing. "Thanks Molly. You've given me an idea, as to how we might catch these guys."

Her nose wrinkled, as she watched me leave. "I did?"

* * *

Once I was back in my office, I opened up the department issued laptop and put out a BOLO, to all the hospital emergency rooms, in the surrounding counties. I listed the descriptions and possible symptoms, to be looking for and asked them, to call the Monroe County Sheriff's Department, if they had any suspects.

I then got out the camera and uploaded the photographs, to my computer and printed physical copies of them. I spent the next hour going over every still, looking for anything that might've been overlooked, but nothing was revealed. I collected the pictures, in the order I took them and got down, to my least favorite part of the job: paperwork.

I began filling out the official report, referencing my notes, as I went along, making sure they correlated with the photographs I had taken. I could easily assign this task to another deputy, but as tedious and monotonous as this is, it helps me work through the case in my mind, as I slowly go over it all. Sometimes, I will notice a detail, I had overlooked, in my initial run through, other times, I won't find anything new. As I was finishing this report, it looked like this go around was going to be under the latter heading. I saved the report and made a copy to place with the crime scene photographs, before securing them all in a folder, labeling the case number on the tab.

It was past seven in the evening and the growling of my stomach reminded me I hadn't eaten anything since breakfast. It also made me realize, I needed to get home to make sure Mick had something to eat. Deciding it might do my brain some good to take a break, from the O'Brian case, I grabbed my coat and made for my truck. I spotted Jack, still at his desk, finishing his daily reports. "I'm calling it a night, Jack. You almost done?"

Jack looked up and scratched the scalp of his shaved ebony head, while stifling a yawn. "Just about to be. Oh, by the way I made some calls and found out the house that crushed the victim, did belong to Gary Winchell. He was married to a Felicia Baxter, for fifteen years, until they split in August of 2000. They had one son, Patrick. Gary died in February of 2001, due to complications from a stroke."

All of the information jived, with what Saul had told me, so there was some solace, in that he was honest, about this aspect of the investigation. "You find anything on which bank foreclosed on the property?"

He pointed to the steno pad setting beside the keyboard of his computer. "It used to be the Vonore City Bank, but it was bought out by People's Bank, ten years ago. I called them earlier today, but the loan officer was out of town, at a meeting and wouldn't be back, until tomorrow. I left a message on his voicemail. If he hasn't called back, by ten tomorrow morning, I'll try him again."

I scratched the skin just above my eye, forcing back the yawn working its way up my throat. "Sounds like you have a plan. If they give you any grief, patch them through to me."

"Roger that."

I was at the front door, when I snapped my fingers and returned to my sergeant's desk. "Hey Jack, we get those statements from the VCPD yet?"

He rolled his chair back, to the desk, against the right wall and grabbed a binder of folders. "They came in around two and gave their statements."

I held the folders and looked at him, my stomach beginning to feel like the inside of a basketball. "They all three came in, at the same time?"

Jack folded his arms on the desk and propped himself up. "I thought it was a bit odd myself."

I took the binder and placed it with the casefile, I had just compiled. "I'll look at them later tonight. Although, I believe the VCPD have already started fortifying the blue wall."

Jack looked at the binder of statements, in my hand. "You think one of them is lying?"

I tapped the binder, with my finger. "At the crime scene, Officer Hensley gave conflicting reasons, on how he discovered the body. When I tried to press him, Saul immediately stopped me, saying I needed to get "on board.""

Jack released a groan, as he sat back. "That doesn't sound too good. They didn't hide the fact no one wanted Alston in Vonore and now the man has been found dead, just a stone's throw from the police station."

I stared up at the ceiling in faux exasperation. "You know, just once I'd like to have a murder investigation, that's easy. Just to know what it feels like."

Jack gave me solemn face, as he held up his hands. "If it was easy Jonas, then anybody could do it."

* * *

I took Mick for a quick walk around the edge of my property, where he lifted his leg to every other tree and squatted once, before I took him back in and fed him supper. While he ate, I took out some frozen chicken tenders and placed them in the microwave, as I got out the lettuce, radishes, and tomatoes for a nice salad. I sprinkled some cheese on my salad and put a dash of bacon bits on top. When the tenders had cooled enough, I cut them into tiny quarters and spread them evenly along the greenery, before adding the dressing.

I tore into the food, as my stomach growled. Even when I was scraping the last bite from my plate, I only felt half full, but opted to eat an apple instead of anything heavier. After placing my plate in the dishwasher, I took a seat at the desk, in my home office and began reading over the statements.

Saul's and Hensley's statements were almost identic, with just enough variations in their words, so as to not be suspicious. When I got to Elvis Gentry's statement, I stared at the closed folder. At the crime scene, I felt like he was trying to tell me something. Though he seemed to lack discipline, when it came to his donuts, but when I spoke with him, I got the impression he was an honest man. Maybe I was reading too much into it. I let out a light sigh and flipped open the folder to read his statement, even though I already knew what it would say.

In my second read though, something seemed off, about Gentry's statement, but I couldn't place my finger on what it was. So I read it again and still, couldn't figure out what was nagging me. It wasn't until the fourth read, that I finally noticed it. It was in the section where Gentry said Officer Hensley's probable cause for searching the property. In his remarks, Gentry said, *Officer Hensley radioed in that he noticed buzzards circling over the house, but I never saw the creatures upon arriving at the scene.*

I reread the sentence again, before retrieving Saul's statement, in which Hensley reported seeing vultures in the sky. He made no mention of looking for the birds at the scene. That was the second time Gentry had said something to cast suspicion on Daniel's statement. Why did you add the afterthought Gentry? Was it an accidental slip of the tongue or do you know something more? Not all of the flying scavengers head south for the winter and their sense of smell can detect the beginning stages of decomposition a mile away. But, with the cold slowing the decaying process down, I'm not sure if Alston had been dead long enough to alert the vultures. One thing is for sure: I was going to have another conversation with Elvis Gentry.

My BlackBerry chimed, I had a video chat request. I opened up my laptop, to discover it was dead, because I had forgotten to plug in the charger. So I had to opt to prop my phone up on the lamp and hit accept. Lydia's face came up on my screen, with slight frown on her face. "Why are you looking down?"

I pointed to the useless computer before me. "I forgot to plug in my computer. This was faster. How was your day?"

She shook her head, as she narrowed her eyes. "The picture could be better. I wish you'd get another smartphone. I don't know anyone, besides you that still uses a BlackBerry."

"Well, I guess that makes me unique." I shook my own head, not really looking forward to repeating this seemingly endless conversation. Lydia wasn't the only, one who has been on me to "get with the times" over my choice of smartphones, but she was hands down, the most vehemently enthusiastic, about me trading it in, for either an Android or I-phone. I've listened to the arguments about the broader selection of apps and higher resolution photographs, and I see her point. The thing is, I've never been one of those people, who need to have the right amount of applications on their phone, nor do I care, if my pictures are a half a pixel less than the other camera phones. Maybe it is complacency or fear of change, but my phone makes and receives calls and texts. I can do a web search on it and the pictures are clear. What more can you ask for?

She cocked her head over her right shoulder, jutting her chin out. "Stubborn is more like it."

"As I asked earlier: how was your day?"

I could tell by the firm line her lips had formed, she didn't want to change the subject, but she eventually shook her head in defeat. "My day was tame compared to yours. I heard the VCPD found Alston O'Brian's body this morning."

I told her they had and gave her the summation of my day, down to Gentry's statement. "He left his statement open to interpretation."

The side of her face was cupped in her right hand as she listened. "You think it was intentional?"

I shrugged, reaching back to scratch the base of my neck. "Who knows? It may have not been intentional, but I intend to speak to him again."

Lydia nodded. "If you need any help, Mr. Deland has asked me to tell you don't hesitate to ask."

I stretched my shoulders and yawned. "He's made that clear several times. This case has him worried."

I watched her carefully pull a loose thread from the sleeve of her sweater. "I can't say I blame him, if he is. This whole thing is a powder keg. The assistant state solicitor, chief of police, and the first officer on the scene, all have connections to the victim. One spark and the whole thing can blow up in their faces."

I smiled at her. "Nice pep talk."

She playfully rolled her eyes. "*You* can handle it. But you do need to keep that in mind, as you work the case. The sooner you close it, the better."

There was a brief intermission, while Lydia stared down at her desk, lightly scratching the desk blotter with her thumbnail. "What is it?"

"Nothing," she said.

I knew that look meant it was something and said as much. "So why don't you go ahead and tell me what it is?"

She lay both arms in front of her and shook her head. "It really is nothing. Janet McMahan was telling me, about a cabin, she has on timeshare, near the Blount County line, just before you get into Sevierville. She and her husband were scheduled to go up there two weeks from this Saturday, but he fell off the ladder, cleaning out his guttering. Poor man broke his leg and dislocated his shoulder. She said we could go, if we wanted to. Of course she told me this before you found the body."

I smiled at her. "You got to thinking about, that weekend we had planned, that was ruined by the ice storm."

She smiled back at me arching her eyebrows. "Yeah. Looks like it's not meant to be this winter."

I found my hand involuntarily touching the top drawer of my desk again. "Well, let's not jump ahead of ourselves here. It's over two weeks away. A lot can happen between now and then."

The wrinkle in her forehead and the look of disbelief on her face, told me she wasn't buying it. "Jonas, I know you mean well, but what are the odds of you being able to solve this case in two weeks? Plus, I heard those two jokers wearing their underwear on their heads struck again, so you still have them to deal with."

I picked up my phone, so I could look her directly in the eye. "There is always something for me to deal with, Lydia. The job takes up most of my life, but every now and then, I have to put the job on the backburner. We've got two weeks. Let's see what happens, before you say no."

Her face was a mask of skepticism, but there was a subtle layer of hope in her voice when she said, "You really think you might close it, in two weeks?"

I leaned back in my seat, praying I hadn't gotten her hopes up for nothing. "Have a little faith."

Chapter Thirteen

I woke up fifteen minutes before my alarm and decided to get out of bed. Considering the promise, I had made last night, I couldn't afford to waste any time. Despite the teeth chattering cold, I took Mick for a walk over the trail. Once we were back home, I did a light workout in the small gym I keep in the basement. After giving Mick his breakfast, I showered and shaved, threw on some clothes, while my coffee was brewing up. I put on my badge and gun and poured the coffee into the stainless steel traveling mug, before grabbing a breakfast bar. I looked at Mick, who was sitting at attention, those brown eyes glued on me, his tail sweeping the floor. "You want to come along?"

A light bark was his reply, before sprinting to join me at the door. I made a stop at the Quick Mart gas station, but with a three quarter full tank, I didn't need fuel. After purchasing a copy of the Monroe County Buzz, I took the change over to the real purpose for my stop: the payphone. A side effect of the ever-growing cellphone market, is that payphones are now becoming extinct. As a child growing up, I could remember seeing several of the silver and black phones mounted onto the walls of public areas and the standalone metal boxes planted on the sidewalks in Madisonville. Now my memory tells me, there are only about three or four left.

The reason I needed the public phone, was simple; I needed a phone that couldn't be traced back to me. I inserted the quarters and dialed the number for the Vonore City Police Department. After the first ring, a woman answered the phone. "Vonore City Police Department. How may I direct your call?"

I did a recon glance, to make sure no one was close by, before pinching my nose together, as I spoke in a low voice, hoping to disguise my identity. "Yes, I'd like to speak with Officer Gentry please. Is he in?"

There was a mild wave of static before the woman replied. "No sir, I'm afraid he's not. May I take a message?"

"No thank you. I'll call back later." I hung up and looked back to see Mick staring at me through the front windshield, his head squared and cocked to the right. The look on his face, left little doubt, that his sensitive ears had heard the change in my voice and couldn't deduce what had happened to me. Even when I got behind the driver's seat, he was still watching me, like he wasn't sure about me. "For crying out loud boy it's me," I said in my normal voice.

This seemed to set his mind at ease. He sat back in the seat, which still allowed his massive head to look over the dash. Starting the engine, I turned the heat down to medium and pulled onto Highway 411, heading north toward Vonore. Our destination was Elvis Gentry's home. I was taking a leap of faith, that he would be more forthcoming with me, one on one, outside the presence of Saul and the rest of the VCPD.

According to the address he gave on his statement, Elvis lived in Meadows subdivision on Rolling Ridge Road, just up from the Vonore Elementary School. His house was the third one up the small hill, on the left. I saw a green Nissan Quest in the driveway, as I pulled in and parked. When I got out, I went to Mick's door and attached the leather leash to his harness, before I let him jump down. After guiding him to the edge of the driveway, where he was compelled to lift his leg on a patch of dried grass, we proceeded to the front door.

It was a clear morning, with the sun out, giving the blue sky and white clouds an almost three-dimensional effect. The icy cold that Mick and I had experienced at six this morning, was now a more comfortable cool. A light breeze whistled through the dead weeds, in the field, beside Gentry's house. Arriving at his front door, I pushed the doorbell. After a brief pause, I pushed it again and added two firm knocks to the red door.

I was about to look in through the front window, when I heard footsteps coming closer to the door, followed by someone releasing the deadbolt and unlocking the doorknob. The door opened two inches, where half of Elvis Gentry's face appeared in the space. "Officer Gentry. I'm sorry to disturb you so early on your day off, but I was hoping I could ask you a few more questions, about yesterday."

Elvis, scanned the area behind me, like he was looking for a surveillance team. "Didn't you get my statement?"

"I did."

"Then you know everything I know sheriff." He started to close the door.

I inserted my foot in the opening, placing my forearm along the door, stopping it. "The questions I have are about your statement officer. There are a couple of things I'd like to go over with you."

He once again looked over my shoulder, but there hadn't been a car pass by, since I had pulled into his driveway. "Sheriff, don't take this the wrong way, but I don't think it's a good idea for you to be here, at my house."

I felt my eyebrows elevate up to my hairline, at his brazenness. I was always taught to never waste an opportunity, I decided to turn his discomfort to my advantage. "Why? Are you afraid someone will see us talking and tell Saul or Hensley?"

A pained expression crossed his face, as he looked at me, speaking in a whisper. "I'm not afraid of anything, but I don't need to get caught in the middle of y'all's pissing contest."

I nodded, pursing my lips. "Did Chief West direct you to not answer my questions Officer Gentry?"

"What? No he didn't order me to not answer your questions."

I shuffled my feet, but kept my left foot securely inside the doorframe. "Then I don't see the problem sir. If you don't want anyone to see me, invite me in. I'll ask my questions, you answer them, and I'll be on my way."

Gentry looked at me, for a long moment, before his shoulders drooped and he closed his eyes and rested his forehead against the edge of the door. "You're not going away until you do, are you?"

I smiled at him, shaking my head. "No. I don't like being intrusive, but I have a murder to solve. So shall we?"

He looked down at Mick, who had been sitting patiently by my side, shifting his head between us, as if he was watching a tennis match. "I suppose you want to bring him in, too?"

I shook my head. "I can tie him to a tree in your front yard if you'd like. He is house broken though, so he won't make a mess."

Gentry opened the door and headed into his living room. "Bring him on in. Let's just get this over with."

Gentry was wearing a blue terrycloth robe over a white t-shirt and blue pajama bottoms. He stopped in front of his flat screen TV, with his hands tucked in the pockets of the robe. "You want some coffee? I *had* intended on sleeping in, but since I'm up, I can make a quick pot."

I pulled out my Moleskine notebook and said it wasn't necessary. "This shouldn't take too long."

He used the heel of his hand, to rub his eye, as he yawned. "Okay let's get to it. You said this was about my statement?"

"Yes. It's about how Officer Hensley said he found the body." I looked down at my notes, more for effect than recollection, hoping his annoyance might aid me, if I played it right. "According to Hensley, he said he saw vultures circling the lot. Chief West said the same."

Gentry nodded, as he licked his lips. "Yes. And I corroborated that in mine."

I had my notes turned to the page, where I had interviewed Officer Gentry, not even twenty-four hours earlier. "Yes, that's why

I'm here. When I asked you about how Hensley discovered the body, you said when he called it in, it was because of the vultures, but you also noted you didn't see any signs of the birds around the scene. What was that last part about?"

He rolled his tongue along the inside of his cheek, as he slowly moved, to the gray couch and sat down. "I meant nothing by it. I just didn't see any vultures, at the scene."

"Then yesterday, when I asked you about Hensley seeing the vultures, you asked, *can you believe that*? What was that about?"

His eyes took on a pained look, as his hand gripped the armrest, making indentation in the fabric. "I don't think I like your tone sheriff."

I closed the distance between us, so I was standing over him. "And I don't appreciate being treated like an idiot officer. I get the sense that everyone on the VCPD knows more than they're telling. A man was tortured, for several hours, before his death. Is that something you want to just let slide by?"

Silence had now filled the gap between us. Gentry's jaw was locked in place, as he continued to glare at me. His breathing was becoming more agitated and his face was flushed. "I stand by the statement I gave to your deputy yesterday."

Mick, who had been lying on his side, licking his privates, stood up shook his body, causing his vaccination tag to jingle. He let out a large yawn, like he was bored and moved to Gentry, resting his chin on the edge of the armrest. The officer looked at the large bulldog for a while, before he reached over and rubbed his head. After a few moments of this, I noticed the muscles around the base of his neck, seemed to relax and his breathing returned to normal. I took a seat across from the couch and released a short sigh. "From what you told me yesterday and from Hensley's and Saul's reactions, I don't think there were any vultures up in the sky yesterday."

He continued to pet Mick in silence. The central heat kicked in and I felt a gust of hot air brush the back of my leg. "I also think, in your own way, you were trying to let me know something was wrong."

Gentry stopped massaging the canine's head and looked at me, but continued to remain silent. I reached into my coat pocket to take out the copy I had made of his statement. I unfolded it, so he could see the portion I had highlighted. "Here you made a point of adding; you never saw or heard the buzzards yesterday morning. Neither Saul nor Hensley said anything like that in their statements. Why did you say that, Elvis?"

Looking to the ground, he hunched his shoulders and looked at his bare feet. "Because I didn't see any buzzards."

I crossed my leg, resting my hand on my knee. "Why mention not seeing them? In the official statements, you were the only one who said that."

The beeping of a garbage truck could be heard, as it backed into the driveway, of the neighboring home, to remove the trash. I waited patiently, as he tried to form an answer, casually looking around the room. There were no photographs of a wife or kids on the walls or on the shelves. Gentry didn't have a wedding band on his finger, so it was a safe bet he was a bachelor. However, there was no visible dust on the furniture, nor were there any stains on the upholstery or on the floor, as is sometimes the case, when a man lives alone. From where I sat, there was a good view of the kitchen, I saw no dishes on the kitchen table or lining the edge of the sink. Perhaps Elvis was a neat man, but when I remembered him eating the donut the previous day, sprinkling glaze all over himself, I was inclined to believe he hired a maid service. I remained silent, until I heard the garbage truck gear up and drive down the road. "Why did you say that Gentry?"

Gentry looked at the wall across from him, his eyes vacant of an expression. Mick had grown tired of having his head rubbed, so he laid on his stomach, at our feet, resting his head on his paws, gently wagging his tail. "Sheriff, I don't understand how any of this is pertinent, to the investigation."

I took my pen and started to lazily draw figure eights on the edge of my notepad. "It may seem trivial, but I've always believed in the saying: *God is in the details.* That one sentence stood out like a sore thumb in your statement. Why did you mention not seeing the buzzards, when no one even asked you, if you did?"

He exhaled a deep breath through his nostrils, rubbing the center of his forehead, like a headache was beginning. "Sheriff, you don't seem to understand what you're asking of me."

I turned my head to look at him. "I'm asking you to tell the truth."

He blew out a scoff, as if what I said was amusing. "Truth. The truth is I didn't see any vultures in the air."

I was feeling the snake of impatience beginning to coil up inside my belly, forcing the muscles in my shoulders and neck, to tighten. I sat on the sofa, gently tapping my pen on my notepad, focusing on my breathing, not wanting my impertinence, to increase the invisible fissure between the two of us. I thought about what he had said, which ignited a small lightbulb inside my head. "You said you didn't see any vultures when you *arrived*, at the crime scene? How about before? The house isn't that far from the stationhouse, so the birds could be easily seen from there. Is that what you meant?"

Gentry stood, stepping over Mick's supine body, as he started to pace the living room. It was on his third lap across, that he stopped to look at me. "What if I were to say, hypothetically, that about a half an hour before Officer Hensley reported in for work, I had to go the Shell gas station for some aspirin, because we had run out at the stationhouse. And on the way back, I saw *nothing* flying over the house, where the body was found."

"I would have to hypothetically ask if you were certain. That was early and it was still fairly dark."

Gentry shook his head, his tone serious and morose, as if this was the last thing he wanted to talk about. "Hypothetically, there was enough light from the predawn, for me to be able to see, if there were any large, dark birds flying around."

I didn't know how far he had planned to take this game, but I had reached as far as I intended to go. "So, when Hensley stated he saw vultures, that's when you knew something was wrong."

Gentry looked the tops of his toes, before nodding. "Yeah."

I sat on the edge of the couch scratching the tip of my chin, with the knuckle of my thumb. "How did Saul seem when he came into work, yesterday?"

I watched his face wrinkle from his scowl of confusion. "What do you mean how did he seem?"

I thought it was a pretty simple question, but I elaborated for him, as I sat back. "Was he at ease or agitated? Was he acting like this was business as usual?"

I watched Gentry stare to his left, taking his time to think about the question. "He seemed to be worried."

I narrowed my eyes, as I wrote this down. "Worried?"

"Yeah. I mean he wasn't shaking like his nerves were on fire or anything like that, but I could tell something was wrong."

I made a reference in my notes, before looking at Gentry. "And how did you feel when you realized he and Daniel were lying?"

He ran his hands through his unkempt hair, with a pained look on his face. Gentry rubbed his stomach and headed into the kitchen. "I need to take my heartburn medicine, but I have to eat something before I do. Which is kind of silly to eat something on an upset stomach. Come into the kitchen."

Mick jumped up to follow, but I told him to stay, which he reluctantly acquiesced. He had to make a show of his disapproval, by throwing himself down on the floor and exhaling along sigh. In the kitchen, Gentry had the cabinet over the sink open, pulling out a bottle of pills. After placing one of the capsules on the counter, he got out a loaf of bread from the breadbox on top of the refrigerator and popped two pieces into the toaster, then pushed the button down. Grabbing a glass from the cupboard, he then took a half gallon of milk from the refrigerator and filled his glass. "Want some?"

"No thanks. How long have you been a police officer?"

He took a long drink and wiped his mustache, with the back of his hand. "Almost fifteen years."

I leaned back against the kitchen counter and watched the wires, inside the toaster turn bright red, from the heat. "It'll soon be fourteen years for me. I remembered how nervous I was, the first time I put on the badge. It just didn't feel right, you know?"

Gentry shook his head, taking another sip of his milk. "No I don't. "

"I can't really explain it myself. It just didn't seem like I should be wearing it. Like I wasn't really a cop, despite the fact I went to the academy. Even today, it still seems unreal, that I'm the sheriff."

The toast popped up, revealing dark brown sides. Gentry took a plate from his cupboard and placed the two pieces on it, before swallowing his pill. He ate his bread in silence, so I opted to continue the conversation. "I eventually figured out what it was. In fact, I told your chief my theory, on the day Alston O' Brian went missing. I told him I realized, I had to earn the privileges and responsibilities, that come, with the badge, every day. It is something that should never be taken for granted, nor easily forgotten."

Gentry had finished one piece of toast, but seemed to be transfixed, with the second untouched piece of crusty bread. I kept my gaze focused on the wall across from me allowing him another moment to think. "Do you agree Officer Gentry?"

He pushed the plate away and braced himself on the counter. Closing his eyes, he rested his chin, in the cushion of his robe, taking slow deep breaths. "Yeah. Yeah I do agree with you, sheriff."

I couldn't help but feel some sympathy for Elvis Gentry, watching him stand there, with slouched shoulders and his head hung down, like it was tied to an anchor. I didn't envy the position he was in, but I also couldn't abide it either, so I pressed on. "Then answer my question please. How did Saul's and Daniel's statements make you feel?"

Pushing himself off the counter, he took a seat at the kitchen table, clasping his hands in front of his face, as if in prayer. "It made me feel…bad all over. I know what I heard on the radio, but I also know what I saw. There were no damn buzzards flying over that area."

I joined him at the table, turning my chair to face him. "You were trying to tell me yesterday, weren't you? That little side remark, about believing he saw vultures, wasn't just an idle comment."

He grinned at me racking, his knuckles on the table. "And *you* knew something was off yesterday, didn't you? When you acted all forgetful, saying you didn't write down Daniel's reason, for searching the property."

I shrugged and leaned back in my seat. "Did Officer Hensley say anything about you altering your statement or making sure your stories were the same?"

He shook his head, leaning back and crossing his arms. "No, but I mentioned not remembering seeing any buzzards that morning. Daniel said they were there, but he refused to look me in the eye for the rest of the day. That told me all I needed to know."

I wrote this down. "Did you ever hear Saul or Hensley mention Alston O'Brian's name?"

"Daniel mentioned him on the day you and your deputy came into the stationhouse, after the incident at Hardees. Said he couldn't understand why you were defending Alston, after all he had done, to the families, he had grifted. He said he thought you should mind your own business."

I shook my head. "I can't say I'm surprised by that. Where were you that day, Alston was being attacked, at Hardees?"

He turned back to the counter and retrieved his glass of milk. "I had the morning off. I didn't even know about the fight until after I started my shift. I was in the breakroom getting a cup of coffee, when I saw how upset Daniel was and asked what had happened."

I made a quick note, of this, in my chicken scratch writing. "And you never heard the chief mention the victim?"

Gentry shook his head. "Not until yesterday, at the crime scene."

I read over my notes, still confused about the scenario. Why all the confusion about how they discovered the body? It was making no sense and I said as much to Elvis. "Can you think of any reason, why there would be so much commotion, about the discovery of the remains? Why they changed their story?"

Elvis shook his head again, tapping his fingers on the table. "I don't know sheriff. It makes no sense to me, either. I mean, Daniel wasn't even supposed to be patrolling that section yesterday."

I looked up from my notes. "He wasn't?"

"No, he was supposed to go across the bridge and patrol that area." He stared out his kitchen window, for a few seconds, chewing his bottom lip. "Which is another thing that has bothered me. The house sets down at the bottom of a hill and the weeds and grass are so grown up, you can barely see it from the road anymore. So, if there weren't any buzzards, then how could he see it?"

I recalled the geography from the day before and agreed the real estate was practically invisible from the road. "So, if they were to discover the remains, then they would have to find a probable cause, to go onto the property. Since you can't see the house, then you'd need another excuse. Like buzzards, for example."

"It's the only scenario I can think of. Of course, why would anyone leave the body there in the first place, you'll have to figure out that answer."

I had been saving this next question for last, but couldn't put it off any longer. "I have to ask this next question, Officer Gentry, so please don't take it personally. Did Alston O'Brian take any money from you or your family?"

I watched the corners of his mouth curve upward. "No. As far as I know, no one in my family was a victim of Alston O'Brian's scam. I can understand why you're asking, especially after the way, the VCPD has been acting lately."

I made a note to double check Gentry's background, but I believed him. Why lie about something that was easy to verify? He had also stated he wouldn't publicly contradict Saul's and Hensley's statements, but I asked if there was a way, for us to reach a compromise. Gentry's jaw set as he shook his head. "I told you, I won't speak out against the chief or Hensley."

I raised my hand, signaling for him to dial down the tension. "I understand, if you can't do it, now. But what if, I find strong evidence, that suggests, they were involved in the circumstances surrounding the victim's murder? Understand Gentry, I don't want that to happen. I'm hoping there is a simple explanation, for all of this, but if there isn't, can I count on you to recant your statement and tell what really happened?"

I watched him chew the corner of his mouth for several heartbeats, as he considered my proposal. I waited, silently, trying to quell the small squall of anxiety and impatience brewing in my stomach. When he finally looked at me, he slowly tapped his fingers on the tabletop and blew out a deep breath. "If you find hard evidence. I mean evidence, so damning even Jesus himself would condemn them, then I might recant. That's the best offer I can give, sheriff."

I slowly released my breath, allowing a small smile to spread over my face. "Well, that'll have to do."

* * *

Mick and I were back in the truck, heading to the stationhouse when my BlackBerry beeped, indicating a text message. I waited until we were stopped at a traffic light, before opening the message. The text had come from Karen, who wanted to see me at the morgue ASAP. "Looks like we've got another fieldtrip to go on, Mick."

The large bulldog looked at me panting slightly, his doe brown eyes shining, with the keen excitement he always got, when he rode shotgun in the truck. Licking his lips, he discharged a light bark, signaling his OK.

The light turned green and I put the truck in gear. "Let's go then."

Chapter Fourteen

The county morgue is located in the basement of the Sweetwater Hospital Association, or Sweetwater Hospital, as we Monroe natives say. I stopped by the Duck Pond and let Mick out to do his business, while I walked lazily behind him. The small park was desolate, on this winter morn, but in the spring and summer, you often see people using the trail across the wooden bridge, that spans the creek, or just eating, at the numerous picnic tables. Concerts are held on the outdoor stage, especially around the Memorial Day, Fourth of July, and Labor Day holidays. The park is also famous for the ducks, that can often be seen floating down the creek or walking around, demanding food, hence the name. Usually there aren't any fowl around this time of year, so I was mildly surprised to see one approaching me. Now, I'm not a duck expert, so I have no idea what the species was, but it was a large one with white feathers, mixed with black paint strokes. He looked up at me, imploring for some food scraps. "Sorry pal, I don't have anything for you."

The duck just stared at me, twisting his head from side to side, as if he was trying to decipher a foreign language. Mick saw him and brought his ears up to high alert, a small, but powerful growl bellowing from his throat. "Mick, don't. This is his park, not yours."

I hooked the leash to his harness and we returned to the truck and headed for the hospital. I took the closest parking space near the door, facing Mick away from the sun, so he wouldn't get too hot. Pets aren't allowed inside the hospital, so I would have to leave him in the cab, but with the cool temperature outside, I didn't have to worry about him overheating. I gave him a quick head rub, before I got out. "Be back, before you know it."

Inside, I went to the elevator and pushed S1 and felt the gravitational shift, as the large box descended to the basement. I exited the elevator and took the first door to my right. Inside, I removed my overcoat and wrapped a paper thin hospital gown around me. I put on a hair net, and shoe covers, before I proceeded to the end of the corridor, where the letters morgue were written, in standard black letters on the door.

Crossing the threshold of the morgue, my nose was invaded, by a mosaic aroma of industrial sanitizer and the sickly sweet scent, of bile and other bodily fluids. Karen was standing over an examination table, which contained the deceased Alston O'Brian, nude and lying face up under the examination lamp. Karen, was wearing the same outfit I was, but with safety glasses carefully positioned over her eyeglasses. She was putting the final touches, on the stitches she used to close the Y incision, made for the internal examination. On the stainless steel workbench behind her were sealed plastic containers. At first glance it, looked like they contained samples of the stomach contents and blood, along with the organ and tissue samples, she had collected for analysis. "Good morning Karen."

She looked up from her work and nodded, "Morning. Glad you got here so fast, thought you'd want to know about this right away."

There was an inventory of the victim's effects, which included the keycard to the Madisonville Motel, located on Highway 68. It must have been where Alston was hanging his hat during his brief stay here. I guess I'll be making a quick stop by there. There was one notable item that was missing from the list. "Did you not find a cellphone, in his clothing Karen?"

"No. Everything I found is on the list. I've already sent them to Molly for analysis."

I stepped closer to the table, for a better look at Alston. The once pinkish tone of his skin, while alive, was now an ashen blue. His midsection was concaved, from the impact of the house. However, the bruising on his shins and lower thighs was a surprise. Karen noticed the injuries had caught my attention. "That's why I called you in. After opening up Mr. O'Brian for examination, I discovered, what was literally, a Pandora's box."

I turned toward the good doctor, to give her my full attention. "I'm listening."

She snipped the final stitch, with a pair of scissors and placed them on the table. "I'll start at the top. Someone tied this old man up and beat him."

Karen pointed to the biceps of both arms, where red marks, about an inch wide were visible. The skin was blistered from abrasions. "From the size of these markings, I'd say someone used a good old fashioned rope, to restrain him, while they worked him over. There are several bruises on the chest, face and sternum, that are consistent, with someone using both their fists and a weapon on him."

I followed her hands as she detailed each wound. I pointed to the larger contusion, about the size of a half-moon, just above his heart. "Was it a baseball bat that caused that one?"

Nodding, she walked down the table to the midsection. "Most likely. The wound fits the shape and diameter of your average baseball bat. But it's in his abdomen, that things start to get interesting."

I moved to stand directly over his abdominal region, patiently waiting for her oration. "At first I found pretty much, what I expected to find. His spleen, stomach, and liver were, for lack of a better word, smashed, from the weight of the house. His intestines ruptured, etcetera. But upon examining the pelvis, I found injuries, that didn't quite add up."

Karen moved to the wall, where a set of x-rays were illuminated by the backlight. She pointed to the pelvic bone, where lines of fractures crisscrossed over the black and white images. "You see these fractures here? Well, they shouldn't be there."

I elevated my eyebrow, but kept any sarcastic comments to myself. I had worked with Karen enough, to know she wasn't just going through the motions, so I patiently waited for her to elucidate at her own accord. "I examined the photographs I took at the scene and I had Jack send me copies of the photographs you took. Noting where the house was placed on the body, the pelvic region should've been left untouched."

"Meaning the pelvis should not be broken," I said.

She gestured to me, but kept her eyes focused on the x-rays. "Right." Karen stepped to the side where another set of x-rays were on display, which indicated the bones along the shin had been fractured as well. "There should be no broken bones in this area either, but here they are."

Noting the broken legs, I calculated the distance, from the impact site, to his shattered pelvis and soon realized what had caused them. "He was hit by a vehicle?"

Karen turned around, resting her hands on her hips, as she looked at me. "Got it in one guess. So, shortly before Alston O'Brian left this world, he was bound, beaten, run over, and had a house dropped on him."

I studied the x-rays, for a moment longer, before turning back to look at the remains. "Someone had a lot of anger issues."

"And that old man had to pay the price. You should also know we got the toxicology results back and we found heavy traces of melatonin and L Theanine in his system."

I thought about it for a moment, unable to make the connection. "What's that?"

Karen moved to the head of the corpse. "Sleeping pills. The kind you can get at any pharmacy. With all the other injuries to his face, it's difficult to be certain, but there appears to be some slight bruising to the base of his nose and around his mouth."

I stared at his face, as I realized what happened. "Someone forced him to swallow the pills."

"That would be my guess."

I thought about my last conversation with the victim. "We know Alston had been missing, for a couple of days. Maybe, whoever did this, had to sedate him, while they went out to get supplies or something. That way, they didn't have to worry about him escaping."

Karen nodded, as she pointed to the injuries. "Some of these wounds show signs of healing. My guess is, this went on for at least twenty-four hours. And judging from the levels of the sedative, he was, most likely, still under the affects when he died."

I returned to the cadaver, looking into the gaunt pallid face. "So, what is the official cause of death?"

Karen joined me at the table, staring at Alston's remains, as she spoke in her professional monotone voice. "He died from severe internal injuries, followed by massive exsanguination and eventually shock. He would've expired between 11:00 p.m. and 1:00 a.m. the night before the body was discovered. The cold temperatures make it difficult to pinpoint the time any better."

I nodded, as I crossed my arms over my chest, my eyes still focused on the body. "Which was it that killed him? The beating? The impact from the collision or the house dropping on him?"

She shook her head, a frown covering her face. "That's a chicken and egg question I'm afraid, Jonas."

Imagination is a key part to being a forensic investigator. Not only do you need to catalog the evidence, but you also have to try to deduce, what it all means and how the evidence got there. This is where science meets art, as you have to let the information filter through you mind to reach plausible answers. "So he was tortured, then sedated. Tortured some more. Sedated again, before being hit by a car and finally squashed by the house."

Karen nodded, as she too crossed her arms over her chest. "Most likely. But why run over him?"

I casually paced the length of the corpse, as I felt the synaptic highways in my brain begin to light up. "Maybe that wasn't part of the plan. What if Alston somehow managed to get lose from his restraints and made a run for it. His abductors tried to catch him, but ran over him instead. Whether by accident or design, we can't say."

Karen raised an eyebrow at me, pointing to Alston's body. "Accident or intentional, it still yielded the same results. I can't speak for you Jonas, but this is the first time, I've had to conduct an autopsy, on a man, who was kidnapped, beaten, run over, then flattened by house."

As you can see, Karen doesn't have my restraint on sarcasm, but no one is perfect. "It's a first for me too, Karen. The kidnapping and torture seems to indicate someone, who is organized."

Karen pinched her eyes together, slowly nodding her head. "But putting the body under a house isn't too smart, Jonas. Or organized."

I held up my forefinger. "One: if they were smart, we'd be out of business." I held up my second finger. "Two: what if dropping the house on the cadaver was a crazy attempt, by the killer, to conceal the impact of the vehicle?"

Karen looked at me for a moment, as if I was speaking a foreign tongue, but slowly, I watched her ebony eyes take on a sheen of ingenuity, as she began to grasp my train of thought. "That...might be true. It's an unorthodox way of going about it, but you could be onto something there."

I pointed to the x-rays, noting his injuries once again. "It's just a theory, but it seems to fit with the evidence we have, so far. They probably believed, if they dropped the house on top of him, it would cover up the injuries sustained from the impact of the collision. Only, they didn't put enough of him under the house, to conceal the pelvis and leg fractures."

Karen rolled her eyes, staring up at the ceiling. "Ah, how the best laid plans go awry."

I shook my head, waving my hand over the body. "Like I said, the abduction was planned. The torture was planned. The victim getting run over is where everything started going sideways. They had to start improvising."

Karen scoffed, as she took the sterile sheet and began to cover the remains. "Which is why they were so sloppy about it."

"It's when they improvise, that mistakes happen. Which is a good thing for us, although it didn't do Alston any good."

Karen turned toward her office. "His fate was sealed no matter what, Jonas." She came back with her full report and handed it to me. "If he hadn't been killed by his injuries, Alston probably wouldn't have made it another six months."

I opened the report and saw her preliminary findings, on the tissue samples removed. The word carcinoma stood out. "He had cancer?"

Karen's expression showed empathy, for the first time, as she looked over at the canopied remains. "It looks like it started in his liver and had spread to the kidneys and lungs. I don't know what kind yet, but it appears to have been an aggressive strand of the disease."

I closed the folder and tapped my fingers on the edge. "Did the body show any signs he was receiving treatment?"

"There were no physical signs he was taking any treatments. But we'll know for certain, if he was taking chemo, after we get the results from the samples I took"

I found myself looking over my shoulder, at Alston's remains, again, feeling an uncertain sense of sympathy, for the man. Having relatives that had succumbed to this indiscriminative disease, I knew Alston didn't have a pleasant ending waiting for him, as the malevolent cells ravaged his body. I can't help but ponder, if this end, as painful as it had to have been, wasn't a better one. "Is it possible he didn't know he was sick?"

She closed her eyes, shaking her head emphatically. "There's no way. He'd have experienced episodes of severe pain. There is absolutely no way he wouldn't have suspected something was wrong."

I turned to look at the sheet draped over the remains, finding myself once again lost down the rabbit hole. If Alston knew he was sick, then why wasn't he receiving treatments? More importantly, if he knew he was dying, why come back to the very scene of the crime, that put him in prison to begin with?

This question kept playing in my head, as I drove back to the stationhouse, with the radio on NPR, not really listening to what was being discussed, as I tried to pinpoint Alston's reason for returning to Monroe County. A man, with only months to live, decides to return, to the place, responsible for his years behind bars. Was it the alleged money, that went missing, during the trial? Did Alston want to live out his final days, in as much ease and comfort, as he could afford? If so, then he could've returned, removed the money and left a long time ago. No, he had remained, in the county, for a reason that we hadn't deduced yet.

There were some gray clouds moving in from the north, when I parked the truck, in my reserved space at the stationhouse. When Mick and I stepped out of the truck, the wind was more fierce, than it had been an hour earlier. I thought perhaps winter was about, to sprinkle more snow on us, this afternoon.

Phil Woody was standing in the front vestibule, as we entered the stationhouse. His navy blue parka was hanging over his enfolded arms, covering the upper part of his blue jeans. I walked up to him and shook his hand. "What brings you out here, Phil?"

He gripped my hand with a strong, calloused fingers. "I was headed into town for some groceries and thought I would check in, about my robbery."

Mick's nose began to twitch, as he sniffed the ambient aroma surrounding Phil. I wondered, if he was detecting a whiff, of more than, just the usual scents, a body produces. "I'm afraid we're still looking for the guys, who broke into your house, Phil. They've been wreaking havoc, all over the county, these last few weeks. I wish I had better news."

Phil shook his head, a sympathetic smile spreading across his face. "It's all right sheriff. I thought they might still be at large. With this murder in Vonore, I'd say your plate is full."

"We're still working on it, Phil. We take home invasions very seriously here."

Phil again shook his head, only more emphatically. "I wasn't insinuating that anything was wrong, Jonas. I know you'll do your best to catch them."

My coat was becoming an oven, standing in the vestibule, so I removed it, to mimic Phil's position. "I think we might be zeroing in on them, though. With just a little luck, I might have them in custody soon."

Phil's silver eyebrows, arched up, genuinely surprised. "Really?"

I spread my hands out, palms down, not wanting to get his hopes up too much. "It's just a hunch, for right now, but I feel pretty good about it. Keep it to yourself, for now."

Phil raised a hand to the heavens, as his voice dropped, to the deep baritone level, he took on when he preached. "You can count on me sheriff. Like it says in the good book, *The man who can keep a secret, may be wise, but he is not half as wise as the man with no secrets to keep.*"

I looked down at the floor, to see Mick now had his nose pressed firmly against Phil's pants, as a scent had really captivated his attention. I grasped his leash and pulled him back. "I believe it was Edgar Watson Howe, who originally said that Phil, but I get the point."

I thought our conversation had come to a close, but Phil remained where he stood, his face having a perplexed look, like he didn't know how to say, what was on his mind. "Something else I can help you with, Phil?"

He glanced over his shoulder to Jack, who was at his desk working on his reports, before turning back to me. I took this as a cue he wanted some privacy, so I invited him back to my office. "I'll be with you in a minute."

I walked back to Jack's station and leaned on the counter. "Jack anything on Patrick Winchell?"

He shook his head, as he entwined his fingers. "Nothing yet. Glen and Tom are checking out his old hangouts, but so far, they've not found anything. He might've decided, to leave town."

"Because his old family home was used to crush Alston?"

Jack rubbed the hair of his eyebrow, with the pad of his thumb. "It does make him look complicit, at the very least. Think we need to put out a BOLO on him?"

I drummed my fingers on the counter, as I pondered the idea, but eventually shook my head. "Not yet. Let's see what Tom and Glen turn up. If they don't find him by this afternoon, then we'll issue the BOLO."

I returned to my office and closed the door, as Mick took one of the seats in front of my desk, leaving Phil with only one place to sit down.

I had wisely taken the precaution of covering the pegboard, profiling the evidence of Alston's murder, with a sheet last night, before leaving. After putting my coat on the rack by the door, I took a seat behind my desk. "What's on your mind, Phil?"

He had his hands resting on top of his folded coat, as he looked at the corner of the desk. "It has to do with the man, who was found under the house, yesterday."

"Alston O'Brian?"

He nodded, clearing his throat before replying, "Yes."

I straightened up in my seat, as I took a pen from my desk and slowly rotated it in my hand. "Did you know the victim?"

Phil looked at me, his face stoic, speaking in a low translucent voice. "Not for long. I mean, I only met him, a few days back. Of course, I remembered the case from years ago, when he conned the people in Vonore, but at that time, I had only seen him on the news or pictures in the papers."

I took a legal pad from the top drawer and scribbled the date and time, along with Phil's name in the top left corner. "In what capacity, did you know Alston O'Brian?"

Phil, crossed his leg, as he blew out a deep breath. "He came to me, about two weeks ago, on a Sunday, after I had given a sermon at a local church. Saying how much he enjoyed my sermon, he told me his name and that he just got out of prison."

I wrote what he said, making sure my handwriting was legible. Phil didn't seem to mind the interlude. "Did he talk to you about anything else?"

Phil looked down at the top of his shoes, scratching the skin above his left eye with his thumb. He looked back at me, the corners of his mouth, set firm. "He said he was sick and didn't have a lot of time left in this world."

I decided to feign ignorance, for a while, to see what I could learn. "He was sick?"

Phil nodded, rubbing his abdomen. "It was cancer. It had started in his liver, but it had spread throughout his body, while he was in prison."

I had intended to speak with the warden, of the prison, to see if Alston's medical condition was known to them, but this revelation suggested it was. This led me to wonder, if the warden had divulged Alston's prognosis, to the attorney general, when she gave him the heads up call. I made a notation to call the warden, after I finished my interview with Phil. "Did he know how much time he had left?"

Phil picked at a piece of lint on his coat, as he uncrossed his leg. "He said the doctor's best guess was maybe ten months, on the outside. Realistically, it was probably about six or seven months."

So far this seemed to jive with what Karen had discovered. Alston did know he was sick and on his way out and still chose to come back here. Of course as always, the why was elusive. "Why did Alston tell you this Phil? Was he seeking spiritual advice, before the cancer took its toll on him?"

Phil cleared his throat and once again cast his eyes away from mine, as he started to tap his heel on the floor. "In a way, I suppose it could be seen as spiritual advice."

I focused my eyes on him, noticing his face was beginning to turn red. "Phil, just out of curiosity, did Alston come to you because of your, let's say organic proclivities?"

The color of his face turned ketchup red, and he got a sheepish grin on his face. "A discussion might've arisen about my botanical excursions."

I set the pen down, working hard to conceal my impatience. When it came to Phil's ganja use, we always had to do a delicate dance, so as to not get him in more trouble than was necessary. Lord knows, he didn't need any assistance, in that regard. "What were the circumstances surrounding this discussion?"

Phil paused, as he seemed to be choosing, how to phrase his response appropriately. "It was in regards…to his medical condition. He wanted to know, if there was a way to alleviate the nausea, from his treatments."

I rolled the pen on top of the legal pad, as I sat back and propped my foot, on the open bottom drawer, of my desk. "Nausea? You mean, from the chemotherapy?"

He nodded, as he rested his palms on top of his knees. "Yes. He explained how unbearable it could be at times. I had an uncle, who lost his battle with bone cancer. I remembered it seemed the treatments were as bad as the disease. So, I gave him two bags of…medicine."

I pointed to the file on the corner of my desk. "This is Alston O'Brian's autopsy results Phil. Dr. Long confirmed he was indeed in the advanced stages of cancer and probably only had a few months left to live. She also felt pretty certain that he was not receiving chemo treatments."

The preacher's mouth opened, but he spoke no words. He looked toward the corner of the office, his forehead wrinkled in confusion. "He wasn't getting any treatments at all? You're sure?"

I scratched the back of my left ear, giving him a slight nod. "They'll run more tests, but Dr. Long felt pretty positive, that he had received no cancer treatments at all."

Phil's whole body slouched in the chair, staring at me with a blank expression. "Then why did he ask for the...stuff?"

Thankful for his quick use of the word "stuff," I shrugged my shoulders, as I gently rocked my seat back and forth. "Maybe he wasn't lying about the nausea. As advanced as his cancer was, he was most likely feeling some discomfort and maybe your organic medicine made it more bearable. Then again, and I hate to say this Phil, Alston was a conman. Maybe he thought he could use his condition, to score an easy batch of the stuff."

Phil shook his head, as he let his eyes focus on the top of my desk. "I just can't believe that sheriff. He seemed so sincere, when he said he was in pain. I can't believe he would use such a tragic disease, for his benefit."

"Did he pay you for your medicine?"

"No. I said there was no need seeing as he…. Oh geez." He rested his forehead inside the palm of his hand.

I gave him a sympathetic smile. "Don't be too hard on yourself, Phil. Alston once conned about a third of the population of Vonore."

Phil had his face partially covered with his hand, shaking his head. "I can't believe I fell for it Jonas. I'm old enough to know better than that. I can't believe I let him swindle me like that."

"Phil, he played on your charity and generosity. If you had to be conned, would you rather it have been because of selfish greed or because you were trying to help someone?"

Closing his eyes, he turned his head toward the ceiling, whispering a prayer I was unable to understand. "Amen. I suppose there is some wisdom in your words, though no one likes to look like a fool. But then in Ecclesiastes it is said: *The misfortune of the wise is better than the prosperity of the fool.* I suppose in his own way, Alston was prosperous."

I grinned at him. "In a way he was. And it was Epicurus who said that not Ecclesiastes."

The mask of confusion, I had seen on his face more times than I can remember, was once again in place. He scratched the back of his head. "Really?"

"Yeah." I took up my pen, deciding it was time to move on to a more pertinent topic. "Phil, when you were talking with Alston, did he mention why he came back to Monroe County, after all these years? I would've thought he would never want to return."

Phil interlaced his fingers on his lap, as his expression became that of a funeral director. "When he told me who he was, I did ask him about his return. I was wanting to know, if it had anything to do with, seeking forgiveness from those he harmed."

I waited a moment, for him to continue, but it seems he was expecting me to prompt him. "How did he reply?"

"His answer was ambiguous. He said he was like the salmon, swimming upstream. That he had some unfinished business to attend to, before he finally met his maker."

I felt my brow furrow in confusion. "Like the salmon?"

"Those were his words, Sheriff."

I stared at the word on my legal pad, having no clue as to its significance, assuming there was one. "Were you able to get him to elaborate on his meaning?"

Phil shook his head, scratching his upper lip with his finger. "I tried to get him to divulge more to me, but he refused to say anything else on the matter. Whatever it was, it was obviously very personal to him."

The central heat kicked on, releasing a subtle gust of cool air into the room, before the air turned warm. Mick looked up at the ventilation shaft, in the ceiling for a moment, before exhaling a deep breath and closing his eyes, to take a nap. "Phil, is there anything else you can think of that happened, while you were talking with him?"

He started to shake his head, but held up his hand and leaned forward. "Well, I don't know if it means anything, but I'm pretty sure when he drove off, there was someone following him."

My interest piqued, I gave the preacher/delusional apostle, my full attention. "You get a look at who it was?"

He shook his head, with a grimace on his face. "It was too far away and I couldn't swear to it, but I noticed a green pickup truck pull out, after Mr. O'Brian left. The driver was wearing a baseball cap, that much I can remember. Everything else, I'm afraid is kind of fuzzy. My memory isn't what it used to be."

I looked at my notes, after scribbling down what he had said. "That's all right Phil. You've been a big help. If you wouldn't mind sticking around for a bit longer, I'll have a deputy write this up, as a formal statement, for you, to sign."

Phil nodded as he stood up. "That's not a problem."

I led him to the door, but he stopped to face me. "That quote was really from Epicurus?"

I smiled, nodding at him. "Yeah it was."

He wrinkled his brow, staring at the floor. "When in the hell did I ever read Epicurus?"

* * *

Once I had Phil's statement, I spent the rest of the morning, tracking down Elizabeth King, the warden of Whiteville Correctional Facility. When I had her on the phone, she was able to confirm, that Alston had been diagnosed with his cancer, while he was incarcerated and it did have some sway in the parole board granting him early release.

"How long did the doctors give him?"

"According to his file, six to eight months," she replied.

I wrote this down, as I continued my questioning. "Did he receive any treatment while he was still incarcerated?"

"We offered it to him, but he declined. Said there was no sense in it. He was probably right. The doctor said, at most it would've bought him a month or two and he'd be in bad shape by then."

Mick was now sitting up and giving me, what I call his statue stare. It was pushing noon, so my guess was he wanted something to nibble on. I turned to the filing cabinet behind me and got out a bowl, before taking a small bag of dog food from the bottom drawer. Placing a palm full in the bowl, I sat it beside my desk. Mick jumped out of the chair, shoving it back two inches and quickly inhaled the contents in under ten seconds. "So there was no doubt in Alston's mind he was going to die?"

I heard sheets of paper sliding across one another, telling me she must be reading the report as we talked. "No sheriff. Mr. O'Brian knew his condition was terminal and there wasn't much that could be done for it."

I returned the dogfood bag back to the drawer and removed a bottle of water. Dumping the crumbs into the trashcan, I poured some water for the dog and set it before his paws. "How did he react to the prognosis?"

Elizabeth, exhaled a deep breath and spoke more directly into the line. "I wasn't there when he got the news, Sheriff Lauer, but I imagine he wasn't too happy learning he was going to die soon."

It was a poor way to phrase the question on my part, but she still didn't have to get snippy with me, on the phone. I rose above the instinctive need, to reply with a snide remark of my own and proceeded with the conversation. "What I mean, did he file a petition, for early release or was that at your suggestion?"

"It was a mutual arrangement. He only had a year left on his sentence and he had never caused any trouble during his stay here. Given his condition, I saw no reason for him to spend his remaining time incarcerated, so I recommended him for early release."

Mick's vaccination tag, was clinking against the stainless steel bowl, as he lapped at the water with his tongue. I gave him a quick stern glance, but he looked up at me, with water dripping from his chin, his eyes indicating he didn't see the problem. "Warden, just a few more questions and I'll let you go. While he was there, did Alston receive any visitors?"

"Let me see." There was a brief intermittence. "It looks like other than his attorney, Mr. O'Brian received no visitors."

My pen moved along the legal pad, as I took my notes. "According to the court records his attorney was Eugene Collier.

"That's the name we have on record as visiting him."

"When was the last time his attorney was there?"

"His last contact with his attorney was October12, 2002. The day his final appeal was denied."

I lightly tapped the back of my pen on the desk, listening to the humming static coming from the long distance call, as I re-read my notes. So far, this avenue of inquiry had revealed very little new information, however I wasn't quite finished yet. "Did Mr. Deland know about Alston's medical prognosis?"

"Yes, Mr. Deland was aware of his cancer. I saw no reason not to inform him."

Then why didn't the prosecuting solicitor show me the same courtesy? I made arrant doodles on the edges of the legal pad for a moment, pondering the question. Having no answer at the moment, I asked for one last favor from the warden. "Did Alston have a cellmate?"

"Let me see." There was another brief pause in the conversation. "Yes, he was housed with a Max "Gearjammer" Bandon."

I wrote this down and felt my eyebrow cock. "Gearjammer?"

I heard her emit a low sigh, laced with impatience. "Yeah, he was convicted of stealing three semi-tractor trailers and the manifest. He's halfway through his ten-year sentence. He spent the last three of those years, as Mr. O'Brian's cellmate."

"When it is convenient, I would like to speak with him. It can either be on the phone or video conference, whichever is easiest for you."

"I have a meeting with the state legislator this afternoon. Would tomorrow morning, at 9:00 a.m., your time, be good?"

I told her it would and gave her my cellphone number, if she needed to contact me to reschedule. "One last thing ma'am. On the day of Alston's release, did anyone pick him up?"

"Let me check." I heard the typing of buttons on a computer keyboard. "According to the guards, he was a walkout. A lot of them do that. Especially the ones, who have been in here a while."

I wrote this down and thanked the warden for her time. "Your welcome, sheriff."

After I hung up, I read the section of my notes about Anthony Deland knowing that Alston was terminal. I found myself wondering why he hadn't told me. It could've been an oversight on his part, but that didn't jive. He made the point to speak with me privately, about Alston and it would only seem logical, for him to mention his medical condition. I had to push down the conspiratorial thoughts that wanted to mushroom inside my head. A difficult process, considering I had a police chief and the first officer, on the scene, hindering the investigation. Was Anthony in league with them as well?

I shook my head, shaking the incriminating thoughts from my mind, as I recalled what Bill Hays had once told me, way back, when I was a rookie forensic investigator. He said: "never let your theories, get in the way, of what the facts are telling you. If the facts are slow in coming, don't use your own personal theories to fill in the gaps." I repeated those words inside my head once again, as the balloon of anxiety, slowly deflated.

I did another initial review of the case file, not gaining anything of significance, but that was probably because I couldn't seem to get past Alston's illness. Why would Alston O'Brian come back to Monroe County, as he reached the end of his life? Plus, we still didn't know how he was able to afford a good car and clothing. If he had help, on the outside, he took painstaking steps, to keep their identity a secret.

I ran a search on his attorney, only to find Eugene Collier had retired from practice seven years ago. I vaguely remembered seeing him in court, when I had first joined the sheriff's department. He had a thick mane of red hair, that was fading to gray along his temples, with a neatly trimmed beard. He was a very methodical attorney, with a high success rate. Eugene was also a resident of Madisonville, so it didn't take me long to find his home address and phone number.

Jack knocked on my office door, just as I was about to call him. "Jonas, I just got a call from Oscar Horton. He says he's got a car, that he thinks might be stolen."

An occupational hazard of a scrapyard and parts yard from time to time, is receiving stolen property. Even when the owners comply with the law, there is always a chance someone will steal some metal or a vehicle, for a quick buck. "Send a deputy over and have them fill out a report."

Jack stepped into my office, hooking his thumbs under his. "I was going out there to do it myself, until he told me it was a gold 2014 Toyota Camry."

I dropped the reports on my desk. "A gold Camry? We ever get the Vehicle Identification Number for Alston's car."

"TDOT hasn't gotten back to me on that one."

Never being a fan of coincidence, I stood up and grabbed my coat. "Why don't you and I go have a look at this car."

Chapter Fifteen

When we pulled into the scrapyard, a large blue tarp had been secured over the massive opening, caused by the robbery. Oscar came out to meet us at the pay window, his unbuttoned blue, plaid shirt hanging loose on his shoulders. I grabbed my field kit, as Mick and I exited the truck. "Sheriff. We just keep on meeting after someone's committed a crime."

I smiled, as I shook hands with Oscar. "That's usually how I meet most people anymore. Is it all right if the dog joins us?"

Jack was there by then and Oscar shook his hand also. "Won't bother me none. The car's around back. Follow me."

At the back of the facility, stood three rows of cars and trucks gathered to be sold for parts. Most had seen better days, which made the 2014 Camry, stand out like a diamond in the rough. "It came in first thing this morning."

Jack opened the field kit and removed the digital camera. I wrote down the VIN number in my notebook, as he began to take some photographs. "Who was the seller, Oscar?"

"It came in, with that red Tacoma over there, on the left, the blue Civic on the right, and silver F150 just over there, all from Gillian Motors."

I carefully walked around the car, observing no signs of forced entry around the doors or trunk. Peering through the windows, the tan leather interior revealed no signs of blood and neither did the floorboard. "Are the other three vehicles legit?"

Oscar tucked his hands, in the pockets of his coat and flicked his tongue across his teeth. "Yeah. This is partly my fault too, sheriff. I've been so busy, trying to get everything in order since the break-in, I let this one slip by me."

"How do you mean, Oscar?"

He adjusted his faded outback hat, to shield his eyes, seeming a bit embarrassed. "State law says, that any car made, within the last twelve years, has to have a title, before I can purchase it. This one did have a title, but I didn't notice the VIN numbers didn't match up. I've been working with the insurance company and contractors to get that huge hole fixed, while trying to run this place and it just got overlooked. As soon as I realized my mistake, I called Robert Gillian and asked for the correct title."

A quick gust of wind come out of the north, sending a shiver of ice down my spine. "And he said?"

"The man said he didn't have any idea what I was talking about. He said he never sent me a Toyota Camry, that I must've misplaced the paperwork." Oscar spat on the ground, a scowl on his face. "Lying bastard. I didn't misplace nothing. Hell fire, the car was delivered, on one of his rollbacks. I got it on camera, so who's he trying to fool?"

"If I had to hazard a guess, Oscar, I would say it's about possession," I said.

Oscar looked at the car. "Possession?"

Jack was making notes for the report, when he said, "I'm assuming you've paid for the car right?"

Oscar nodded his head.

"Then that means you own the car now. So therefore, it is your problem, not his," replied Jack. "Or at least he thinks it is. We're going to have a chat with him, after we leave here."

I stood to the side of the Camry, watching Jack process the car. "Am I correct in assuming you made out a bill of sale, when you purchased these vehicles from Gillian Motors?"

Oscar nodded. "Yes sir. I've got them in my office. You need to see them."

"We'll need copies for the report, which will aid in proving, they owned the car first. But since the Camry has been purchased by you, I need to know if we have your permission, to search the vehicle."

Oscar tilted the brim of his hat toward the gold sedan. "I called you down here to check it out, so go on ahead."

Jack put on a pair of gloves and opened the driver's door and popped the trunk. Inside we found a section of the tan carpet, the size of a football, stained a rusty brown color. "I think we might have something here, Jonas."

I nodded as I pointed to the kit. "Get the phenolphthalein and run a swab over it."

Jack took a sterile Q-tip from a cardboard box container and removed the plastic cap. After dousing the cotton end with distilled water, he gently ran it over the stain. He then pulled out the bottle of phenolphthalein and put one drop on the edge of the swab and watched as it remained white. Oscar took a pack of gum from his pocket. "What does that mean?"

I looked at the scrap dealer, as he removed a sliver of gum from the pack. "It means it's most likely not blood. We'll have a sample taken to the lab. Molly will figure out what it is."

Oscar nodded, as he put his wrapper in his pocket. "I saw that police bulletin, about the Toyota Camry, belonging to that guy, who died and then this car showed up. I knew it was going to be a part of that."

Jack took pictures of the carpet, before putting a marked scale. "Gillian Motors is that place beside Wendy's on Highway 68?"

Oscar released a light sigh, as he chewed on his gum. "That's his main yard. He has another one in Vonore, that he opened two years ago."

I felt a small quiver in my gut, as I turned toward Oscar. "Am I correct, in assuming, this shipment of vehicles came from the Vonore location?"

Oscar's forehead wrinkled, under his hat, as he stared at me, like I was a carnival act. "Yeah, it did. How did you know?"

I shrugged, as I looked at the vehicle. "It was a lucky guess. Jack after you're through here—"

"You want me to go and talk to Bob Gillian and the driver about the shipment. You'll also want me to see, if they have any surveillance cameras on their property, that could reveal how the Camry got there."

"Sounds like you've got it covered. I'll call a tow and have the vehicle taken to the lab, so Molly can go over it for trace evidence."

Jack gently closed the trunk lid and put the camera and swab in the forensic kit. "You want me to search the vehicle or head on to Vonore?"

I shook my head and pointed toward the road. "Note the time you're leaving. Then go to Vonore and check out the parts yard. I'll do the search."

As Jack made his way to his cruiser, I called Atkins Body shop for a rollback, to retrieve the vehicle, then put on my own set of gloves. I opened the passenger door and pulled the lever to the glove box. Inside was the owner's manual, a large bottle of aspirin, and a plain white envelope. Opening the envelope, I found the registration, with Alston O'Brian's name, issued by the county clerk in Meigs County. I placed it inside my coat pocket and looked at the bottle of aspirins. When I shook it, the inside didn't sound like a baby rattle. I opened it and found a small bag of grass. Knowing where this would lead, I shook my head and placed the bag back inside the bottle, praying, Phil's prints were too smudged to be lifted.

"Looks like the driver liked a little "pick me up"," Oscar said.

I opened the back passenger door, kneeling down to look under the seats. "He doesn't need it anymore."

Oscar shifted his weight on his feet and spoke, with a more somber voice. "You're certain this belongs to the dead guy."

I checked the VIN number from the factory seal with the registration and nodded. "I'm afraid so Oscar."

I heard him shift his weight again, the rubber from his steel toe boots kicking the tiny beads of gravel along the asphalt. "Any idea why someone dropped the house on him?"

There was nothing under the passenger seat, so I moved around to the driver's side. "I can't comment on an ongoing investigation, Oscar."

I hunched down and looked under the seats, but found nothing that caught my attention. I checked under the floor mats, to found flecks of dirt and dried grass. I made a note to have Molly analyze these when the car was taken to the lab. I checked the spare tire compartment in the trunk and found the tire and jack were all in their proper place. I made notations, to this fact before closing the trunk. "Oscar, I noticed the key in the ignition. Is it the only one you have?"

The scrap dealer nodded his head, taking his hat off and tunneling his fingers through his hair. "Yeah. The motor still works on it too. It's a darn shame, it was stolen. I could easily get eight hundred for the engine alone."

"Afraid there's not much I can do about that Oscar. Has anyone else, besides you, touched the car?"

"No. I personally inspect the vehicles."

I put my notebook in my pocket. "Would you mind letting us take your prints, so we can eliminate yours, from the ones found inside the car."

He ran the pad of his thumb over his forehead, a slight frown on his face. "If I have too. You want me to come by after work?"

I took a small fingerprint kit from the stainless steel case. "We can do it right now, if you want."

We walked over to the F150, where I opened up the kit and removed a fingerprint card. I put Oscar's name on it along with the date and time then removed the black inkpad and took off the lid. "Let's start with your right thumb."

I took his right hand and rolled each digit, in the black pad and proceeded, to do the same on the card, in the assigned box. I watched as the ridges and valleys of his fingers left their charcoal black stencils on the card, making sure each was clean and decipherable. I did the same with his left and gave him a sanitizing wipe, which did a half decent job, of removing the ink. "Thanks, Oscar."

He stared at his stained fingertips, before wiping them again. "I hate getting this stuff on my fingers. How come you don't have a digital scanner? We have one, for the prints we take here after purchases."

I grinned and closed the fingerprint kit, latching the plastic locks. "We do have one at the stationhouse. But we don't have it in the budget, as of right now, to buy a portable one for the field. At least not yet. We're hoping to get ourselves one, by the end of spring or early summer."

My explanation seemed to have abated his anger. "Yeah, that stuff does get on the expensive side. I've been reminded of just how much it cost, from the insurance reports, I've had to file."

From where we stood, you couldn't see the tarp over the massive crater, the boxer boys had left in their wake. I glanced back at the main office, as I placed the kit and card back inside the stainless case. "Has the accident affected business much?"

"Not much. We had to shut down for a day, to get the safe back inside and secured. We have a backup computer system in my office, so we set up a desk next to the front door and put the computer and printer there. The digital camera and signature plate still work, so we hooked them up to the computer and we were back in business the next day."

"Time waits for no man?" I said.

He shook his head, a grin spreading across his face. "Not in this business. We're not the only dealer in the area. If we wait too long, we could lose our customer base and contracts. A lot of people make light of it, but scrap is a cut throat business."

The red cab of the rollback, from Atkins, was entering the gate and I waved him over to where we stood. I grabbed Mick's leash firmly, to keep him from charging the diesel truck, as he had a tendency to do. I saw the owner Ron Atkins, was behind the wheel, as he came to a stop. Stepping out of the cab, he adjusted his blue company logo baseball cap down over his red hair, as he came toward me. "Which one do you need me to haul, sheriff?"

I pointed, to the gold Toyota sedan, in front of me. "That one right there. But you need to wear gloves, on this one Ron. We want to preserve any prints that might be on it."

Atkins Body Shop and Wrecker Service has been in business in Madisonville, for as long as I can remember. Ron's father Larry started the company before I was born and Ron took the reins after his death several years ago. Their service was always good, so the sheriff's department contracted the vehicle removals with them. This wasn't Ron's first rodeo, so he knew the drill, when I said we needed to preserve prints.

He put on a pair of gloves and backed the rollback up to the Camry. When the backend was aligned with the front of the car, Ron got out and opened the driver's door. "You want to do the honors?"

I handed the leash over to Oscar, Mick who was failing in his attempts to stifle his barks, was digging his back feet into the ground, like he was about to charge the truck. "If you wouldn't mind. Hold it tight, he's stronger than you think."

I retrieved a boot cover from the evidence kit and moved to the sedan. I put it on my right foot before pressing the brake pedal, without getting in the seat. I turned the ignition with my still gloved hand and put the gear in neutral. I stepped back outside and shut the door. "She's all yours, Ron."

After Ron set the cable, he rolled the sedan onto the rollback. Once the chains were set on the wheels, he opened the door and put the gear in park. He jumped down to the ground and groaned, as he rubbed his knee. "Man, it wasn't too long ago doing that wouldn't have hurt."

I smiled at him, as I removed my gloves. "Time catches up with us all, Ron."

He took off his own gloves and scratched his freckled face. He was about ten years my senior, with a thin frame and strong thick calloused hands. "You want it taken to the storage lot behind the lab?"

I took the leash from Oscar. With the diesel engine off, Mick's sole purpose now, was to try and get Ron to pet him. "Yes please. Give the paperwork to the deputy and we'll make sure you get paid. Thanks again, Ron."

"You're welcome." He turned to Oscar and nodded. "You doing all right, Oscar?"

Oscar smiled, as he looked at the Camry. "You mean besides someone busting down my wall and receiving a stolen car? Other than that, I'm good. Your business doing all right?"

Ron adjusted the bill of his cap over his forehead. "Been good. Cold weather is good for the wrecker service. People's batteries die on them or they slide into a ditch and need me to pull them out."

Good times all around, I thought. "I guess there's a season for everything."

Ron headed to the cab of the rollback, waving to us. "Well I better head out. Y'all have a good one."

"Same to you," I replied.

"See you Ron," Oscar replied.

Once the engine was in gear, Mick started to bark, jerking at his restraint in a valiant, but vain effort to follow the truck. "Mick settle down." I watched the rollback head out the front gate, before grabbing the evidence kit and heading for the main office. "If you wouldn't mind Oscar, I'd like to take a look at the paperwork."

He joined me. "Follow me and I'll get it for you."

I fought the shiver, that was trying to run up my spine. Picking up the pace, Mick was running ahead of us. "Thanks."

When he unlocked the door to the office, I immediately saw, that the debris from the assault on the wall had been cleaned up nicely, considering the circumstances. There was still some flecks of concrete dust along the corners of the walls, but the large chunks had been removed and the furniture, that hadn't been destroyed was back in place. Sitting at the desk in the broom closet was Katy Spear, with her coat cinched up tight, her gloved hands waving back and forth over a space heater. "Good morning to you, Ms. Spear."

She looked back at me and the dog, nodding, as she kept herself hunched over the space heater. "Good morning. I see you've brought a friend."

The blue tarp concealing the rupture, popped and snapped, from the wind rolling along the surface. It was doing a good job keeping the moisture out, but it did nothing for the cold wind. "Yes ma'am, I did. He likes to get away from the house every once in a while. I'll bet you'll be glad to get that wall back up."

A cloud of white blew from her mouth, as she sighed. "Lord yes. Though I shouldn't complain. I'm still working, so there is that."

Again there was something about her tone of voice that piqued my interest. I can't put my finger on it, or even put it into words, but something has bothered me about Ms. Spear. The background check on her came back clean, but I wasn't satisfied. "How long before you start the repairs on the building?"

She hooked her thumb over her shoulder, in Oscar's direction. "As soon as Mr. Horton gets through dealing with the insurance company. They're haggling over the price, of course."

I shook my head, closing and opening my hands inside the coat pockets. "That's no surprise there. Some adjusters would squeeze the copper out of a penny, if they could."

Oscar came back with the forms. "Amen to that. You ask me the insurance companies are licensed thieves. Here you go."

I looked at the bill of sale, for the vehicles he had purchased, and found the Ford F150, Toyota Tacoma, and Honda Civic and the Toyota Camry. "You mind if I make a copy of these?"

Oscar shrugged. "Go on ahead."

Katy took the papers from my hand and took them to the copy machine. As I waited for the bar to scan the documents and eject the printed copy, I looked over to the computer. "You said you checked the VIN numbers, on the other three vehicles and they checked out OK?"

She shivered as she nodded. "Yeah, they're good."

I would run a check on the numbers myself, to verify, back at the office, just to be thorough, but I wasn't expecting there to be any other discrepancies. Katy brought me the copies of the documents. "Thanks. Oscar if you get anything else about that Camry, please let me know."

Mick and I were back in the cab of my truck, when I got a call from Jack. "Jonas, I just finished here at Gillian Motors."

"And what did Bob Gillian have to say about the car?"

Jack let out a light sigh. "When I got him to realize we could trace the car back to him and that it was involved in a homicide, he finally admitted the vehicle came from his property. He said he didn't know where it came from. He got a call from the yard manager, the same morning, Alston's body was discovered, saying the Camry was wedged between the other vehicles that were scheduled to go to Oscar's scrapyard. They were afraid of getting caught with a hot car, so they pawned it off on Oscar, thinking it would be his problem, then."

I leaned against the headrest. "That was cordial of them. Why not just call the police?"

"They realized the car matched the description we sent out and didn't want to get caught up in a police investigation."

Out of the frying pan into the fire. "Well, they're in it now."

"But I got some good news. They have security cameras on the front and they let me take a look at the footage, from the night of Alston's murder."

I felt a mild wave of jubilation. "Did you get a look at who brought in the Toyota?"

He let out a long sigh, which quickly shattered my expectations. "The camera didn't have a night lenses on it. You see an SUV pulling up to the trailer, with the Toyota pulling in behind it at 2:22 a.m., but there were too many shadows, to see who the drivers were."

I smacked the bottom of the steering wheel. "I suppose we couldn't be that lucky."

"Whoever it was, parked the car and got into the SUV, then they drove off. The whole thing took about a minute."

I thought about the situation, for a second, before coming to a decision. "Jack, call the VCPD and have them arrest Bob Gillian, for the transportation of stolen goods and hindering prosecution. It's their jurisdiction and we don't need any more animosity between our agencies right now."

"I already did that. Saul and Daniel are here right now taking him into custody."

I put my seatbelt on and started the engine. "Good work Jack. I'll see you back at the stationhouse."

"I've got more for you Jonas."

I sat back, letting the engine warm. "I'm listening."

"The cameras couldn't see the drivers, but the back end of the SUV was under the street light. I was able to make out the license plate."

I stared at my phone in frustration. "Why didn't you say that first?"

Jack let out another long sigh, which made the inside of my stomach feel as hollow as a steel drum. "Because, I figured I'd save the bad news, for last."

199

I lightly tapped my thumb on my cellphone. "How is finding the license plate a bad thing?"

"Because, after I ran the plates in the computer, they came back belonging to a silver 1998 Dodge Durango. The problem is, the record says, it's supposed to be at the county impound lot."

Chapter Sixteen

The Monroe County Impound Lot is located next to the Wil-Sav Drug store, just off of Niles Ferry Road. This is where impounded vehicles, for DUIs or abandoned cars are placed. Twice a year the vehicles and other property confiscated in arrests and seizures, are auctioned off, to make room and collect much needed revenue. There were motion sensors and security cameras on the lot, but no alarms had sounded, therefore there had been no report of a break in.

Jack and I arrived at the impound lot at the same time. Both of us spotted the silver Dodge parked ten yards away from the front gate. I left Mick in the truck and stood at the double gated entrance. The lock was set and didn't appear to have been tampered with, but when I checked the closest surveillance camera, I found they had been splattered with white paint, as if someone had fired a paintball gun at them. "I guess it's safe to say, we won't be getting any usable video footage from here."

Jack looked up at the cameras and shook his head. "Yeah, I guess whoever was monitoring the screens, at the security company, fell asleep at the wheel. How come the motion alarms didn't go off? Even with the camera's down, those should've still worked."

Using my ink pen, I went to the keypad and accessed the menu. I scrolled back to the access code menu and brought up the last entry code into the lot. I felt my shoulders droop with a binary sensation of confusion and disappointment. The number used was an old universal code, I had thought was deleted long ago. "Jack, you remember that old universal code that Bill had programmed into this thing, when it was first installed?"

His face grew stoic, in concentration, as he searched his memory. "I think so. Wasn't it 9499? Bill had the security company create it, when the alarm kept going off all the time. We had to use it for what? Three months?"

I shook my head. "Four. I thought it had been deactivated, but looks like I was wrong."

Jack placed his hands on his hips, as he looked at the key pad. "You mean that code is still active? That was nearly six years ago."

I nodded, exhaling a long breath. "I know. So now, we've got to decipher, who knew the code, who they told and who that person might've told."

Jack sighed and uttered a little chuckle. "Looks like we're going to be burning the midnight oil on this one."

It also looks like I might be breaking my promise to Lydia, but I kept that one to myself. "I have a feeling we're going to be burning several gallons of oil on this one."

My deputy nodded as he rested his hands in the pockets of his bomber jacket. "Okay. What's the plan?"

I looked to the keypad. "We dust this thing for prints first. I know they'll probably be a smorgasbord of smudges and partial prints, but we have to try. Maybe we'll get lucky. I doubt it though. The weather and elements will have taken their toll, plus our guys may have been using gloves, so I'd say it's next to nil on getting anything usable."

Jack nodded staring at the keypad. "It'll be a pain, but we really don't have a choice do we?"

I shook my head. "No we don't. After that, I'll get Tom up here to take a look. Let's hope that computer science degree of his can help us out."

Jack headed to the car, to retrieve his forensic field kit from the trunk. "That degree does come in handy."

I photographed the keypad, before Jack dusted for prints. There ended up being twenty-two different fingerprints, on the keypad, most of them partials. Some were smudged beyond recognition. We had to scale and mark each, for the record, which is one of the most tedious aspects of the job, that annoys even me. Once we had the fingerprints lifted and placed on individual evidence cards, Jack dusted the galvanized steel gate, but no discernable prints were discovered. I entered my access code, into the keypad, which released the lock.

The impound lot is covered in gravel, which extinguished any hope of finding any shoe impressions. I looked up at the cameras positioned around the lot and removed my BlackBerry to dial Tom's phone extension. "Deputy Kirk."

"It's me Tom, I need you to drop what you're doing and pull up the security feed to the impound lot. We've had a break in."

I could hear the ruffling sounds of papers being moved. "Someone broke into the impound lot? What did they take?"

"One of the SUVs was taken and returned. It looks like they shot a paintball capsule at the cameras, so I doubt we're going to get much from the video feed. Let's hope we get a glimpse of them before the camera lens was covered. When you're done with that, I'll need you to come down to the lot and run a diagnostic on the keypad. Whoever did this had a code. I want a record of all codes entered here, going back at least a month, to see if there may be a pattern."

"I'll get there, as soon as, I'm finished here," he said and hung up.

I put my phone back in my pocket and moved toward the SUV in question. The silver Dodge had a large dent in the front, which wrinkled the hood and cracked the front grill. There was a line of gravel parallel to the radiator, that was stained from a slow leak of antifreeze. The left headlight was busted, reminding me of the glass fragments, I had found at the crime scene, the day before. The fender well on the driver's side had a crack in it and there were traces, of what looked to be blood, on the hood. A quick examination through the window of the cab revealed tan leather seats, that had sweat stains along the edges, where the driver's arms had touched. The floor of the vehicle was faded and littered with flecks of dried grass, leaves and small pieces of gravel. I knelt over and examined the tires. "Jack, when you were at Gillian Motors, were there any tire tracks in mud?"

"They just had a fresh load of gravel. I think I remember seeing some clumps of mud on them, but I can't be sure. Why?"

"I need you to get over here and take some photographs please."

I heard his large feet, crunching the gravel, as he made his way over to me. As I repositioned myself, to ease the strain on my thighs. Jack grunted as he lowered himself to ground level. "What am I shooting?"

I pointed to the tread of the Bridgestone tire, where clumps of red clay clung to the exterior. "Take a few shots of these."

He did so as I placed an evidentiary scale next to them, for reference. I also asked him to take a picture of the wheel well, which looked like it had been painted dingy orange by the back spray of mud. Jack was giving me a quizzical look from the corner of his eye. When you live in Monroe County, mud on pickup trucks is the same as flies on manure. "I have my reasons for this Jack."

My deputy shrugged, as he rested the camera on top of his knee. "I've never known you to do anything, without a reason, Jonas."

I slowly stood, feeling the stiffness work out of my knees, as I flexed them to loosen the tendons. I moved to the back and found there was a hitch on the truck, with a two-inch ball attached. I knelt down once again, squinting my eyes, as I looked at the metal ball that had, what appeared to be, fresh marks on it. "Take a shot of the hitch, too."

I used my pen to identify the markings, as he snapped the photo. Jack scrolled through the pictures, to make sure the resolution was clear. "I take it you think the mud on the tire and markings on the hitch are connected, to the crime scene."

Jack had set his kit down, just to the side of the truck. I opened it and took a specimen jar and a disposable scalpel. "At the crime scene yesterday, there were tire tracks in the mud, from the presumed vehicle, that moved the house. This would've left a lot of mud in the tire well and the tread too."

I placed the specimen jar, under the tire and scraped a sample of the mud into the evidence jar. "This mud looks fairly fresh. I know what you're going to say, Jack. This entire valley is covered with red clay. But this specimen, takes on a different meaning, when you factor in the tool marks on the hitch."

I sealed the specimen jar and wrapped it in red evidence tape, before initialing and dating the white label on top of the black lid. Setting it beside the kit, I moved back to the hitch pointing to the markings around the base of the ball. "These markings look recent. There aren't any signs of corrosion or weathering inside them. Plus, look at how they wrap around the ball."

Jack bent over, eyes narrowed, as he looked at the scrapes. "Kind of like the markings a chain would make."

I nodded, as I stood up looking over at the United States flag flying over the Veteran's Flag Memorial, at Sunset Cemetery. The red, white, and blue fabric was damp and limp as it swayed with the breeze. "If that's the case, then not only was this vehicle used by the killers, to move the victim's car, it was used to kill him and possibly used, in disposing of his remains."

Jack shook his head and he looked at the truck for a long time. "I hate to say this, Jonas. But this is looking more and more like an inside job."

By inside job, he meant a cop, unfortunately, I had to agree with him.

* * *

After fingerprinting the outside of the doors, I opened the truck and took out the floor mat. Jack placed a large evidence bag over the mat before sealing it. We did the same for the passenger side floor mat. The forensic coveralls were at the stationhouse, so I improvised by using another sheet of plastic, to cover the seat, before getting behind the wheel. The first thing I noticed was, that my knees were rubbing against the dash. I'm a quarter of an inch shy of six feet, indicating there was a good chance that the driver, was probably around five feet nine inches. Of course the last driver could've pushed the seat up to throw us off, but it was something to keep in mind. A quick examination of the ignition switch, revealed how the vehicle was jimmied. From the scratches around the ignition, it appeared someone used a screwdriver or knife as a universal key. The keys that belong to this truck were locked in a safe, at the stationhouse, along with the other keys for the impounded vehicles. I lowered the sun visor and found it was empty. I did the same for the passenger side. I got out of the truck and peered under the seat, where I found a screwdriver lying on the carpet. Jack took a photograph, before we placed it in a plastic bag, to take back to the lab for fingerprints.

A quick examination of the glove box revealed nothing, save for the registration and owner's manual. I jotted down the mileage on the speedometer, before closing the door. I next moved to the interior of the back storage space, under the hatch. Compared to the outside exterior, it appeared to be cleaner. As if, someone had recently washed it. I drew closer to the interior and inhaled a breath of air, detecting a faint chlorinated aroma. "Jack, take a whiff and tell me what you smell."

Jack stuck his head over the tailgate and did a heavy sniff. "That smells like good old Clorox to me. Think this is where the body was put?"

I shrugged as we walked around the vehicle once again, searching for more anomalies. "I'd put money on it, if I were a betting man. The bleach will deteriorate any chance of DNA, but we'll have Molly go over it anyway. We might get lucky and she can pull something out of her hat."

The House Of Cards Murder

Jack started filling out the evidence report, shaking his shaved head in disbelief. "So if we're reading this right. Someone came in here, took the Durango and kidnapped Alston. They took him to the Winchell house, beat him and eventually ran him over with the Durango. Then they placed the deceased's body under the house and used the Durango to pull the house down on the body. They cleaned the bed with bleach, then brought the truck back to the lot."

I nodded, as I took the tape measure from the field kit. "It may not have been in that particular order, but it sounds about right."

Jack emitted a sardonic laugh. "Well, whoever it is, has a set of brass ones, I have to give them that."

It was a strong possibility Jack was right, about the assailant's fortitude. It could also be interpreted, that whoever we were looking for, was desperate enough to risk the break in, to get a vehicle that was untraceable. Extending the yellow metal tape to the edge of the tire, I measured the width and told Jack to put it in the report. "It's the same width as the tracks we found at the house yesterday."

Jack made the notation. "Can't say that wasn't to be expected."

Hearing the engine of a vehicle parking near my truck, I turned to see Tom exiting his cruiser. It was then I saw the fogged up windshield of my truck, and I remembered Mick was in there. It had only been about thirty minutes since we started processing the truck, but he gets restless, if he's alone in the cab for too long. Tom joined me at the passenger door, as I let Mick out. "I looked at the footage of video, but it's not going to tell us much. Like you said, someone used a paintball gun on the cameras."

I rubbed the dog's head and walked him over to the power pole near the side of the road, so he could do his business. "Were you able to make anything out?"

Tom's full lips dropped downward, as he placed his hands in his pockets. "There was one perp, who could be seen walking to the gate and punching in a code. From there he got into the Durango and drove off. That was at 10:30 p.m. the night of the murder.

Then at around 2:45 a.m., two people can be seen returning the vehicle. I was able to determine they were wearing ski masks and gloves. After they left the SUV, they closed the gate and moved out of the view of the camera. I'm almost sure I saw headlights flash somewhere on the lot, so there had to be another vehicle there, waiting for them."

I scratched the back of my head, recalling the autopsy report. "Thirty minutes to eleven, is close to the timeframe Karen said Alston died. One stole it, but two returned it you said? Were you able to tell their height from the truck?"

Tom shivered from the growing chill in the air. It was almost four o'clock and the sun was working its way toward the western ridge, where it would disappear in an hour. "The paint made that impossible. But I did see one of them, near the edge of the camera's range, where there was no paint and this individual appeared to have a small build. I just can't swear to it."

The seat adjustment of the truck came to mind, as I guided Mick back to the truck. "Other than the headlights, were you able to see anything, of the vehicle they were driving?"

Tom rolled his eyes. "You know we're not that lucky. It was just out of sight of the camera. It's like, they knew, where the blindspot was."

I reached down and rubbed Mick's head, as he lay near my leg. "I can't say that surprises me, at this point. Do what you can with the keypad. Maybe the codes will tell us something."

Tom turned to leave, but stopped. "Oh, I nearly forgot. Glen and I finally located Patrick Winchell and Harrison Birch."

Opening the door, I helped Mick into the passenger seat. "Where were they?"

Tom got a sardonic smile on his face. "Winchell was bunking on Birch's couch last night."

I shut the door and leaned into my truck. "So, they're each other's alibi. That's convenient."

Tom winked. "According to Mr. Birch, he said Patrick has been staying over at his place, for the last couple of days."

"Did he tell you that, before or after you told him the body was found under Winchell's old house?"

Tom hooked his thumbs under his belt. "We told them the body had been discovered in Vonore, but never mentioned the house. As soon as they heard that, Harrison gave his friend an alibi."

I drummed my fingers on the roof of the cab. "We had kept the details about the house out of the press, but the news of Alston's body being discovered, in Vonore, made the local papers and there was a segment on all three news networks last night. It wouldn't take Patrick long, to realize that we would be getting in touch with him."

"We got them to agree to come to the stationhouse, but they haven't been questioned yet."

I had two suspects at the stationhouse, but there was also a crime scene that needed to be processed here. It was against my nature, to leave an active scene, but in all honesty, there was very little else I could do here. I was barely proficient in computers, in this digital age. Tom could handle the keypad and Jack was more than capable of securing any more physical evidence, so that made the decision easy. "I'm going to head back to the stationhouse, to talk with Winchell and Birch. You and Jack finish up here. If you need anything call me."

* * *

After noting the time, I left the scene and headed to the stationhouse. Seated on the bench, near Jack's station was Patrick Winchell and Harrison Birch. From the annoyed expressions on their faces, I'd say they would've preferred to be visiting a proctologist. I decided to let them stew for a moment longer, as Mick and I moseyed over to Glen's desk. "Have our guests behaved themselves?"

Glen leaned back to stare at the two men, rolling his tongue around the inside of his lips and shaking his head. "For the most part.

They've been informing me of how I've been wasting the taxpayer's money. Then they gave me a few lovely annotations, about how I couldn't find a certain part of my anatomy, with both hands."

I gave him a lighthearted smile, as I sat on the edge of his desk. "Well, it's good to know that the classics are still around. Other than that, have they volunteered any useful information?"

"Only that they didn't have anything to do with Alston O'Brian's murder."

"We'll see about that."

I moved toward the two men, Mick beside me, frowning at Patrick and Harrison. "Gentlemen, I appreciate you coming in. I'll be speaking with you individually. Mr. Winchell, I'll begin with you. Mr. Birch, you can help yourself to a cup of coffee, while you wait."

Harrison and Patrick stared at one another, obviously taken aback by this development. Harrison ran his hands up and down the thighs of his blue jeans. "You want to speak with us separately? Wouldn't it be quicker, if you talked to us at the same time?"

I nodded, as I patted Mick's head. "Yes, it probably would, but right now I'm not so much concerned about the speed of things, as I am, about getting to the truth. So Mr. Winchell, please follow me to my office."

Mick and I walked into the office, where the big dog, immediately took his customary seat, in the chair in front of my desk. Patrick followed tepidly behind me, glancing around the office, as if he was stepping into a lion's den. I hung my coat on the rack by the door and pointed to the only remaining vacant chair. "Take a seat sir."

Patrick looked at Mick for a moment, before he grabbed the wooden chair and moved it a few inches away from him. "If the dog makes you uncomfortable, I can have him wait outside, Mr. Winchell."

He adjusted himself in the chair, slowly rotating his shoulders, while shaking his head. "No, it's all right."

I opened my bottom drawer and pulled out a yellow sheeted legal pad. "Would you like something to drink, before we begin?"

"I'm good. I am wondering, if I need to have a lawyer here."

I took out my pen and put the time and date, along with Patrick's name on the top line. "That is your right. If you want, we can wait until your attorney arrives and then we can proceed."

He looked at the edge of my desk, his forehead wrinkled in thought. I waited with my hands resting on the legal pad and Mick laid his head on the armrest and closed his eyes. After a half minute went by, I asked him again, if he wished to have his attorney present. Patrick let out a long sigh and leaned back in the seat. "No. I've done nothing wrong, so let's get this over with."

"Very well. This inquiry is about the death of Alston O'Brian. From what my deputies have told me, you seemed to be expecting us."

He was gently gripping his kneecap through his blue jeans, as he nodded. "It's been on the news and the local papers. It doesn't take a genius, to figure out why you guys were there. I'll tell you right now, I'm not sad that old man is dead, but I had nothing to do with it."

I wrote this down. "We still have to ask you some questions. Especially, since you were in an altercation with the victim, a short time before his death."

Patrick's jaw locked and his eyes took on a hard glint. "You mean, when you stopped my friend, from giving that no good thief, the ass whooping he deserved?"

I kept my face impotent of any emotion, but wrote down animate anger and circled it. "Yes I do. It's no secret you and Alston had a history."

Patrick shook his head. "That morning, in Hardees, was the first time I had ever met the man, face to face."

I looked at him, allowing a moment of silence to build between us, before pressing on. "Do you know where the body was discovered, sir?"

He hunched his shoulders, while simultaneously shaking his head. "Yeah, in Vonore. It seems kind of poetic, that he died in the very town he ripped apart."

"His remains were found underneath a house on Church Street."

I watched, as his face became a mask of confusion. "Under a house? You mean it was a house trailer?"

I shook my head, gently tapping the tip of my pen on the legal pad. "No. The house was on braces, ready for removal. In fact, it's been sitting up on braces ever since the bank foreclosed on it, some time back."

His brown eyes expanded and his bottom jaw dropped. "You don't mean he was found under my family's house do you?"

"I'm afraid, that is exactly what I mean Patrick. And before you say it is just a coincidence, understand I know that Alston ripped off your father's employer, which caused him to lose the house."

Patrick inhaled a deep breath and released it slowly. He repeated this action twice before speaking. "It also led to my father dying from a stroke and my mother leaving us."

"I'm sorry for your loss, Patrick. But it also, indicates that you have a more extended history with Alston, than just the confrontation at Hardees."

He raised his hands in mock surrender. "All right. You got me. The son-of-a-bitch destroyed my family. But I wasn't the only one in town that hated him."

I shook my head, as I pointed at his chest. "No sir, but it was your family home, his body was discovered under."

He spat out a gust of breath, stomping his foot on the floor, causing Mick to jump up and frown at him. "If I was going to kill the man, do you think I would be stupid enough, to leave his body under my house, where you could easily link it back to me?"

"No one is accusing you of murder, Mr. Winchell. But you understand, why I have to ask for your whereabouts on the day, before yesterday."

Patrick slowly lowered his head. "I already told your deputies where I was."

I held out my hand palm up. "Then it should be no problem, for you, to now tell me. Please, be as precise as you can."

He leaned forward and rested his hand on the edge of my desk. "I worked overtime, that day, from seven in the morning until six that evening at the Phizser Pharmaceutical factory. I then went to the Teddy Bear for a lousy cheeseburger and a warm stale beer around 6:30 p.m. I left there around eight. I met up with Harry at The Laffing Goat around 8:45 p.m., where we remained until closing time. From there I spent the night at Harry's place, on the couch and the next morning I went home, for a quick shower, before going to work. I spent the better part of the weekend there."

I dictated all he said, pausing a moment to read over the statement. I could hear Patrick's respiration slowly accelerate, as he waited. "Is it normal for you to spend the night on Harrison Birch's couch?"

The wooden chair moaned, as Patrick leaned back. He kept his eyes focused on me, like he was trying to burn me out of existence. When I looked at him, I pretended not to notice. "I wouldn't say it's normal, but from time to time, I do stay over. Besides, I wasn't in the mood to listen to Justine read me the riot act."

"Justine?"

"My girlfriend. We've been arguing a lot lately. I didn't want to hear her preach to me about my drinking, so I decided it was best, that I spend the night somewhere else."

"Did Justine see you, when you returned for a shower, before going to work?"

He snorted out a quick gust of air. "Yeah, but she didn't say a word to me. Made a point of letting me know she wasn't talking to me, if you know what I mean."

Every man does, but that was a moot point. "What time did you arrive at your house?"

He shrugged. "Maybe 6:10 a.m. Somewhere around then."

I flipped to clean page and wrote down Justine. "I need your address and the girlfriend's last name."

From the way his forehead wrinkled, you would've thought, I had asked for the keys to the kingdom. "Why do you need to know Justine's last name?"

"It's just to verify, you were at your place of residence, when you said you were."

Rolling his eyes upward, Patrick laughed emphatically, before looking at me again. "Do we really need to involve her in this? Things are rough enough, without having the police involved."

I placed my hands on top of the legal pad, staring at him. "Sir, I know this is intrusive, but—"

"You're damn right it's intrusive and an invasion of my privacy. I mean when you talk to Harrison, he'll tell you, that I spent the night at his place, so why not leave it at that?"

Ignoring the redundancy of his remarks, I lay my pen down and aligned my arms with the armrests. "Mr. Winchell, I know you don't like this and a part of me understands why. But the fact remains, I have a murder to solve. So, the sooner we can check you off the list, the sooner we will stop bothering you."

The hinges of his jaws contracted, as he grinded his teeth. You didn't need to be a detective, to realize he was using all of his willpower, to avoid screaming at the top of his lungs. I suppose, if the roles were reversed, I'd feel the same way. No one likes a stranger coming into their lives and poking around, but that is exactly what this situation calls for. After a few seconds, Patrick's shoulders seemed to relax, as he looked toward the door and exhaled a short breath. "Fine man, have it your way. Her name's Justine Kymel. She's at work now, but she gets off at 5:30."

I wrote the time down. "Where does she work?"

"She works at The Alternative Way, across from O'Reilly's."

"The holistic medicine shop?"

Rolling his eyes again, Patrick rubbed the bottom of his nose with the back of his finger. "Yeah, she's in to all those herbal remedies and the aligning of the chive energy."

I looked up and shook my head. "I believe you mean chi."

"That too. She's all the time saying, I need to release the negative energy that's inside me. Says my anger at Alston O'Brian is stifling my inner life. Whatever the hell that means."

I looked at him, rubbing my chin with the tip of the pen. "Was it Alston O'Brian that the two of you were arguing about?"

Patrick rolled his tongue inside his cheek and he nodded emphatically. "Ever since the fight at Hardees. Justine kept saying I needed to forgive him and move on, but she don't understand. Some feelings don't go away, no matter how hard you try. There ain't no prayer, or natural remedy, that can make it go away."

Since he had opened the door to his state of mind, I felt it was only natural for me to ask the next question. "Did you kill him, Patrick?"

His lower lip trembled, as his left heel tapped a silent Morse code on the tile floor, before he shook his head. "No. A part of me wanted to kill him. But…I didn't have the balls, I guess. It's like I said before sheriff; I'm not sorry he's dead, but I didn't kill him."

I set the tip of my pen on the legal pad and slowly spun it around. "Have you heard the rumors, about the cash, that Alston had allegedly stashed away before his arrest?"

Patrick scoffed, shaking his head. "Oh yeah. *The O'Brian Treasure* is what it was called, there for a while. It doesn't exist sheriff."

"Still though, it would be an added incentive."

He slouched back in his seat, tilting his head over his right shoulder. "What good would that money do? My parents would still be split up. My dad dead. Our home foreclosed on. Honestly sheriff, what good would any of that money do me or Harry?"

"How did Mr. Birch seem that night?"

He shrugged as he pursed his lips. "Same as usual."

I made one more note with my pen. "Where were you last Friday?"

This seemed to have caught him off guard. "Huh? How does last Friday have anything to do with the old man's murder?"

"Please answer the question Mr. Winchell."

"The weather gave me an excuse to play hooky from work. I called in, saying my car was acting up and the roads were too slick. It was Harrison's day off, so went along some of the back roads and watched the deer out in the fields."

I analyzed his statement on the paper, for a moment, before looking at him. "Deer? You spent the day looking for deer?"

He nodded. "Yeah. They come out more in the wintertime, looking for food."

"You remember what roads you took?"

He shook his head. "Not really. Just sort of drove around. Saw a good sized buck out there. Wished I had my rifle with me."

I started making doodles with my pen. "And I'm sure Harrison will confirm this."

He pursed his lips and nodded. "Yes sir."

I leaned back in my seat resting my hands on the armrests. "If you wouldn't mind Patrick, hold up both of your hands, so I can see them, please."

After a brief pause, he acquiesced, holding them up, palms out. "The backs too, please."

He swiveled them around, revealing no scratches or bruises. Someone had repeatedly hit Alston with their fists. Even with gloves, there would've been some bruising on their hands. "Thank you. I'll need you to stay in town Patrick. I may have more questions for you. If you wouldn't mind, ask Mr. Birch to come in."

He got up to leave, but I stopped him at the door. "One last thing, remind me what kind of vehicle do you drive."

Standing with his hand on the doorknob, Patrick turned around. "A GMC Sonoma. Why?"

"What color is it?"

"Blue."

"May we take a look at it?" I asked writing down the information.

He stuck his chin out at me and opened the door to leave. "You want to search my truck? Get a warrant, sheriff."

* * *

Harrison Birch was the next contestant. Mr. Harrison entered the room, with his head held high and his shoulders squared. Stopping in front of my desk, his hands clasped behind his back, Harrison looked down on me with expressionless eyes. "Sheriff Lauer."

I returned his stare, sitting relaxed in my seat. "Please have a seat Mr. Birch."

He kept his gaze focused on me and his voice firm. "I'm comfortable standing, if that is all right."

I recall, reading somewhere awhile back, about tactical advantages, of how to conduct yourself in an interview. One way to turn the tables, was to stand above your subject, so they were looking up at you. It had something to do with people feeling intimidated, by looking up at an individual, who is standing in a position of power. I don't know if that was Harrison's game here, but I didn't care to play along with it right now. "I would appreciate it, if you took a seat, Mr. Birch."

Moving to the vacant chair, Harrison sat down, keeping his profile rigid. I pretended to not notice his gaze, as I wrote his name at the top of a clean page of the legal pad. "We need to know where you were the night before last, Mr. Birch."

He crossed his leg, stacking his hands on his thigh. "I don't work weekends, so I spent the day home alone. I got restless that night, so I went to Krystal for supper at 7:30 p.m. Then I met up with Pat at the Laffing Goat, just before nine and we stayed there until closing. He'd had one too many and was arguing with his girlfriend again, so I let him sleep it off on my couch."

"And what time was it, you arrived home with Mr. Winchell?" I asked, scribbling what he said in my chicken scratch writing.

He shrugged. "I'd say it was around 2:30 a.m."

"And where do you work, Mr. Birch?"

"I operate the forklift at the Amazon.Com factory in Athens. I work the twelve-hour shift, from seven to seven. You can speak with the floor supervisor, Terry Gibson, to verify."

I wrote this down, as the courthouse clock chimed. "Had you intended to meet up with Mr. Winchell that evening?"

"No sir. We just happened to bump into one another that night."

I wrote down unintended meeting and underlined it. "And the two of you were together from the time you met in the bar, until you returned to your home."

Harrison nodded, as he licked his dried lips. "Yes sir."

I flipped over to another sheet of paper and smoothed out the creases. "What did the two of you talk about?"

This seemed to cause him to pause for a moment, in order to think about his response. "What does that have to do with anything?"

I waved my hands, like it was no big deal. "It just gives me a sense of what state of mind the two of you were in. Was Mr. Winchell in good spirits?

The question seemed to amuse Harrison, as he blew out a sardonic sigh, while shaking his head. "No, I wouldn't say that. He and his girlfriend got into a fight and Pat needed to blow off some steam. Again."

The ringing of the crossties from the railroad tracks could be heard, as a train from out of Sweetwater passed through town. "Am I to understand, that it's not uncommon for Mr. Winchell and his girlfriend to have disagreements."

"Try every other week."

I slowly rotated my pen between my forefinger and thumb, as I reviewed my notes. "Patrick said on that night, at the Laffing Goat, he and his girlfriend had an argument about Alston O'Brian. Did the two of you talk about him?"

His chest inflated, as he drew in a deep breath and set his feet flat on the floor. "I wondered when you were going to get to the point. Yeah, Pat talked about Alston O'Brian. There isn't any law against that."

I nodded, continuing to roll the ink pen between my fingers. "For talk? No. Murder? Yes."

If he was worried, that he might be implicated in a murder investigation, he gave an award winning performance of not showing it. Harrison merely gave his head a slight shake, as he once again crossed his legs. "But all we did was talk."

"There was more than talking going on that morning at Hardees Mr. Birch. Things got violent very quickly."

His left foot, which was dangling loosely over his right leg, began to shake back and forth. "I admit tempers got the better of us that day, but no one got seriously hurt."

I felt my left eyebrow elevate, despite myself. "The only reason no one got seriously hurt is because my deputy and I intervened."

He held out his hands. "Like I said, tempers got out of control."

"With all due respect, you threw the man into the wall. Your friend didn't do anything to discourage you from attacking Alston, that day."

The muscles along his neck, grew taut. He swallowed hard, his Adams apple bobbing, as he licked his lips. "Pat's my friend, but not my keeper."

I wrote down what he said. Harrison was turning out to be an interesting individual. The man attacked Alston one day, but claims it was no big deal, despite the fact the man is now dead. "How long have you and Mr. Winchell known each other?"

"About nineteen years."

It didn't take long for me to do the math. "You two first met around the time Alston came to town?"

"At his sentencing hearing, to be precise." He stared at the floor for a moment, before clearing his throat and returning his gaze to me. "Dad was too embarrassed to be there. He barely had it in him to testify. He lost all of his spirit after what Alston did to him. I felt someone from our family should be there to see that man go to jail. Though, it wasn't nearly long enough. Pat was there too. None in his family were directly involved with Alston, but he left his mark on them anyway. We got to talking and we've been friends ever since."

"How did it make you feel, when you heard that Alston O'Brian had been released?"

A smirk developed on his lips, as he scratched the top of his head. "Like any red blooded man would feel, sheriff. *Angry*. The man destroyed people. My father died from it. It may not have held up in a court of law, but he killed my dad and he gets to walk free. Wearing those slick clothes and driving that nice car. The man had no decency at all."

"Do you think the stories were true about the missing money?"

He seesawed his head back and forth emphatically. "*I* never really believed it. But it sure would explain how he could afford all those nice things."

I made a reference to this, as I moved on to the natural follow up question. "Did it make you curious?"

The foot he had been shaking, began to move faster. "You mean, did it make me curious enough to kill him?"

I rested my chin on my interlaced fingers. "Revenge and money, are two of the most popular reasons for murder, Mr. Birch. It is amazing how often the two intertwine."

He continued to shake his foot, as he cupped his knee with his hand. "I've been hearing about that money for years, sheriff. Like most people, I've wondered if it was true, but it doesn't really matter if it was, because neither me nor Pat killed him."

"Can you give me any reason, as to why, someone would put Alston's body underneath Patrick Winchell's old family home?"

His mouth opened in surprise. "It was Pat's father's house he was found under?"

There was something off in his tone of voice. A lack of conviction. "Yes sir, it was. Can you think of why someone would do that?"

He started to say something, but then thought better and instead cleared his throat. "That isn't my job sheriff. It's yours."

I nodded and pointed to his hands. "Let me see your hands, please."

He held them up, flipping them back and forth, so I could see no marks on them. "Is there anything else?"

"Yes. Where were you last Friday?"

He stared at the door. "Me and Pat went out looking for some deer. Saw a buck and a few does."

I paused, to think about what he had said. "Was it because of the weather that you missed work?"

Harrison nodded, hunching his shoulders. "Sort of. We decided to play hooky and used it as an excuse."

"The roads were slick, but obviously not so bad to prevent you from cruising for deer?"

He rubbed his thighs with the palms of his hands, as the flesh of his face grew crimson. "We waited until the ice melted, before we left."

I took a moment to examine my notes. "One more thing for now. What kind of vehicle do you drive?"

"A Mazda B2300."

I scribbled this down. "What color is it?"

"Green."

I wrote this down and underlined it. "May we examine it?"

Smiling he got up and put his hand in his blue jean pocket. "Sure. Right after you get a warrant. That all, now?"

I returned his smile, as I too stood. "Yes, but stay in town, please. I'm sure we'll have more questions."

I waited until he had left the stationhouse, before I walked to the glass doors to watch him get into his truck. Once Harrison was pulling out of the parking lot, I went to the monitor room and brought up the survelliance footage around the stationhouse. I got a clear image of the truck and printed a copy of it, to see if Harrison Birch's truck matched the one that Apostle Phil had seen tailing Alston.

Chapter Seventeen

After Harrison and Patrick left, I asked Glen to check out their statements, to verify their alibis. Two hours later I had Tom and Jack sitting in my office, with Anthony Deland on speakerphone. I told him about the Toyota Camry being found at Horton Recycling and that a Dodge Durango used, to pull the braces from under the house, most likely was stolen from the county impound lot. I also informed him the perpetrators also used the Durango to dispose of the Camry at Gillian Motors.

"Do we know that the Camry is definitely Alston's car?" Anthony asked.

Jack leaned forward in his seat. "Yes sir. The vehicle identification number matches the registration, that is in Alston O'Brian's name."

"Where did he purchase the car?" asked the solicitor.

"He bought the car at Denton's Used Cars, just south of Meigs County," Jack replied "He paid nineteen thousand cash, right there, on the lot, on January eighteenth."

There was a brief pause, as Anthony's seat whined from his movements. "He paid nineteen thousand cash, just two days after his release?"

Jack rested his hands on top of his knees, as he leaned closer to the phone. "That's what the owner said. They will fax us the paperwork, first thing in the morning."

Anthony let out a long sigh. "How sure are you that the truck, in the impound lot, was used in the disposing of the Camry?"

I ran my fingers along the top of my desk. "There isn't any doubt about that Anthony. The license plate was visible on the security cameras at Gillian Motors. And there is 57.4 miles more on the speedometer."

Anthony's chair squeaked again. "How can you tell that?"

"Whenever we impound a vehicle, we do an inventory of its contents and check the mileage. When the Dodge was impounded, it had 123,341.8 miles on it. Now it has 123,399.2 miles," I replied.

"What is this about, it being used, to pull the house down?"

With Jack and Tom occupying both seats, Mick was lying by my leg. He raised his head, nudging my knee. I rubbed his crown as I spoke. "There was fresh mud on the truck. And the width between the tires matches the tracks found at the scene. I've got the car at the lab now, where Molly's going over it, with a fine tooth comb. If there's a trace on the Durango, she'll find it."

Anthony was silent for a while, before asking, "How did they get into the impound lot, without setting off the alarm?"

All three of us looked at each other, equally dreading this next part. Since it was my responsibility, I was the one who answered. "It appears the thieves had a pass code for the alarm system, Anthony."

"Now what?"

I explained about the universal pass code and how we didn't realize it was still active. "This was before I was sheriff, Anthony. But it's still on me, for not checking it out."

"Man, this just keeps getting better and better. Did the cameras get any pictures of the thieves?"

I lowered my head, massaging the skin between my eyes, with the pad of my thumb. "They shot the cameras with paintballs. Even if they hadn't, they wore ski masks."

Anthony's voice ascended two octaves. "How come we weren't alerted about the cameras being inactivated?"

I pointed to the phone, as if he was there in the room with us. "That was the responsibility of the security company, the county hired. To save money, the county commission contracted with a company in Athens, to cover the departments property, instead of using a local company. Whoever was watching, dropped the ball big time. I'm recommending, that we drop their contract and route the video feed here to the stationhouse"

The solicitor released an audible gust of air, as he slapped his desk. "What good does that do us now? We still don't know which cop was involved in the theft."

I raised my head, so the microphone could hear me clearer. "That's not true sir."

"What do you mean?"

"Deputy Tom Kirk can explain it better than me, Anthony, so I'm handing it over to him."

Tom cleared his throat and scooted to the edge of his seat. "I ran a diagnostic on the keypad, Mr. Deland. From the timestamp on the cameras and the clock on the keypad, we know that the thieves entered the impound lot at 10:30 p.m. Now, everyone here knows, we're most likely looking for a cop, but there is also a way to eliminate a lot of them."

"I'm listening."

Tom clasped his hands together, as he cleared his throat. "All of our cars and police issued mobile devices have GPS on them. We need to obtain a list of everyone, who was on duty the night the SUV was stolen and track their whereabouts. That'll eliminate quite a few officers right there."

The line was dead again, for a few moments. "Yeah, it would. But which department are you going to check?"

I decided to get back into the conversation. "All of them, Anthony. It's the only we can say, we were impartial. Anyone who knew that code is a viable suspect."

Anthony discharged another deep breath, his chair squeaking once again. "But we do know which department is at the top of the list, sheriff."

I looked at my deputies, who were all nodding in agreement. "Yes sir, we do. With all of this going on and it looking more and more like a police officer is involved, I feel I have to put the option of calling the T.B.I. on the table."

Emitting another long sigh, Anthony took a long moment to consider my proposal. "I'd really like to keep this in house, if possible, Jonas."

"I'm not a fan of the idea either, Anthony, but given the circumstance we find ourselves in, we have to consider it."

The room was silent, save for the sound of Mick's panting. After a while, I was beginning to wonder if we had lost the connection, when Anthony finally spoke. "Before we make that call, let's see what Ms. Newman turns up from her investigation. I also want to see what Deputy Kirk's idea yields. If it doesn't help narrow the field any, then we call the T.B.I. in."

I wasn't quite sure how I felt about his decision. I've always been a proponent of keeping as much work, as we can, in house. Early in this investigation I was insistent on keeping it that way. However, with the evidence pointing to law enforcement officers, confiscating police property, for their own nefarious enterprises, I'm wondering if some outside help might be needed. For now though, I opted to go with Anthony's decision. "If that's how you want to play it, we'll go along sir. Tom get started on tracking the GPS coordinates. Jack go over all the surveillance footage again, to see if anything was overlooked."

My deputies nodded and left my office. Anthony was about to hang up. "Well, I guess I need to let you get to work, sheriff."

I stood up, stepped over Mick and closed the office door. "Wait a moment Anthony, I need to talk to you for another second."

"What about?"

I took the receiver off the cradle and turned off the speaker. "I spoke with the warden from Alston's prison. He had terminal cancer, with only a few months to live. She also informed me that she told this to you."

For a few moments all I heard was a buzz from the overhead fluorescent light. "That's right. Ms. King did inform me about his medical condition."

I tightened my fingers on the phone, before relaxing them, slowly nodding. "May I ask, why you didn't inform me of this?"

"I guess I didn't see the relevance of it, sheriff."

I sat back, thumbing the phone cord. "You didn't think it was odd, a man who was terminally ill, would come back to the very place that led to his imprisonment?"

"When it comes to people's personal motivations, there is no telling what drives them, sheriff. I assumed the money was his reason, for coming back to town."

I was slowly curling the phone cord around my finger. "So you believe the stories, about the money, are true?"

"I have no proof it exists, if that's what you mean. Why else would Alston return here? He had to have known there would still be people here, who resented him. Why else risk it? The money could be the motive, for his murder."

His words mimicked my own thoughts on the case and that scenario was entirely plausible. Yet, when it seems everyone involved in this case is holding something back from me, skepticism, becomes second nature. "I suppose it could be. Right now I need to have two warrants to impound and search Patrick Winchell and Harrison Birch's trucks."

"You think they might be our guys?"

"I can't rule them out Anthony. They both had motive to kill Alston. We also have a statement from a witness, who says he saw a green truck following Alston, a few days before his disappearance. Plus, both men were involved in the altercation in Vonore, just days before Alston's murder."

"Say no more. Get the paper work on my desk and I'll get a judge to sign it."

"It'll be on your desk in an hour." I paused, as I had one more bit of bad news to deliver. "There's one more thing, Anthony."

There was a delay in his reply, like he didn't want to ask. "What sheriff?"

I flexed my fingers along the phone, before gripping it tighter. "We looked into the history of the Dodge Durango to discover the reason it was impounded. Turns out it was placed there after a DUI bust late last year. The arresting officer was Chief Saul West."

"Jesus, this just keeps getting better. Who else knows about this?"

"As of right now, you and my deputies. We're going to keep a lid on it, until we see how it all plays out."

Anthony blew out another long sigh, followed by a groan. "Lord, I hope Saul's not involved in this mess."

"We don't know anything yet, Anthony. Let's see what Tom's investigation yields, before we get ahead of ourselves."

"You're right. You're right. Keep going and call if you need anything."

I hung up the phone and stared at it for a few seconds, still unsure of what I thought about the prosecuting attorney's omission, concerning Alton's medical condition. It appeared there wasn't anyone on the investigative front of this case, who didn't have something to hide, save for me and my deputies.

I got the paperwork started on the search authorizations and sixty minutes later, I handed them to a trustee, who walked them over to the courthouse. It was now 4:47 p.m., meaning the judges were gone for the day. It would be morning before we'd get the warrants signed.

I spent another hour reviewing all of the statements and reports, when Jack knocked on the door. "Jonas, Warden King called and said she can set up a video conference with Max Brandon at 10:00 in the morning, if that's all right with you."

I nodded, stretching my arms. "Call her back and tell her I'll be ready."

"Yes sir."

"Before you leave, Jack in the morning I want you to conduct a little experiment for me."

He rested his hands on his belt, as he squared his shoulders. "What experiment?"

"I want you to find out how many miles it is from the county impound lot, to the crime scene. Then note the mileage, from there to Gillian Motors."

Jack bobbed his head, shifting his weight to his left foot. "You want to see, if that mileage will match the difference between the recorded mileage, at the time the Durango was impounded, with the mileage it now shows."

"I do. Use as many routes as you can think of to do so. My guess is, whoever stole the truck, kept to the backroads, as much as possible, but check every route and write the mileage down."

He gave me a salute, before leaving my office. "I'll get on it first thing."

I looked over at Mick, who had reassumed his rightful spot in the guest chair. He zeroed those dark brown eyes on me and let out a long sigh, letting me know that he was bored and ready to go home. There wasn't much more I could do at the office, so I placed all the casefiles in a folder. Mick raised his head, his tail wagging, when he saw me put on my coat. "Come on boy. Let's go home."

Mick had just settled in the passenger seat, when Jack called out. "Wait up Jonas."

I turned to find Jack, Glen, and Tom running out of the stationhouse, their jackets zipped and heading for their cruisers. "What's going on?"

Jack got out his keys and opened the door to the white Sheriff's department SUV. "We just got a call from the custodian at the courthouse, saying that someone has stolen the Ten Commandments from the storage room."

My chin fell to my chest. "Don't tell me."

"The custodian made it to the window just in time, to see Gary Dawson, get in his Jeep with the commandments and drive off."

I gave him a hard stare, as I got behind the wheel of my truck. "Didn't I tell you not to tell me?"

* * *

We arrived at the courthouse, in less than a minute. Glen was the first to spot Gary's blue Jeep Cherokee. "The suspect is heading north, down Warren Street," he said over the radio.

Glen and Jack turned to follow him, while Tom and I took Tellico St. to run parallel to him. I spotted him just as he drove past White's Marble Works. I pressed the accelerator and grabbed the microphone. "I see him. I'm going to try and cut him off on Deacon St."

"Roger that," Glen replied.

I got to Deacon St. and turned in front of O'Reilly's Auto, where some of the customers had come out, to see what the commotion was about. Just as I made it to the end of the street, Gary cut the turn hard and passed me, using the auto parts store parking lot. Glen and Tom followed him. I saw in the rearview mirror, Gary had turned to head north, so I floored the accelerator and headed in that direction on Warren Street. "Be advised, the suspect is heading toward Highway 411," Jack said on the radio.

I came around the curve in time to see Gary pass the Madisonville Cemetery, heading for the bypass, that would put him onto the highway. I had my light bar on, casting blue and black shadows over the road, as I gained some speed. Mick was sitting up, his tongue hanging out, dripping droplets on the leather seat cover, which I had purchased for that very reason. He swallowed hard and let out a bark, as we proceeded down the road.

Traffic was light on the highway, so Gary was able to merge onto the road with little effort. When the deputies and I reached the double lane, we started making some speed. Gary, so far, was able to keep his Cherokee four car lengths ahead of us, but he had to stop and swerve over to the right lane, when an oversized truck started to turn into the Dollar General Store parking lot. This allowed us to gain some much needed territory. Glen was able to barely miss the truck's front bumper and actually pass Gary's Cherokee. Jack pulled up beside Gary, allowing me and Tom to pull in behind him. I turned on the loudspeaker of my radio and brought the mike to my mouth. "Pull over and turn off your vehicle, right now."

Gary didn't slow down. In fact, he tried to sideswipe Jack, but the deputy didn't give any ground. I took this to mean he wasn't going to comply peacefully, so I decided it was time, for a more aggressive approach. I glanced over at Mick as I tightened my seatbelt. "It's time to get ugly, so hold on boy."

I pressed down on the gas and brought the ram bar on my truck into contact with Gary's back bumper and kept it there. Mick jumped up in his seat, emitting a short bark, before sitting up in the seat and whimpering. I unhooked the microphone and pressed the talk button. "Pull over and shut off your vehicle."

Gary swerved his car to the left and made contact with Jack's SUV, causing him to swerve into the passing lane. Thankfully no one was there, but I believe being hit, irritated the usual affable deputy. Jack turned his wheel hard to the right, hitting the front fender of Gary's Jeep. Gary didn't like being attacked from two fronts, so he made a hard right into the parking lot of the Mexi Wing restaurant, and took Tyler Road that led to Niles Ferry Road.

Tires shrieking along the pavement, I took a hard turn and gave chase. Mick almost fell out of the seat, from the sudden shift in gravity. Watching as Gary turned onto Niles Ferry, I could see Tom was still on 411, waiting to follow Glen and Jack. I took the microphone to the CB and pressed the button. "Tom, double back to 411 Chapel

Baptist Church. He's heading south on Niles Ferry. You might be able to cut him off."

"Ten four."

I continued in pursuit, quickly catching up with Gary's Jeep. I spotted my deputies' lights reflecting in the rearview mirror and tried my best, not to marvel at the ridiculousness, of the situation. A sheriff, his dog, and three deputies were chasing a man, who stole a copy of the Ten Commandments, from the courthouse. I knew somewhere in all this convolution, there was the makings of a great country song.

I was a car length from Gary, when we arrived at the intersection, where Niles Ferry feeds into Highway 411. Thankfully, just as he was about turn, Tom came roaring up the hill, forcing Gary to turn left. Tom was right behind, him and I followed, with Glen and Jack finishing the caravan.

At the top of the hill, the road divides into two directions. One was toward Ball Play Road, the other was Sunset Cemetery. Gary appeared to be veering left towards Ball Play, but a supersized truck stopped him. The roads in this part of the county are narrow, so he had no way to pass the truck, forcing him to turn right, into the cemetery.

This road also feeds onto Ball Play Road and I have no doubt, that is where Gary intended to go, but a hazard of the cold temperatures, had caused limbs from the older trees surrounding the cemetery, to fall onto the road. Unfortunately for Gary, one was now blocking his escape. He turned right, cutting it short and actually tracking through the cemetery. Fortunately, Haven Hill, is lined with flat, ground level gravestones. With Tom directly behind him, I turned right onto the paved side road, which curved around to a junction in the cemetery. I made it there just as Gary was about to turn, forcing him to keep going west towards the cul-de-sac rotary.

It was here, I felt for certain, Gary would stop, but he decided to follow the rotary, with Tom behind him. For a few seconds, I had to watch from the cab of my truck, as the two vehicles continued on their orbit around the rotary, that was no more than two hundred feet in circumference. Finally, having enough, when Gary and Tom had passed for their sixth lap, I moved my truck into the line of fire. Gary, realizing what I had done, braked hard, his tires squealing, as he slid to a stop, just an inch from hitting my truck. Tom did the same, but turned his cruiser so Gary couldn't back up.

Once again we had all underestimated the tenacity of Gary Dawson. Throwing open the driver's door, he ran down the hill, with the framed commandments in hand. I put my truck in park, and gave chase with the rest of my posse behind me. I must've left the driver's door open, because soon Mick was trotting beside me. Gary was headed to the Veterans Flag Memorial, constructed in 1995, where the second largest United States flag in Tennessee, waved two hundred feet in the sky, as a salute for all, who had perished in war from Monroe County. Each of the brick used, to create the monument, had the name of a soldier from the county who had served in the Armed Forces.

Gary set the frame on top of the wall, before climbing up on the ledge. The wall borders a steep drop off, which leads directly onto highway 411. One slip and Gary could find himself in the north bound lane, directly in the path of a car, going forty-five miles an hour. I held up my hand, for the others to stop. "Gary, you need to come down from there."

He held the Ten Commandments above his head, like he was Sally Field in "Norma Rae". "Someone has to do something sheriff. If you don't have the guts to do so, then it's up to me."

Mick was sitting beside me, with his head rotated to the left, staring up at the man. I was glad to know I wasn't the only one confused. "Do what Gary? What is the plan here?"

"The," he paused to burp, his legs swaying in the wind, as he stumbled to the right.

I closed my eyes, as I leaned into the flagpole. "Gary, are you drunk?"

He placed the frame in front of him, like a shield and pointed his finger at me. "Don't try to change the subject sheriff. This nation was founded on these principles. They should be displayed with honor and not covered with a musty sheet, hid in a storage closet."

The red, white, and blue banner was flapping in the wind, sending small concussive waves down the pole, vibrating my hand. I looked up at the stars and took a deep breath, wishing I was anywhere but here at this moment. I moved closer to Gary, my hands on my hips and stared up at him. "Gary, you know where the law stands on this. So, other than a grand chase, what did you hope to accomplish tonight? You had to know that we'd catch you."

He tapped the glass on the frame, swaying in the wind, while I waited, certain he was going to fall backwards, at any moment. "This is the first step to getting back to the principles that this country was founded upon."

I stood there, feeling anger rising in my chest, constricting the muscles along my neck and shoulders, as the words he was saying became all jumbled in my head. I got to thinking about all of the paperwork, we were going to have to fill out, about the theft and chase through Madisonville. All of this because of a man who can't accept the fact, that we have to comply with the law, so he got liquored up and stole state property. Adding more to the irony, is the fact that Gary wanted the country to go back to God's laws, but the word God isn't mentioned in the Constitution of the United States. Thomas Paine, George Washington, Benjamin Franklin, and Thomas Jefferson, were all raised in religious homes, but worked hard, to make sure the new country they were founding, was secular. I could've been drawn into a long debate, but I had had enough religious philosophy, for one evening. "Enough Gary. I've heard enough. Now step down from the wall, put the Commandments down, then turn around and put your hands behind your back."

The House Of Cards Murder

I watched his face transition, to the glass eyed stare, I had seen on numerous inebriated people over the years as sheriff. His forehead wrinkled, like he had lost his train of thought, so I said once again, "Step down Gary. Right now."

He stared at me for a moment, before his shoulders drooped and he let the picture frame hang loosely in his right hand. He started to bend over to balance himself with his left hand, then his foot slipped and he fell backwards down toward the highway. Somehow, he managed to grip the edge of the wall, with his fingertips, before completely falling. "Jesus! Help!"

I ran to the wall, jumping and pulling myself up over the edge, only to see Gary, swinging back and forth like a pendulum, the Ten Commandments, no longer in his hand. The illumination lights from the memorial, made it impossible for me to see, if they had landed on the steep embankment or the pavement below. I reached out and grabbed his hand and began to lift him. "Hold on Gary. I've got you."

Tom had jumped on the wall with us and reached down to hook his hand under Gary's other arm. Together we pulled him up and over the wall, where Glen and Jack were waiting to assist his descent. Tom and I were leaning up against the wall, trying to catch our breath, while Gary was on his hands and knees, on the ground. "Jesus all mighty, I thought I was a goner."

I stood up and moved around to the edge of the wall. With my flashlight, I shined my light along the steep slope, and paused, when I saw the jet black frame shining in the damp grass. I moved back around and saw Jack handcuffing Gary, as Glen read him his rights. "Well the good news is, the Ten Commandments didn't shatter on the highway. Bad news is, the frame is nestled almost halfway down the slope."

Tom narrowed his eyes, giving Gary a cross look, as he placed his hand on his hips. "How do you want to handle it?"

I took a moment to think about our predicament. "I've got some rope in the toolbox in my truck. If we tie the end off to the front bumper, I can shimmy down the slope and get the Commandments. Once they're secured, one of you can put the truck in reverse and pull me back up."

Tom nodded, sucking on his cheek. "Good plan, but I think you need to let me go Jonas. I'm lighter than you. Not that you're fat, it's just that you're bigger. I mean—"

I cut him off, before he dug himself to China. Tom was taller than me, but had a thin, frame and I was more Simian in shape. Many of my relatives, on my mother's side of the family were similar in shape, so it just goes to show, genetics is a key factor in life. "I get what you mean Tom. If you're volunteering to go down, the slippery, grassy knoll, then I won't stop you."

While Jack was helping Gary into the backseat of his SUV, I pulled my truck up to the wall, leaving the headlights on, to help illuminate the area. I put Mick in the passenger seat, so he wouldn't get in our way, as we attempted our recovery. I took the rope from my toolbox and tied one end to the bumper guard. Tom removed his gun belt and wrapped the other end of the rope around his waist, then tied a knot. I found an old pair of leather working gloves and gave them to him, to protect his hands from rope burn.

When Tom was at the edge of the slope, I backed the truck up until the rope was taut. Tom looked down the steep incline, and shook his head. He gave me a thumbs up and I put my truck in drive and slowly moved forward. Glen was the spotter, watching Tom, so I would know when to stop. After one minute, Glen held up his hand. "Stop."

I gently pressed the brakes and waited, while Glen peered over the edge. A few seconds later, he held up his hand, thumbs up. "Okay go."

Shifting to reverse, I carefully backed up, having to stop twice, as Tom almost lost his grip on the prize. Soon, I saw him stepping up on the edge, the Ten Commandments tucked under his left armpit. When he was on solid ground, I put the truck in park and got out to check on my deputy. "You good?"

He nodded as he handed me the frame and started to untie the rope. "Yeah. Lost my footing once or twice, but other that, it wasn't too bad."

Glen and I both noticed his voice was shaky and there were ribbons of perspiration running down his face. Glen craned his neck, to look over the incline once again. "You want to go for another ride?"

Tom shimmied the rope off of his hips. "Once was enough."

"I agree." The display frame was in surprisingly good condition, considering the fall it had taken. There were some scratches, along the edges and the back board was wet, but the glass itself was still in one piece.

Jack pulled his SUV closer to us and got out. "I'm heading back to the stationhouse, to book him."

"Go on ahead. Perform a breathalyzer on Gary while you're at it, please. I'm willing to bet he's been driving under the influence tonight," I said.

Jack pointed to the frame. "How's it look?"

I held it up for him to see. "Surprisingly intact. I thought there would've been more damage to it."

"It was by the Grace of God it was saved," Gary shouted from behind the partition window.

I rolled my eyes and pointed to Tom. "It was by the grace of Deputy Kirk, that saved them Gary. It was because of *you* they were almost destroyed. However, you got your wish, The Ten Commandments will be back on display in the courthouse."

Even through the shadows draping the back seat, I could see his eyes expand in jubilation. "Really?"

I bent over, so he could see my face. "Yes sir. They'll be on display, as evidence, at your hearing. Take him away please, Jack."

Chapter Eighteen

After filling out the incident reports and conducting an investigation into the theft, it was after eleven o'clock before I got home. The courthouse surveillance camera revealed Gary entering through the front door and hiding in a broom closet, as the building was being closed for business. He waited, in there, for over an hour, until he came out and walked up the stairs, to where the storage room was located. The lock on the door was old and hadn't been updated. The reason for this was most likely because other than the Ten Commandments, the only other items in the room were some old paintings and photographs, most had forgotten about. I intended on submitting a request for new locks, by the end of the week.

I reviewed the casefile, one last time before going to bed. I learned long ago, to keep the facts fresh in my mind, because one never knows what little detail will break a case wide open.

In the morning I had just barely finished breakfast, when my BlackBerry vibrated on the kitchen counter. When I saw it was Jack's extension number, I got a bad feeling in my stomach. "What's up Jack?"

I could hear women screaming at one another, shouting out obscenities, that would make the worst of the worst blush. Jack had to shout to be heard over the commotion. "Jonas, you need to get down here, now."

I put my dishes in the sink, before grabbing my forty-five off the counter and holstering it. "What's going on there?" I asked putting on my coat.

"Gary Dawson stealing the Commandments made the local newspaper this morning. Then he made his one phone call for his wife to come down and see about bail."

Mick didn't seem interested in riding with me today, so I left him on the rug by the fireplace, with food and water in his dishes. "Is that her I hear screaming?"

"She's one of the women screaming."

At that moment a woman emitted a scream so loud, it made my eardrums ring. It was followed by the sound of something being thrown to the floor, soon to become a crescendo, of women calling one another a familiar biblical names. I chose not to ask any more questions. "I'm on my way."

I arrived at the stationhouse, in just over fifteen minutes, when I entered the door, I saw Jack wasn't at his desk. The next thing my eyes spied was paper strewn all around the floor of the vestibule and the computer screen from Glen's desk dangling, by the power cord. Heavy scuff marks lined the floor, from the vestibule, to the door that led to the holding cells. Three purses in plain sight, were lying on the floor. Resting my hands on my hips, I observed the carnage, before Glen, Jack and Tom opened the door to the cells. All three were flushed, with tiny beads of sweat sprinkled over their faces. Tom's shirt was wrinkled and untucked, the pocket on Glen's had been ripped and Jack's shirt was missing the first two buttons. "Looks like I'm a little late to the party. What happened?"

Jack, hooked his thumb under his belt and shook his head as he exhaled a deep sigh. "Last night, after I booked Gary, he called his wife and asked her to come by in the morning, to post his bail. Around 7:45 a.m., a woman with blond hair came in, saying she was Gary Dawson's wife. Said her name was Vicki Dawson and she wanted to know how to go about posting bond for her husband. I explained the judge would set the bail later this morning, at the arraignment. I told her we'd be taking Gary up to Sessions court at 9:00 a.m. She said she would wait and took a seat over there by the wall. It was maybe five minutes later, a brunette came in waving a copy of the Monroe County Buzz, like it was the state flag, saying she wanted to know why Gary Dawson had been arrested."

I nodded. "Who was she?"

Jack let out a sardonic laugh, as he stared at me. "She said her name was Amy, and she was Gary's wife."

It felt like my eyes were going to pop out of the sockets, as I processed this information. "She said she was his wife, too?"

Jack rolled his tongue along the inside of his cheek. "Uh-huh. According to Amy, they've been married two years. Needless to say this was a complete surprise to Vicki, who by now, was up at my desk, demanding to know who Amy was."

I closed my eyes, rubbing the bridge of my nose. "And that's when things started to get messy."

Glen let out a laugh, as he picked up his computer monitor and placed it back on his desk. "He ain't finished yet, Jonas."

I glanced over at Glen, before focusing again on Jack's oval, obsidian face, that now exhibited the look of exasperation. "While the two of them were at it, another petite blond came into the room, shouting over Vicki and Amy, saying she was Gary Dawson's wife and wanted to see him."

I slouched back on my left foot, the palm of my right hand resting on the hammer of my sidearm. "He had a third wife?"

"Apparently," Jack said.

I stared at the floor, my forehead lined with wrinkles. "Who was she and how did she find about Gary's arrest?"

"She said her name was Jane and like Amy, she read about her husband's arrest in the local paper," Jack replied.

It was now twenty past eight, as I took another look at the room and my deputies' disheveled uniforms and quickly pieced together what had happened, in a span of thirty-five minutes. "And then it really hit the fan."

Tom looked down at his shirt, shaking his head. "And splattered all over us."

Jack closed his eyes, nodding with Tom's assessment. "They started tearing into one another, like nothing I've ever seen. I got out there and grabbed Jane to pull her out of the ring. And let me tell you, she's a lot stronger, then she looks, for her size."

Tom leaned back against the wall, rubbing his left wrist. "That's when me and Glen stepped in. I grabbed Amy and Glen secured Vicki. We had to put them in holding, so they could calm down. In separate cells, of course."

I sat down on the edge of Tom's desk, slowly shaking my head. "Gary Dawson, has three wives and none of them had a clue the other existed?"

Jack shook his head. "From the way they acted, I'm inclined to believe they didn't."

I got to thinking of the numerous times Gary had been arrested for his protests in the courthouse and it wasn't adding up. "We've arrested him several times over the commandments. How come their paths haven't crossed until today?"

Glen, who had been at his computer scrolling through the files, had the answer. "Because in all of those instances, he called his brother Jeremy Dawson, to bail him out."

Tom crossed his arms over his chest. "I know that name for some reason."

Jack snapped his fingers. "Jeremey Dawson passed away six or seven months back. We had to block traffic, for the funeral procession, remember?"

Tom nodded his head, emphatically. "Yeah, that's right. I think it was a heart attack that killed him."

I stared up at the ceiling, trying and failing, to not roll my eyes. "Jeremy was his cohort. Probably lied to the wives, giving Gary alibis, when he needed them."

Tom was shaking his head, his face a mosaic of confusion and frustration. "I just don't get it Jonas. These women are good looking and a few years younger than Gary. What did they see in him?"

I took a moment to ponder his question, not really having an answer. "I haven't a clue Tom. I've never understood, what it is that brings people together. Obviously, there is a side to Gary Dawson, we've not been privy too. Speaking of which, does he, know his *wives* are here?"

Glen's chair squeaked, as he swiveled around toward us. "I can't believe he didn't hear the commotion, but none of us has officially told him."

I stood up, waving my hand over the floor. "Let's clean up this mess, then you guys get back to work on the O'Brian case. Have those search warrants come in, yet?"

"No. But Mr. Deland left a message, just before, all hell broke loose. He said he'll have them here within the hour."

"OK. While we're waiting on that, I'm going to check the records and see if there are three different marriage certificates for Vicki, Amy, and Jane. If so we may be charging Gary with bigamy."

Tom went to the broom closet and got out a broom and dustpan. "Gary Dawson, the crusader for the Ten Commandments. Turns out he's been married to three different women, at the same time. What a hypocrite."

Glen got down on his knees and began gathering up the files. "That's usually the way it turns out."

* * *

Once we had the floor cleaned up, I took the purses into my office and got out the driver licenses, of the three bridezillas. Tom was right in his assessment, that the women were all attractive and younger than Gary. Vicki was thirty-two, Amy thirty, and Jane just turned twenty-nine. All three women lived in different parts of the county.

Vicki lived up in Coker Creek, a small town way up in the mountains of Tellico Plains. Amy lived in Sweetwater and Jane here in Madisonville. A quick background check on each revealed Vicki, was the only one native to Tennessee. Amy was from Las Vegas and Jane was from Cherokee, North Carolina. Apparently Gary was a traveling man.

Someone knocked on the door. "Come in."

Jack opened the door, with two documents in his hand. "We just got the search warrants for Patrick Winchell's and Harrison Birch's trucks."

My watch revealed the time was now 8:58 a.m. I had the conference call with the warden and Alston's cellmate in just over an hour. "You and Glen go and secure the vehicles. Bring them back to the lab, so Molly and her people can go over them. Call me if you need anything."

"Yes sir."

I stood up and stretched my back, as I walked to Glen's desk, where he was putting on his coat to leave. "Before you go, did you get a chance to check on Harrison and Patrick's alibis?"

He flipped open his steno pad. "So far both of their stories check out. Their bosses at both places, confirmed they were off from work. I lucked up and got the cashier at Krystal who checked Harrison out and she remembered seeing him around 7:00 p.m. The waitress at the Teddy Bear remembered Patrick coming in for dinner. Patrick's girlfriend Justine confirmed they were arguing." Glen stopped to look up at me. "That girl's a bit off Jonas."

"What do you mean?"

Glen pointed, at the air around him. "She kept going on about the energy around me was negative or something."

I nodded, recalling my conversation with Patrick, the previous day. "Yeah, Winchell said she was really into the new age movement."

Glen shrugged his shoulders, as he looked back to his steno pad. "Kind of annoyed me. Anyway, it's at the Laffing Goat, that things start to get murky."

I tucked my hand in my pockets as I listened. "They weren't there?"

Glen shook his head, tapping his pad with his finger. "No, they were there. I stopped by there last night and the owner, bartender, and waitress all confirmed they saw both men there. None of them however, are sure when they left. It was a busy night, so none of them could remember, for sure, if Patrick and Harrison left around closing time. I'm still working on finding some other patrons at the bar, to see if they can verify their story, but that's going to take a while."

I nodded as Jack moved to the front door. "Keep at it. Until we know for sure they were there until closing, we can't rule them out as suspects. Pick it up after you and Jack get back with the trucks."

"Will do."

Tom was in our computer room, working on syphoning through the GPS of the cruisers and phones of the officers on duty. "How goes it, Tom?"

He exhaled a long exasperated breath, as he stared at the screen. "It's working, but it is also going to take some time. I've been able to eliminate twenty officers, so far."

I stared at the digital map of Monroe County on the computer screen, watching the blinking blue dots move across the roads and highways. "Well, that is a start. I don't suppose Saul West and Daniel Hensley have been disqualified?"

He typed on the keyboard, shaking his head. "Afraid not."

I studied the map for a moment. "Officer Hensley was off duty that night. Can you tell me where Saul was that evening?"

He punched in some keys on the keyboard. "Give me a minute."

A few seconds later he pointed to one blue dot that was on Church Street. "There is Saul's cruiser. It drives down 411, stops for five minutes, then proceeds down 72 East, where he stops again at 10:01 p.m."

I peered over his shoulder, to study the blip. "The cruiser stops? For how long?"

Tom punched a key and fast forwarded the images. "Looks like for five minutes, then he continues on his patrol. Moving at a very slow speed, from the looks of it."

"How long does he patrol the area?"

Tom tapped a few more keys. "For an hour. Then he heads back to the main highway."

I did my best to recall the geography of the city. "If I'm remembering it correctly, that's a part of the city, that has very few residents or traffic, especially at that time of night. That's a long time to patrol that area."

"Especially, at such a slow speed. He couldn't have been going more than twenty-five miles an hour," Tom replied.

"Where was Office Daniel Hensley, during all of this?"

Tom punched some more numbers into the command window. "He has a department issued phone, which we can access. According to its GPS he was at his home from 7:30 p.m., until he went to work, the next morning."

I shook my head. "All that proves is his phone didn't move from the vicinity of his house. Daniel could've left it there, so his movements wouldn't be tracked."

Tom nodded "That's true."

I let out a light sigh. "It's still not enough to pin anything on them or clear them. The GPS doesn't place either one of them, at the crime scene, yet."

Tom flexed his fingers, before he resumed typing commands into the computer. "I've just begun to scratch the surface, Jonas. If there is something there, I'll find it."

I smiled at his confidence. "You get everything you needed from the Vonore PD?"

Tom let out a dry laugh. "Yes and no."

"What does that mean?"

Tom looked over his shoulder at me and shook his head. "We got the calls for the night of the murder, but there are gaps."

I stared at him. "Gaps? You mean static?"

"I mean complete silence. There is a period from 12:00 a.m. until 4:00 a.m., where there was no communication at all, with dispatch, or any of the other officers on patrol."

"Did you crosscheck with the reports for that night?"

Tom turned around and gave me a slow, but strong nod. "There were three arrests that night, Jonas, during that timeframe. Two DUIs and one for driving without a license."

I walked over to the empty chair by the wall and took a seat. "The officers involved should've called those in, for sure. I don't suppose one of the officers involved in those arrests was Saul?"

"I'm afraid not. In fact, save for when Saul started his patrol, his voice wasn't heard again until 6:15 a.m. when he came in for the morning shift."

I leaned back, resting my head against the concrete wall behind me. "And I thought things were bad before."

Tom rotated his neck, the vertebra making audible pops. "I know. But even with the radio silence though, it still doesn't prove anything."

I pointed to the screen beside him. "I'm hoping GPS will prove they weren't anywhere near the crime scene. Was there anyone near the impound lot, at the time the Durango was taken?"

"Not yet. I'm going to keep looking at the other GPS trackers of the officers on duty that night, so we can officially eliminate them. I'll try to see if the radio track was tampered with, after I finish here."

I got up and headed for my office. "I might have a line on that one. Keep up the good work, Tom."

I closed the office door behind me, I looked up the contact information for Elvis Gentry and used my BlackBerry to dial up his cellphone. "Officer Gentry," he said on the third ring."

"Officer Gentry, this is Sheriff Lauer. I need you to answer a question for me."

There was a moment of stale silence, before his reply. "What are you thinking, calling me on my personal phone?"

"Are you alone?"

"I'm on patrol right now, but I could've easily been back at the station."

"Take a deep breath officer. No one will know about this call. I need you to clear something up for me."

He released a long sigh into the phone. "What?"

"You said you worked dispatch the night of Alston's murder, right?"

"Yes. How many times do I have to tell you that?"

I could empathize with his situation, being caught between the hard place and the rock, but there wasn't much I could do about it. "Just bear with me a few more minutes, Gentry. Do you remember there being any problems with the CB radio that night?"

"No, there weren't any problems that night. It was working just fine."

I wrote this down in my notes. "There were no blackouts? Communications always went through?"

"Like I said, everything was running smoothly that night. Except for the prank call."

My hand stopped writing. "There was a prank radio call?"

Elvis scoffed. "Yeah. Someone got on the radio that night that wasn't a cop, but they were talking so fast, I couldn't understand them. I tried to get them to respond again, but no one ever did. I figured it was someone making a prank call. You know how some kids are?"

"Could you tell it was a kid's voice?"

"No. Like I said, they were speaking too fast for me to really understand."

I tapped the tip of my pen on my desk. "One last question. Who made the copies, of the radio logs, that were sent to the sheriff's department?"

There was another long pause, before I heard him clear his throat. "It was Chief West who made the copies. Why are you asking these questions? Was there a problem with the call logs?"

247

"I'm afraid I can't go into that right now, officer. But I do have another question. Saul was patrolling that night also. Was that unusual for him?"

"No, not really. I mean Saul usually works a graveyard shift once or twice a month. Although, he usually spreads them out more."

"Oh? When was the last night Saul worked a graveyard shift?"

"Two days before the night of the murder. Usually he works a shift at the beginning of the month and the middle of the month."

I wrote this down as well, feeling the onset of a headache begging to take root in my head. "Was this a last minute change in the schedule?"

"Yeah. It was supposed to be Hensley, who patrolled that night, but he and Saul switched at the last minute."

"Did Saul mention why they switched shifts?"

"No. And I didn't ask. Figured they worked it out amongst themselves."

I wrote this down and underlined it twice. "Thank you Officer Gentry. I'll do my best to make sure no one knows you've been helping me."

"See that you do." He hung up, leaving me staring at the phone.

I set my BlackBerry on the desk, then used my fingers to massage my temples. The information I had just learned was a blessing and a curse, all intertwined into ball of trouble. What was the prank call Gentry had mentioned? No matter how you looked at it, I was going to have to talk to Saul and Daniel again. I was praying for a rational explanation for everything, but I had a feeling, we weren't going to be that lucky.

* * *

At five past ten, I had my laptop open with the video conference set up and was speaking with Warden Elizabeth King. She was a very handsome woman, in her late forties, with auburn hair, which had strands of gray along her temples. Her round face was emotionless, as was her voice, when she spoke. "Mr. Brandon will be here in just a few minutes, Sheriff Lauer."

From the way she kept checking her watch, it was obvious she didn't want to be there, so I decided it was a good time to extend my gratitude to her. "Thank you again, for setting this up, Ms. King, under such short notice. Being the warden of a prison, I imagine you have a full plate."

Her shoulders appeared to relax a bit, as she crossed her leg and rested her left palm on her knee. "It's usually overflowing, but this is no trouble sheriff. We'll assist you in your investigation any way we can."

"Again it is appreciated."

I heard a buzzer sound, before the door behind her opened, and two guards escorted in a man wearing an orange jumpsuit, with leg irons and wrist restraints. Warden King stood up so the inmate could take her place in front of the camera. "Mr. Brandon, this is Sheriff Jonas Lauer, from Monroe County."

Max "Gearjammer" Brandon, had his head shaved, with a brown goatee covering his chin and mouth. His forearms had flame tattoos peeking out from under the sleeves of his jumpsuit and there was a spider web tattooed on his neck. Three years into his seven-year sentence, he was twenty-nine when he entered the prison, so that would make him thirty-two now. Looking at the deep creases on his face, he looked older, maybe late thirties or early forties. Prison time takes its toll on the body and the soul. He stared at me, shrugging his shoulders, as he leaned back in the chair. "It's your show man, so what do you want?"

"It's my understanding, that you were cellmates with Alston O'Brian, until his release a few days ago, Mr. Brandon."

Max, let out a light laugh, as he shook his head. "Alston? Man has he gotten into trouble again, already? You'd think a man his age would learn how to not get caught again. Look, we were put together by the prison. Whatever he's into, I have nothing to do with it."

I observed him through the screen for a few seconds, before I shook my head. "Alston doesn't have to worry about getting caught anymore, Mr. Brandon. I'm afraid he was murdered two nights ago."

He had a good poker face, his eyes betrayed nothing, but even through the screen, I could see, the flesh around his temples and jaw, tighten. "Murdered? How?"

"I'm afraid I can't go into any specifics. As I said, you were his cellmate up until his release. When he learned of his release, did he mention any plans he may have had once he was out?"

He shrugged his shoulders, lightly tapping his feet on the floor. "Man, we were *placed* together, not roommates. We didn't have a lot of heart to heart chats."

"This may be true, but you two spent a lot of time together, in a confined space. You can't tell me that you didn't talk at all."

Max looked over to the left, like he was debating something in his mind, before he shook his head. "It was just prison talk, man. We talked about the things we missed from the outside. Like good food, fresh air, women, stuff like that."

I was making doodles on my notepad, as I listened. "And he never once spoke about his intentions, when he was free? Never said where he'd go or who he might try to look up?"

He paused and stared into the camera for a moment. He started to speak, but quickly closed his mouth and shook his head.

I leaned forward in my seat grasping my laptop with both arms. "Mr. Brandon, if you're concerned about betraying a fellow inmate's confidence, don't be. Anything you tell me will stay confidential. All I'm concerned with is finding out who killed Alston O'Brian."

He stared down at the tops of his legs and cleared his throat. "If I help you, can this shave some time off of my sentence?"

I fought the urge to roll my eyes, staring into the screen. Whoever came up with the concept of honor amongst thieves, must've been writing about an extinct breed. "If what you tell me, leads to an arrest, I will put in a word with the parole board. That's the best I can do."

Warden King stepped forward from the wall, with her arms crossed. "And I'll make sure that the board knows this as well. But if you are not forthright, Mr. Brandon, I'll personally see to it, that you serve the full length of your sentence."

Max looked to his left again, before he lifted his hand to scratch the underside of his nose. "All right, sounds like a good deal. Alston wasn't much of a talker, until recently. The doctor told him he had cancer and didn't have much longer. Once he heard that, it was like he talked nonstop."

I took my pen and placed it over the yellow sheet of paper. "What specifically did he talk about?"

"Mainly about the wrong he had done to those people in Vonore. He said he wished he could go back and give the people he stole from all of their money back."

I wrote this down, followed by the word regret and underlined it. "Did he ever mention any names?"

Max "Gearjammer" Brandon shook his head, as he propped his hands on the table. "No, he never said any names. Just kept going on about how he hadn't been a good example, when he was younger."

I stared into the camera, my forehead, wrinkled. "He said the word example?"

"Yeah. I think his exact words were, *I wished I had set a better example*. I asked him once what he meant, but he never did say."

I underlined the word example and stared at it. "So basically, Alston wanted to make amends before his passing?"

Max seemed to ponder the question, staring at the wall behind the computer, before he nodded his head. "Yeah, I guess that would be a good way to put it."

I tapped the notepad with the tip of my pen, making a collage of black dots in the corner. "And Alston never mentioned any names?"

Max started to shake his head, but stopped, elevating his eyebrows, holding up his restrained hands. "Wait, I think he might've mentioned a name one time. It was a few days before his release. It was after one of his pain episodes and he was mumbling."

Leaning back, I ran my finger along the edge of the laptop. "Whose name did he say?"

"Like I said sheriff, I can't swear to it, but I'm pretty sure he said *I'm sorry Clare.*"

I wrote the name down. "Clare?"

He nodded. "He kept saying over and over under his breath. Like I said, I can't swear that was what he said, but I'm pretty sure it was. I figured it must've been his wife or something."

The problem with that is Alston, was never married, as far as anyone knew. "Did he ever say anything about coming back to Monroe County? Or to Vonore?"

"No. Like I said he wasn't a big talker."

I had one last avenue of questioning, that I wanted to pursue before closing the interview. "Some of the money Alston stole, was never recovered at trial. Did he ever mention it to you?"

Max laughed, leaning back in his chair, quickly stomping his feet on the ground. "Oh yeah, he did mention that once or twice. There were more than a few of the cons in here threatened his life over it. Saying they'd offer him protection, for information about the money."

"How did Alston reply?"

He leaned forward, like he was about to whisper a secret to the camera. "That there was no money. Everything had been seized by the cops. The stories about there being thousands of dollars stashed away, was nothing but smoke. According to Alston, most of them didn't take too kindly to this. They all believed that he was just holding out, until the end of his sentence, so he could have the money for himself. Spent some time in the infirmary over it."

I looked up at the screen into Max's face. "Alston was assaulted?"

He hunched his shoulders. "He never said that. He just said he was inside the prison hospital more than he was out, when he first got here."

I studied his face through the screen, looking for any signs of deception, but as before, his face was stoic. "I don't suppose Alston told you, who the fellow inmates were, that gave him trouble."

From the look he gave me, you would've thought I had walked into the room with a banana in my ear. "Come on man. No one sees or hears anything in here. Shit man, if it ever gets out that I talked to you, could get me a beating or worse."

"One last question Mr. Brandon. Did you believe Alston, when he said there was no money?"

He smiled and pointed at the screen. "Another rule in here, sheriff. Trust nobody."

I could sympathize with him.

Chapter Nineteen

It had been over two hours since the wives of Gary Dawson had been placed in holding. I was hoping, that was enough time, for them to settle down. For obvious reasons, the women had been placed in individual cells. I stood near the back wall observing them through the shatter resistant glass, unable to fathom the situation. Gary Dawson, was by no means, a man who would be nominated as the sexiest man alive, but somehow he had been able, to marry three beautiful women, at the same time. I couldn't understand how and I had a feeling it was going to be one of life's mysteries, that I would never solve.

So far Vicki, Jane and Amy were so busy talking to one another, that they had been oblivious to my presence. Evidently during their time in closed quarters, their anger had combined and metamorphosed, into a singular hatred, for their shared husband. The words they were using to describe, what they would like to do to Gary, would've made Gloria Steinem blush. I won't go into detail about their plans for him, but it is suffice to say, that once the trio were done with Gary, fatherhood would no longer be an option. I had other things on my plate, so I stepped forward and cleared my throat. "Ladies, may I have your attention?"

All three of them, were up at the glass partition, announcing their displeasure, at being incarcerated, even it was for a brief period. Amy had her right palm on the glass, with her left hand resting on her hip. "How long are you going to hold us in here?"

Vicki, crossed her arms over her chest, her full lips almost flat with anger. "I want an attorney."

Jane stood with her hands tucked in the back pockets of her pants. "If we're under arrest, don't we get a phone call?"

I held up my hand, which silenced them for a moment. "None of you are under arrest. We detained you, after the three of you got into a brawl, in the middle of the stationhouse. I'm prepared to release you, but we have to get a few things sorted out."

Vicki, pushed a strand of her blond hair behind her ear, as she scoffed. "What is there to sort out? We are all married to the same slimy snake and he finally got caught."

Amy rolled her eyes. "Girl, he's no better than the dog shit you get smeared on the bottom of your shoe."

"Lord I'd love to get my hands on him," Jane chimed in.

We were quickly getting off point, so I turned the bow around, before the ship was adrift, once again. "Ladies, all I need to know is do any of you wish to press charges against each other, with regard to the fight that happened upstairs?"

They all looked at one another, before turning to me. Amy, once again was the first one to speak. "Why would we be pressing charges against each other? It's that lying maggot you have in the other cell, that caused all of this."

"Is that how you all feel?" I asked.

All three of them nodded. "Okay. You'll be processed and out within the hour. Given the extenuating circumstances and the fact no real damage was done to the premises; I'm opting to not file charges against you."

The line Amy had drawn across her brow to represent her eyebrow was smeared from the scuff, so when she elevated it, it didn't have the same impact, it would have otherwise. "Press charges against us? What about Gary? He's not a two timer, the man is a three timer."

Jane and Vicki were cheering her on. I had to nip this in the bud, before it blossomed into a flower of retribution. "Ladies, rest assured, we will be looking into all three of your marriages. Most likely your husband will be charged with bigamy."

Vicki stepped closer, her fists pressed firm into the shatter resistant glass. "Lock the man in a room with us for fifteen minutes and you won't have to bother with pressing charges."

The icy tone of her voice made a chill run down my spine. "Ladies, it is understandable that you're upset with Gary. However, if and when, he makes bail and any of you assault him, you'll wind up back in here."

Jane stomped the concrete floor, before she started pacing the cell. "I can't make that promise sheriff. He's made a fool of me."

"He's made a fool of all of us," Amy retorted.

"If you don't mind ladies. How did the three of you initially meet Gary?"

Vicki rolled her eyes. "I met him at one of the car shows in town. We got to talking and seven months later we were married. God I'm an idiot."

Jane stepped forward, crossing her arms. "I worked dispatch for a trucking company in Charlotte. Gary came to town to buy a couple of International rigs. We got to talking and nine months later we were married."

Amy let out a sigh. "I was a cocktail waitress at a business convention in Las Vegas. Gary was there and we got to talking—"

I held up my hand. "I get the picture. And I understand that you are justifiably angry with your husband." I thought about it for a moment, as an incendiary idea began to take root in my mind. "I can understand wanting to exact revenge on him ladies, but think about this, all three of you can now divorce him. Maybe even file a civil suit against him, for damages."

This made all three of them stop and ponder the possibilities. It wasn't long before subtle, malevolent smiles were scrawled on all three of their faces. Amy crossed her arms over her chest, slouching back on her left leg. "You think we can file a civil suit?"

I hunched my shoulders. "I'm not a civil attorney, but I imagine so. These days, you can get sued for just about anything."

Jane nodded. "It would sure be worth looking into. Even if we didn't get much, it'd be worth it to see that bastard squirm."

Realizing the idea was taking root, I decided to make my exit. "Just do me a favor. You didn't get the idea from me."

* * *

I decided to make a quick visit with Gary, before going back topside. The men's holding cells were located on the other side of the women's, separated by a three-foot concrete wall. I know I should've kept my mouth shut, with the three wives, about the possibility of a lawsuit, but Gary has done very little, to garner any sympathy, from me since I've been in office. It may have not been ethical, but I do believe it was just. Besides, it was the only thing I could think of, that might keep the women from killing him, if and when, he makes bond.

Gary was lying on the cot, with his arm draped over his eyes and a low snore coming from his nose. His blood alcohol had been .75, nearly three times the legal limit, so he was probably still sleeping it off. "Gary."

His snoring didn't miss a beat, so I knocked hard on the glass partition. "Gary Dawson, wake up."

He jumped up from the cot, almost falling to the floor. Squinting, he turned his head toward me and scowled. "Leave me alone, damn it."

"It's time to rise and shine Gary. You'll be going up before the judge in a little while, so you might as well get up."

He groaned again, turning his back to me. "I'll be up in a minute. Lord my head hurts. Can you keep it down?"

I inserted my hands into my pockets, shaking my head, as he clearly didn't understand, just how difficult his life was about to become. "You should know your wife has come by to post your bail. Vicki I believe her name is. Or is it Amy? No it was Jane."

He rolled over to face me. I could see fear slowly overshadow his resentment at my presence. He licked the inside of his lips, before swallowing hard, his eyes darting back and forth. "What is that supposed to mean?"

I stared down, at the tops of my shoes, hoping to conceal the smile on my face. "Gary, I don't have time to beat around the bush. All three of your wives came to post your bond, at the same time. Meaning the cat, or I guess cats, are out of the bag."

He sat up straight in his cot, rubbing the side of his temples. "You mean all three of them are here, right now?"

I nodded.

"And they all know that…." His face suddenly turned pale green, like he was about to be sick at his stomach.

I nodded again. "I hate to be the bearer of bad news, but you're up a particularly stinky creek, with no paddle. And the boat's got a leak in it."

He placed his head between his legs, groaning. "God help me. They are going to kill me."

My sympathy well was completely dry, when it came to Gary Dawson's fate. The man who had done nothing but give me grief, over the Ten Commandments, had broken number seven, two times, and still had the audacity to call me unchristian. Give me a sinner any day of the week, at least I know where I stand with them. "They are considering it. If I were you, I'd watch your back when you get out."

He looked at me, quickly shaking his head. "I can't leave here. The only thing keeping me alive right now, is this cell."

It was becoming harder, not to smile at his predicament. I know it is unprofessional to behave in such a way, but this falls under the heading of exigent circumstances. "Gary if it'll make you feel better, I can put some extra patrols on your street, when you get out."

He looked at me and must have seen the humor I was trying to conceal. "You think this is funny? My life may be in jeopardy and you think it's a joke?"

"No sir. But the hell you're in, is of your own making. I'm just here to inform you, that your secret is out and that the charges against you may be amended, with the additional charge of bigamy."

"Bigamy?"

I crossed my arms over my chest. "Simultaneous marriages are illegal in Tennessee, Gary."

He braced himself against the shatterproof glass, hanging his head down low. "You must think I'm nothing more than a hypocrite. Spouting off about the Ten Commandments then going out and marrying three different women, at the same time."

"If it walks like duck and sounds like a duck, Gary."

He nodded, closing his eyes. "I meant every word I said, about this country needing to go back to the principles it was founded on. And I love all three of those women. I never meant to fall in love with any of them, much less marry them. I just couldn't imagine my life, without any of them in it."

I sensed truth from his words. When it comes to matters of the heart, I'm as confused as everybody else. I suppose in the end, we just don't want to be alone. "A deputy will be down to escort you to sessions court Gary. Good luck to you."

* * *

I called Alston O'Brian's former attorney, Eugene Collier and was lucky enough to find the man home. After explaining the nature of my phone call, he agreed to meet with me at his home in an hour. As I was about to leave for our meeting, I saw two rollbacks leaving our forensic storage facility, at the bottom of the hill, telling me that the search and seize authorizations had been implemented on Patrick Winchell's and Harrison Birch's trucks. I drove to the lot and signed in, at the sealed storage shed, where Jack and Glen were signing the transfer forms. "Did you have any trouble executing the warrants?"

Jack shook his head. "No. Patrick griped the whole time, but he offered no resistance."

Glen rolled his eyes, as he took out his handkerchief and wiped his nose. "Harrison didn't cause any trouble, but he filmed the whole thing with his camera phone, saying he was documenting the entire thing, in case we violated his civil rights."

The vehicles in question were on opposite sides of the garage, with an industrial plastic curtain draped around them, to block cross contamination. I looked at the front of Patrick Winchell's blue Sonoma and found no dents or scratches along the grill or hood. The same could be said for Harrison's green Mazda pickup. "Neither one of them appeared to have been in an accident."

Jack shook his head, tucking his hands in the pockets of his bomber jacket. "Neither one of those vehicles has dents or scratches, that you'd expect to see, if they had hit someone. In fact, they both look like they've been taken to a carwash, within the last day or two."

"I mentioned as much to Harrison and he said he wanted to wash all the salt off of his truck, before it ruined the paint job," Glen interjected.

I furrowed my forehead, as I looked at my deputy. "Wash the salt? It was over a week ago, the county salted the roads and he just now washed it off of his truck?"

Glen gave me a long side glance. "That's what he said."

I turned to head back to my truck. "We'll have Molly go over it anyway. Glen when you get back to the stationhouse, continue trying to verify Harrison and Patrick's alibi. Jack, you need to release Gary's three wives when you get back. After that, I want you to go over Alston O'Brian's case file, to see if you can find any reference to a woman named Clare. His cellmate said he heard him mention her name once."

"I'll get on it," Jack replied.

"And I'll see, if I can find, a few more people, who were at the Laffing Goat," Glen said.

"Good. I'll be speaking with Alston's former attorney. Maybe he can help shed some light on this case."

Glen smiled. "It would be nice if a defense attorney helped us out for once."

* * *

With an eighty-five percent success rate, Eugene Collier was one of the most reputable solicitors during the time of Alston O'Brian's trial. After graduating Tennessee Wesleyan College, then graduating from the University of Tennessee School of Law, Eugene worked for three years with the attorney general's office, before opening his own private practice. Though he was a very competent prosecuting attorney, he was an even better defense attorney. I had watched him eviscerate witnesses on the stand, with such ease, they barely knew what had happened. We had crossed swords a few times while I was still a forensic investigator, and he had tried to discredit the evidence I had collected. I am more than a little proud, to say, he never succeeded in doing so. However, I always had to keep my guard up while sitting in the witness box. After retiring, he and his wife Donna, moved closer to Madisonville.

I parked beside his Mercedes XT3 and walked up to his front door and rang the bell. A minute later Donna opened the door, her reading glasses were hanging from a silver chain around her neck. "Good morning, sheriff. Come on in out of the cold."

I wiped my feet on the black floor mat with Welcome written across it, before I entered the home. Donna Collier was in her late sixties, with straight silver hair, cut short around her rectangular face. You could still see vestiges of her youthful looks, in her oval cheeks. Retiring as a manager from People's Bank, three years ago, she now works part time as a volunteer at H&R Tax assessors, helping people with their taxes and finances. "Thank you Mrs. Collier. I appreciate you and your husband seeing me on such short notice."

She rolled her eyes, while taking my coat. "Please sheriff. My husband is retired now and on blood thinners. In wintertime, he spends most of his days indoors, so I should thank you. Eugene gets stir crazy after a while, this gives him something to do."

"Well, thank you just the same, ma'am."

She put my coat on the coat rack by the front door. "Please call me Donna. You can wait in the living room, while I get my husband."

I felt small beads of sweat begin to line the back of my neck, as the room was beginning to feel stuffy. The thermostat must've been set high, a result of Eugene's blood thinners, no doubt. I stood there near the loveseat, with my hands clasped behind my back. On the wall, opposite the flat screen TV were family pictures of his twin son and daughter, now grown up. Last I had heard, the son lives in Virginia and the daughter in Lenoir City. There were other photographs of Eugene and Donna, from various places they have traveled during their retirement. This of course reminded me of the impending weekend Lydia and I had planned, which I still held out hope, we would be able to enjoy.

I heard the change jingle, in his pockets, before Eugene Collier entered his living room. Thick gray socks peeked out from under his blue jeans and I could make out the white collar, of a thermal shirt under his gray sweatshirt. His face was adorned, with a gray beard. His curly hair had receded over the years, revealing a small dime sized birthmark on the top of his head. He smiled and shook my hand. "Sheriff Lauer, it's good to see you again."

I took his hand and shook it twice. "Same here Eugene. You can call me Jonas. Retired life treating you well?"

He nodded, but angled his head, in the direction of the other room. "It's good, save for the honey-do-list, she keeps adding to. There are days, I would rather be back in the courtroom."

"Nothing's stopping you from going back to work. Besides this is your house too, so it won't hurt you to help maintain it," Donna shouted from the kitchen.

Eugene's face grew red, as he looked toward his wife's direction. "She's got the ears, of a fruit bat. So what can I help you with, Jonas?"

He gestured to the loveseat, as he sat, in the powder blue Lazyboy recliner. I took out my notebook and I sat down. "Like I said, on the phone earlier Eugene, it's about Alston O'Brian. Our records show you were his attorney during the trial and through his appeals. I'm sure you're aware of his death."

He nodded while pointing, to a file on the coffee table, in front of me. "I saw it on the news. I don't know how much I can help you though, Jonas. Here is all I have left on the case. It's just a summation of the trial and a few discovery motions. It's yours, if you want it."

I looked down at the file, as I clicked my ink pen. "Thanks Eugene. I was curious if you could give me your impression of Alston, when you first met him. How did he seem when the trial began?"

Eugene leaned over and propped his head on the knuckles of his left hand. "Surprisingly calm, all things considered. After getting caught, when he was so close to being home free, you'd think he'd have been bitter. He was always polite and well mannered. It was easy to see how he fooled so many people. He had an air of authority about him and was quite knowledgeable about a lot of subjects. Alston was very active in his own defense."

I made references in my notebook. "Yet he still lost, for all the good it did him. No offense meant to you Eugene."

"None taken. I knew that case was going to be a loser, when the judge refused to change venue."

I pointed the end of my pen at him. "I always wondered why the judge decided to have the trial in Monroe. Why was that?"

Eugene allowed a sly smile to flicker across his face. "Because the honorable Mendel Walsh, said the good people of Monroe County came from good stock and would be able to remain impartial. I'm paraphrasing of course, but you get the point."

"I take it you disagreed?"

He waved his hands out, speaking in his assertive courtroom voice. "How could you expect anyone in this county to have been impartial? It was on all the local news stations and newspapers. Most everyone knew someone connected, to the original crime. It was the gossip of the county and Walsh, thought the people were going to be able to keep their emotions in check? One of the jurors, I had disqualified said, if he had a rope he'd have hung Alston from the tallest tree he could find."

I made a note of this. "You remember the juror's name?"

He shook his head. "That was a long time ago Jonas. He was full of piss and hot air anyway, so I don't think he's a likely suspect. I'm just trying to give you an idea of what we were up against. It didn't help that Walsh denied just about every motion we presented him."

"Sounds like you had some good grounds, for an appeal. How come none of the appeals you filed went through?"

Eugene held out his hands, releasing a long sigh. "I'm sure you are aware, of the blue wall of silence, among cops. The same can be said for judges. Rarely does one judge overturn the ruling of another sitting judge, Jonas. It has to be an egregious offense for a judge to grant such an appeal. Besides, all of Walsh's rulings were within his bounds, as a judge. Plus, it didn't help that Alston was caught, with the money, and that he had a record, as a confidence man."

I held up my hand to correct him. "Most of the money. Most of the money was recovered. Almost six hundred thousand wasn't ever found, according to the court records."

Eugene, leaned his head back and released a light laugh. "Oh, yes. The vanishing fortune. I had almost forgotten about that. He never mentioned anything about the cash, Jonas. The prosecuting attorney offered him a good deal, if he surrendered it, but Alston said all the money had been recovered. That it was a miscalculation on the police's end of the investigation."

I tilted my head, tapping my notebook with my pen. "Was that a possibility?"

He shook his head. "I had two independent accountants go over the figures and both came up with the same number. There was six hundred grand, that disappeared, from the time Alston left the county, until his arrest. But he wouldn't deal."

I adjusted the collar of my shirt, feeling the heat of the room drenching my shirt. "Do you think he had it stashed away somewhere, with a plan to get it, after he go out?"

The former lawyer gave a light shrug, as he set his hands on the tops of his knees. "He never said anything to suggest that. Then again, I wouldn't put it past him, either. He was a shrewd son-of-a-gun. He had to know there was a good chance he was going to prison, for quite some time. That might've been his retirement package, so to speak. Have you found it? Is that why you're asking these questions?"

I smiled at him. "Just gathering information, Eugene. During your inquiries into the case, did you ever come across a woman named Clare?"

His gray eyes expanded, a sheen of shock filtering through them. "Yeah. I'm surprised to hear that name, after all these years."

I started scribbling in my notebook. "Who was she?"

Eugene leaned forward, the palm of his hand sounding like sandpaper, as it stroked his beard. "We're getting into some gray areas here now, Jonas. May I ask how this will be documented in your investigation?"

I couldn't fathom what the gray zone could be, considering the benign nature of my questions. Then again, there had been a lot of curve balls thrown at me, during this investigation and I had a feeling another one was about to come my way. "I'm not looking to jam anyone up, Eugene. I'm just trying to get a better understanding of the situation. My only concern is catching those responsible, for Alston's murder."

He took a moment, eyes cast down in deep thought, as I waited. After thirty seconds passed, his shoulders relaxed, as he came to a decision. "Her full name was Clare Hensley. Alston and her had an intimate relationship, while he was in Vonore. He never contacted her, after his sudden departure, nor did he try to after he was arrested."

I searched the caverns of my mind and didn't recall reading the name Clare Hensley, in Alston's casefile from 1999 and said as much to Eugene. "How come her name was never mentioned in the trial or investigation?"

He stared down at the coffee table, sucking in a deep breath. "In many ways Clare was viewed as a victim too. Alston told her they were going to have the perfect life, living in a fine house and wearing the best clothing. When he left town, it destroyed her. Chief Udall felt that it benefited no one, by putting her name in the file."

I looked up from my notes, my mouth forming a small O. "Chief Udall made this decision? Nobody told this to Sheriff Hayes?"

"No. We saw no point in mentioning her involvement with Alston."

I made notations of this, circling Clare's last name and putting a question mark beside it. "So basically, you, Alston, and Chief Udall, all decided to keep Clare's name out of the investigation. Even concealing her name from Bill. Is that correct?"

Eugene nodded, holding his hands up, like he was surrendering. "I know how it sounds Jonas, but there was nothing to suggest she had anything to do with Alston's criminal activity. Besides she was only twenty years old. Hell, we all made some stupid decisions, when we were that age."

His arguments were valid, as always. Who amongst us didn't make some bad decisions when we were young? Eugene took my moment of silence, to ask his own question. "How did you learn of Clare's name?"

I stared at him for a moment, but saw no harm, in telling him about my recent discovery. "Alston O'Brian had terminal cancer, that gave him sudden seizures of intense pain. It was during one of his attacks, that he was heard whispering the name Clare. No one knew what to make of it. At least until now, that is."

Eugene, slouched back in the recliner, a somber look washing over his oval face. "He was dying? And he was thinking of Clare?"

"So it would seem."

Scratching his neck, he slowly nodded his head. "You know now it makes sense."

I narrowed my eyes, placing my pen on the paper. "What does?"

"Alston's behavior. He insisted that Clare's name be kept out of the trial. He was adamant about it. He said she had no part in or knowledge of his criminal activities and that she had been through enough. It was the only time I saw any sense of regret in him. If he was mentioning her, all these years later, you think it is possible, he had genuine feelings for her?"

I gave my head a slight shake, as I rolled my pen with my thumb and forefinger. "The human heart is well out of my jurisdiction counselor. This Clare Hensley, is she still in Monroe County?"

He nodded his head crossing his leg. "Yeah. Still lives in Vonore, if you can believe it. Lives with her brother, as I recall."

I stared at the name Hensley for a moment. "I don't suppose her brother is Officer Daniel Hensley by any chance?"

Eugene smiled as he gave me a wink. "Yeah. You know him?"

I pursed my lips, feeling tiny balls of lead, drop in my stomach. "We've met a couple of times."

* * *

I was thankful for the cold air washing over my face, after leaving the intense heat of Eugene's home. I placed the file he had collected, for me, in the passenger seat and started back to the stationhouse. Suddenly Jack's voice came over the CB. "Jonas, you got a copy?"

A brief wave of dread slithered down my spine, as I feared Gary might have had another wife come to bail him out. I took the receiver and mashed the talk button. "Right here, Jack. What's the situation?"

There was a bar of static, before his voice came through again. "We have a hit from Sweetwater Hospital, concerning that BOLO, you sent out the other day. There was a patient who came in matching the symptoms you described."

I turned left on Warren, heading to Highway 411. "Tell the administrators I'm on my way, right now."

Fifteen minutes later, I was standing at the admission desk, with my badge out. "Sheriff Lauer. I believe someone called my office, about the notices we faxed out?"

A rotunda of a woman, with curly red hair, nodded as she put on a pair of reading glasses and took a file out from behind the computer screen. "Yeah, it's right here. Sorry it took so long for us to get back to you, but the staff's got hit hard by the flu bug, so we didn't get around to it until yesterday."

I shook my head. "Better late than never."

"If you'll wait in the conference room to the right, I'll have Dr. Solarin meet you there."

By the time I hung my coat over a chair, a dark skinned woman, with ebony hair, entered the room. She looked at me over the rims of her square glasses. "Sheriff Lauer," she said with a heavy Nigerian accent. "I'm Dr. Sanouk Solarin."

I shook her hand. "Nice to meet you doctor. I understand you may have a patient who matches my description."

She opened the file for reference. "It was two patients actually. They were admitted to the emergency room two days ago, with respiratory problems. We treated them for smoke inhalation, yet neither of them was in a fire."

I couldn't help but grin, as I sat on the edge of the table. "Let me guess, there was traces of ash inside the nasal cavities?"

Sanouk looked up at me, the skin between her eyes wrinkled. "Yes, both of the men did have ashes in their nasal cavities and throat. We had to keep them overnight, on oxygen, trying to clean out their lungs. Both men checked themselves out, against our advisement."

I removed my pen and notebook and flipped open to a clean page. "Did they drive themselves home or were they picked up by someone?"

She read the chart again. "A woman signed them out, yesterday afternoon."

I held out my hand. "May I see that please?"

Reading the signature of the woman, who discharged the patients, I was surprised, but at the same time expecting it. I wrote her name down in the notebook, along with the names of the two men. "So this Thomas Kinderman and Frederick Brentwood, were both admitted for the same respiratory problem?"

The doctor nodded her head. "Yes, I prescribed medication for the respiration, but according to the pharmacy, they haven't filled them yet. When the young woman, Katy Spear, signed them out, I explained to them, they needed to take all of the prescription or else they could develop a serious infection."

I closed my notebook and returned it to my pocket. "Dr. Solarin, I think it's safe to say we're not dealing with the sharpest knifes in the drawer. May I have a copy of this please?"

She nodded, returning the release form to the file. "I'll have one printed for you." She paused a moment, staring at me before inquiring, "Might I ask, how you knew to ask about these particular symptoms, Sheriff Lauer?"

I smiled, as I crossed my arms over my chest. "If I'm right, Thomas Kinderman and his friend Frederick Brentwood are responsible for a series of robberies, including the theft of the cremated remains of woman, in Madisonville."

I watched her eyes widen, as she deduced, where I was going with my train of thought. "You don't think that they..." Her face scrunched up, as mild shiver ran down her spine.

I shook my head, as I released a long sigh. "We have evidence, that suggests, they have a penchant for drugs. I believe when they saw those ashes, in the plastic bag, they thought they hit the motherlode in cocaine."

She stared at me, open mouthed, lightly tapping the folder on the leg of her blue scrubs. "How dumb are they?"

"Well doctor, they've been committing robberies, using men's boxers for masks, so what does that tell you?"

She removed her glasses and rubbed her left eye, with the pad of her thumb. "You meet some interesting people in your line of work, Sheriff Lauer."

I pointed to the file in her hand. "They were your patience Dr. Solarin. So I think the same could be said for you, too."

* * *

An hour later, I had Jack meet me at Horton's Metal Recycling. We entered the office and found Katy Spear sitting at her desk, with her space heater on high. The plastic cover was lightly concaving, in the breeze outside, as we shut the door behind us. When she turned to see us standing there, her eyes were startled, before they began to well up. "Ms. Spear. Do you know a Frederick Brentwood and Thomas Kinderman?"

She closed her eyes, allowing a line of tears to roll down her cheeks. I moved closer to her desk, while I had Jack stay by the door. "Did you check them out of the hospital yesterday afternoon?"

Katy wiped her eyes with a tissue and started to reply, but Oscar's entrance into the office stopped her. "Sheriff, you find something out about that Camry?"

I looked at Oscar, who was waiting, with his hands tucked in the pockets of his tan coat. "We're here about that robbery, Oscar."

His eyebrows arched, as he stepped closer. "You find them?"

"We're getting closer," Jack replied.

"Well that's good news." When Oscar saw the somber face of Katy, he furrowed his forehead and looked to me and then Jack. "Well isn't it?"

Katy stood up and took Oscar by his arm. "I'm sorry Oscar. I never wanted this to happen. You've always been good to me and it tears me up inside, that I had a part in hurting you and this company."

Oscar stared at his secretary, shaking his head in confusion. "Katy what are you talking about? Did you have something to do with the break-in?"

I stepped beside her, gently taking her arm in my hand. "Katy, we need to finish this at the stationhouse. Oscar, I'll explain it all to you later."

I was advising her of her rights, as we walked to Jack's squad car. "Do you understand Katy?"

She stared at the plastic draped office and let out a long sigh, her breath billowing around her. "I understand, I hurt a good man and just lost one of the best jobs I ever had."

I helped her into the back of the cruiser, propping myself up with the open door. "Frederick and Thomas have been the ones committing burglaries and wearing boxer shorts for masks, haven't they?"

She remained inert for a few minutes, her eyes impotent of emotion. "Yes. The most lame-assed disguises, I've ever heard of."

I looked to Jack, who nodded in agreement with her. "Do you know where they are right now?"

"Yes. I'll tell you where to go."

"Jack tell Glen and Tom to get ready for a raid."

Katy snorted out a curt breath. "They're both pretty sick, from snorting those ashes. You won't have any trouble arresting them."

I let out an internal scoff, as those famous last words, echoed in my head.

Chapter Twenty

After returning to the stationhouse, I did a criminal background search on Thomas Kinderman and Frederick Brentwood and wasn't surprised, to find, they both had criminal records. However, it was from when they were both juveniles and the records were sealed after their eighteenth birthdays, which is why their fingerprints didn't get a hit in the database. After having the records unsealed, I learned Thomas was expelled from school, for bringing marijuana to class and stealing school property. He did six months in juvenile detention at age fifteen. Frederick, did seven months, for destruction of property and vandalism. Both were placed in foster homes, where their crimes only got worse. There were charges for assault, petty theft and various other crimes. You didn't need to be a psychic to decipher where things were headed. Both, now twenty years old, had evidently decided, it was time to step up their game, by becoming the Boxer Twins. What sparked their ingenuity, I haven't a clue, but maybe I could answer that, after they were in custody. Their last mugshots were at age seventeen. Thomas was six feet tall, with sandy blond hair. He had a spider web tattoo, on both of his forearms, and the slogan Rebel Forever, on the right side of his neck. Though he was underage, no one was able to discern, where he got the ink for his tattoos. Frederick was five feet eleven inches tall, with dark hair down to his shoulders and no visible tattoos or scars. Looking at them, you wouldn't think they could cause so much trouble, but that is where the old saying of appearances and deception comes into play.

Thomas and Frederick, both resided at 245 Alden Street, in a faded blue house directly across from the Madisonville Primary School. The school held over six hundred students, which presented a problem. Having no desire, to deal with several hundred irate parents, if we put the school in lock down to apprehend the Boxer Twins, I opted to postpone the raid until five o'clock. Katy said both were still recovering, from their failed attempts, to get high from the cremated ashes, of Hannah Cathcart's mother. Thomas, in particular was plagued with heavy bouts of coughing and Frederick was so severely congested, he sounded like the cartoon character Elmer Fudd.

The residence was a one story shotgun house, with a red Chevy S10 parked in the driveway. The back of the property was flush with Adam's Feed warehouse. The only way to enter or exit the property was the front driveway, which was a double edge sword. Our quarry only had one way to leave the premises, but if we weren't careful, they could be alerted to our presence, before we were in positon. Fortunately, we didn't alert them, to our locations, as we prepared to breach the residence. Tom quietly peeked in the windows of the house, in an attempt to locate the whereabouts of the suspects. He immediately returned to my truck where Glen, Jack and I waited. "Frederick is on the couch in the living room. Thomas is in the bedroom on the west side. Both are sleeping."

Jack and I took the back, while Tom and Glen approached the front door. Glen and Jack each had a battering ram in hand and waited for my command. I approached the back doorway of the house and immediately found it unlocked. Jack pulled out his S&W M&P 40, while I clicked the safety off of my Benelli M4 shotgun. Two seconds later, the front door burst open, as Tom entered with his sidearm up and ready, followed by Glen with his Remington 870. Jack entered from the back, and I stayed in place, in case one of the suspects made it past my deputies.

The front and back door aligned perfectly, giving us all a direct sightline to each other. Tom had Frederick on the floor, with his hands behind his back, before he had a chance to react. Glen joined Jack at Thomas' bedroom door, just before Jack opened it. A nanosecond later, I heard the distinct sound of glass being broken. "He's jumped through the window," I heard Jack yell.

I peeked around the corner and saw Thomas, blond mane wild and tatted, clad in his white briefs, running barefoot toward the front. He had gotten more ink since his last arrest. On his left leg there appeared to be a green dragon reaching, from the top of his foot, all the way up to his upper thigh. I hoofed it hard and made it to the front, just in time, to see Thomas jump into the red truck. There was no way I was getting into another high speed chase, not after last night's fiasco. "Get out of that truck, right now!"

He refused to listen as he ignited the engine. I aimed the ghost ring of my sights on the front tire and squeezed the trigger, delivering a direct hit. I did the same for the back tire, before centering the gun directly on the driver. Thomas lowered his head and covered his face with his hands. He then erupted into a fierce coughing episode, as he peeked at me through slits of his fingers. "What the hell man!"

I raised my voice, so he could hear me over the engine. "Turn the truck off and throw the keys on the ground."

Jack and Glen were outside surrounding the truck, by then. Thomas eyed the deputies, with weapons trained on him, then brought his brown eyes back to me. He turned off the engine and threw the keys on the ground.

My rifle trained on him, I slowly moved to within twenty feet of the truck. "Exit the vehicle, hands out where I can see them."

Thomas suddenly moved his right arm, causing me to take a half step back, as I slid my finger along the grooved edge of the trigger. "Hands where we can see them."

Thomas opened the driver's door, with his left arm extend, as he stepped out. Suddenly he charged toward me, with a tire iron in his right hand, screaming like a banshee. I dropped the rifle sights to his upper thigh, now covered by the dragon tattoo, and squeezed the trigger. Chunks of the dragon's scales blew away, in a red starburst. Thomas screamed, releasing the tire iron, as he fell to the ground, hands clutching the neck of the dragon. Blood was spurting through his hands onto the ground around him. He uttered a deep moan of pain and rocked back and forth on his back.

Jack called for an ambulance, as I ran to my truck for the first aid kit. Leaving the Benelli locked in the back seat, I locked the door, before returning to Thomas. I slipped on the thick nitrate gloves and proceeded to apply pressure, to the wound. Glen stood over him, his sidearm still aimed at him, as I administered emergency treatment. When the bleeding was under control, I stared at Thomas, unable to comprehend his actions. "You don't bring a tire iron to a gunfight, you moron."

His face red from the pain, with adrenalin surging through him, he spat out a series of long, deep coughs, before he spoke through gritted teeth. "It was under twenty-one feet."

I frowned at him, as I glanced up at Glen, who also shook his head in confusion. I looked at Thomas while keeping pressure on his wound. "Say that again, please."

He looked at me, like *I* was the idiot. "Twenty-one feet man. I read on the internet that if you're twenty-one feet or less from a cop, you can take him out, before he gets a shot off."

There is some proven data to support this claim. If the officer's weapon is holstered and the assailant's weapon is out and within twenty-one feet; the assailant does have a chance. But not in this particular case. "Son, that only works if the officer doesn't have his weapon drawn. I had my shotgun loaded and aimed at you."

Ambulance sirens echoed through town, as the red and white van made its way down College Street. Thomas moaned, his body beginning to tremble, from shock and blood loss. "I don't remember reading that."

Glen and Jack both rolled their eyes at our prisoner's ignorance. Jack shook his head and turned to leave. "I'm going to help Tom secure the one, in the house. You two good here?"

I nodded, as I kept the pressure firm on the upper thigh. "Go ahead, we got this. Glen you do the honors."

Glen read Thomas his Miranda Rights, as the ambulance pulled into the driveway. "You understand your rights, Mr. Kinderman?"

His teeth chattered, as his tremors grew stronger. "I understand I'm screwed, if that's what you mean."

* * *

Glen accompanied Thomas Kinderman to the hospital, while Tom took Frederick Brentwood to the stationhouse, to be processed. Jack and I searched the house and found not only the boxer shorts, that were used as disguises, but several of the stolen items, including Phil's flatscreen TV and the remnants, of the cremated ashes, of Hannah Cathcart's mother. Now, I had to find a way, to explain to her, why there was a bit less of her mother, than before. I would cross that bridge later.

After securing the evidence at the lab, I filled out a report for the officer involved shooting. This was the fifth time I had done this, since becoming sheriff and it never gets any easier. The T.B.I. would send an investigator, to conduct an investigation. With Glen and Jack corroborating the altercation, there was little doubt, the shooting would be ruled justified. Still, it was a deterrence I didn't need, with this active murder investigation.

It was after seven, when I joined Katy Spear in interrogation room one, to record her statement, concerning her connection to the Boxer Twins. She had waived her right to counsel and she told me everything. Her connection to Frederick and Thomas traced back to their days in high school. She had briefly dated Frederick during their senior year. After graduation, they had kept in touch, but their lives had gone down two different paths. Katy had gone on to junior college, earning a degree in business administration, whereas Frederick and Thomas had chosen to pursue careers in crime. It was upon learning Katy worked at a scrapyard, that things began to head in the wrong direction.

"We were having lunch one day and I mentioned, that the Sweetwater City police, had been to the yard, because someone had reported their copper stolen. Turns out a couple of guys had stolen some used copper tubing from a man, while he was away on vacation. The police were able to trace them to us and later arrest them for theft," Katy said, as she stared at her bottled water.

I nodded, checking the digital recorder, to make sure it was still operating. "How did they react to this information?"

She wrapped her arms around her torso, as if she was very cold. "They wanted to know how often the police arrested, these kind of customers. I told them not often. That it is almost impossible to trace scrap metal back to the original owners, unless it is a car or something that is traceable. I thought they were asking out of curiosity."

"But instead, it gave them an idea to bring stolen metal, to the scrap yard, for a quick buck," I retorted.

She sighed, lowering her chin to her chest. "It never occurred to me, that they would do this, sheriff. I swear to God, I never thought they would actually rob people."

The evening train sounded its horn, as it passed through the first of the three railway crossings, near the stationhouse. Miniature shockwaves shook the walls, rippling the water in her bottle. "You knew it was them, who stole the aluminum wheels, from O'Reilly's, didn't you?"

For a moment she stared mutedly at me. "Yes. Or at least I suspected it was them. I thought I recognized their truck, that day. Then when Mr. Horton described them to me, I knew for certain. When I approached Thomas and asked him what he thought he was doing, he acted like it was no big deal. No one got hurt and the parts place could just write it off."

"But then they decided to rob the safe." I was taking notes as she spoke, pausing my pen for a moment, as I read over what she had said. "Did you ever mention how much money was in the safe?"

She shook her head, emphatically. "No. I never once talked about what happened inside that office. I couldn't believe it when I saw the huge hole, in the wall, that morning. I swear to God, I felt like someone had torn a hole through me. "

"Why didn't you tell Oscar or me about Thomas and Frederick then?"

Katy looked up at the ceiling, rolling her eyes. "I was afraid I would be arrested too. It's selfish, I know, but that's why. I didn't want to go to jail, which is exactly where I wound up anyway."

"Did you have any contact, with them, after the break-in at Horton's Metal?"

Katy swallowed hard, before running her tongue along the interior of her lips. "No. At least not for a while. I called them and told them I wanted nothing more to do with them. I still can't believe they did that. I knew Fred and Tom were having trouble with the law, but I never dreamed they would do anything, to me, or anyone I knew."

I thought about saying, that people with the criminal records, like Thomas and Frederick, weren't usually known for their consideration, but I felt it wasn't appropriate. Instead I opted to move on. "How did you find out they were at the Sweetwater emergency room?"

The muscles along her jaw grew tense and the plastic bottle popped and cracked from the tightening of her grip. "Thomas called me, saying they needed me to drive them home. The stupid idiots, thought ashes were cocaine and made themselves sick. Served them right, if you ask me, but they didn't want to risk anyone at the hospital getting the license plate number off their truck, so they had a friend drive them to the hospital. Then when the doctors said they wanted to keep them overnight, what did they do? They called me, to sign them out. It was all right for my information to get out there, but not theirs."

Moving my pen along the paper I drew a figure eight, in the side column, before asking, "Why did you go Katy? If you hadn't there is a good chance, we would never have connected you to them."

279

She slowly oscillated the water bottle on the table top, leaving overlapping rings of water in its wake. "I didn't want to go there at all. They could've choked on those ashes, for all I care, but Thomas said I could be blamed for the break-in. He said he would tell you, it was my idea to steal the aluminum rims and sell them, to the scrap yard. For all I knew, you might believe him. In a way it is my fault. I should've stopped hanging around them years ago, when they began getting into trouble with the law. Run around with dogs and you get fleas."

I wrote this down and concluded the interview, stopping the recorder. "What's going to happen to Tom and Fred?" she asked, as I closed my legal pad.

"When they are physically able, they'll be charged and arraigned. My guess is they'll plead down to a lesser charge, but no way they avoid doing some jail time. "

She stared at the tabletop, placing her hands together and wedged them between the knees of her blue jeans. "And me?"

I gave her a light shrug. "I'll have to discuss this with the attorney general, Katy. It doesn't look like you physically robbed any of the locations, but you didn't come forward with your suspicions, even after they admitted to you they were the robbers. I don't think you'll do any jail time, but there may be some probation or community service involved."

She tunneled her fingers through her yellow hair, pulling the skin on her face back, as she exhaled a deep breath. "Considering what happened to Mr. Horton, I deserve worse."

I remained seated, staring after her, as the deputy escorted her back to her cell. This wouldn't be the first time someone got arrested, because they associated with a bad element. It's easy to lump all of these cases into the category, of they should've known better, and they deserve whatever punishment they get. The truth is, we never really know what is waiting for us just around the curve, nor how we'll react when the dominos start falling. Despite the circumstances, I sympathized with Katy Spear and her predicament.

* * *

The next morning, I found myself sitting in a conference room, at the courthouse, recanting the circumstances surrounding the shooting of Thomas Kinderman to a T.B.I. agent After four hours of reviewing the circumstances surrounding the discharge of my firearm, I was permitted to go back, to my duties, as sheriff. Glen would be next to be interviewed, along with Tom and Jack. A week later they would come back with their findings. I felt confident in my decision to shoot Thomas Kinderman, in the leg, and was certain the report would conclude a favorable judgement. The incident would remain in my memory, but there was more than enough work to keep me distracted.

The Boxer Twins were to be charged with three counts of aggravated robbery and destruction of property. With regard to the cremated ashes, I debated if I should charge them with the desecration of a corpse, but realizing it wouldn't hold up in court, I decided against it. In a bizarre turn of events, Oscar announced he didn't want to press charges against Katy. He felt she didn't intend for his business to be robbed and had no desire to see her in jail. It would be up to Anthony, if he wanted to proceed with conspiracy after the fact. Now that I had the two dumdums in custody, I decided to press on in the murder investigation.

I performed a background check on Clare Hensley and discovered she had no criminal record. She had been twenty years old when Alston first came to Vonore, in many ways still a kid. Now thirty-nine, she worked at Lowes warehouse, in Vonore, as an executive assistant for the past twelve years. I wanted to talk to her, but without the presence, of her little brother, so I decided to go to the warehouse, during business hours.

When I entered the main office, at the Lowes warehouse, I spotted Clare immediately. She had similar facial features, to her brother, especially around her cheeks and lips. She had her brown hair tied back in a ponytail, with turquoise eye glasses resting on the bridge of her nose. The smile on her face vanished, as I approached her desk, with my badge exposed. "I'm Sheriff Lauer. Are you Clare Hensley?"

Clare swallowed hard, eyes focused on me. "Yes. How can I help you, sheriff?"

I placed my badge back on my belt, noting the carotid artery along her neck was beating fast. "I have some questions, regarding Alston O'Brian, ma'am. Is there somewhere we can talk? It will only take a few minutes."

There was a slight tremor in her hand, as she removed her eye glasses and placed them on the desk. She gave me a weak smile, shaking her head. "If you're talking about the man who was found dead a few days ago, I'm afraid I can't help you. I never knew the man."

I pursed my lips, as I looked around the office. The general manager's office was to my right, with the door closed. A solo muffled voice could be heard through the wooden door, indicating he was talking on the phone. Clare, must've realized the call could end at any moment and her boss could come walking out, only to find his secretary talking to the sheriff. "Ms. Hensley, I have it on good authority, that you and Alston knew each other quite intimately. In fact, a deal was made, to keep your name out of the official court record."

Clare looked toward her supervisor's door, her breathing labored. She lowered her voice to whisper. "Please. I can't do this here."

I leaned over her desk, so I could look her square in the eye. "I understand ma'am. If you want, we can do this at the stationhouse."

"I don't know anything," she said through gritted teeth, louder than she intended, as she glanced back at the office door. Yet the muffled voice could still be heard on the other side of the door, which was some relief to her. "I haven't seen the man in almost nineteen years, so there isn't anything I can tell you about him."

Observing the fear in her eyes, gave me no pleasure. As much as I would like to leave sleeping dogs alone, I've learned there are times, they just won't stay asleep. "Ma'am, I understand you don't want to talk about this, but we must. Now the sooner you answer my questions, the sooner I can get out of here. Is there a breakroom where we can talk?"

The fear in her eyes, quickly turned to annoyance and frustration. Clare stood up and walked toward the door, opposite her employer's office. "Follow me."

She led me through a narrow maze of doors and rooms, until we came to a cramped storage closet, with shelves filled with various office items. Clare shut the door, and flipped on the light switch, before crossing her arms over her chest. "I've not got long. Mr. Detrick, will be finishing his conference call soon."

I removed my notebook and pen from my coat pocket. "I'll be as quick as I can. You and Alston were involved with each other back in 1998, just before his arrest, correct?"

Her oval face grew red from either embarrassment or anger. "Yes. I was barely twenty years old and had never been more than a hundred miles from Vonore. Alston arrived and just swept me off my feet. I'm not proud of it, but I was still a kid, in many ways."

I scribbled this down, the close confinement of the room, combined with my winter coat, caused thin ribbons of sweat to roll down my scalp. "I'm not trying to judge you, Ms. Hensley. I'm just trying to understand your relationship with him."

Scoffing, she stomped her foot on the floor as she glared at me. "The man talked his way into my pants is what it boils down to. Haven't you ever made a mistake before?"

If she was trying to shock me by her candidness, it wasn't working. "Did Alston ever mention anything about the money, that was never recovered?"

She shook her head, cocking her ear to the door, listening for footsteps. "No. I never saw a dime of that money, if that's what you're asking. I didn't even know about it, until it was brought up at the trial."

I made reference to this, noticing her right forefinger tapping on the bicep of her left arm. "Alston never mentioned anything about his intentions, for the money, he had stolen from the investors he was scamming?"

I watched her eyes grow intense. "Of course not. Don't you think I would've told someone, if I had known he was stealing the money? What kind of woman do you think I am?"

I held up my hand, for her to calm down. "Ma'am, since you weren't questioned during the original investigation, that means I have to do so now. Please bear with me just a few more minutes. Did you have any contact with Alston during the trial or while he was in prison?"

She shook her head, leaning back against the door. "No. I wanted nothing more to do with that man. I still can't believe how naïve I was, to think he actually cared for me."

I stared intensely at her for a moment. "Ms. Hensley, what do you know about the circumstances, that led to your name being omitted, from the original trial?"

Pursing her lips, Clare shook her head, while shrugging her shoulders. "Just that Chief Udall, said there was no reason, for me, to be involved in the trial. He said that enough families had been hurt by Alston and my family didn't need to be dragged through the mud any more than they already had."

I kept my eyes focused on her, as I lightly tapped my pen on the notepad. "Ms. Hensley, I have it on good authority, the only reason your name was never brought up during trial, was because Alston insisted upon it. He was very clear, that your name be omitted, from all the court records."

Her pupils dilated, suggesting she was genuinely surprised. Her mouth formed an O, before she closed it and swallowed. "He did?"

I decided to reveal more information, to see where it led. "Alston was also terminally ill Ms. Hensley. He only had a few months left to live. During an episode of severe pain, a witness said they overheard him repeating your name."

Clare swallowed hard again, as she gasped for breath, then grabbed the doorknob. "I have to get some air."

She almost hit me with the door, as she bolted back toward the employee breakroom, which was still empty. She moved to the round dining table and took a seat. I opened the refrigerator, near the back wall, and got out a bottle of water. "Here you go ma'am."

Clare broke the seal on the bottle, but left it on the table untouched. Her eyes stared intensely at the tabletop, the flesh along her forehead wrinkled with confusion, as the corners of her eyes narrowed. "You have to be wrong. Chief Udall would've told me, if Alston had tried to help me."

I took a seat on the bench beside her, tapping my notebook on the pale blue table. "Ms. Hensley—"

"Please stop calling me that. My name is Clare," she said, before taking the bottle and swallowing a long sip.

I gave her another moment, before continuing. "Clare, I got this directly from Alston's attorney and I believe he was being truthful."

Clare rolled the white plastic bottle cap between her fingers, and looked at me. "Then why didn't they tell me this years ago?"

I turned toward her, resting my hand on my kneecap. "What exactly did Chief Udall tell you?"

"Like I said before. That there was no need for me to testify, because I had no part in the theft. He thought that if I went before the judge, I would embarrass myself and my family. He believed it was a slam dunk case against Alston, so there was no need for my testimony."

I wrote as she dictated. "Did you know the victims well?"

She nodded, staring up at the heavens. "Lord yes. I knew almost all of them. I was surprised they didn't try to run me out of town. I guess they didn't..."

I watched the color evaporate from her face, as she brought her hand up to her mouth to catch her breath. "What is it Clare?"

285

The way her eyes darted back and forth, reminded me of a rabbit, being chased by a pack of dogs. She was clutching the fringes of her shirt, while clearing her throat. "Nothing. I just really don't feel like answering any more questions."

I studied her, noting the way her eyes kept darting down to her watch. She stood to leave, but I moved, blocking her path to the door. "Just a couple of more questions, please. You have any contact with Alston after his release, Clare?"

She twisted her shoulders and moved around me, speaking rapidly, with a quivering voice. "No. Like I said, I haven't seen him, since he was arrested."

I was trailing her, hoofing it to keep up with her pace. "Alston told me the reason he came back to Monroe County, was because he had unfinished business. You have any idea what that might mean?"

"No I don't. Now please leave."

Back in the main office, I saw Officer Daniel Hensley, standing by Clare's desk, holding a red backpack with the Sequoyah High School logo on the front. Upon seeing me, his face grew intense. He opened his coat, exposing his sidearm in the clip-on holster, nestled on his blue denims. Instinctively, I opened my overcoat, and rested my palm on the hammer of my forty-five. "Officer Hensley. You planning on drawing down on me?"

He was grinding his teeth, as he looked first at his sister, then back to me. "What the hell are you doing here?"

I slowly moved closer to the front door, still keeping my hand near my sidearm. "My job, officer."

He returned his eyes to his sister. "Has he been bothering you?"

Clare moved toward her brother and placed her hand on his gun arm. "Daniel, he was just leaving. Don't do anything stupid."

Daniel zeroed in on me again, pointing his finger directly at me. "You stay away from her. You need to talk to anyone in this family, you talk to me."

I squared myself against him, beginning to find his attitude and disrespect a bit irritating. "Officer, I go where the investigation leads. Now if you'll excuse me—"

Just then, the main office door opened and a man with a bald head and red beard stepped into the vestibule, staring at all three of us, with a mask of confusion drawn across his pudgy face. "What's going on here? Clare is there something wrong?"

She shook her head, fear in her eyes. "No Mr. Detrick. Everything is all right. Isn't it Daniel?"

Daniel eyed his sister, before slowly moving his hand away from his sidearm. Mr. Detrick now looked to me, a flicker of recognition registering on his face. "Hey, you're the sheriff aren't you? Why are you here?"

Clare looked from her employer to me, raw fear evident on her face. "I'm conducting an investigation Mr. Detrick and needed to speak with Officer Hensley. He said I could meet up with him here. I'm sorry if this has caused you any inconvenience."

Mr. Detrick scratched the back of his head, his frown deepening. "No, it's no trouble. But from the way you guys are standing, I thought you were about to have a gunfight."

I shook, my head, pulling my coat over my gun. "Oh nothing like that sir. Officer Hensley, why don't we get moving? Again, I thank you for your patience and time, sir."

I held the front door open, for Daniel, who took timid steps in my direction. Suddenly a commode flushed down the hallway. We all stood still, eyes glued on the hallway. A second later the door opened and a teenage boy with light brown hair tied back in a ponytail, walked into the vestibule, as he dried his hands on a paper towel. He stopped when he saw the four adults staring at him. He looked to Clare, shrugging his shoulders. "What's everyone staring at Mom?"

I stared at his facial features, noting the arch in the nose, the space between the eyes, and the shape of the lips, unable to ignore the traces of a young Alston O'Brian standing before me. He threw the soiled paper towel into wastebasket and it was then I observed the scrapes and bruises running along his knuckles. When I saw them, I understood I shouldn't have been asking *what* Alston O'Brian's unfinished business was, but *who* it was about. When I looked at Clare, I saw that she realized the conclusion I had reached. She sent her son back to the breakroom. "Nathaniel go on back and start on your homework."

Clare closed the door behind him, gripping the doorknob, as she kept her eyes closed. Daniel had an ashen sheen on his face, as he looked to his sister. I had no reason at the moment, to bring the three of them in for questioning, so I could see no reason to prolong their anguish. "Well, we'll get out of your way. Nice to meet you sir. Ms. Hensley."

I closed the door behind Daniel and we walked silently to our vehicles. When Daniel was at his blue and white Vonore Police cruiser, he turned, as if to say something to me, but no words came out. I made no effort to say anything, the silence told us both what we needed to know. I got into my truck and exited the parking lot. I looked in the rearview mirror, Daniel was still by his car, staring in my direction.

Chapter Twenty-One

I called Jack and asked him to check out an unmarked car, then head over to the Hensley residence and wait until further notice. The Hensley family was no doubt scared by now. Spooked animals have a tendency to run and the last thing I needed was a manhunt, so if they did try to take off, I wanted to nip it in the bud.

"By the way Jonas, I finally got around to checking those routes, that would add the extra mileage to the Durango," Jack said.

"You find a likely avenue of travel?"

"Best I can tell, they took 411, until they got to Vonore, then they pulled onto Church Street. You factor in the distance to the house and back to the impound lot, it is almost an exact match."

"Pretty slick of them to travel the open road. It was dark and if they kept the speed limit, they would have drawn no attention to the vehicle or themselves."

"That's what I was thinking too," Jack replied.

"That's good work, Jack. Let me know if anything happens, at Clare's house."

Molly said she would have some results from the search of the two trucks later in the evening, so until, then I opted to go visit with Bill. He sat across from me, listening as I related all that had happened during the last few days, plus what was discovered at the Lowes warehouse. I watched the disbelief in his blue eyes, as I divulged how the relationship between Alston O'Brian and Clare Hensley had been covered up by Chief Udall and Eugene Collier. If there had been any doubt about Bill's involvement, it was erased. He contracted his jaw and placed his thick calloused hand on the table. "You mean Alston was sleeping with Clare Hensley and the chief of police and the defense attorney covered it up?"

I nodded. "Not only that, Bill. She was pregnant at the time."

His mouth opened, as he sat back in his seat. "Alston has a child?"

I rested my arms on the table, interlacing my fingers. "I met him just over an hour ago. His name is Nathaniel and he's the spitting image of his father."

The chains jingled, as Bill leaned over to rub his eyes with the pads of his thumbs. "So it's safe to say, this situation may be the unfinished business, that brought Alston back to Vonore. He wanted to see his son, before he died."

I was tapping my thumbs, as I continued the story. "When I saw Nathaniel, he had fresh scrapes and bruises on his knuckles. Exactly the kind you get when you're in a fight."

Bill looked at me, as he assumed the translucent face of a policeman. "Or, if you're beating a man, while he's strapped to a chair."

I grimaced, nodding my head. "I've got Jack watching the house in an unmarked, in case they try to run. I want to bring them in, but I've nothing to charge them with."

Bill scratched his chin, while staring out the window, deep in thought. "You really think the kid had something to do with Alston's death? I mean, maybe he got into a fight, at school or something?"

That thought has occurred to me and I said as much. "I'm going to call the school in the morning to see, if he's been involved in any physical altercations. I'm hoping he has, because I really don't want to arrest an eighteen-year-old boy, for murder."

Bill shook his head as he released a deep breath. "I don't blame you. I wouldn't want that job either. But if he's involved, he didn't do it alone, Jonas. There's no way he could've stolen the Durango from the impound lot and dropped the house on Alston."

I rested my head in the center of my hand. "There were two people, spotted on camera, breaking into the impound lot. The ski masks and paint on the cameras made them impossible to identify, but we were able to ascertain, that one of the intruders was taller than the other. It's possible, it could've been Saul or Daniel, but I can't say that for certain."

Bill, interlocked his fingers and slowly twiddled his thumbs. "It fits. With them being cops, they would've known about the universal pass code. I still can't believe, that thing, was still activated. I could've sworn, I had the security company deactivate it."

"Don't beat yourself up about it, Bill. I had completely forgotten about that code or else I would've made sure it was deactivated. There is plenty of fault to go around on that one. The problem with my hypothesis is, that Daniel and his nephew Nathaniel, are roughly the same size."

The former sheriff, took a moment to think about where I was going, before he slowly shook his head. "They wouldn't have involved the boy. From what you told me about Daniel's reaction, to the questioning of his sister, he would never involve the kid in breaking and entering a police impound lot. Even if it was to help cover up a crime."

I drew invisible squares on the table with my fingertip. "So, if it was cops, who broke into the impound lot, which is almost certainly the case, then it stands to reason, it was Saul and Daniel."

"From what you've told me, they are the only suspects, that could've entered the impound lot, undetected."

I sat up straight and stretched my back. "Then, there is Harrison Birch and Patrick Winchell. Harrison is the one I had to subdue during that altercation at Hardees. Patrick is a friend of his, who didn't go out of his way, to dissuade him from accosting Alston. Plus, both of them have family members, who were victims of Alston's."

Bill pointed his finger at me, his eyes beginning to sparkle, as they often did, when his detective juices began to flow. "But, could they have gotten into the impound lot, to procure the vehicle, used to transport the body?"

"So far, that is a no. The most viable suspects we have, for that, are Saul West and Daniel Hensley."

The courthouse clock rang seven in the evening, but as it has been for years, it was actually 7:15 p.m. The cars passing along the road, cast shadows through the window, as they flickered in and out of the streetlights outside. "Have you been able to pinpoint where Saul and Daniel were, the night of the murder?"

"Tom's working on that. According to the GPS on Daniel's phone, he was at his house the entire night. But really, all that proves is his phone was there. Chief West's cruiser was on patrol on Highway 72 East around the time of the murder, putting him near the crime scene and within the M.E.'s window, of the time of death."

Bill's eyebrows canopied his eyes, as he frowned. "I don't recall there being, that much traffic, on that road during the day, much less in the middle of the night."

"Neither do I. It would be a good place to meet up and maybe come up with a plan, but I've nothing, that connects them, to the stolen vehicle or crime scene. Even if I did, they were both first responders to the house, so that would explain away traces of them."

Bill got a smirk on his face, as he scoffed. "That was convenient, of them, being first on the scene."

I gave him a dry smile. "It was, wasn't it? I would love to take a look at the GPS of Nathaniel Hensley's phone, to see where he was, the night Alston was murdered, but no way I have enough for a warrant."

He nodded in agreement, but saw a silver lining crack through the overcast. "No, but you know which direction, to aim your investigation in now. The kid's the key. It's probably the reason Alston came back here. Keep digging on that and you may get the break you need."

I had to give him points on that one. "Well, I suppose there is only one way to find out."

* * *

Molly texted me she had some results, but my growling stomach made me decide, to ask her to meet me at my office, in thirty minutes. I got some chicken tenders for supper at Bo Jangles. As soon, as I entered the stationhouse, my deputies had their noses in the air, inhaling the seasoned aroma, of the spicy chicken and buttery biscuits. "Dinner's on me guys. There's plenty for everyone."

I put together a plate for me and Molly, before grabbing a couple of sodas, out of the fridge, and headed to my office, where she was waiting. Upon seeing the plate of chicken and fries, Molly smiled. "I've not had anything since breakfast this morning."

I set the plate and drink before her and got out some paper towels for napkins. "My treat."

She took a bite of chicken, with a sigh of appreciation, as she wiped her mouth. "Man, that is good."

I had my mouth full, so all I could do was nod, in agreement. After swallowing a sip of soda, I got down to the business at hand. "So what did you learn from the two trucks?"

Molly swirled her french fries in the cup of ketchup, shaking her head. "Neither of them had been in a collision of any sort. There were no dents, scratches, or blood, on the outside or underside. The truck beds also revealed, no presence of blood."

I took another bite of chicken and wiped my fingers. "How about dirt in the tires. Were you able to get anything from that?"

She nodded her head, after taking a long sip. "Yes. On the Mazda was red clay, which is typical in this area. But there were also significant traces of coal mixed in with the clay."

I wiped my mouth and placed my napkin on my desk. "Coal?"

"Small traces, but significant enough for spectrometer to pick it up."

I thought about the conundrum, for a moment, but enlightenment soon filled me with euphoria. "About six years ago, the last train car from a CSX train, got lose and overturned in Vonore. Remember, it was a miracle no one was hurt and there was no serious property damage?"

Molly snapped her finger, as she pointed to me. "Right, I had forgotten about that. It was near the crime scene, wasn't it?"

"There abouts. CSX cleaned it up and paid for the repairs. I bet that's why there were traces of it in the soil. Still doesn't mean, it was at the house, where Alston was found. The spill affected a lot of areas."

Molly elevated her eyebrow, as she smiled at me. "In the bed of the Mazda, we did find traces of a polyester coated material, which also had traces of dyed green urethane. In other words, a heavy duty plastic tarp. We found similar samples, of the same tarp, on Alston O'Brian's clothing."

Ironically a CSX train engaged its siren, just before the railway crossings began to ring. I felt my own eyebrows elevate, at this news. "Traces of the same tarp, in the bed, of the truck and on Alston's clothing?"

She nodded. "And in Patrick's truck, we found threads of Alston's coat, in the backseat."

I pushed my food to the side, leaning back in my chair, allowing my mind, to process this information and put it into context. "So we have trace evidence, that connects Alston, to both vehicles. So... maybe, they abducted him in Patrick's truck, then after he died, they used Harrison's truck, to move the body. The tarp could've been used, to slide him, under the house."

Molly thought about it, before agreeing with me. "It's a plausible theory. It's far from a slam dunk, but it for sure, puts the victim in both trucks."

I scratched my chin, the small stubble of a five o'clock shadow brushing under my fingernail. "And since Harrison Birch and Patrick Winchell were part, of the lynch mob, that attacked Alston a few days, before his death, I seriously doubt the two just offered him a ride."

"We also concluded, that fibers from the victims clothing matched the samples, you took, from the house. The blood samples were AB negative, the same blood type, as the victim. There were also traces, of the same tarp, mixed in with the blood."

I interlaced my fingers over my abdomen. "You match, that shoe impression in blood, to any of the exemplars, we took at the scene?"

She shook her head. "None of the foot ware impressions, you took from the scene, match that shoeprint, in blood, found in the carpet."

Not the answer I was hoping for. "How about the Durango?"

"The tires match the casts you took, from the crime scene. No surprise there and we found similar traces of coal, in the soil samples." She turned the page of her file. "The blood, on the grill and bumper, matches the victim's blood type and the glass you collected, at the crime scene is a match, to the headlight of the Durango. The markings on the hitch are fresh. There was no corrosion, as you'd expect, if it had been sitting in a lot, for months at a time. I also looked at Karen's autopsy report and the measurements, of the Durango's grill, matched the wounds on the victim. It's definitely the car, Jonas."

"I don't suppose the thieves were sloppy enough, to leave their fingerprints behind?"

Molly smiled, as she shook her head. "We fumed the entire car, with superglue and could not find a single print. No smudges or partials. Whoever did this, wiped the entire vehicle down thoroughly."

This was no surprise. I slowly turned the paper plate, in a circular motion, on my desk. "You had a chance to look at Alston's car yet?"

She nodded her head, in the direction of the forensic lot. "I've got people working on it as we speak. We're pulling an all-nighter, so we should have some results, by morning. We checked the bag of marijuana, for prints, like you asked."

I rocked in my seat, waiting. "And?"

"We found two sets. One was from Alston, the other isn't in any database."

I was mildly relieved. I was afraid Phil's fingerprints would be on it. Having been arrested a few times, his prints are on file, so they would've definitely popped up. "Good work Molly. If the Camry is GPS enabled, let Tom know and he can upload the car's whereabouts. We might get lucky and find out where Alston was abducted, before he was killed."

She handed the folders, across the desk, to me, as she stood up. "Will do. Here are your copies of the reports."

I took the reports and set them beside my laptop. Thanks and I appreciate you working through the night, Molly."

She waved it off, like it was no big deal. "Comes with the territory, Jonas."

After she left I walked, to the squad room, to see Glen had returned and was now eating a plate of chicken tenders. Not wanting to disturb his meal, I stopped by Tom's station, to see if he was still working on the data, from the police cruisers. I sat down in the empty chair near his desk. "How's it going Tom?"

He nodded, catching his yawn in his hand. "I've just about finished with them all. Another hour or so and I should know where all the vehicles and department issued phones were located, during the night of the murder."

Watching the blinking dots on the screen, I saluted the major task Tom had performed. It was a flash of genius, for him to come up with such an idea and to execute it, so well. I'm proficient, when it comes to computers, but when I'm in Tom's presence, I always feel a wave of humility, as I watch him punch a few keys on the computer and move several megabytes of data. With the plethora of new mobile devices, computers and various other electronics that come out each year, you would be foolish, to believe you didn't need a computer expert, on your side. "Tom, I don't know how you do it."

He grinned, as he continued to punch the keys and scroll the screen, with his mouse. "Oh you could do this. It's easy, Jonas."

I laughed, stretching my neck. "For you maybe. Me, knowing my luck, I'd wind up accidentally hacking a government facility or something."

This made him laugh. When he looked at me, I could see the fatigue in his red eyes. "When's the last time, you took a break, from this?"

"I'm all right. Like I said, I'm almost done. Besides, when was the last time you took a break, from this case?"

Touché, I thought. "We may have some more GPS work for you tomorrow. Molly's going over Alston's car tonight. If the car has a GPS system, I want you to map it out, as well."

"I'll see what I can do."

Glen came from his desk, with his steno pad in hand and a ballpoint pen tucked behind his ear. "Jonas, I've been talking with some of the patrons, who were at the Laffing Goat, the night of the murder. I've been showing them the driver's license pictures, of Patrick Winchell and Harrison Birch. So far, no one can say they were there until closing time. Some of them remember seeing them, but not one can vouch, for when they left."

"So it's a soft alibi.

"It's sure looks that way."

Rocking the chair on its back two legs, hands behind my head, I stared at the upper corner of the wall. "Glen start the paperwork, on a search warrant, for Harrison Birch and Patrick Winchell's place of residence. I want Mr. Deland, to take it before a judge, first thing in the morning."

Glen made a note in his steno pad. "I take it we've developed some leads."

I was still staring at the ceiling, slowly shaking my head. "Molly found trace evidence, that puts Alston, in both Patrick's and Harrison's trucks. I want to see what else we can find, on their properties."

Glen let out a low whistle, as he started back to his desk. "I wonder, if those two will be more cooperative, when they realize, they're in our crosshairs?"

It might be enough to get one of them talking or maybe drive a wedge between them. It wouldn't be the first time, two friends turned on one another, at the prospect of a better prison sentence.

I quickly pushed those thoughts aside. No sense in getting ahead of ourselves. I was hoping the warrant, would reveal the actual tarp Alston had been wrapped in, or any other trace evidence, that might connect them, to the victim. Yet, despite these solid leads, I still found myself coming back, to Nathaniel Hensley and his bruised hands. My gut was telling me he was involved in this somehow, but I had no physical evidence, that validated my theory. An idea suddenly sprouted in my mind.

I returned to my office and got online, to search the website, that in today's world, is the quickest way to research an individual: *Facebook*. A rather ubiquitous fact of today's modern society, is people's need to share, the most intimate aspects of their lives, online. The department uses this from time to time. People voluntarily post their pictures and thoughts, on the social media site, and we don't need a search warrant. I was betting since Nathaniel was a teenager, that meant, he was an avid user of the site. Typing in his name quickly revealed, I was correct.

His biography said, he was born on July 31, 1999, he went to Sequoyah High School and he worked at Fastenal. The posts didn't reveal anything related to Alston, but the photos and videos, he posted revealed quite a bit of information. He was a shortstop, for the Sequoyah Chiefs and had hit several homeruns. There was one photograph of him, with some other teenagers, in the woods wearing camouflaged fatigues, that were stained, with multi colored paint, obviously, from a paint gun. My mind immediately jumped, to the paint covered cameras and the cylindrical shaped wounds, on Alston's torso.

I read the forensic reports Molly had left behind, learning no more than she had told me already. When I saw it was after nine, I took what was left of the tenders and fries, microwaved them and wrapped the plate in aluminum foil. I packed up the casefiles and put them in my bag and headed out, to where Jack was on stakeout, at the Hensley residence.

Daniel and Clare lived, in a doublewide trailer, on the edge of Vonore Estates. Jack was parked along the curve of the road, in a faded red 1999 Honda Civic. It wasn't the most luxurious of vehicles, but when you're conducting a stakeout, you don't want a car, that will attract a lot of attention. I parked a few feet behind him. I quickly extinguished my headlights, before exiting my truck and making my way to the passenger side of the sedan. He was still looking ahead when his nostrils, came alive and he inhaled a long breath. "Tell me, you brought that for me."

I handed him the plate, which he gladly accepted. I pulled out some fast-food napkins I had stashed in my coat pocket. I handed him a bottle of water. "I thought you might be hungry. How's things going here?"

He swallowed, a whole tender in two bites, pointing to the house, with his chin. "It's been all quiet, so far. I got here, about thirty minutes, before Clare and her son arrived. Daniel arrived five minutes after they did. He stayed for an hour, then left and hasn't returned yet."

In the streetlight, the tan siding on the Hensley trailer appeared white. The dogwood trees in the yard, cast stenciled outlines, across the dead grass. One could see the rectangular shape of the trailer windows, as the light peeked out, from under the edges, of the shades. "How did Daniel seem when he left?"

Jack cracked open the bottle of water and took a sip. "The way he was moving, you'd think someone, lit a match, to his backside. He slammed the door, of his truck and squealed the tires, as he backed out onto the street. I was worried he might've seen me, but he raced up the road, away from me. I've been watching, in case he doubled back, but so far I've seen no sign of him."

I nodded, adjusting my position, so my coat wasn't bunched under my hindquarters. "And the mother and son? How did they seem, to you, when they got home?"

"All right I suppose. But when I looked at the mother, with the binoculars, her eyes looked like she had been crying. The boy was quiet and kept his head low, as if he was trying to be invisible."

I folded my hands over my lap, as I studied the surrounding real estate. "I rattled them all pretty good, at the Lowes warehouse. Daniel may have gone out, to clear his head, or go to Saul for advice. I just wanted some eyes here, to gage their reactions, from our encounter."

Jack finished his food and folded the paper plate, so it could be wrapped up in the aluminum foil. "What's made you suspect Clare Hensley and her son?"

I leaned my head, against the cushion of the seat, and kept my eyes focused on the doublewide. "I discovered Alston and Clare were lovers. When I questioned her about this, she became very nervous. At first, I didn't think too much of her reaction, since she had believed this had all been buried. But as I was leaving, Daniel was dropping her son, Nathaniel off from school. Jack, the boy is spitting image of Alston, when he was a young man."

My deputy turned to me, his eyes protruding, as he dropped his baritone voice an octave. "You think Clare had Alston's baby?"

"I think it is a strong possibility. To make things even more interesting, the kid has bruised knuckles, on his right hand. He's also a baseball player and likes to shoot paintball."

Jack's face grew long, as he closed his eyes. "So, maybe, it's possible the kid might've had a hand in the beating Alston received, just before his death and maybe even stealing the Durango."

"It sure is looking that way."

"How come her name was never mentioned at the trial?"

I gave him a brief summation, of what I had learned, from Eugene Collier, earlier in the day. After listening to me, Jack slowly shook his head. "That just doesn't seem right to me, Jonas."

I nodded scratching my leg, just above the hem of my sock. "I know, it's probably an ethical violation, on Eugene's part, but the man's retired now and I don't see any reason to bring him up before an ethics committee."

Jack tapped his long finger, on the dashboard of the car. "Not that. The idea that no one knew Nathaniel was Alston's son. Vonore, is a small town and Alston left a big mark there, that has still left a bad taste, in some people's mouths. You are not going to convince me, that there weren't a few people, who knew about Clare and Alston being together and made the connection, as to who her son's father was."

My deputy was making a very compelling argument, for which I was silently scolding myself, for not realizing sooner. There had to be people in Vonore, who knew or very strongly suspected, as I do, that Nathaniel was the son of Alston O'Brian. This leads to some very interesting questions. Like, why had Clare chosen to stay here during and after the trial? If the man, who caused the people of Vonore so much pain, wasn't readily in front of them; wouldn't it stand to reason, they would take it out on the next best thing, the mother and son? Living in a rural county all my life, I had witnessed this plenty of times. I would like to think, a good mother would never allow, such tribulations to fall upon her child. From what I saw at the warehouse, Clare genuinely cares for her son. Perhaps, that means the town accepted, the fact, Nathaniel was the offspring of the man, who destroyed so many families. Did the citizens of Vonore rise above the primal need, for retribution and not blame the son, for the sins of the father?

I stopped the train of thought, before my mind was sent into a tailspin. "Maybe they did Jack. It might've been an open secret, if you will. Right now, though, our concern is that they stay in town, until we get this sorted out."

Jack nodded, as he took another sip from his water. "How long do you want me here?"

"You can call it quits at midnight. I can't authorize a full stakeout on just the fact, the boy happens to look like Alston. In the morning,

I want you to call Sequoyah High School and find out if Nathaniel was involved, in any school fights or sports activities, that could explain away, the injuries I saw on his hand."

He nodded, placing the bottle in the cup holder. "And if it turns out he doesn't have a school related reason, for his injuries?"

I gave him my dead stare. "Then, I'll go to Mr. Deland and tell him my suspicions and we'll proceed from there. I'm hoping the injuries can be explained away, because believe me, I don't want to be responsible, for putting a teenaged kid behind bars, for possibly the next twenty years."

Jack reached over and patted me squarely on the shoulder, with his massive hand, sending ribbons of concussive shocks down my arm. "If the boy did it Jonas, you're not responsible. You didn't make him do anything."

Once again, Jack's wisdom was as sound, as the roots of a mighty oak tree. However, what wisdom has often taught me is, what we know in our heads and feel in our hearts, is often two very different sets of emotions.

* * *

I was on my way home, when I realized I had missed a text message, from my mother, saying her computer was acting up, so I dialed them up and said I'd swing by on my way home. Mom was in her PJs, with her red flannel robe on, her reading glasses, resting on the top of her head, when she opened the door. The cool wind forced her to wrap the robe tighter around her. "Get in here and shut the door."

I closed the door and removed my boots, so as not to track up the house. Dad was sitting in his chair, reading the newspaper, but really eyeing, the cooking show, that was on the television. "Hey son. You didn't have to come over here, tonight, to look at the computer."

I placed my boots on the hearth and placed my coat on the chair, by the computer desk. "It's no problem. Like I told Mom, I was on my way home. What's it doing?"

Mom's face grew serious, as she pointed to the computer screen. while propping her other hand on her hip. A similar gesture she often gave me, when I was being scolded as a child. "We can't get the keyboard to type anything. I was practicing my typing, using MS Word and everything was working perfectly and then it just stopped."

I brought the screen up and studied it, for a second or two, before quickly deducing what the problem was. I punched the shift key five times and then the keyboard was working again. "You hit the shift key, too many times in a row. Probably by accident. When you do that it locks the keyboard up."

She stared, at the shift key, a heavy frown on her face. "Why does it do that?"

I shrugged my shoulders, as I stood allowing her to sit down. "I don't know, Mom. I can ask Tom, if you want."

Waving her hand, she took a seat and typed a few more words across the screen. "Don't bother. It would probably be over my head, anyway. I swear everyone says these things make everything so much better, but I get more headaches from them, then I did the manual typewriters, we used in school. Even when the ribbons snapped, I never wanted to scream the way I do, when this thing freaks out on me."

I was standing behind her, arms folded across my chest, nodding my head along with her speech. I had heard it more than once, over the years and no doubt I would hear it again. In truth, I agree with a lot of what she says, with regards to technology and it's supposed benefits, which I am not debunking. Yet, when something goes wrong, it is like the whole world stops in its tracks. Then again, who am I to pass judgement? "It's probably over my head too, Mom. You two doing all right?"

Dad turned to the next page of the newspaper, glancing down at it, but quickly casting his eyes on the television once again. "Everything

303

is good, now that you've solved that catastrophe. How have you been doing?"

"Fine."

Dad cast his eyes away from the TV, in my direction. Mom, stopped her typing and turned around in her seat. I hunched my shoulders. "What?"

Mom swung her hand back, tapping me in the stomach. "Son, don't "what" us. We've been with you since day one. We know when everything is not *fine*."

I looked back at Dad, who concurred with his wife of forty-four years. "What your mother said."

It still nagged me, as much now, as it did, when I was a child, how my parents always seem to have x-ray vision, when it came to me. "It's just been a rough day."

Mom closed out the screen and returned to the sofa, where her novel was resting. "It's about that man, who was found dead, under the house, isn't it?"

I took a seat, in the old chair, that had been mine, when I was still living here. "Yeah. I can't go into detail, but the case has taken a turn I wasn't expecting."

Dad folded the newspaper on his lap and hooked the earpiece, of his glasses, inside the collar of his shirt. "What direction is that?"

I closed my eyes, resting my head against the cushion, of my favorite chair. "We've been here before folks, so let's just speak in hypotheticals."

Mom blew out a deep breath, as she enfolded her arms. "That's fine by me. Though I don't see why we have to do that. I've never once, told a secret, you trusted me with."

I looked over at her, fighting the temptation to say something dry and sarcastic. "Then we're all agreed. I've got a situation, in which I believe an eighteen-year-old kid is involved in an investigation."

Dad nodded, keeping his voice low and even. "Involved how?"

"He may have a connection, to the victim and also may have been involved, in the death of the victim."

Mom cocked her eyebrow, as she pursed her lips. "There has to be more to it than that, to get you so upset."

I smiled. "There is. Let's say the teenager has family connections to the police. There are two other very good suspects as well, which I can connect to the crime scene. The problem is, I can't figure how all these pieces fit together."

Dad stared off into the void of the hallway, lost deep in thought. "Do you think they did it together? The teenager and your other suspects?"

I furrowed my forehead, as I stared him. "There is nothing that connects them to one another. Wait, that's not true. All involved have deep connections to the victim. I suppose they could've gotten together, to get revenge. But would they drag the kid into it?"

"You're assuming, the men dragged the teenager, into the scenario. What if it was the other way around?" Mom said.

I thought about what she had said, but I still didn't see the full picture, she was attempting to draw on the canvas. "You're thinking, an eighteen-year-old boy, could convince, two grown men, to commit murder?"

Mom rolled her eyes, resting her reading glasses on her thighs. "Son, I was a teacher for over thirty years. I can tell you, from personal experience, kids are much cleverer, than most adults tend to believe. It seemed to me every year, they got smarter and more deceptive, than the previous year."

I focused on my mother's words, playing out the scenario, she was suggesting. "Yeah, but how could he get them to drop the house on the victim?"

Dad stared at the top of his armrest, for a few seconds, thinking about the question. "It doesn't make sense, that's true. But, what is the advantage of dropping the house on the victim?"

I shook my head, but stopped as a crazy solution came to mind. "It could take our focus away from the kid."

Mom wrinkled her forehead. "Say that again?"

"With the house being used on the victim, it made us look into the previous owner, which in turn, led to my two primary suspects," I said, feeling the wheels turning. "We didn't know about the teenager. The mother's name was never mentioned in the trial, so there was no record. It's possible, the kid could've believed, we'd never connect it to him."

I stood up and started pacing the room. "But to do everything, you're suggesting, he'd have to be very clever and very devious."

Mom leaned forward, pointing the rim of her glasses at me. "Son, kids grow up a lot faster now, than they did, when you were boy. You've been a cop a long time, now. I'm not saying that is what happened. I'm just asking is it possible, that it could've happened that way?"

I had to admit, it could be possible, but I would have to do some more digging into Nathaniel Hensley, before I could be certain. It is natural to want to see everything linear, from point A to point B. The reality is, we all know life comes at you, from all directions, most of which, you cannot predict. I was still going to need more information, before I could see the entire picture, but as Bill had said earlier, I did know, which direction, to look.

"There is one more wild card you need to consider too, Jonas," said Mom.

I turned to her and rested my hands on my hips. "What's that?"

She smiled, shaking her head, like I should already know the answer. "The mother. I can tell you from personal experience, a mother will do anything, to protect her child. It is a primal instinct, that takes root in us, while the child is still in the womb."

I instantly recalled the feral gleam in Clare's eyes, when she realized, I knew Nathaniel was Alston's son. "Any advice on how to handle the mother?"

Her smile evaporated and a hard gleam enveloped her eyes. "Very carefully. Getting in the way of a mother trying to protect her child, is like standing in the pathway of a tornado, son."

Dad smiled at me nodding his head, in his wife's direction. "She's right on that one, son."

Indeed, she was.

Chapter Twenty-Two

I told Jack, I would speak with the principle of Sequoyah High School. I learned Nathaniel Hensley had not been involved, in any physical activities, that would explain the injuries to his hand. The school counselor had questioned Nathaniel, about the bruises, on his knuckles. Nathaniel said he had sustained the injuries, while doing chores around the house. I suppose that was a plausible explanation, but it didn't set right with me. This excuse didn't implicate him, in anything nefarious, but it didn't exonerate him, either.

Further background, on Nathaniel, revealed that he was a member, of a school sponsored junior police squad, which matched students, with officers for observation purposes. It was no surprise, to find, Nathaniel had been assigned, to the Vonore City Police Department. My mind kept returning to the conversation I had with my parents, the previous night. I found myself wondering if Saul or Daniel had taken Nathaniel to the impound lot.

The hospital called and said Thomas Kinderman would be in recovery, for a few more days, at which time his leg would be well enough, for transport to our holding facilities. Frederick Brentwood, would be arraigned, by the end of the morning, for his compliancy, in the robberies and destruction of property. My next phone call was to Anthony Deland, where I discussed the evidence Molly had discovered.

"So we can place Alston, in both Harrison Birch's and Patrick Winchell's vehicles?" Anthony asked.

I took a long sip of coffee. "Yes. It's circumstantial, but it's a solid lead, nonetheless."

Anthony exhaled a long exasperated breath. "It's not enough, for an arrest, but I should be able to get a search warrant."

I smiled as I set my cup on the desk. "I've got Glen working on the request. He should be at your office in a few minutes. That sound good to you?"

I took a paperclip from my desk and traced the edges between my fingers, as Anthony replied, "You should have your search warrant in an hour."

"Thank you," I said replacing the phone in the cradle. I sat there for a moment, trying to decide what my next move should be, while I waited for the warrant. My eyes landed on the picture of Harrison's green Mazda, which reminded me, I needed to speak with Phil Woody, about the truck he saw, on the day, he spoke with Alston.

Phil answered on the fourth ring and after explaining why I called, he agreed to meet me in my office. Twenty minutes later, Phil, wearing a plaid coat and blue toboggan, walked into the stationhouse. I stepped into the hall to greet him. "Come on in Phil."

He came into my office and declined a cup of coffee. "Thanks, but I'm fine. You said you had a photograph, you wanted me to look at?"

I took the 4x6 photo, from my desk and placed it before him. "Is this the truck you saw, the last time, you spoke with Alston O'Brian."

Phil took out his reading glasses, before taking the photo. He rested the jet black bifocals, on the bridge of his nose, and focused on the truck. He frowned, as he peered intensely at the photo, then rubbed the bottom of his chin, with the back of his hand. "It might be Jonas. It might be. You and I know, that my mind isn't exactly, as sharp as a tack, anymore. That said, I think it might be the truck. It's definitely the same size and color. Who does it belong to?"

I retrieved the photograph, placing it face down on my desk. "I can't divulge that right now, Phil. But I can tell you, we have the guys, who broke into your house. We're dealing with another investigation, but I have no doubt, that their prints are going to match those we lifted, from your house."

Phil pulled off the toboggan, smoothing his unruly silver hair. "I read in the paper you had made an arrest. I appreciate that sheriff. Lord knows you've had your hands full, with all of this other stuff going on. I can't imagine it was easy."

I hunched my shoulders and waved my hand. "It's the job, Phil. It was also a team effort, so I can't take all the credit."

Phil smiled, shaking his head. "I've never seen a man refuse a compliment, like you do, Jonas."

I returned his smile, as I propped my right foot on the open bottom drawer of my desk. "I want to make sure I don't get the big head."

Phil smiled, as he looked down at the corner of my desk. "I suppose that is a virtue unto itself, keeping a person's good deeds to himself. It says so in the book of Isaiah, *The person who talks most of his own virtue is often the least virtuous.*"

I cleared my throat and worked hard to keep my face straight. I sifted through my memory, for the true author of the quote, but wasn't having any luck. "That's not from the Bible Phil. I'm not quite certain, where you got that one. I believe it was some politician, who said that."

Phil lowered his chin to his chest, as he pushed out a long sigh. "You're right. I was watching a documentary on TV about Jawaharlal Nehru, the prime minister of India. I think they did mention that quote."

I nodded, pursing my lips. "It's an easy mistake. But thanks for the compliment."

Phil smiled and stood up. "You're welcome. Well, I won't take up anymore of your time."

I stood and shook his hand. "Come on, I'll walk you out."

After walking Phil to the door, Tom stood up and waved me over to his desk. "Jonas, I've got the results from the GPS on the police personnel."

I waited, as he brought up the database on the screen. "Dazzle me Tom."

He pointed to the list of names on the screen. "All of these officers have been cleared. I was able to confirm their whereabouts, through the roll calls and reports. The second column are the names, whose GPS report, show they were miles away from the crime scene. Since we've been unable to make any connections to the victim, I feel pretty sure we can mark them off the suspect list."

I folded my arms over my chest, watching him scroll the screen. "Who does that leave us with then?"

"You already know the answer to that, Jonas." Tom brought up the names I had grown all too familiar with. "Chief Saul West and Officer Daniel Hensley."

The courthouse clock chimed the time. "You have anything that directly connects them to the crime?"

Tom's shoulder's slouched, as he looked at the screen. "Unfortunately no. Hensley's phone has him at his house. Saul's patrol car had him on Highway 411, for about an hour, then he spent just over an hour on 72 East, before making that brief stop."

I shook my head. It made no sense, for Saul to spend that much time on that road. "Why was he there for over an hour? Was he looking for something?"

"That's what I was thinking," Tom replied. "You said it yourself, there's not much traffic on that road."

I pointed to the gray lines on the digital map. "What do those lines represent?"

Tom squinted at the scrawls, hunching his shoulders. "Nameless backroads. That one looks to be about two tenths of a mile long."

"And what time did Saul arrive there?"

Tom zeroed his vision in on the timestamp. "According to the GPS, he entered the area at 10:01 p.m. and left at 11:02 p.m."

Running the timeline through my head, it didn't take long for me to do the math. "So that eliminates him, from being the one who took the Durango from the impound lot."

Tom's chair popped and creaked, as he leaned back. "Plus the cameras show that only one individual stole the Durango, but two were present, when it was returned. Maybe Daniel stole it, while Saul was on patrol. The GPS on Daniel's phone says he was at his house, but he could've easily left it there, just to throw us off the scent."

"Was there any contact between Saul and Daniel that night?" I asked.

Tom brought up a screen, on the computer, with a time stamp on it. "They spoke around 7:45 that night, for about five minutes. There was no other contact between them, at least not with their phones. Which brings me to the part, you're not going to like."

I looked down at him, as the wings of trepidation began to flap inside my stomach. "What?"

Tom brought up the first screen, that had all the GPS devices listed. "After 11:10 p.m., Saul's phone is no longer active."

I stared down at my deputy. "You mean he went off grid?"

Tom shrugged, as he pointed to the screen. "That's what it looks like. From 11:10 until 5:30 a.m. his phone's GPS was in active. Either he turned the phone off or he deactivated the locations feature on the phone."

I stared at the computer, arms draped across my chest. "Remind me again, but wasn't that the exact same time frame, that the CB radios were down as well?"

"Almost the exact same time. It certainly appears, he didn't want anyone to know what was happening during that six-hour period."

"That is definitely enough time to kill Alston, place the body under the house, and then return the Durango, to the impound lot," I said.

"Either way Jonas, that's a huge period, for which the chief has no alibi," Tom said.

The word conundrum isn't a sufficient enough expression for this situation. On one hand, we have physical evidence, that connects the victim to two suspects. The same two suspects, that attacked him, just days before his murder. The only problem is, they did not have access to the impound lot. However, on the other hand, we have two cops, refusing to cooperate, have a past history with the victim, access to the impound lot, and weak alibis. But we have no physical evidence, to link them to the victim. It was like I was walking through my own version of the Chaos Theory. "How about Alston's phone? You ever recover it?"

Tom shook his head, crossing his arms over his chest. "No. I was able, to trace the number back, to a prepaid cellular telephone company. Alston bought his phone at a gas station, in Meigs County, the same day he bought his car. Paid cash of course. The last activity on the phone was when Alston called you, the day he disappeared."

"So either the phone has been turned off or it's destroyed," I said.

"That's the way I see it."

I shook my head, as I sucked in some air. "We're still missing something here, Tom."

"Yeah, we still can't exclude Saul or Daniel."

"No, that's not what I mean. We're missing a piece of the puzzle. We have physical evidence that connects Harrison Birch and Patrick Winchell. Then we have Saul going off grid and all radio calls, on the night of the murder, vanishing."

Tom looked at the screen, frowning in concentration. "Is it possible, that they were all in on it together? Patrick and Harrison with Saul and Daniel?"

I rubbed the base of my chin, with my thumb, carefully considering his theory. "It's plausible Tom. All of them had a grievance against Alston. They could've gotten together and devised the plan."

"Having two cops, on your side, does help," Tom retorted. "Who better could clean up a crime scene?"

I took a seat beside him, with a frown on my face. "That's where it doesn't fit though, Tom. If Harrison and Patrick were working with Saul and Daniel, would they have left the trace evidence, in their own trucks?"

Tom slowly nodding his head. "Could Saul be trying to frame them?"

I cocked an eyebrow at him. "Well, if that was the plan, it's working. But the thing is, if Saul tried to frame them, then the two of them could simply turn the tables on him."

Tom thought for a moment, before shrugging his shoulders. "You're right. There is something missing."

My BlackBerry vibrated, indicating I had a text from Molly. It said the GPS in Alston's vehicle had been activated and the footage was ready for Tom to analyze. She had the results from the sample taken from the trunk of the Camry. "Turns out the stain, in the trunk, is burned cooking oil and grease. It was pretty old. I guess the previous owner must've put their garbage in the back and it leaked. Now, I need you to go to Anthony and get a warrant, for the GPS on Alston's car, then head to the garage and download the GPS coordinates. Maybe we can find out where he was abducted."

He stood up and grabbed his coat and laptop. "I'll let you know what I find."

I called Jack and Glen into the conference room, to let them know a search authorization would be coming soon and they would be in charge. I would remain at the stationhouse and hold down the fort. I needed time to think and the solitude would do me good.

* * *

After Glen and Jack left, I sat behind my desk, with the door closed, staring at my notes, reviewing the timeline. There were several pieces missing. However, Einstein said, imagination was more important than knowledge. I too have found, that imagination is a very important tool and I was putting it to good use right now. I propped my foot on the bottom drawer of my desk and slowly swiveled my chair, from side to side, as I placed my hands on my abdomen. Closing my eyes, I replayed the sequence of events, in my head, in slow motion, beginning with the phone conversation, I had with Alston, on the day, he was most likely abducted, up until the discovery of his body. Mapping out a scenario, of how that fateful evening might have happened, I realized as bizarre as it seems, it wasn't entirely out the realm of possibility. The main characters' faces were still unclear, but my gut was telling me, that I was moving in the right direction.

I began going over the time line once again. Phil said he saw a green truck leaving the church parking lot, right after Alston left, the morning, he gave him the marijuana. It was at that moment "logical thinking" came to an abrupt halt.

I sifted through the folders on my desk, until I came to the autopsy report. After reading it from cover to cover, I saw there was no mention of THC found in Alston's bloodwork, but there was six ounces, of the drug, in his car. According to Phil, he gave Alston four bags of marijuana, a few days before his death and I had found three bags, in his car. Even if he had only been smoking it for a short while, THC would be present in the blood up to ten days. Dr. Karen Long was an excellent pathologist, so I have no doubt the blood tests were conducted professionally. So that begs the question, if Phil gave Alston marijuana and he didn't use it, where was the missing bag?

It was then, I became aware of a familiar scent. I looked up to see Lydia standing at the corner of my desk, her hands tucked in the pockets, of her navy blue pants. There was a light smile on her face, as she shook her head. Clearing my throat, I closed the file and gave her my best grin. "You've been standing there a while, haven't you?"

She nodded, sitting on the edge of my desk. "For about five minutes. I knocked on the door and said your name. Twice."

I dropped my head, feeling the back of my neck grow warm from embarrassment. This was not the first time I had gotten so deep in thought, that I was oblivious to my surroundings. A fault I am not proud of. "Sorry. I got—"

"Lost in the rabbit hole." Lydia ran her fingers along my scalp, straightening a lock of my hair. "It seems you must've found something pretty interesting in that file."

I took her hand in mine and kissed it lightly. "It's what I didn't find actually."

"Do tell?"

I started to divulge my discovery, but quickly decided to postpone it for the moment. "How about we talk about why you're here?"

She smiled, cocking her head over her right shoulder. "Thought I'd stop in and see how things were going with the case. Mr. Deland said you had requested search warrants. I was curious if maybe you were closing in on a suspect."

"The weekend getaway is still a possibility."

Lydia's golden brown eyes focused on my face, like she was trying to read my thoughts. "You doing all right?"

I frowned and leaned back in the chair. "I'm fine. Why are you asking?"

She let her hand gently rest on top of mine, her fingers brushing the hair on the top of my hand, while casting her eyes down at the floor. "No reason. I know you've been under a lot of pressure and I've not exactly been helping you, by wanting to go on that romantic weekend."

I leaned back in the chair, swiveling in her direction. "You didn't make me do anything. Besides we both know, it wasn't exactly etched in stone it would happen."

"So everything is good?"

I was the one now examining her face, trying to see what was beneath the surface. I've never been very good at reading women. Whereas men are more singular in their actions and line of thought, I have found the fairer sex more multifaceted, especially in the emotional reasoning category. The stereotype assumption that women are flighty and incapable of making serious decisions, therefore not suited for positions of authority, is completely false, in my humble opinion. The honest truth is, I've often felt, that if the roles were reversed, Lydia would make a better sheriff, than me. That said, I believe there was something more to her sudden concern, about my state of mind, and I believe I know where the root of this concern has sprouted. "Did you talk with my mother today?"

Her lips formed a small O, her eyes expanded, before she gave me a halfhearted shrug. "She didn't call me. I called her, wondering if they'd like to have dinner with us later in the week. Your mom asked how you were doing, saying you looked tired, when you stopped by last night."

"And you thought you'd stop by and see how I was doing." I propped my head on the knuckles of my left hand. "The concern is appreciated, but I am OK."

She pointed to the file, I had been so engrossed in, just few moments earlier. "From the way you were reading that, I assume you have made a breakthrough, in the investigation."

I eyed the casefile in question. "I think I may have found something, that could possibly aid in the investigation. It's too early to say if it'll help us, but you know many times, it is the smallest details that can often crack a case."

Crossing her leg, her leather boot, touched the edge of my chair, while she folded her hands on her knee. "Then why are you not excited? Usually, it's a good thing, when you catch a break."

I seesawed my head from shoulder to shoulder. "Because I still can't see how all the pieces connect. I'm also afraid, when those pieces do fall into place, this case is going to have a bad ending."

"As opposed to the other murder investigations with happy endings?"

I had to concur with her logic. "Not the best choice of words, but I believe you get my meaning."

Lydia scratched the flesh on her thumb. "I know what you mean. I also know, that you have no control over the actions, of other people. When you arrive on the scene, it's too late to do anything, but clean up the mess and find out who the perpetrator is." She leaned over and looked me directly in the eye. "However, this plays out, it's not your fault. I don't want you blaming yourself."

I can always count, on the women in my life, to give me a swift kick to the butt. My mother has the left cheek, Lydia takes care of the right one. I met her gaze and smiled. "I will take your advice to heart."

She smiled, giving me a light peck on the cheek. "See that you do."

I rubbed my chin with my finger. "You know taking it "easy on myself" isn't exactly my strong suit."

Lydia gave me a frown that was a disapproving, yet cute at the same time. "Alcoholics stop drinking. Drug users stop using. I'm pretty sure, if you put your mind to it, you can find it in yourself, to stop placing the world's problems on your shoulders."

My telephone beeped, I had a call from Tom's workstation. "What can I do for you Tom?"

"I've been going over the GPS data, from Alston's Camry. I think I have something. Is it all right if I come in? I saw Lydia go into your office a minute ago."

I hit the hold button and rested the phone on my shoulder. "Tom thinks he's got something from the GPS on the victim's car."

Lydia stood and straightened her blazer. "Tell him to come in. I can leave."

I shook my head and pointed to the seat across from my desk. "I'd like you to stay, if you can."

Lydia stared at the worn, vacant chair. "I can do that."

"Take the other seat. That's the one Mick likes. You don't want dog hair on your backside for the rest of the day." I released the hold button. "Come on in, Tom."

A minute later, Tom brought his laptop into the office and nodded to Lydia, when he saw her. "Lydia."

Lydia smiled, crossing her legs. "How are you doing Tom? He's not working you too hard, I hope."

Tom grinned, as he opened his computer. "He's not cracking that whip any more than usual."

I kept my face neutral and pointed to the laptop. "I may get to cracking it, if you don't show me what it is you found."

Tom scrolled his finger across the trackpad and double clicked on an icon. "After I downloaded the Camry's software, I was able to track Alston's location, right up until the time, we found the car at the scrapyard. According to his phone, you last spoke with him four days, before we discovered his body"

"Yeah. He sounded like he had something serious on his mind."

Tom angled his laptop, so I could see the digital map. "I was able to use the time stamp, on his call log, and the GPS on his car, to get a pretty accurate idea where he was abducted."

I sat up and studied the map. "Show me."

He pointed to the East Tellico Parkway Road, about three miles west from Highway 411. "Right there.",

I recalled, this was the road I had gone down that morning, searching for Alston. "How can you be sure this is where he was abducted."

"From the call log on the phone, you two started talking at 11:45 a.m. and you spoke for three minutes and four seconds. The GPS from the Camry indicates he was driving on this road. When he stopped talking to you at 11:48 a.m. his vehicle continued on this course, for about one more minute, then it stops right here, about a mile and a half from the highway. After a minute and a half, the car crosses Highway 411 and stops here."

I stared at the blinking light, that represented Alston's vehicle, and its final destination on East 72. "That's pretty close to where Saul spent so much time on the night of Alston's murder."

Tom shook his head, tapping the location on the screen, with his finger. "It's the exact location of Chief West"

I stared at the screen for a while, letting the information sift through my brain. "Saul stopped his cruiser, at the exact same spot, that Alston O'Brian's car was taken? That's too much to be a coincidence."

"I'm inclined to agree with you."

Lydia was slowly rocking her leg up and down. "Where did the victim's vehicle go after that?"

"It remained parked there, until the night of the murder. At 1:45 a.m., it moved maybe ten feet, before going off line, until it was discovered at the scrapyard."

Lydia sat forward in her chair pointing to the computer. "Did the GPS place either Saul or Daniel near the site of the abduction?"

I interjected for Tom. "Saul for sure couldn't have. When all of this was going down he was at the McDonald's in Vonore. Daniel came in not long after I did, so I'd say it's unlikely he was involved in it either."

Lydia's forehead began to wrinkle, as she stared at the corner of my desk, deep in thought. "Neither Saul nor Daniel were near the area of abduction, but Saul's patrol car was at the exact spot the Camry was placed. I agree this is too much of a coincidence. Is it possible that Saul and Daniel were conspiring with someone else? Maybe Harrison Birch or Patrick Donovan? I understand there were a lot of hard feelings when it came to Alston O'Brian. Is it possible these gentlemen got together and decided to get revenge?"

Like I said, she'd make a great sheriff. "Or we have two different sets of perpetrators acting independent of one another. That is, before they crash into one another."

Lydia and Tom looked at each other, a light scowl on each of their faces, indicating they didn't quite understand my point. Tom, scratched his forehead with his thumb, as he slouched back on his left leg. "Care to run that by me again."

"You mean that someone else abducted the victim and killed him. But another person tried to cover it up?" Lydia asked.

I nodded. "I know it's out there on the edge, but it's not implausible. For now, I want to focus on what we do know. And for me, that means a trip to the place Alston's car was stashed, before it was taken to the scrapyard."

Tom closed his laptop and placed it under his arm. "You want me to go out there and process it?"

I shook my head, standing up. "No thank you. I'll go. It'll do me good to get a firsthand look at the scene. I'll grab a forensic kit and head on out. Tom, you let me know when Glen and Jack get back with the results from the search."

Tom gave me a thumbs up, before leaving the office. "You got it."

"Is it all right if I join you?" Lydia asked. "I'm sure Mr. Deland wouldn't mind."

I hunched my shoulders as I grabbed my coat. "It's fine with me. I'll meet you at my truck in five minutes."

Chapter Twenty-Three

We didn't speak after we got in the truck. I felt like there was more to her insistence on accompanying me, than just wanting to keep the AG in the loop. But I had also learned, that Lydia would let me know, in her own good time, without me prying. We were at the traffic stoplight at the Food City in Vonore, before she asked the question, I knew had been bothering her, since we left the stationhouse. "What gave you the idea for two different sets of assailants?"

I turned on the defroster, to keep the windshield from fogging up. "Something my parents said last night, actually." I gave her the abridge version, of my discovery of Clare Hensley and my suspicions, about her son Nathaniel, plus the background, I had discovered about him.

She cocked her eyebrow. "So you believe, there is a possibility that Nathaniel is Alston's son. You also think he may be involved in the murder?"

"I know how it sounds, believe me. I just can't shake the feeling, that the kid's involved." I flipped on the turn signal before switching lanes. "You didn't see Clare's reaction yesterday, when I first met Nathaniel. I'm telling you there is something more to this, Lydia."

She nodded in agreement, but skepticism was etched all over her face. "You've got a good track record, Jonas. I just don't see the connection to the murder."

"I'm not placing any bets on it. I'm just keeping it as an option."

Silence filled the cab, as Lydia seemed content to look out the window at the passing cars. The sun felt good, beaming through the front windshield, warming my chest. The warmth, along with the confines of the truck, made her perfume more aromatic, but not overwhelming. I felt like I should say something more, but no words came to mind. I glanced over at my passenger, noting she seemed at ease. A few minutes later we were crossing the Highway 411 bridge and turned onto 72 East. I had entered the coordinates, from Tom's computer, into the GPS of my BlackBerry, before leaving the stationhouse. When we came to the spot, the first thing I saw was a road, that led up a hill.

Parking the truck, I took the forensic kit, from the back seat and grabbed a pair of rubber boots, from the aluminum toolbox on the bed of my truck. I swapped my shoes for the boots and took out a pair of leather work gloves, before grabbing the kit. Lydia came around from the other side of the truck, with a pair of shoe covers concealing, her leather flats. I stopped and stared at her.

She returned my stare, with elevated eyebrows. "I said I wanted to join you. You didn't think I was going to stay in the truck, did you?"

I kept my eyes focused on her for a few seconds, before heading toward the dirt road. "All right, but I don't want to hear you complain, when you get dirt on that business suit."

The terrain was firm, but covered with a thin, slick coat of mud. The sun peaked through the barren trees and cast charcoal shadows across the hills. The squishing from our steps was mixed with the occasional snap, crackle, pop of a fallen twig. I slipped once, on some wet leaves, causing me to utter a silent obscenity. I glanced back at Lydia, who was trying to stifle a laugh. "You all right?"

I felt a scarlet wave of warmth drench my face, as I revealed a sheepish grin. "I'm fine. Grace was never one of my best traits."

"We can't be good at everything."

We had walked another thirty yards in silence, before Lydia stopped and scanned the surrounding real estate. "Are you sure this is where Tom said the Camry and Saul's vehicles were located? I've not seen any signs of a vehicle being parked anywhere."

I was inclined to agree with her, until I saw an evergreen tree, with the tips still white, indicating recently severed limbs. About seven feet to the left, was another evergreen tree, also exhibiting missing limbs. Crouching low to the ground, I slowly oscillated my eyes all around the area, until I saw a line of green needles heading to the left of Lydia. I gently put my hand on her shoulder. "Excuse me for a moment."

She rubbed her arms for warmth, as I walked passed her. "What is it?"

I hooked my right thumb over my shoulder. "Those evergreen limbs appear to have been cut. Judging from the tips, I would say they've only been exposed to the air, for a short time. Why would someone cut so many?"

"Maybe someone wanted the needles for potpourri. Ouch."

I turned back, just in time to see a branch had snagged the cuff of Lydia's coat, scratching her neck in the process. I smiled at her. "You see what a good time you have, when you go out with me?"

She ran her finger along the scratch, and found a string of blood. "You sure do know how to sweep a girl off her feet, Jonas."

I turned and continued down the trail. "I must've done something right. You're still here."

She let out a long sardonic sigh. "You're just about broken in. I've put too much work into you, to let you go, now."

"Ha ha," I said emphatically.

Six feet farther, I arrived at the site of a huge mound of evergreen limbs. I held up my hand for her to stop. "I think I know why the limbs were cut."

Lydia stood beside me and stared at the mound of limbs. "They cut the branches, to cover the car, until they could come back and get it."

Looking back toward the road, I could see a thin wall of dead, wild hedges, with webs of deceased honeysuckle patches. "The overgrowth, along with the limbs, could easily camouflage a vehicle.

There isn't that much traffic, on this road, so it is unlikely, anyone observed the perpetrators."

Stepping carefully, I searched the surrounding area, for any unusual markings, in the muddy soil. About seven feet along the mound, I noticed a faint ridge pattern in the mud. Opening the kit, I took out the magnifying glass and held it over the area in question, which revealed a barely visible tire impression, untouched by the rain. The problem was, how to document this evidence. The indentions in the mud were too faint for a traditional cast, so that left only a photographic means of extraction.

I removed the tripod, from the stainless steel case and attached the camera. Next, I connected the extension cord to the flash, so I could angle the light. I centered the tripod over the impression and flipped on the camera's digital screen. At first, only bare, red, mud was revealed. Turning on the flash, I was able to bring the image closer, all the while being careful, not to disconnect the black cord, from the camera. Using a forty-five-degree angle, I snapped a shot, but again I saw no display of the impression on the screen. It took twelve attempts, before I perfected the right light angle, to produce an image clear enough, to reveal the tread pattern. "Lydia, get me one of the evidence markers, from the kit, please. I don't want to move, now that I've found the right angle to take the photograph."

She pulled a numbered yellow cone from the kit and brought it to me. "Where do you need me to place this?"

I peered through the screen, until the yellow marker was in frame. "Set it there, please."

After taking two more photographs, I removed the camera, from the tripod, and scrolled through the pictures. I felt certain, the ridge detail, was clear enough, for evidentiary purposes. Examining more of the surrounding area, I discovered a separate set of tire impressions, which I photographed and cataloged, as well.

While examining the rest of the area, I found faint footwear impressions, which I was able to photograph and scale. Finding no other usable physical evidence, I took out my BlackBerry, made sure the reception was strong enough, then called for a forensic unit.

"Why are you calling in a forensic unit? What else is there to collect?" Lydia asked, after I ended the call.

I pointed to the cedar limbs, stacked on the ground. "Each of those limbs has to be matched to the tree and to the exact location, they were cut from. Glen and Jack should be about completed with the search of Patrick Winchell's property. I want to be at the stationhouse when they return. Plus, I assumed you didn't want to stand around another two hours, while I marked and measured each limb."

I watched her eyes slowly scan the decapitated limbs, her mouth open. "*All* of them?"

I nodded and started back to the truck. "Uh-huh. You must document everything, so all bases are covered, should the case go to trial. Plus, you never know what other latent evidence may be present, but hidden. The devil does like to dwell within the details."

"You're going to ask Molly to compare the photos of the tracks to the vehicles at the lab?"

I nodded, placing the equipment back in the case. "This may be the break we're looking for."

Back in the truck, I took out the department issued laptop and uploaded the photographs, then connected the wireless router. When the computer was in sync, I attached the documents to an email and sent them to Molly Newman's email address. Taking out my cellphone, I sent Molly a text, asking her to compare the tire treads, to the three vehicles in custody. I also asked her to compare the footwear impressions, to those taken, at the primary crime scene.

Lydia had removed her shoe covers and placed them on the tailgate of my truck. "For a man who is so detail orientated in his work, why is your desk always in disarray?"

I sat down on the tailgate, removed my boots and replaced them with my shoes. "I'm a complicated guy."

She looked back at the search area and shook her head. "Where do you find the patience for all this?"

I followed her gaze. "For what?"

"The limbs. Measuring each and determining, which branch, they belonged to. You really did this detailed work, before becoming sheriff?"

I nodded, as I synched the knot of my shoelace. "Yeah. Not necessarily tree limbs, but other things over the years. It's part of the job."

She sat on the edge of the tailgate with me, as we waited for the forensic detail, to arrive. "It's a part of the job, that I could never get my head around."

I smiled, as I let my feet dangle from the tailgate. "I take it, you weren't drawn to the world of forensics."

She rolled her eyes and smiled. "Hardly. When I started at C.I.D., I had to work with the crime scene department for six months and it didn't take me long to decide, I wasn't going to be a C.S.I. candidate. I hated the tediousness of it. Collecting blood samples and trace evidence, all that time working, to find the exact angle of the flash, would drive me nuts. I just don't have the patience for it."

I was listening very intently, as Lydia has only rarely mentioned her tenure in the Army. I have learned to never press her on it, so whenever she talks about it, I make sure to pay attention. "What did you like, about the C.I.D.?"

She stared off in the distance, for a moment, taking time to reflect. "Putting the pieces together. Making sure it all fits. That was what I enjoyed the most. I suppose that's why I like my job, as an investigator at the Attorney General's office. I get to go over all the evidence and see how the dots are connected. Though, I don't have the knack you do."

I stared at her, my mouth falling open. "Come on Lydia. I've seen you work before and you are an excellent investigator. I've learned quite a bit from observing you."

She smiled and punched me on the arm, as was her custom. "And I have from you, too. But, you can walk in both worlds, in way I can't, Jonas. You can gather the evidence and interpret it, all by yourself. You've been doing it for so long, that you've don't realize, how unique that is. To see the details and the big picture. It's a rare bird who can do both."

I was about to deflect her compliment, but she nipped it in the bud. "Don't you dare try and shrug it off. It's true and you know it."

I opted to keep my opinion to myself and held up my hands in surrender. A few moments of silence passed, before I looked at her again. "Was there something else you wanted to say? I mean was there another reason, you came along with me this afternoon?"

Lydia took her fist and gently punched me on the shoulder, again. "No. Our schedules are so hectic, at times, that we don't get much time alone together. I just found a way to spend some quality time, with my boyfriend, Jonas. That's the only hidden agenda here."

I slid my hand over to take hers. We sat there, listening to the cars sail along the highway. I gave her a side glance, still unable to understand what this intelligent and beautiful woman was doing with me. I thought about the item, I had in my desk drawer, at my house and what it would mean. I was about to mention it to her, but my BlackBerry vibrated.

It was a picture message from Glen, revealing a discovery found at Patrick Wilson's home. When I brought up the picture, I jumped up, as I felt a jolt of endorphins run through me. Lydia stood beside me, trying to peek over my shoulder. "What is it?"

I shifted the screen toward her, so she could see the picture of a cell phone. "Glen found this at Patrick Winchell's home. It belongs to Alston O'Brian."

Lydia's eyes flashed with amazement. "He didn't get rid of the phone? What happened, did he forget about it?"

I read Glen's message. "According to Glen, Patrick insists he doesn't know how the phone got there. He is being brought in for questioning, right now."

My phone suddenly received another text, this time from Jack, who was at Harrison Birch's place of residence. "Jack says they found a plastic tarp matching the material found in the truck bed. There also appears to be dried blood on the tarp."

Lydia stared at me for a moment, her eyes wide. "Let me guess, he doesn't know how it got there."

I shook my head. "Nope. Jack's bringing him in for questioning."

I then got a call from Molly's extension at the lab. Lydia and I both looked at the phone. "Man aren't you popular, right now."

I answered the call. "Molly, Lydia's here with me, so I'm going to put you on speaker." I hit the feature. "Okay go."

"Hey Lydia," she said

"Molly," Lydia replied.

"Jonas, I just finished comparing the tire impressions and shoeprint you sent me. The first picture matches the tires of the Dodge Durango, to a tee. The second picture is a match to the Toyota Camry."

"And the shoe impression?" I asked.

"They match the exemplars taken from Chief Saul West's boots."

Lydia and I both stared at the square box in my hand, shock evident on our faces. "You're sure Molly?" I asked.

"I double checked Jonas. They belong to Saul West."

"Thanks Molly. Good work, as always."

"You are welcome," she said and ended the call.

I placed my phone in the cocoon of my coat pocket and slammed the tailgate shut. Lydia, her hands in her pockets, gestured toward the cab. "Are we going to see Saul West?"

"Oh yeah."

* * *

When the forensic unit arrived and I explained what I needed documented. I have to admit, I felt a bit like a cad, for having them perform such an arduous task. I had performed similar tasks, as a forensic tech, but it's different, when you're the one giving the orders. But I quickly pushed that useless thought to the back of my mind and headed to the stationhouse, of the Vonore City Police Department.

Inside the stationhouse, I observed Officer Gentry, at the front desk. His face took on a gaunt expression, when he recognized me and Lydia. He was about to speak, but I didn't give him a chance. "I need to see Saul. Is he in?"

From the tone of my voice, Gentry decided not to argue with me. He swallowed and pointed to the closed door of Saul's office. I stepped around the desk and knocked on the door. "Saul, it's Jonas. We need to talk."

I heard a chair move a few seconds, before the door opened. Saul stood there, hands at his side and dark circles under his eyes. "What is it, Jonas?"

"I need you to come to my office, Saul. I have a few questions about you and the murder of Alston O'Brian."

He looked at me for a moment and then to Lydia, who had remained near the front door, her hands hanging loose by her side. Saul looked at me again, inhaling a long breath, before exhaling it heavily through his nose. "What questions?"

I unbuttoned my coat, so I had access to my sidearm, if necessary. I hoped it wouldn't come to that, but in law enforcement, you never know what to expect. "I'll explain when we get there. If you want, you can have an attorney present. I'll also need to confiscate your weapons, before we leave Saul."

The chief stared at me, his eyes cold as ice, as he inhaled several deep breaths. His face became flush, as he looked down at his gun belt. I was expecting more of a fight, but he surrendered and gave me his gun. He put on his bomber jacket and zipped it up tight. "You want me to follow you or take your truck?"

I looked over at Lydia, her expression, indicated something was not right. I stepped to the side allowing Saul to pass. "We'll take my truck."

On the way out, Saul removed his mobile phone and began to send a text. "Who are you contacting Saul?"

"You said I could have my attorney present. I'm texting him, to meet, us at the stationhouse," he said.

A cold feeling began to grow, in the pit of my stomach. Lydia, too seemed uneasy, as she turned to look at the chief. "You are asking your attorney to meet you through a text?"

Saul hit the send button on his phone. "Yeah. Welcome to the new age. No one talks to anyone, anymore."

I stared at his phone for a second and opened my left palm. "May I see your phone?"

Saul looked down at my hand, before casting his eyes on his phone. "Why?"

I kept my hand extended, as I studied his eyes, which revealed the first stages of panic. "I'd just like to take a look at it, Saul. May I?"

Saul smiled and shrugged. "Sure."

He threw the phone on the asphalt as hard as he could, obviously forgetting he had a protective shell around it. When the phone hit the ground, the case cracked open along the seam, with the phone ejecting from the case and landing unharmed beside it. Saul lifted his foot to crush it, but I lunged, shoving him toward my truck and away from the phone. His arms pushed out, extending his elbow towards my head, but he missed. He swung wild with his right, all the while, screaming at the top of his lungs. I stepped into the ark of his arm, blocking it, while bringing my right fist up into the center of his solar plexus. Air escaped Saul's mouth and soon he was doubled over, wheezing. I took out my cuffs and restrained him, while Lydia checked the phone. "Is it still working?" I asked.

She picked the phone up and nodded. "Looks like it. That protective case did the trick."

I placed Saul in the back of my truck and secured his feet with a zip tie. "We'll need to get a warrant, to see who he sent the text to."

She angled the screen so she could make out the details. "The name of the final text is still in plain sight. It's a woman named Clare."

I stared at Saul through the backseat window, the cold feeling in my stomach growing stronger. "Get in the truck Lydia."

I fired up the engine and floored it. I took Hall Road, which was a straight shot to the Lowes warehouse, from the VCPD stationhouse. Lydia tightened her seatbelt and braced her hand on the dash. "You think he was sending her a warning?"

I kept my eyes on the road, swerving to avoid a motorist, who was attempting to pull onto the road. "Yes I do. He was telling her and Nathaniel to run."

Saul leaned forward, spittle hitting the back of my neck as he spoke. "You leave Nathan out of this. He has nothing to do with anything."

Lydia turned to look back at him, before she looked forward. "No offense chief, but by you saying that, it automatically makes me think, he is *definitely* involved."

Amen to that. One minute later we were at Lowes warehouse, just in time to see Clare getting into her car. Her tires screeched, as she backed out and gunned it for the driveway. I pressed the accelerator harder and pulled in front of her Buick Century. I rolled down my window. "Clare stop!"

Clare's eyes were wide with desperation. She looked around, trying to find a way out. I lowered the back window, so she could see Saul, restrained in the backseat. I watched the shock engulf her face, then finally settle into defeat. I parked the truck and got out, quickly moving to the side of the vehicle, in case Clare got a sudden rush of courage and opted to accelerate the car. I stood by the driver's side window, my hand resting on the grip of my sidearm. "Clare, I need you to turn off your vehicle, please."

She stared at me for a moment, gripping and releasing the steering wheel with both hands. Slowly she put the car in park and killed the engine. I nodded. "That's good. Now remove the keys from the ignition, slowly open the door, and put them on the ground, please."

Opening the door, Clare dropped the keys on the asphalt. "Please exit the vehicle."

She got out, keeping her hands in full view. When she spoke, her voice was barely audible. "I did it."

I looked at her with a sense of pity, for I already knew the answer to the question I was about to ask. "Did what Clare?"

"I killed Alston O'Brian," she said, her voice trembling. "He came back to Vonore and I just got so angry at him, for all that he did. I killed him. I did it all by myself. I'll confess to everything."

I couldn't help but have some admiration for her devotion. I felt the same for Saul too. Both trying to protect their loved ones. Unfortunately, I couldn't allow my admiration to cloud my judgement, no matter how much sympathy I felt. "Clare, you need to consult an attorney, before you say anything else."

Panic was beginning to take over, as she clenched her fists. "I don't need a lawyer. I'll tell you everything that happened that night."

"Clare, I can't let you take responsibility for someone else's actions." I paused a minute, before I asked my next question. "Where were you going just now?"

She became silent now

"Clare, were you going to get your son?"

Her eyes became feral, as a mammalian scream erupted from her throat and she lunged at me, fingers shaped like claws. She came at me at an alarming speed and I was barely able to step aside. Clare quickly pivoted and lunged for me again. I grabbed her left wrist and used her momentum, to swivel her around and press her into her car. "That's enough Clare."

Lydia was out of the truck by now, with a pair of zip ties she had taken from my glovebox. Clare was still struggling, as I restrained her hands, yelling at me with tears running down her face. "You leave my boy alone. You hear me, you bastard, you leave my son alone. He didn't have anything to do with this."

I recalled my mother's words, from the previous evening, about how a mother is a wild card. I guess this proves she was right. "Clare you're under arrest, for attempted assault on a police officer."

I felt something warm running down my cheek. "Jonas, you're bleeding," Lydia said.

I looked at my reflection in the window and saw a streak of crimson running down my face. I had Clare sit on the ground, then called the stationhouse. Tom answered the phone. "I've got two suspects I'm bringing in. It looks like they're connected, to the death of Alston O'Brian."

It turned out Tom had some news for me, too. "Jonas it's a funny thing you should say that. Glen and Jack have returned with Harrison Birch and Patrick Winchell. Two minutes later, in walks Officer Daniel Hensley."

Lydia had pulled a tissue from her coat and handed it to me, to wipe the blood. "What does he want?"

"He just confessed to the murder, Jonas."

I had one Hensley, who had confessed only a minute ago. I have physical evidence that connects my other three suspects, to the crime scene and now I have another Hensley confessing, to the same murder. "Misery always did love to have company."

Chapter Twenty-Four

We only have two interview rooms in our stationhouse. I had Patrick in Interview one, and Harrison in Interview two. Saul was in the conference room and Daniel was sitting in the pressroom, handcuffed to the steel bench bolted to the floor. I placed Clare in a holding cell, charges pending, for my assault. I then asked Glen to do some more research into the Hensley family and since Tom had access to Alston's GPS, I asked him to pull up the other locations he had visited.

I was sitting alone, in the monitoring room, watching the digital effigies, of the suspects on the screens, as I spoke with Kaleb Swafford, SRO at Sequoyah High School, about Nathaniel Hensley. "Have you ever had any problems with him, Kaleb?"

Kaleb was originally from Mississippi, so he had a deep southern drawl, that caused him to elongate his vowels, when he spoke. "No sheriff. At least not officially."

I cocked my eyebrow. "What about unofficially?"

"About two months back, the principal and I felt pretty sure some of the students were smoking pot on campus. They were pretty smart about it, keeping off camera, so we were never able to catch anyone. But we did have a few kids in mind, as to which individuals were actually smoking the pot and Nathaniel Hensley was one of them."

"Marijuana huh? Was there anything else?"

"A few kids came to me and accused him, of cheating them out of their lunch and gas money. They hinted, that he was betting on the baseball games, saying he could guarantee, the outcome. Things like that."

I wrote this down, as fast as my hand would move. "Did anything come of it?"

"I tried to dig, but I could never get the kids to go on the record."

I sat back in my seat, remembering my conversation with the principal earlier in the day. "I spoke with the principal, this morning about Nathaniel and he didn't mention any of this to me. Any reason why?"

"Probably because none of the students, would make a complaint, and we had no physical proof against the boy. I also got the feeling that the principal was cutting the kid some slack."

"What makes you think that?"

"I heard him say more than once, that Nathaniel didn't have it easy growing up. Sounded like the kid's dad wasn't in the picture, but that's no excuse, for bad behavior. My dad split, when I was ten and nobody cut me any slack."

I put my pen down on the table. "What's your impression of the kid?"

There was a brief pause, on the line, before he spoke. "I'm not entirely sure. He always speaks to me in a polite manner and on the outside seemed all right. But there's just something about him, Jonas, that's doesn't feel right."

I thought about what he said, as I looked at the menagerie of suspects, on the monitors. "Thanks for the help Kaleb. If you wouldn't mind bring Nathaniel to the sheriff's stationhouse. If he asks any questions, tell him it has something to do with his mother and uncle. If you can, take the scenic route. I need a few more minutes."

"Will do," he said and hung up.

I put the phone in the cradle and studied my suspects. None had asked for an attorney, which was odd, considering, they were brought in, for questioning involving a murder. Then again, most people believe asking for an attorney is a sign of guilt, so they try to wing it on their own, usually at their own peril. I had maybe thirty minutes, before Kaleb would be here, with Nathaniel, so I needed to move quick.

I left the monitoring room and walked to Glen's desk to find out what he had learned, if anything, about the Hensley family. "You got anything for me, Glen?"

He swiveled around with his steno pad in hand. "Keep in mind, I've only been able to get the highlights."

"I'll take what I can get."

He flipped the page back and started reading. "I checked with the County Register and it appears that even though she and Daniel both live in the doublewide trailer, it is in Clare's name. I called Lowes, to find out if she was working the day Alston was abducted. Her boss said she had that weekend off, because a friend by the name of Beth Vance, was sick and Clare left, to visit with her, in Farragut. I haven't been able to confirm that yet, but if it's true, then she couldn't have killed Alston. That's about all I got, so far."

I ran my thumb along my chin, as I pondered this information. "How about Daniel?"

Glen ran his pen under his notes as he read. "No trouble with the law or associations with any bad elements. One interesting thing, that stuck out to me, was when I looked at his application to the academy, Clare payed for it. It got me to thinking, the application said Daniel went to Cleveland State Community College. I've got a friend who works in the financial aid department, so I called him up. Now this is unofficial, since we don't have a warrant, but he told me, that Clare also paid Daniel's tuition, in full."

An idea began to blossom, in the fertile recesses of my imagination. "She paid it all? No scholarships or financial aid, of any kind?"

"None Jonas." Glen placed his notepad on the desk. "I think I'm going to go work for Lowes. They must pay their administrative assistants, extremely well."

"Keep digging. And keep that friend of yours under wraps for now. If need be, we can get the warrant for the records later."

Glen pantomimed zipping his lips. I next moved to Tom's workstation. "Tom have you gotten anything from the GPS on the Camry?"

He watched the screen as he talked. "Yeah. Alston visited various restaurants for meals and he spent some time on the backroads, near Sequoyah High School."

"Probably, trying to get a look, at Nathaniel," I said.

Tom snorted. "Yeah, he wasn't exactly father of the year was he?"

"The man made mistakes, Tom, and he paid for them. I can't fault the man for wanting to see his son." I paused and spoke under my breath, "Though it may have been a fatal mistake. Anything else?"

"He spent a lot of time at Fastenal in Vonore. A lot of time there."

Glen looked up from his desk. "Why in the world would he spend so much time there?"

I recalled the biography from Nathaniel's Facebook page. "Because that's where Nathaniel works. Tom, tell Molly I'll be in interrogation, so she'll need to text me, about updates on the phone and tarp. I'm going to see what our guests have to say."

I took some photographs from the evidence board in my office and placed them in a file folder. I stepped into the monitoring room, one last time, to observe Patrick and Harrison. Both were beginning to show signs of anxiety, but Harrison was the one who was biting his nails and tapping the heel of his foot on the floor. Meaning, he gets to be my first contestant.

As I made my way to the second interview room, Anthony Deland and Lydia were entering the stationhouse. Upon returning, Lydia had gone to the courthouse, to inform Anthony of all that had happened, during the previous hour, so his visit wasn't a surprise. "Anthony," I said. "Lydia."

Anthony stood in the vestibule, hands resting on his hips. "Sheriff. This place is hopping today, isn't it?"

I shrugged. "What can I say Anthony, when it rains it pours."

"What have you got, so far?"

I pointed to the interview rooms. "I'm about to have a talk with Harrison Birch, right now. He seems the most anxious, so I thought I would take a crack at him first."

Anthony shook his head, a grim expression across face. "This case is going to be a nightmare, when it goes to court. With all of these different suspects and confessions, it's possible it will end in a mistrial."

I took a moment, that I really didn't have to spare, to try and settle his nerves. "Counselor, I know this seems like a convoluted mess, but in reality, I believe it is very simple. I can't get into the details right now, but if I play this right, we'll have the murderer and everyone else involved in custody, by the end of business."

I left him standing there, as I moved to Jack's desk. "Jack I need you to drop what you're doing and go to SQHS and have the principle open both the locker and gym locker, of Nathaniel Hensley. Time is of the essence, so the quicker the better. Make sure you wear gloves."

Jack stood and grabbed his coat. "Yes sir."

Anthony was still in the vestibule, a look of confusion on his face. "Why are you searching the locker of Nathaniel Hensley? Haven't we got enough suspects?"

I waved the file at him, as I headed to the interview room. "I don't have time to explain Anthony. You can watch in the monitoring room, if you want. Tom make sure the equipment is recording properly."

"Sheriff?" I heard Anthony say.

Lydia stepped in for me. "Sir, I know this may sound bias, considering Jonas and I are dating, but I've seen that look in his eyes before. He's onto something. Let him do his job."

* * *

Harrison stood up, when I entered the room, a sheen of perspiration, on his face, which glowed under the florescent lights. "Sheriff, I don't have any idea how that tarp, got in my garage. I didn't kill that man."

I sat down at the interview table and pointed to his chair. "Please sit down, Mr. Birch."

As he slowly took his seat I could see the pulse point at his temples beating, indicating an elevation in blood pressure. "You've been informed of your rights is that correct, sir?"

He nodded his head. "Yeah."

"Do you wish to have an attorney present?"

He shook his head, speaking as he bit his fingernail. "I don't need a lawyer, because I did nothing wrong."

I opened the file, making sure he couldn't see the contents. "You were witnessed, by myself and Deputy Kirk, assaulting the victim, just a few days before his death." I took out a crime scene photo showing the house sitting on top of Alston's body. "The victim was found crushed under your friend, Patrick Winchell's old family home. Evidence suggests, the victim was tortured inside the house." I removed the second photo, which revealed the blood-stained tarp and placed it on the table. "Now we have a tarp that matches samples taken from the victim and your truck. Blood was found on the tarp, as well, and I feel certain it's going to match Alston O'Brian. The same man you held responsible, for your family's misfortune."

The whites of his eyes grew, in diameter, as he looked at each photograph. "I have never been inside that house. Yeah, I blamed O'Brian for my father's death, but that doesn't mean, I killed him."

I closed the folder and placed it in front of me, resting my hand on top. "Besides the house, we've also found other evidence, that connects to your friend Patrick Winchell. He's in the other room."

His licked his lips, his right foot incessantly tapping the floor. "Pat's here?"

I nodded. "I wonder what he'll have to say? I mean twenty years is a long time."

Harrison shook his head, his forehead wrinkled. "Twenty years?"

"That's the state minimum, you'll both have to serve, before being eligible for parole," I explained. "Of course, whoever cooperates, may get a few years shaved off, but that's up to the attorney general."

Harrison looked at the wall, where Patrick just happened to be sitting, on the other side. Beads of sweat formed on his face and neck, causing a damp ring around the neck of his T-shirt. "Pat would never talk. He didn't do anything wrong. We both were at the Laffing Goat."

I lightly tapped my fingers, along the folder, shaking my head. "You see the problem, with that, is no one knows exactly when the two of you left, that night. So, we have no way of validating your alibi. The two of you could easily have snuck out, killed Alston, and still had time to make it home, before dawn."

Harrison slapped the table with both hands, his face as red as a tomato. "This is bullshit. You're setting me up. If you had anything damning on me, you'd have already arrested me."

"True," I said. "It's still thin, but I think after I speak, with Nathaniel Hensley, everything will become clear."

His leg stopped shaking and his red face turned white. Harrison swallowed hard again, slowly rubbing his hands, along the edge of the table. "Who's that?"

I didn't even try, to camouflage my disbelief. "Am I supposed to believe, you don't know, who Nathaniel is, Harrison? No offense, but you have a lousy poker face."

He shook his head, with a grim expression, on his face. "I don't know what you're talking about."

I hunched my shoulders retrieving the photographs and returning them to the folder. "If that's how you want to play it, that's your choice. I'm sure I'll get the full skinny, from Nathaniel, when he gets here."

Harrison's face grew more pale. "He's coming here?"

I nodded. "Oh yes. We can't wait to hear what he has to say."

Harrison's breathing was becoming more erratic, as he gripped the table's edges. "You're going to question him?"

"He should be here within the next fifteen minutes or so." I studied the pallid expression on his face. "Are you feeling OK, Mr. Birch? You look like you're ill."

He looked toward the door, as if Nathaniel Hensley was on the other side. "What's he saying?"

I shrugged, scooting my seat back, about to stand to leave. "I've not spoken with the young man, yet. Why are you asking?"

Harrison continued to stare at the door, both feet tapping the floor. "You can't believe a word, that little bastard says. He's going to pin it all on us."

He was speaking so fast, that I could barely understand his words. "Sir, you're saying Nathaniel is the mastermind behind this? I find it hard to believe that a high school student could outwit two grown men."

Harrison leaned over the table, pointing his finger at me. "Don't let him fool you. He's not just a kid. He's Alston O'Brian's son."

I noted the feral gleam, in his eyes and the desperation in his voice, indicating my instincts regarding what happened to Alston were on target. "I take it you mean, the apple is pretty close to the tree?"

"I'm saying, he's every bit the con man his daddy was." Harrison ran his tongue over his lips, tapping the table with his finger. "Don't believe a thing he says. He's the reason me and Pat are here."

I held up my hand, for him to stop. "So you are saying, Nathaniel Hensley is the son of Alston O'Brian?"

He blew out a puff of air rolling his eyes. "The Hensleys thought they fooled everyone, but we all knew Alston was banging Clare. Then she leaves and comes back with a baby and we're supposed to not know, who the daddy was? Everyone in Vonore knew she was knocked up by that no good sonofabitch."

"Describe how the residents of Vonore treated Nathaniel."

Harrison waved his arms out wide. "How am I supposed to know? I didn't chaperone the kid. I mean I never saw anyone treat him bad, when he was out, but as he got older, he started looking more and more like his daddy. I did see some people give him some strange looks, but I mean, I never heard anyone say anything to him."

I allowed the silence, to fill the void between us, waiting before I began the next phase. "OK, Mr. Birch. Let's say I believe, that an eighteen-year-old, somehow managed, to frame the both of you, for the murder of Alston O'Brian. How did he do this?"

Harrison began to speak, but stopped, rubbing his mouth with the palm of his hand. "Maybe I need to talk to a lawyer, after all."

This was the brainstorm I was hoping he wouldn't get. The right to counsel is a law I do believe in, but with the sand quickly emptying from the hourglass, I needed to move fast. "That is your right Mr. Birch. We can arrange for you to call a lawyer, while I speak with Nathaniel. From that point on, it is first come, first serve."

He leaned forward, splaying his hand on the table. "What does that mean?"

I stood, placing my chair under the table. "I mean whoever talks first, will get a deal. If what you say is true, Nathaniel must be very clever."

I had my hand on the doorknob, before he spoke. "Wait! Wait!" He was on his feet walking around the table.

"Stay over there Mr. Birch," I said.

Harrison returned to his seat, keeping his hands out. "Is there really a deal?"

I remained where I was, my hand on the doorknob. "I can't promise you anything concrete, Harrison. It all depends, on what you have to say and the part you played, in what happened that night. However, your cooperation, here, will be noted."

I could almost hear the synapses firing inside his head, as he debated whether or not to roll the dice and talk. I have no idea how many times, I've been in a similar situation, waiting to see if the suspect will take the bait. Usually it's only a few seconds, but it feels like hours. Harrison released a long sigh, as he sat down, lowering his head to the table. "You need me to write it down?"

* * *

I had the handwritten statement, from Harrison Birch, in hand, fifteen minutes later. After divulging that Harrison was talking, Patrick Winchell decided to give me a statement as well. With no discrepancies between the two statements, I felt certain the two were telling the truth. By then Kaleb had arrived with Nathaniel Hensley, who was now sitting in the breakroom, drinking a soda.

Molly texted me, indicating she found no usable prints on the outside of the cellphone, but did find a set of prints on the battery, which matched the unknown prints found on the bags of marijuana in Alston's car. As for the blood on the tarp, it was a match to Alston's blood type. With so much blood evidence, I had no choice but to authorize her, to send samples to a serological laboratory, for a DNA test. With any luck we would have the results in about three weeks. If we were extremely lucky, we just might have this case closed, by the end of the day.

Just as I was about to talk to Nathaniel, I received a text from Jack. He sent me two pictures of the contents found in both Nathaniel's school and gym locker. I instructed him to get the items to Molly and have her rush the results. Until then, I would have, to stall, this very clever young man.

When I opened the wooden double door, to the breakroom, I saw Kaleb, standing near the entrance, standing at attention, with Nathaniel sitting on the bench, sipping his beverage. "Thank you, Officer Swafford. I'll take it from here."

He gave me a curt nod, before scratching his cheek. "Any time sheriff."

Nathaniel was up and heading in my direction by then. He had his red SQHS jacket unzipped, revealing a red baseball shirt. It was almost eerie, as once again, I noticed the definite similarities between the young man and Alston. His blue eyes were a mosaic of uncertainty, revealing hints of fear, as he stared at me. It was when I noted the constellation of acne across his face, that it dawned on me, just how young he really was. Even with all I knew, it was still difficult for me to believe, that this teenager was a major part, of this tragedy. If it was hard for me to swallow, it was definitely going to be difficult for a jury to believe. Let's hope, I was cunning enough, to outwit Alston O'Brian's son.

"Nathaniel Hensley," I said extending him my hand. "I'm Sheriff Lauer."

He gave my hand a light shake with a flimsy grip, as if he was afraid I was contagious. "What's going on here, Sheriff? Why am I here?"

Indicating for him to follow me, I walked to the door and held it open. "Come with me please and I'll explain."

I had Tom take Harrison Birch to holding, so Interview One was empty. I opened the door for Nathaniel. "Take a seat please, son."

I stood at my chair waiting for Nathaniel. He stared at the room, nervous and unsure. He slowly walked over to the empty seat across from me. The legs of the seat whined, as Nathaniel scooted it across the floor and slowly sat down and adjusted himself in his seat. I did the same, keeping the tone casual.

"OK, before we begin Nathaniel, you need to know that you are not under arrest and that you can have a lawyer present, if you wish," I said.

He looked at me, for a few seconds, before examining the room once again. "Do you know where my mother is? She's not answering her phone."

I ignored the question. "We'll get to your mother in a moment, Nathaniel. Right now, I need to make sure you understand what I've told you. Do you understand that you can leave and you can have a lawyer present?"

He leaned over the table looking at me, with a cold gleam to his eyes. "What do you mean, we'll get to her later? Do you know where she is? Why did you guys take my phone when I got here? I was trying to call her, but got no answer."

"Please Nathaniel, do you understand?"

Nodding his head emphatically, he leaned back in his seat. "Sure man, whatever. I understand."

"Thank you." I placed my hands on the table, interlacing my fingers. "I need you to answer a few questions Nathaniel. Have you ever heard of a man named Alston O'Brian?"

I watched his pupils quickly dilate, before returning to normal, as he swallowed. "No sir. I mean yeah, I heard about him on the news."

"You ever meet him?"

He shook his head, eyes dilating once again. "No. Why would some old con artist want to see me?"

I took out my pen and made a note on my notepad, more for show than anything. "So you have never had any contact with Alston O'Brian?"

"No, I've never met the man. What's this about?"

I made more notes, before tapping the notepad with the back of my pen. "Do you work at Fastenal, in Vonore?"

A questioning look, appeared on his face, as if he couldn't see the relevance of my question. "Yeah."

I made one more note and sat back, pretending to read from the yellow page. "Would it surprise you to know, we can place Alston at the Fastenal, on several occasions?"

The carotid artery in his neck took on a faster cadence, as he hunched his shoulders. "OK. He might've come into the store. But I don't remember him, if he did."

"Does Fastenal have security cameras?"

Nathaniel slowly nodded and stuttered. "Yeah."

I wrote camera and circled it heavily for emphasis. "Have you ever heard of or met a Harrison Birch?"

Nathaniel shook his head, sliding his hand under the sleeve of his jacket, to scratch his elbow. "No."

"How about a Patrick Winchell?"

Again he shook his head. "No."

I acted like I was studying my notes, before asking again. "Are you sure?"

"Yeah." He paused, to compose himself and lower his voice. "Yes. I've never heard of them or met them."

I printed another word on my notepad and circled it, which seemed to agitate the young man, across from me. "Man, where's my mom? You said you knew where she is?"

"Just a few more questions Nathaniel," I said, flipping to a clean sheet of paper. "There's no easy way to ask this question, so I'm just going to lay it out there. Were you aware that your mother and Alston O'Brian knew each other back in 1998?"

The tendons and muscles in Nathaniel's jawbone, swelled, as he grit his teeth together. "No. That has to be a mistake. Mom would never be associated with a criminal."

Observing the steel glint in his eyes and icy tone of his words, I realized, if I had been harboring any doubts, about him being Alston's son, they were erased. "Your mother might not have realized he was a criminal."

"I just said she never knew him." He was clenching his fists. "My mother is a good woman, who would never have anything to do, with a man, like Alston O'Brian."

I pursed my lips, giving him a slight headshake. "I'm afraid I have it on good authority, that your mother did know Alston. In fact, the two were intimate, Nathaniel."

Nathaniel leaned into the table, eyes narrowing like a bobcat, zeroing in on a rabbit. "What does that mean?"

I kept my tone ambivalent, as I played my next card. "I mean I know Alston O'Brian was your father."

Nathaniel shared his mother's quick temper. Shouting a war cry, he lunged across the table and grabbed the lapel of my sports coat, knocking me to the floor, the top of my chair burying itself in my back. Nathaniel was screaming, in my face, as we struggled. "You take that back! My mom's not a whore!"

I grabbed his left wrist and twisted it hard, until he released my coat. I pushed off the floor, rolled over and straddled him, forcing him over on his belly. He was half my age and very fast, but I had weight and strength on him. I locked his arm behind his back, forcing him to surrender. "Calm down, son. Calm down."

By then Tom was in the room, with zip ties out. I shook my head. "Wait one second Tom. Nathaniel, are you going to settle down or are we going to have to restrain you?"

He was grunting, saliva running from the corner of his mouth. "You stop saying things about my mother. She's done nothing."

Clare had said the same thing about her son, an hour earlier, as she lunged for my eyes. Mother and son were loyal to one another, which is admirable. "Nathaniel, no one said anything derogatory about your mother. Now are you going to behave?"

Nathaniel was still groaning, but had stopped resisting. Soon his body relaxed and he released a long sigh. "All right man, I give. Get off of me."

Placing my feet on the floor, I stood, pulling Nathanial up with me. Tom blocked the doorway, in case he attempted to run. I turned him toward the wall and released my hold on him. "Now sit down."

He rubbed his arm through his jacket, his elbow no doubt sore from my grip. He moved around and picked up his chair and sat down. I picked up my own chair and set it upright. "Tom you can go."

My deputy nodded, as he made his way out. I turned back to the teenager and sat down. "That's quite a temper you have there, Nathaniel. It must be hereditary."

Nathaniel stopped rubbing his elbow, the anger in his face turning to confusion. "What does that mean?"

"I mean you're the second Hensley, to attack me today. Your mother is in a holding cell right now, after attempting to assault me." Actually, this was the third time, in one day, someone had attacked me. This might be a record. I wondered if there was something about me, that set these people off.

His face deflated faster than a punctured water balloon. "What? Mom's been arrested?"

I looked down at my torn lapel and silently cursed. "Right now, she's in holding, pending charges."

His mouth fell open. "What?"

I decided, now was the time to add more manure, to this compost heap. "I also have Saul West in custody."

Nathaniel sat up straight, his eyes wild, like a feral cat. "What? You've put Uncle Saul in jail? Why?"

Uncle Saul? I guess that explains why Saul tried to warn Clare. The Wests and Hensleys were evidently very close. "We found evidence, that connects him to the murder." Nathaniel's jaw dropped even further and his shoulders sloped. "We also have Daniel in custody."

Nathaniel looked up to the ceiling. "Jesus, are you arresting the entire family."

I shook my head, as I picked my notebook and file folder up from the floor. "He turned himself in. He said he murdered Alston O'Brian."

Nathaniel remained silent. He looked into my eyes, as if trying to decide, if this was the truth. Eventually he surmised it was. "Uncle Daniel confessed to the murder? You can't believe that."

I flipped the notepad open to the page I was on, before Nathaniel jumped me. "We take every confession, to a murder, very seriously. Even if we know it's not true, it still has to be investigated. Especially, if it is a police officer, who is confessing."

"But he didn't do anything. None of them did anything wrong."

"That remains to be seen." I took out Harrison's and Patrick's statements. "And then there is the statements of these two."

He sat up, lifting his head, attempting to view the documents. "What are those?"

I feigned absentmindedness, snapping my fingers. "Oh I'm sorry, did I not mention that we also have Patrick Winchell and Harrison Birch in custody?"

Open mouthed silence was his response.

"We found evidence that connects them to the victim. Both men vehemently deny they had anything to do with it." I paused, pointing to him. "But when I mentioned that you were here, both of them started reciting a tale about the night of Alston's death."

Silence was still his reply.

Seizing the opportunity, I pressed on. "They began to spin a yarn, about how, after the tussle with Alston at Hardees, they saw him talking to you, in the parking lot at Fastenal. This gave them an idea." I placed the statements back in the folder, keeping my hands flat on the table. "It's a well-known secret, who your father is, Nathaniel. So it got them to thinking, maybe they could use you to get a little payback, for what he did to their families. Problem was, when they thought they were conning you, in reality you were conning them."

Nathaniel released a nervous laugh, as a devious grin spread across his face. "Man this is a bunch of crap. You really believe, that I could con two guys, into killing that old man?"

I smiled at him, remembering I had that same thought, barely twenty-four hours ago. "It is hard to fathom, I agree. Yet, the one thing my job teaches you, is to look for the common denominator. That one thread that will connect everyone and everything."

"Now obviously the victim is where you have to start." I leaned in, tapping the table with my finger, as if I was laying out the game plan. "Everyone involved is somehow connected to Alston O'Brian. Whether it be through the con he ran back in the nineties or other means. However, the more I dug into this case, I found one other person that seems to connect to the participants. That would be you, Nathaniel."

There was a line of sweat tracing his hairline, as Nathanial removed his jacket and placed it on his chair. He cleared his throat, scratching the back of his neck, with his bruised hand. "I don't see how I connect to any of this."

I cocked my head to the left, a quizzical look on my face. "Really?" I started reciting the connection points. "We can prove that Alston drove his car to Fastenal and we have two witnesses who saw you talking to him. You're the spitting image of Alston, when he was a young man. Saul warned your mother, who was attempting to hightail it from work, in an effort to get you out of town. Saul, Clare and I believe, even Daniel, are all in trouble, because they are trying to protect you."

Nathaniel's grin grew more confident, as he sat back in his seat. "You've got no proof of anything. I'd already be arrested, if you did."

The drawback of talking to this young man, who works with the R.O.T.C. program, is he knows about police procedure. I was trying to think of a comeback, when my phone chimed. It was a text from Molly, with results from the newly acquired evidence. You see it often on TV, the detective gets the results, just in the nick of time. A phenomenon, which has rarely happened to me, but I was thankful this was one of those rare times. There was so much information, she had to send two messages. I read every word twice before I resumed the interview.

"You should know we completed a search of both your locker and gym locker at school, while you sat here." He tried to speak, but I stopped him. "Before you say anything about illegal search, you have no expectation of privacy, in a school and the lockers are subject to searches, without a warrant."

He grew silent. I decided to take advantage of his silence and continue. "My deputy found a bag of marijuana, in your locker and a baseball bat, in your gym locker."

Nathaniel shrugged, as if it was no big deal. "My locker doesn't have a lock on it, so the pot could've been planted there by anyone. As for the baseball bat, I'm a ballplayer, of course you're going to find a baseball bat."

I smiled again, a bit impressed with his legal knowledge. I held out my BlackBerry and retrieved the picture Jack and sent me. "So this is your personal baseball bat?"

He looked at the picture, before rolling his eyes. "Yes."

"The reason we're interested in the baseball bat, is because the victim had wounds on his body similar to the shape and diameter of a bat." I brought up the pictures Molly had sent me on my phone and showed them to him. "This photograph, reveals traces of blood found under the rubber grip on your aluminum bat."

Nathaniel shrugged again. "So what? I cut myself all the time."

"The blood type is AB negative, just like the victims. They also found fingerprints in blood, along the grip end of the bat," I said. "The blood, on the black handle was invisible to the naked eye. But the amino black solution revealed them, quite easily."

Nathaniel was silent. "We will run a DNA sequence on that also, to see if it is a match to Alston O'Brian's blood."

He still had no reply. The smug grin on his face had turned to stone. "We also fingerprinted the bag of marijuana and found a set of fingerprints that belong to Alston O'Brian, plus a set of prints that aren't in the database."

I returned my BlackBerry, to my coat pocket, deliberately smoothing out the wrinkles in my shirt. "Those unknown prints also match the set found, in blood, on the baseball bat, which you just said was yours."

His eyelids fluttered, as his skin became flushed. Nathaniel was trying to think of a plausible explanation for this. "I leave the baseball bat in my locker most of the time. It doesn't have a lock on it either, so anyone could've taken and returned it, without me knowing."

This would be his default defense and it was in the realm of possibility, but I had been saving the best for last. "We found the victim's cellphone on Patrick Winchell's property. There were no prints on the outer case. But the battery, in the cellphone, was a different matter. You see we believe, whoever took Alston's phone, removed the battery, to keep it from being tracked. They wiped the phone, but they forgot about the battery. And wouldn't you know it, the prints on the battery match the unknown prints on the bat and the bag of pot."

Desperation was in his eyes. It must've felt like the world was crashing down around him, as his mind, like a pinball machine, was scrambling for a way to escape the blockers. I witnessed a small glimmer of hope emanate in his eyes, as he seemed to relax. "You can't prove those prints are mine. They aren't in the A.F.I.S."

I nodded. "This is true. The prints didn't get a hit in any database. But we can fix that."

He frowned in confusion. "What? How?"

I pointed to my ripped lapel. "You assaulted me in front of witnesses and on camera. If I choose to press charges, you will be fingerprinted and entered into the computer. From the look on your face right now, I'm willing to bet all the money in my pocket, that those prints will belong to you. And when the DNA matches to Alston, I'll arrest you for murder."

Nathaniel stared at me, swallowing hard, remained silent. No doubt he was using the silence, to try and devise an angle, to free himself from this jam. I had no intention of allowing that to happen. "After you are processed, charges will most likely be filed against Saul and Daniel, for concealment of a crime and possibly aiding and abetting. As for your mother—"

He broke his silence. "You leave her out of this."

I shook my head. "I'm afraid I can't do that, son. We'll have to investigate her."

He let out a groan and smacked the table top. "God damn it! It wasn't supposed to go down like this. You weren't supposed to even know that I…"

I studied him for a moment, waiting for him to finish, but he refrained from speaking. "I wasn't supposed to know what?"

Silence was the reply once again.

I thought about it for a moment, then the light bulb moment came. "I wasn't supposed to know you existed? Is that what you mean? Because Clare was kept out of the trial and there was no mention of her in the records, you thought no one would dare suspect you?"

His face grew more flushed and drenched with sweat, as the minutes passed. "She didn't have anything to do with this."

I shook my head, pointing at myself. "*We* have to determine that."

He slammed his fists on the table. "I said leave her alone. She didn't know what was going on. She wasn't even in town that weekend. She was in Farragut visiting with a sick friend, until Monday morning."

"If you give us the friend's name we can check that out. Of course we'll have to determine, if she knew anything, after the fact."

"She didn't know. She didn't know anything, until yesterday, when you came to her office."

I held up my hand for him to stop. "Son, I feel I need to tell you again, you have the right to remain silent and have an attorney present."

Nathaniel waved his hand flat over the table, as the words poured from his mouth. "I don't want a lawyer. I'm eighteen, legally an adult and I waive my right to a lawyer, but only if you leave my mother out of this. Uncle Daniel and Saul too."

I studied him for a moment, noting the fear and determination in his eyes. I believed in his sincerity, in wanting to protect his mother. I don't believe he ever intended for her to get involved in this. Probably the same could be said for Saul and Daniel. The problem was, there was no way I was going to be able to meet all of his demands. "I'm afraid it's not that simple Nathaniel."

His voice was as cold as ice. "It is, if you want my confession. You leave them out of this and I'll tell you everything. Patrick and Harrison can fend for themselves. They tried to dupe me, so they can take whatever punishment you throw at them. You don't let her go, I'll get a lawyer and this case will be tied up for months and you know it. Maybe even years."

I couldn't help but note the irony, in the fact that both Alston and Nathaniel's primary concern, was the wellbeing of Clare. I was also amazed, at how Nathaniel turned the tables on me and took control of the interview. He was right, even with the fingerprints, the case would be difficult, if it went to trial. It looks like father and son were indeed very much alike. I thought about his proposal and knew I should stop the interview and talk with Anthony, but I also knew the outcome of that conversation, so I bypassed it all together, sure I would hear about it later. "Maybe I can keep Clare out of jail. That is, if it can be verified, that she was indeed out of town, when all of this happened, then I'll forgo pressing charges. Saul and Daniel, however, are a different matter. With them being police officers, they will be held to a higher standard. If they cooperate, I'll do everything in my power, to make sure they get a good deal. However, if you recant the confession later, we can still charge her."

He started to protest further, but I held up my hand. "That's the best I can do. So what will it be?"

Nathaniel thought about it for one minute, then sat back in his chair. "Give me that notepad and I'll tell you everything."

Chapter Twenty-Five

Two hours later I was sitting in front of Saul, repeating Nathaniel's confession. I was met with silence, from the no doubt, soon to be former chief, as he listened. "According to Nathaniel, Patrick and Harrison first approached him the day after the incident at Hardees. They pretended to be random observers, complaining about Alston's return to Vonore. Both were trying to draw Nathaniel into the conversation. Their goal was to gain his trust, before revealing to him Alston was his father."

Saul was still silent, his eyes devoid of emotion. I wasn't even sure he was listening to me. "Patrick and Harrison didn't realize Nathaniel already knew Alston was his father and had immediately recognized, what they were trying to do. The amateur conmen were being conned. Nathaniel first gained *their* trust, then he gained access to the information they possessed. Such as, the Winchell family home being on stilts and hidden away, unseen from the road."

Saul scratched at his wrist under the cuff of his uniform shirt, breathing and exhaling in slow deep breaths. Acknowledging his silence, I continued with my summation. "Fact was Nathaniel was playing all of them. Alston visited the Fastenal, where Nathaniel worked, and struck up a conversation. According to Nathaniel, he quickly turned the tables on Alston, by telling him he knew he was his father. He pretended he wanted to get to know the old man, in order to gain his trust, so he could put his plan into motion."

I sat back, adjusting my position in my chair, attempting to relieve the tension in my lower back. "What no one had realized was, Nathaniel already knew Alston was back in town, thanks to his access to the police station. He overheard you and Daniel talking about the old man's return. He said that was when he began to plot a way to get even. Then along comes Harrison and Patrick. It wasn't too difficult to get them on his side. Their anger and resentment of Alston was more than enough fodder for Nathaniel, to reel them in on the abduction. He easily guided Patrick toward using his old family homestead, as the hideout, once they had Alston."

Saul shook his head, as he rubbed his temples with his forefingers. "Stop this. He's just a kid. Don't let him ruin his life."

I corrected Saul, by reminding him, Nathaniel was eighteen years old. "I also read him his rights and asked him if he wanted an attorney, which he declined. This is going to hold up in court, Saul."

Clearing my throat, I reached for a bottle of water and took sip. "Nathaniel easily convinced Alston, his feelings for him were genuine. Alston purchased the marijuana, to get close to Nathaniel. It wasn't long before the plan was ready to be executed. The weekend of the winter storm provided the perfect opportunity. Clare was out of town visiting a sick friend and Daniel had to work a double shift the day of the abduction. So he called Alston, on a throwaway cellphone, he had purchased in Sweetwater, asking for a meeting. He chose the spot on the East Coast Tellico Parkway road, because it was desolate that time of day. Alston must've sensed something was wrong, because he called me, while on his way, to the meeting. I guess he began to wonder, if he was being conned. We'll never know, the real reason he called."

"The three kidnappers had used Patrick's truck and parked it behind some foliage, along the side of the road. When Alston showed up, Nathaniel was standing alone. Alston got out of the car and asked what was wrong. By then Patrick and Harrison ran out and grabbed him. According to Nathaniel, the old conman put up quite a struggle, landing a swift kick to the crotch of Harrison. But his age and illness prevented his escape. They were on him and soon had him restrained. After placing him in the truck, Harrison hid Alston's Camry in the densely wooded area along 72 East."

Saul's forehead furrowed and suddenly raised his hand, signaling silence. "What do you mean illness?"

"Alston had cancer, Saul. He had a few months to live."

The chief stared at me, with pure shock scrawled over his face. "Cancer?"

I nodded. "Yes."

Saul slouched silently back in his seat, which I took as a cue to proceed. "After the car was secured and hidden by the evergreen branches, they took the backway through the woods, to reach the house. No one saw them enter the house. Once inside things started to get out of control. With Alston tied to the foldout chair, Harrison had brought, Nathaniel began the assault. He was punching and slapping Alston, and yelling obscenities. Nathaniel's statement supported this. When the first round of torture was complete, he crushed sleeping pills and mixed them with water and forced Alston to drink it. With Alston sedated, only one person was needed to guard him. They took shifts at night, so he was never alone. Nathaniel took the first one allowing Patrick and Harrison to go eat, which we were able to verify."

"Harrison and Patrick took the day off from work, using the weather, as an excuse, plus neither worked weekends. With Daniel working and his mother away, no one noticed Nathaniel wasn't home much, that weekend. He checked in with his uncle and mother on his cellphone, just to keep them from getting suspicious. The torture continued throughout the weekend. Sunday evening, when Harrison and Patrick arrived at the house, they found Nathaniel using a baseball bat on Alston's chest."

I paused a moment to take another drink of water. I could barely hear the courthouse clock chime, indicating it was only two o'clock in the afternoon. With everything that had happened throughout this morning, it felt like it should be much later. "It turns out for all their bravado at Hardees, Patrick and Harrison were finding out, they didn't quite have the stomach for the violence they were witnessing. On the day of the murder, Nathaniel took over for Patrick and Harrison and sent them to get some food. When they returned Nathaniel had really worked Alston over with the baseball bat. At the sight of the bruised and battered Alston, the two kidnappers lost their nerve. They wanted out, but Nathaniel told them it was too late. They were all in it together. He even explained how all trace evidence would lead back to them. If they did what he said, he'd make sure nothing would link them to the crime scene. Of course, that turned out to be untrue."

Saul stood up. "I need to talk to him. He needs to recant this confession."

I stood up also and pointed to his seat. "You need to sit down, Saul."

He stared at me, in open mouthed disbelief, that I was giving him an order. I pointed to his seat again. "Sit down. You need to hear the rest of this."

We spent the next ten seconds in a staring contest, before Saul eventually sat down. I did the same, and continued with the story. "What happened next was, Nathaniel took a duffle bag from the trunk of his car, before he had Harrison drive him to the county impound. They parked out of the security camera's line of sight. Nathaniel pulled out a mask and paintball gun and shot the cameras. He rode with you in the R.O.T.C. program, so he knew about the universal code. You also taught him how to break into cars with the jimmy bar. He hotwired the Dodge Durango and they drove through the woods to the house."

I inhaled a long deep breath. "Only when they got back inside, Alston wasn't there. Patrick was busy scurrying through all the rooms. He had gone outside to relieve himself and when he came back, Alston was gone."

I shook my head, a sad smile on my face. "The old man was sick, beaten, and drugged, but he still had the capacity to give them the slip. That is admirable in a way. Of course it didn't do him much good, did it?"

I sat forward, pointing at a scar in the wood of the tabletop, pretending it was the road in front of the house. "According to Nathaniel, Patrick and Harrison, they searched the immediate grounds, but found no sign of Alston. They believed he was either on the main road or using the dense overgrowth around the home as cover. Nathaniel took the Durango, while Patrick and Harrison searched through the woods. Nathaniel said he was so focused on searching the tree line, that he barely noticed the shadow, that crossed the headlights. When he looked up, he had no time to see Alston, before hitting the brakes. He was going fifty miles an hour and was only four feet from Alston, physics played a part in the rest."

"From what I gathered, Patrick and Harrison had located Alston and began to chase him. Alston made it to the road and collided with the Durango, still sedated from the sleeping pills, it's not for sure he even knew he was on the road. It really didn't matter, I suppose. Alston's problems were over. The same can't be said for the other three. Their troubles were just beginning. Nathaniel knew they couldn't leave the body on the road, so he took a tarp from his duffle bag and rolled it out. The three of them lifted the body onto it and set it in the back of the Durango. I believe you know what happened after that, don't you Saul?"

The chief looked at me, with cold eyes. Having remained silent during my story, I was mildly surprised when he replied. "Yes I do."

I arched my eyebrows. "So, you're admitting to the part you played that evening?"

Saul rolled his tongue along his cheek, while flexing and relaxing his hands. "It's over for me. We both know that. Now Daniel, he still has a chance at a future. Give him a break. The only thing he's guilty of is trying to protect his nephew."

Look where that got him. "I'll talk to Anthony, Saul, that's the best I can do."

With a disheartened smile on his face, he shook his head. "I guess that's all I can ask."

Saul corroborated Nathaniel's story. His statement also correlated with the GPS information Tom had collected. Daniel had gone home for a late lunch that afternoon and didn't see Nathaniel. Curiosity getting the better of him, he called his nephew, but it went straight to voicemail. Daniel became concerned for his nephew, who always had his phone with him and always answered, whenever he or his sister called. Using the Vonore P.D. computer, he attempted to use the GPS on Nathaniel's phone to track him, but the teenager had been smart enough, to deactivate his location feature and with the phone off, he could not remotely reactivate the GPS. Daniel mentioned this to Saul at the stationhouse, but the chief said, the kid probably just let the battery die and don't worry.

Saul's tune changed when Daniel came into his office at around four. He had just received a call from his nephew, who said he and his friend had been hanging out at their house since before lunch. That's when the two of them decided to switch shifts, for that evening. Daniel would stay home, in case Nathaniel returned and Saul would start tracking the kid down.

He went to all of Nathaniel's usual haunts, but found nothing. It wasn't until eight o'clock, that Saul remembered the conversation he and I had at McDonalds about Alston not showing up for our meeting. A cold thought slowly crept into the recesses of his mind. Alston's sedan had been seen in Vonore on several occasions and Saul had taken the liberty of jotting down the license plate number. He illegally used the car's lowjack to track it to its location. When Saul found the car, his heart sank. Not knowing what else to do, he started scouring the roads looking for any signs of the young man. It wasn't until he received a call from Nathaniel, telling him where he was. Patrick and Harrison were beginning to panic and the boy needed help controlling them. Nathaniel had brought a police radio to monitor the calls and in a panic Harrison grabbed it and called for help, which explains why the dispatcher's log was erased. The reason my guys had missed the call between Saul and Nathaniel was because, we had been concentrating on calls between Daniel and Saul. That had been an error on our part.

Saul was quiet again, his eyes vivid and feral, as he replayed that night in his mind. "I couldn't believe it when I saw Alston's legs protruding out from under the house. I must've stood there for…I don't know how long, holding my breath. Nathaniel, Patrick, and Harrison were all talking at the same time, so I couldn't understand what they were saying. I told them to shut up, so I could have a minute to think."

He took a moment just then, which I allowed him, before asking the question that had been perplexing, me since this case began. "Did they tell you why, they dropped the house on the body?"

Saul rolled his eyes, shaking his head emphatically. "Yeah. They thought that by using the house on the cadaver, it would mask the injuries from the car collision. Problem is they didn't get enough of the body underneath the house."

I looked at him solemnly, before re-reading Nathaniel's statement. Saul narrowed his eyes, and gave me a quizzical look. "What? What did Nathaniel tell you?"

I swallowed and lightly clicked my teeth together. "He told me that Harrison and Patrick were in a panic. They didn't know what to do, so Nathaniel had them help pick up Alston's body and put it in the back of the Durango. He insisted the tarp would keep any trace evidence from getting on the interior of the bed. He told them they needed to search the woods, in case they had left anything that could be traced back to them. They then returned to the house to clean up. While they were doing that, Nathaniel placed the remains under the house. He took a heavy duty chain from his duffle bag and wrapped it around the hitch and one of the stilts supporting the house. He dragged the body under the house, and took the tarp, waited until Patrick and Harrison exited the house... you know the rest."

"But his motive wasn't to conceal the automobile injuries Saul." I paused again, realizing I was about to diminish a man's faith, in someone he had known his entire life. "He used the Winchell family home, as a way to guide the investigation toward Patrick and Harrison. He knew after the debacle at Hardees, we'd immediately zero in on them. The reason no one heard the house fall is because of two factors. One the location and the dense woods surrounding the site. The second is the railway. You can just about set your watch to the trains that go through the county. He waited until the eleven o'clock train blared its horn, before he gave the Durango gas and yanked out the stilt. The house was nothing more than part of the plan from the very beginning. If you don't believe me, then look at the statement."

Saul's face grew pale and his posture slumped, and some of the light left his eyes. I believe deep down, he had always known this was what happened, but was just now accepting it. Nathaniel had called him uncle. Judging from Saul's reaction, I believe he thought of the teenager as his family. "I'm sorry Saul. I'm afraid I also have to tell you that the main reason he called you that night was because—"

"He knew I'd clean up after him." Saul inhaled a deep breath and groaned and shook his head. "He knew I'd clean up his shoe print on the carpet and I would wipe down the walls. I was in such a hurry, I forgot the ceiling. I was trying to save him."

I decided to do some more probing into Nathaniel's background. "From what I've learned, it sounds like this isn't the first time. The SRO at Sequoyah believes Nathaniel was using pot on the premises. Possibly involved in some other illicit activities. He seemed to think that maybe you, had something to do, with him not being punished?"

Saul pursed his lips, closing his eyes while shaking his head. "It wasn't easy on him, being Alston's kid. No one said anything, at least if they did Clare didn't tell me. But as he got older and resembled

Alston more, I could see some of the old timers give him strange looks. Nearly twenty years later and there is still anger brewing about that man. I heard Daniel and Clare discuss how some of the kids at school gave him a hard time and I just felt like the kid…needed his space. Someone to cut him some slack. I guess that didn't work out too good, did it?"

"I'm sure your intentions were noble, Saul."

He scratched the table with his forefinger, releasing a long sigh. "You need to let Clare go, Jonas. She wasn't even in town when it all happened. We kept it from her, knowing it would be better, if she had deniability."

I had not told Saul about the deal I had made with Nathaniel and saw no reason to now. From the tone of his voice when he said Clare's name, I believe there was more to his motivations for protecting her. Yet, when I got to thinking of Lydia and what I would do for her, I felt those motivations were his own. "In the end that's up to Anthony, Saul. I'll put in a word for her, but that's all I can do."

Saul nodded. "That's all I can ask."

"What were Patrick and Harrison doing while you were cleaning up the house?"

He cleared his throat and licked his lips. "I told them to go home and forget everything they had seen. That I'd take care of it, leaving no physical connection between them and the crime scene. They were to say Patrick spent the night at Harrison's place, so they could alibi one another. The next morning, they were to clean their trucks as thoroughly as possible, of any trace of evidence. I coached them on how to answer your questions."

"Where was Nathaniel?"

"I had him go home and tell Daniel, to meet me at the house, so I could go over the plan with him. First, we got the Camry from the location on 72 East and took it to Bob Gillian's place. We've investigated him several times over the years about illegal purchases of vehicles and I knew he would take the car and not report it. Then we took the Durango back to the impound lot. After that, we planned how we would be the first on scene, wearing the same boots as the night before."

"So the footprints at the scene could be explained away."

"I thought my department would be taking the lead on the investigation. That way, I could control the case and clean up what I may have missed, the night before." Saul let out a long sigh. "I didn't think Anthony would hand you the lead."

I could only stare at him.

Saul braced himself, on the table and closed his eyes, as if trying to erase the events of that night. "It wasn't right Jonas, I know. I was trying to make the best of the situation. I believed all three of them had let their tempers get the better of them. I was just trying to keep everyone out of jail."

I leaned into the table, so Saul could see my eyes. "That's what Nathaniel wanted you to believe, Saul. Two days after the murder, Nathaniel planted traces of the tarp used to move the body in Patrick's truck and put fibers from Alston's clothing in Harrison's. Then last night after my visit with Clare, he slipped out and planted Alston's cellphone on Harrison's property."

He was silent, save for his heavy breathing. "The kid was doing his best to set them up. He did a pretty good job of it too, except his hubris got the better of him. Kind of like it did his father, back in the day. It wasn't until he saw me yesterday, that he started to panic, which is when he got sloppy. He planted the cellphone, but forgot to wipe his prints off the battery. He left the marijuana Alston gave him in the school locker. He also didn't get rid of the baseball bat, that has his fingerprints in Alston's blood. Maybe it was because you've covered for him so many times, he felt like he was invincible. Or perhaps, because Clare was never mentioned in the original trial, he believed her anonymity was passed onto him and we wouldn't find out about him. I don't know. All I know is, he nearly got away with it and you did nothing to deter him."

Saul ground his back teeth, as the color of his face drained. "You think I don't know that? You think I like any of this. Is rubbing my nose in it making you feel better?"

I slowly shook my head. "No, Saul. I hate everything about this. Unfortunately, there is very little I can do though. You were read your rights. Do you want an attorney or do you wish to make an official statement?"

He looked to the ceiling, like he was praying, before his shoulders deflated and he held out both hands, palms up. "Give me a pen and notepad."

* * *

Three hours later, I had Anthony and Lydia, in my office going over the statements I had received. They had witnessed all of the confessions from the monitoring room, but it is always prudent to read over them, to make sure it all coalesces. Forty-five minutes after sitting down, Lydia and the prosecuting attorney closed the files and placed them on my desk. A touch of a smile crossed Anthony's face, as he looked at me. "I can't believe you were able to wrap it up like this, Jonas. I thought for sure it'd be a judicial nightmare. Instead, you got all of them to confess."

I slowly rotated my neck, leaning back in my chair. I felt tired. I had been talking for the last four hours, and in many ways, that drained me more, than manual labor. "I was a bit surprised, myself. I felt for sure that Nathaniel would give us more problems than he did."

Anthony nodded. "I thought so too. I hope he's not going to throw in a monkey wrench, later down the road."

Lydia stretched her shoulders, before settling back in her own seat. "You heard him sir. If we don't prosecute his mother, then he'll play ball. I believed him, when he said, he wouldn't recant, if we keep her out of it."

Anthony's forehead wrinkled, as he looked at the corner of my desk. "About that. I'm not fully convinced that Clare wasn't aware of the events that led to Alston's murder."

"I've got Glen looking into the story about her sick friend. So far it seems to be checking out," I said.

"Yes, but what about after she came back." Anthony slowly shook his head. "You really believe, it is possible she didn't have a clue, about any of this?"

I recalled my first encounter with Clare at Lowes and how her demeanor changed during our interview. She went from a reluctant participant to completely stonewalling me. I don't think it even registered what happened during that weekend, until then, which is why she was trying to usher me out of the building, because she knew her son would be arriving soon. The mother in her took over and all she thought about was protecting her child. I related my suspicion to both of them. "She didn't want me to see Nathaniel, because she knew I would see the resemblance to Alston and start digging."

"Which could be seen as concealing a crime, after the fact, sheriff. Don't you think we should at least consider that as a charge?" Anthony replied.

I pointed to the four confessions on my desk. "We could. But if you do, this nice package, as you called it, will all unravel. Nathaniel will recant his confession and most likely so will Saul and Patrick and Harrison. It'll turn into a trial, which could go on for years. Is that what you want, Anthony?

I watched fortitude of his convictions begin to subside, at the prospect of a long trial. Yet his adamancy would not ebb quietly. "Of course it isn't. However, in the end I'm the one who has to go before the judge and explain this. It will be a hard sell, is all I'm saying."

Lydia seemed to have a different perspective on the situation. "If I may, sir. The only definitive crime we have to charge her with, is the assault on Jonas. We've yet to get a warrant for the text that Chief

West sent her, so we don't know for sure what her motivations were. If Jonas doesn't press charges, then there will be no need to bring it up before a judge."

Anthony seemed to favor this idea, as he slowly nodded his head. "That's true. I'm assuming you have no trouble with this, sheriff?"

I shook my head, slowly rocking my chair. "None whatsoever."

Anthony raked his knuckles on the edge of my desk. "Good. Now that leaves Officer Daniel Hensley."

I swiveled my seat around, so I was facing him. "I've been giving that some thought, Anthony. If you would indulge me, I'd like to put a possibility on the table?"

He leaned forward in his seat, giving me the floor, so to speak. "I'm listening?"

I inhaled a deep breath, praying this idea would satisfy everyone. "Daniel confessed to the murder and helped cover it up. We charge him with giving a false confession and the concealment of a crime. You give him a deal where he has to serve six months in a halfway house and the rest of his time on probation. Obviously, he'd have to forfeit his badge and could never be a cop again."

Anthony shook his head, waving his hand flat over my desk. "No. He's a police officer and needs to be held to a higher standard. He willingly covered a crime and misdirected an investigation. He should be prosecuted to the fullest extent of the law."

I had been expecting his argument and had already come up with what I hoped was a good counter. "He and Saul are also well liked among the Vonore community. Now, their chief is going to jail for his part in covering up Alston O' Brian's murder. The man who swindled a fair amount of relatives and loved ones in Vonore out of their money. The man Saul is going down for protecting, is the Nathaniel, the son of Alston. This could bring a lot of bad blood to boil in a community, that has already taken some serious blows. Saul's fate is sealed. However, if Daniel is shown leniency, then it might make all this go down smoother."

Anthony sat back, shaking his head again. "We can't let him get off scot free. I know Vonore has been through a lot, but that doesn't allow us, to let the man go unpunished."

I sat up straight in my seat, not ready to yield my case. "He won't be going unpunished, Anthony. The man's going to lose his job and have a record for the rest of his life. His friend and mentor is going to have to spend at least the next decade of his life in prison. His nephew is going to have the spend the first half of his life in prison, for murder. Plus, he's got to live with the guilt of what has happened."

"Why do you think he confessed in the first place?" I asked, but the question was rhetorical. "Yes, it was to cover for Nathaniel, but I believe it was also out of guilt. He knew what happened that night was wrong, but he couldn't bring himself to turn in his own nephew, so he did the next best thing he could think of. Six months in a halfway house and probation isn't a slap on the wrist Anthony. Nothing we do will bring Alston back, but neither will throwing Daniel to the wolves. All I'm asking for, is for you to think about it."

Anthony stared at me, blankly. The second hand on the clock behind me, ticked away it's autonomic rhythm, as I waited for his reply. Lydia remained silent this time, allowing her boss to reach his own conclusions. He inhaled a deep breath, before releasing it, crossing his leg and resting his hand on his knee. "You should've been a defense attorney, instead of a sheriff. You make a hell of an argument."

I smiled, shrugging. "Did it work?"

He looked to Lydia who hunched her own shoulders. "Sir, I'm with you, when you say Daniel can't get off easy. That said, the people of Vonore have had a lot dumped on them and when word gets out about their chief being arrested, it will cause strife. The sooner we can put this behind us, the sooner the town can heal."

Anthony looked down at his hands, rolling the idea over, as I waited in anticipation. "Eighteen months in a minimum security facility. Then the rest of his sentence on probation. That is the best I can do for him."

It was actually much better than I originally thought I would get. "All right."

Anthony shook his head, pursing his lips. "You're forgetting one thing, Jonas. You have to convince Daniel to take the deal and recant his confession."

I stood and headed to the holding cell. "I've got just the person to do that."

* * *

I escorted Daniel to the interview room where Saul waited. I explained the deal that was on the table and as expected, Daniel refused, insisting his nephew was innocent. Saul had to work hard, but he finally got through to his former officer. He told him the jig was up and there was nothing more to be gained, from him falling on his sword. The best he could do was take the deal, so he could eventually get out and help his sister.

I had refrained from speaking, believing that the former chief, would be better at bringing Daniel back into the fold. An hour later, Jack escorted Daniel back to his cell, his agreement to the deal assured. Saul stood up and held out his hand in appreciation. "Thank you."

I shook his hand, saying nothing in return. What was there left to say? Besides, I was preparing for my next visit. There were no other female occupants in the women's holding cell, and remembering Clare's attempt to alleviate me of my vision earlier, I decided to keep the shatterproof glass partition between us, as I told her the fate of her son, brother, and Saul.

Clare slammed the partition with her fist, the blow echoing through the empty room. "You sonofabitch! I told you to leave my son alone."

I remained where I stood, hands clasped behind my back. "That was never an option, Clare."

She pressed her finger into the glass, like she was pressing it into my chest. "When I get out of here, I'll get the best lawyer money can buy. You're not destroying my family.

I placed my hands in the pockets of my pants. "How exactly will you be paying for that attorney, Clare?"

The question ebbed her righteous rage. "What?"

"Where will you get the money? As a matter of fact, how did you get the money to put down half the amount for the property and house and pay for your brother's tuition, on just a secretary's salary?"

She offered no reply, which told me my suspicions were correct. "Because the missing money went to you didn't it? Did Alston leave it to you before or after he left?"

Again she offered no response, merely looking at me, while chewing on her bottom lip. "It's just you and me here, Clare. No one is recording this. Was it you, who met Alston when he was released from prison? Keep in mind, I can check to see if you were absent from work on that day."

She was breathing hard, no doubt fighting, to control her emotions. Slowly, she paced the cell before scoffing. "What does it matter. The statute of limitations is up. Yeah, it was me. Alston got someone from the inside to get a message to someone who got the message to me. Said he was getting out and asked me to pick him up."

"You brought some money with you too, correct?"

She didn't say anything again. Just stood there slowly shifting back and forth on her feet. "You said it yourself Clare, the statute of limitations is over. Did you bring him some money?"

"Yes." Her voice was one octave below a shout. "It was the least I could do. I was telling the truth, when I said I didn't know about the con. I didn't. When Alston knew he was about to be arrested, he called me and told me where he had hidden the money. He said I had to use it sparingly until after seven years, so I wouldn't draw attention to myself."

I looked at her keeping my face stoic, which seemed to upset her further. "I don't need your judgment, Sheriff. I had a baby on the way and no real job. I needed all the help I could get."

"Did Alston tell you he was coming back to Monroe County?"

She rolled her eyes, staring at the ceiling. "God no. If he had, I would've tried to stop him. He said he didn't want to upset my life any more than he had and just needed some cash to get a fresh start. It was so weird to see him again, after all those years. He was older, but still…."

She trailed off and I saw no need to press it. "I'm not filing charges, so you'll be free to go soon. As for hiring an attorney, that is your choice, but understand, Nathaniel was informed of his rights and waived his counsel. He confessed to everything on his own volition. It's going to be difficult for any defense attorney to get it thrown out."

Clare was breathing hard, before miniature concussions started to reverberate up her body. I saw tears filling her eyes, as she struggled to keep her composure. I'm not even going to pretend to say I understand the kaleidoscope of emotions she had to be experiencing in that moment. Nor, was I proud to be a part of the cause for her discomfort, but the dye had been cast long before my involvement. I was just trying to guide the vessel toward smoother waters. Clare cleared her throat, planting her hands on her hips. "I want to see Nathan. I want to talk to him."

It was strictly against protocol, but we had bent so many rules on this case, I didn't see the harm in doing it once more. Fifteen minutes later, Clare and her son were sitting in the interview room. Nathaniel was now wearing a county issued green jumpsuit. The two hugged for a long time before Clare broke away, cupping his face in her hands. "Baby, you need to take back the confession. I'll get a lawyer and we'll get through this. I can help Daniel and Saul too. We'll can get through this, but you have to take the confession back."

Nathaniel smiled, at his mother taking her hands and kissing the fingertips. "It's all right Mom. I want to do this."

Clare jerked away from him and shook him by his shoulders. "No you don't. Do you realize you could do twenty years or more before you're out? I can't let you do that. We can fight this?"

"Mom, it has to end." Nathaniel smiled at her, holding her shoulders with his hands. "I want it to end. All these years with the kids in school picking on me, the snide looks people gave me, as I got older. I want it to end."

Clare lowered her head to her chest and sniffled. "How did you find out about Alston?"

"About three years ago, a kid started giving me a hard time in the cafeteria at school. Kept going on about how I was a snake, just like my old man Alston O'Brian. Ranting about how my family stole his family's life savings. I was just starting to work, with Uncle Saul then, but there was no mention of the case on the computer. So, when he took me to the courthouse one day, I was able to sneak back to the records and look the name up. When I saw a picture of him I knew he was my dad. I read what he did and I can't explain it. I got to thinking off all the bullies and pranks the kids pulled on me all my life and I suddenly realized it wasn't me they were mad at, it was him. He was the cause of their pain and mine. Then, he came to see me."

Clare took a long breath. "Why didn't you tell me he came to see you?"

Nathaniel shrugged. "I suppose for the same reasons you never told me who my father was. He thought I didn't know who he was, so it made it easy, to manipulate him." He paused, swallowing hard, as a tear rolled down his face. "When I had him in the house, I just released all my anger on him, Mom. Then on the night he died, just before he escaped, he said something that set fire to my brain. He called me son."

Nathaniel stared trembling, tears now flowing down his face. "I lost it Mom. I got out the baseball bat and pounded his chest. I hit him in the face with my fists. I...was so mad at him for what he did to us. I saw the way some people treated you and I never understood why. I took it all out on him. And when I accidently hit him with the car, he didn't die instantly. He acted like he wanted to tell me something. I knelt down and he whispered, *I'm sorry you became like me*. Then he died."

No one said anything for a while, as we absorbed this new information. Nathaniel smiled, his voice trembling. "It was then I realized he was right. I had become just like him. I was scamming the kids at school, I lied to you and Daniel. I got those two idiots Harrison and Patrick to kidnap Alston and I made Uncle Saul help me cover it up. I'm a conman, just like my father."

Clare used the back of her hand to wipe away her tears, as she listened to her son. She sniffed as she shook her head. "No, you're not. It's my fault, son. I should've told you the truth a long time ago. "

"I don't think it would've mattered Mom.," he replied, still smiling. "But do you understand why I have to do this? All of these people are in trouble because of me. I have to be punished for that, Mom. I have to own up to it. Maybe then, we can finally break this cycle."

Clare stared crying profusely, as she clutched her son to her chest, rocking them both back and forth. I believe it was in that moment that she realized the fight was over. Later I was standing with her outside, as we waited for Tom to pull around, to drive her back to work, where her car was. For a long time she stood there with her arms wrapped around her, staring at nothing. "I should've never come back to Vonroe. After I had him, I should've gotten as far from Tennessee as possible."

I looked down at her and asked, "Why did you come back?"

She let out a light maniacal laugh, looking at me. "This was the only home I've ever known. When I went away to have Nathaniel, I only thought about coming home to my parents and Daniel. I thought over time people would forget. That they surely wouldn't take it out on my son. How naïve. The past is never in the past is it?"

    I had no answer for her and was thankful to see Tom bring the cruiser around. I opened the door for her and helped her in. She kept her vision forward, as they drove off. I found myself watching the cruiser until it turned at the stop sign, driving out of sight.

Chapter Twenty-Six

Though it was late, I decided to go see Bill Hayes and update him on the events of the day. I watched his facial expressions, as he listened. "It was Alston's son who was behind all of this?"

"I'm afraid so." I stretched my back, feeling some tiny pops along my spine. "All of this came, from a son's blind rage, at his father. He blamed him for everything, only to realize he had become the very thing he hated."

Bill nodded, stroking his beard. "It happens more than we care to admit. In the end we have to own up to the sins we've committed."

I gave him a halfhearted smile in return. "Yeah I suppose we do."

"What's wrong?" Bill asked.

"It's nothing Bill." I looked up at the window, as twilight crept across the county. I could tell by the look on his face, that he wasn't going to let up, so I decided to tell him what had been bothering me. "In order for me to get Nathaniel to confess, I had to put his mother into play. During the interview, I mentioned we had his mother in holding and she could be charged for assault. I thought that might get him to confess."

The old sheriff nodded, the beard on his chin bristling, as he scratched an itch. "And it worked. You also weren't lying. She was in jail and she was acting suspicious."

I shrugged. "Yeah, I know. But I felt like a lying bastard, for basically using their love for one another. In fact, all the wheeling and dealing I've done today, I'm beginning to wonder if I'm letting the power go to my head."

Bill rolled his eyes, his chains scrapping the table. "Jonas—"

"I'm serious Bill. Four years ago, it would've never entered my mind to take such liberties. I all but dictated the fates of four people. That's not my job. I'm just supposed to catch them."

Bill closed his eyes and slowly shook his head. "Yes, it is, Jonas. You're also responsible for seeing that justice is done. What you're not responsible for, is the actions of other people. From what you have told me, you warned Alston to leave and tried to get Saul to do his job. Everyone involved, in the events leading up to and after that night, are responsible for their own actions. As for you using the mother for leverage, in my opinion you should've charged her anyway."

I sat up straight, slightly taken aback by his last statement. "She and Saul conspired to obstruct justice, Jonas. When Saul texted her, it was to warn her, so she could flee with Nathaniel. You know that's true. But I've known you long enough, to know, you had a good reason for not charging her."

I gave him a slight grin, as it was nice to see Bill's instincts were still sharp as ever. "Nathaniel's going away for quite some time. So is Saul. Daniel's got eighteen months of time to serve. The way I see it, that family's been through enough.

Bill stared at me for moment. "I suppose that is true." He shook his head, staring at his shackled hands. "All those lives, ruined because of that boy. It's almost impossible to believe."

"Yeah it is," I said with little exuberance.

Bill shook his head, as he continued. "Jonas, you've not let the power go to your head. When you're the sheriff, in a rural county or anywhere for that matter, you have to do what is right for the people you represent. For the most part we deal with, for lack of a better expression, some really shitty situations. Not all of it is going to be covered by the book. There are times you have to make decisions that affect people's lives."

"Did you ever do that?"

"More than once. So did the sheriff before me and the one before him. I worked with you, for nearly ten years, Jonas. If there was ever a person, who I wasn't worried about having power, it is you."

* * *

When I got back to the office, it was very late, but I was too wired to go home. I buttoned up my overcoat and decided to take a walk down the block. There had been a light snow falling, while I had been talking to Bill, and it was just barely covering the sidewalks. There was a glow from the streetlamps, reflecting off the ice crystals.

As I passed the courthouse and on down to the Methodist Church, I noticed there were homes that still had up their Christmas decorations, even though we were now into the second half of January. With all the robberies and the murder, it was hard to believe that only three weeks ago, we were all celebrating around the Tanenbaum with our loved ones. It was hard to believe the kaleidoscope of acts that had taken place in this town, were rooted in a conman's grift nearly two decades ago. I found myself thinking about the parallels of Alston and Nathaniel's fates and wondered if our destinies are determined by the blood in our veins. Clare had tried so hard, to give her son a better life and keep him on the straight and narrow, only for him to wind up in jail, just like his father. It was either Shakespearian irony or tragedy, but it did make you wonder, how much is free will and how much is already predetermined.

I dragged myself out of my head, when I noticed the sounds of footsteps on the sidewalk, that weren't my own. I turned to see Lydia walking behind me, her hands tucked in her sky blue winter coat. "How long have you been there?"

"I spotted you at the courthouse." She stood in front of me, her face expressionless. "I could tell you were in deep thought and knew you needed a moment. The moment's past now, Jonas."

I stared down at her, not quite sure of what she meant. "Come again?"

She punched my shoulder, as she always does. I believe it was her version of a wake-up call. "You're thinking of all the bad that's happened and of what you could've done to change it. Nothing. There's nothing you could've done. It was a bad situation and you made the best of it. Keep in mind, none of them did the kid any good by covering for him, all those times, he got into trouble. Maybe if they hadn't, he wouldn't be where he is now, but that is beside the point. You went to extremes, to make sure everyone got the best deal possible, which is more than most sheriffs would've done. You did all you could do."

I looked at her through the amber light of the streetlights, marveling how she could still look so beautiful, while chiding me. "You sound like Bill. You're both right, but that's not always how I feel."

She placed her gloved hand over my heart and smiled. "You have a big heart, Jonas. Always have and I wouldn't have it any other way, even if it means your heart often bleeds for others. In the end, you can only do so much before you have to let it go and move on. You know this. You're too smart not to."

I looked into her eyes for a long spell, wanting to say something in my defense, but a wise man has to know when to cut his losses and when he's out gunned. "Thank you for your help with Anthony. I don't think I could've done it without you."

Lydia shook her head, as she straightened the collar of my overcoat. "It was the right call. I meant what I said about Daniel being charged. But there's been enough heartache for now. Everyone needs to move forward. That includes you."

I took a deep breath, slowly feeling a lot of the weight, from the last few weeks leave my body. I took her hand in mine, which she gently squeezed. "You really like me, just the way I am?"

She moved closer and stood on her toes to kiss me. "Definitely."

The wind was picking up, sending chills down both of our spines. She took my arm inside hers and guided me back toward the stationhouse. "Come on. It's too late to be out here in this cold."

We walked in silence for a moment, allowing the serenity to encompass us. "You do a lot for me, Lydia. I often wonder if I do enough for you."

She punched me in the shoulder again. "You do plenty for me, Jonas."

We walked a few steps in silence, before I suddenly remembered a very good revelation. "Well, there's one good thing that came out of this day."

She looked up at me, her forehead wrinkled in confusion. "What's that?"

I smiled, looking ahead. "With the case solved, we can make it to the cabin next weekend."

I saw her smile from the corner of my eyes and felt her grip tighten on my arm. "That's more like it."

Epilogue

We did get to go on that romantic getaway, which did us both a world of good. The calendar rolled along and as the winter ebbed, I felt more at ease. Lydia and Bill were both right, in their assessment, that there was nothing more that I could have done, for anyone involved in the death of Alston O'Brian. The man had been a sore spot to so many people in this county, even after spending years behind bars. People say the past is the past. I believe though, that much like Dickens' *Jacob Marley*, that some of the chains we forge in life are forged with an impenetrable steel, that cannot be broken, no matter how much time has gone by.

As for the robbery of the Ten Commandments and DUI, Gary Dawson, got his driver's license suspended and two years probation. He had to pay a total of five thousand dollars in fines and court costs, for the charges of bigamy. That's not including, the financial assault he will receive, from the inevitable divorce proceedings and civil suits, by his soon to be ex-wives. It was times like these I thanked the Lord, I wasn't in civil law.

Thomas Kinderman and Frederick Brentwood will both receive six years each for the robberies. Thomas received an additional year tacked on, for charging at me with the tire iron. As much as I would've liked to, I couldn't get them charged with the desecration of a corpse, by snorting the cremated remains.

Patrick Winchell pled to kidnaping and conspiracy to conceal a crime, recieved a sentence of sixteen years in prison. Harrison Birch will receive the same, both eligible for parole in fourteen years. Saul West and Daniel Hensley both lost their badges. Saul was charged with obstruction of justice, in aiding and abetting and concealing a crime, plus the attempted assault on me. Since he confessed and it was exigent circumstances, Anthony was able to get him seven years in a low security facility. Daniel was charged with obstruction for giving a false confession. He'll get eighteen months in a halfway house and serve four more years on probation. Because they had planted the Toyota Camry on Bob Gillian's lot, the charges for moving stolen property had to be dropped. Last I heard, Bob was considering suing the city of Vonore, for false arrest.

Nathaniel Hensley, the architect of this house of pain, will spend over two decades in a detention facility for kidnapping and murder. Clare as promised, remained free. For some, this may not seem like justice, but when you factor in both her brother and son are in prison, you can't say she got off completely free.

As the days started to warm, leaving the damp density of winter behind, I felt a loftiness grow over the valley, that was a welcome change. Lydia was over, one Saturday, helping me dust off my lawn furniture and getting the yard ready for spring. At lunch she was sitting at the kitchen table, while I found myself staring in the direction of my desk, thinking about what was in the top drawer. Lydia had been talking about the kind of plants she thought I should buy this year, but I was hardly paying attention, as I thought about what was about to happen. "Are you even listening to me?"

I looked in her direction, seeing irritation in her eyes. I had better make this quick before the moment passed. "Yes. I was just thinking about you and me, is all."

She placed her fork in her salad bowl and folded her hands across her abdomen. "What about us?"

The House Of Cards Murder

I stood and went into my office explaining myself. "Just about all the events, which had to take place, in order for us to meet. About you having the initiative to ask me out and me being smart enough to say yes. It's quite a correlation of events, that led us to this place, when you think about it."

I opened the drawer and took out the small box. "And where is this place?"

"We're about to find out," I said standing behind her.

Lydia turned around to look at me, her annoyance becoming more apparent with each passing second. "What are you talking about, Jonas? I swear there are times that—"

I opened the box and placed it in front of her. When her eyes fell on the blue sapphire ring, her mouth fell open in a silent O. "I thought you'd appreciate this more than a diamond. You once said, they were over rated. I hope you meant it."

She kept her eyes on the ring, slowly taking it out of the box with her thumb and forefinger. I stepped around and knelt down beside her. "I know this isn't exactly the classical way of doing this. But we've never been conventional, Lydia. Will you marry me?"

She looked at me, over the ring, opening her mouth to speak, but no words came out. Fear was beginning to take root. I found it hard to believe, that she would pick now, to have nothing to say. "Lydia? Did you hear me?"

Lydia nodded her head, as a tear rolled down her cheek. "Do you have a reply?" I asked.

She took the ring and put it on her left hand, ring finger, before taking my face in both of her hands and kissing me. When she came up for air, she kept her nose on mine, smiling, as she looked me directly in the eye, so I could see the jubilation in her face. "Does that answer your question?"

I returned her smile, feeling a light swell within my chest and throughout my body. "I believe it does," I replied, as I kissed her again.

Manufactured by Amazon.com
Columbia, SC
02 April 2017